D0500564

BLUE-SKINNED GODS

Also by the author

I Once Met You But You Were Dead
Marriage of a Thousand Lies
Dominant Genes

BLUE-SKINNED GODS

SJ Sindu

SOHO

Published by
Soho Press, Inc.
227 W 17th Street
New York, NY 10011

Library of Congress Cataloging-in-Publication Data

Names: Sindu, SJ, author.
Title: Blue-skinned gods / SJ Sindu.
Description: New York, NY : Soho, [2021]
Identifiers: LCCN 2021000874

ISBN 978-1-64129-242-9
eISBN 978-1-64129-243-6

Classification: LCC PS3619.I5688 B58 2021 | DDC 813'.6—dc23
LC record available at https://lccn.loc.gov/2021000874

Interior illustrations:
Shell: © snapgalleria/Shutterstock
Lotus: © Katika/Shutterstock

Interior design: Janine Agro

Printed in the United States of America

10 9 8 7 6 5 4 3 2 1

for Geoff

BOOK 1: LAKSHMAN

1

The driver slammed the brakes, whipping my head forward and back. A chorus of honks crescendoed in the muggy New Delhi night.

A few cars ahead, in the middle of an intersection, an auto rickshaw lay on its side, its three wheels still spinning, the metal poles of its sides cracked in half. Tire tracks swirled into a small blue car with its front end smashed. Glass littered the road, glittering pinpricks of light.

People surged around us. My father, Ayya, opened the door of the taxi, and we pushed our way into the crowd.

Ayya weaved to the front. I walked in his wake.

An older woman was sprawled on the ground next to the auto, thrown out as it tipped over. The auto driver was on his back near her. His eyes stared right up at the sky. Red slashes glistened over their bodies.

People shouted in Hindi to call the police, call the ambulance. The woman was still breathing. Two men tried to lift her.

"Stop," Ayya said. He raised his voice and yelled, "Stop! You could make her injuries worse if you move her." He pushed his way into the clearing. I followed out of instinct, as if we had a string tied between us. "I'm a doctor," he said. "Let me look."

The men put her limbs back down. Ayya crouched over the woman. He opened her eyes and checked her pulse.

"She's losing a lot of blood," he said. "She needs help, or she won't last."

"Look," someone said. "Kalki Sami can heal her." A man pointed in my direction. I wondered if he'd been at my prayer meeting earlier, or if I'd healed him before.

A hundred eyes turned toward me.

"Yes, Kalki Sami," another man said. "You can heal her."

I walked toward the injured woman and knelt near Ayya. Up close, the overpowering smell of iron and urine. So much blood. Cavernous slashes in their bodies.

I put my shaking hands over the woman's head, where a pool of blood grew on the asphalt. I chanted over and over, my lips quivering with the words. *Om Sri Ram Om Sri Ram Om Sri Ram.* Some of the crowd prayed with me.

I closed my eyes against the lights. I chanted and chanted. *Om Sri Ram. Om Sri Ram.*

2

Twelve years earlier, a girl named Roopa arrived at our ashram in Tamil Nadu, India, dying from a sickness only I could cure. This, my father told me, would be my first miracle.

It was the eve of my birthday, an important transition. I was the tenth human incarnation of the Hindu god Vishnu, and I was turning ten years old.

Like every Friday, the villagers filtered in with rice and lentils, fresh milk from their cows, spinach, moringa, and bitter gourd from their gardens. They put these gifts in front of me as I sat on the only pillow in the room and took their seats on the bedsheets we'd laid over the cement floor. My father, Ayya, sat to my left, and my cousin Lakshman to my right. We faced the open green door that led to the veranda.

The village kids played outside. As a birthday treat, Ayya had promised to let us play with them after the prayer session, if Lakshman and I were well-behaved and lucky. My mother had wanted to have an eggless cake made to celebrate with the villagers, but Ayya thought it too Western and decadent.

One of the village kids had brought a cricket bat for the first time, and he showed it to the others, beaming as they touched it, demonstrating how to hit the ball. I'd asked my parents for a cricket bat for my birthday. I imagined holding it, showing it off to the boys when they came for next week's prayer meeting.

Ayya nudged me with his elbow and I snapped back to attention, ashamed I'd let myself be distracted. Now was not the time for cricket fantasies. Now was the time to focus and prove myself in whatever test would be demanded of me that night.

Lakshman jiggled his legs up and down, watching the kids too. He was my first cousin, a year younger but almost as big and much braver. He had the round face and big eyes that painters always gave Hindu gods. All I had was blue skin.

The *Sri Kalki Purana*, the Hindu text that prophesied my birth and life, said it was on my tenth birthday that my trials as a living god would begin. I would be tested three times, and I would have to prove myself worthy of my birth. Ayya had reminded me of the scripture that morning, though I read the *Sri Kalki Purana* regularly, and had been anxiously counting down the days to this birthday for over a year.

"I saw a vision," Ayya had said after our morning meditation.

I'd seen a vision, too, early with the sunrise. I'd woken up dreaming of goat blood. In the dream, I'd wrapped my hands around the neck of a month-old kid and held tight as it thrashed, then stilled. I'd pushed my hands through its skin and felt its insides. I'd smeared the gummy blood on my face, my chest, my feet, until my skin prickled and grew fur and my nails knit together into hooves. Until I was the goat.

But I was afraid to tell Ayya about this dream—afraid my vision meant doom.

"I had a vision of your first test," Ayya had said, leaning against a plaster column in our courtyard. "Someone will come to you tonight. A stranger who will need healing."

I'd healed plenty of the villagers already. Arthritis, back pain, bad luck. I could handle one more healing.

"This stranger will be dying," he said.

I watched the angles of his face for clues as to how I should act. I'd only ever healed minor aches and pains. I'd never brought someone back from the edges of death.

"Do not doubt yourself," Ayya said. Disappointment tinged his voice.

I'd let my guard down, shown my doubt on my face. I schooled my expression into something hard and impassive.

"Yes, Ayya," I said.

"You want to travel the world and bring it the healing it needs? The journey starts tonight, with your first trial."

In those days, I wanted more than anything to make Ayya proud. I believed only my own doubts and fears stood between me and my destiny as Vishnu's tenth and final avatar. I believed that if I had enough faith, I could do anything. But doubt crept up on me whenever I laid down to sleep, wrapped its invisible hands around my throat, burrowed into my skin, and refused to let go its hold on my brain.

Now, in the room facing the veranda, as the villagers got ready for our prayer meeting, Ayya reached stealthily toward Lakshman's jiggling, full-motion thigh, and pinched him. Lakshman jumped. The leg-agitating stopped.

Ayya stood and closed the doors of the large room. He lit two five-wicked oil lamps with a small one that fit in the palm of his hand. Lakshman rang the hand bell during the pooja. *Om bhuur bhuvah svah*, we chanted, *tat savitur varennyam, bhargo devasya dhiimahi, dhiyo yo nah prachodayaat*—a prayer from the *Rig Veda*, the oldest Hindu text in existence, calling on the sun god. I gathered up my god energy for the healing session that would take place after the prayers and meditation. If my first trial would begin tonight, I would need as much god energy as I could manage to build. In my mind's eye, I saw this energy like fluffy cotton, accumulating at the corners of how I pictured the inside of my body—an empty room the size of the one I slept in. I walked around the room, squatting and scooping up big armfuls of the cotton, soft and itchy on my skin.

Beyond the veranda, the village kids bowled and batted and ran around, their cries barely audible.

I tried to focus on the chanting.

The kid with the bat had been the hero of this game, and he ran around the others with his bat held high, pumping it up and down.

Lakshman was watching, too, and he sighed, rubbing the spot where Ayya had pinched him.

A man and woman from the village sang bhajans as the setting sun danced through the open windows. Two boys growing shadows above their lips played the wooden harmonium and tablas. When it was his turn, Lakshman sang his favorite Krishna bhajan, his voice achingly soft, arching high across the ceiling. *Enna thavam seithanee, Yashodha, engum nirai parabhrammam Amma endrazhailkka*, he sang. *What great penance did you perform, Yashodha, to be blessed with a God for a son?*

Finally, the bhajan ended and the healing session began. All the villagers stood, lining up. I put the kids and their game out of my head, and focused instead on the room here, now. The villagers would sit in front of me, tell me their problems—sometimes physical, sometimes emotional, sometimes financial—and I would heal them. I spun the armfuls of cotton in my mind into fine, strong god light, blue inside my skin, and focused it outward. I chanted *Om Sri Ram* over and over in my head. This was my prayer to Rama, one of my previous incarnations.

An older hunched woman came forward, holding her lower back. She touched my feet. I blessed her.

"How did you hurt your back?" I asked. Ayya had taught me this. Diagnose early, before they can tell you.

"Too much work for an old woman."

"Your sons should take care of you better."

"My sons don't care."

I prayed and hovered my hands over her. I willed my light to spin into the muscles of her back. *Om Sri Ram.*

She stood up straighter, hands at her lower back. Her face relaxed as I pushed my energy into her.

"Thank you," she said.

I kept an eye on Ayya for his nod, to show me I was doing the right thing. He nodded.

Next, a young boy who was developing too slowly. A regular. Every time I prayed over him, he came back the next week stronger and taller. *Om Sri Ram.*

A man whose textile-selling business wasn't doing well. He touched my feet and I told him he would sell more podavais and veshtis next week. *Om Sri Ram.* A young woman nearing thirty and still not married. Her parents had set her up with an arranged marriage; the groom was scheduled to visit their house on Monday. I blessed her with luck. *Om Sri Ram.*

One family, a young father with his wife and small child, came from many miles away. The child's legs and arms were whittled and thin. Her father carried her in his arms like she weighed nothing, though she was nearly my height, and he placed her on the floor in front of me. I shifted on my cushion to get a better look. This was it. This was my test. I was sure of it.

Roopa's face was sunken in, like she hadn't eaten in weeks. Frail skin stretched over bone. She looked almost like a corpse, but her eyes were pretty and large and she watched me as she lay on the bare cement floor, her chest moving up and down fast, like a songbird's. She was almost beautiful, if I only looked at her eyes.

The god energy filled my skin, filled the inside of me shaped like a room, and I looked around and saw the others filled with their own energies, their own people energies, but Roopa's skin was empty. It was like her soul couldn't find any room inside her fragile body anymore. I didn't know if a person could leave a body and still be a person. And the body they left behind—was that body a person?

But her eyes—I could still see her personness in her eyes.

"Please," her father said. "Our daughter needs healing. We can't afford to pay." He glanced at Ayya, at the ground, and finally toward me. He held pain in his face, and embarrassment. Ayya had told me that a lot of men find it hard to ask for help. The father dropped his gaze to the floor.

"How did she get like this?" I asked. I always knew to ask the question, though I still didn't know what to do with the answer. Ayya knew, and he would tell me what to do.

"She took ill one day. She's not eating." The man looked at his wife, who covered her mouth with her hands. "We have four sons. We can't afford to bring her to the private hospital. The doctors at the clinics don't know what to do."

Ayya nodded at me, a signal to begin my healing prayer. I sat myself next to the girl, the cold of the cement floor shocking my legs through my veshti. When I looked only at her pretty eyes, the rest of her receded.

I took some kumkumam powder and rubbed a red line of it on her forehead. People normally got kumkumam, turmeric, and sandalwood powders from their local market, but we also made them at the ashram. On any given day, my aunt and uncle, Vasanthy Chithy and Kantha Chithappa—Lakshman's parents—would sit grinding sticks of sandalwood or dried turmeric roots on stone in order to make the powders we sold. Villagers bought them for the shrines in their houses, because what we made was purer, made with care, and made in the home of a god.

I put my hands over Roopa's face and closed my eyes. *Om Sri Ram.* I tried to summon up the god energy inside me. Sinewy and blue and gold. *Om Sri Ram.* Blue and gold and bright. I touched her forehead with my thumb. She was dying, and I was the only one who could help. This was my first test. I tried to push the energy inside of her. Gold and luminescent and blue. *Om Sri Ram.*

She didn't move. She lay where her father had put her, eyes darting around the room.

The room had stopped breathing, everyone watching us. My lungs felt too small.

I pushed more god energy, spun more of the mind cotton into light, pushed it all inside her. But still she lay there, with everyone watching. I blinked away the tears in my eyes. I imagined my previous incarnations in the room with me, Rama and Krishna and all the rest, letting their own god energies shine on Roopa's sickness, easing it away.

Ayya was trying to signal something to me, but I couldn't tell what he wanted.

Lakshman took my hand and squeezed it. He leaned over, pressed his shoulder into mine, and whispered, "I'll help," into my ear. I turned back to Roopa and put my thumb back on her forehead while Lakshman held my other hand. Out of the corner of my eye, I saw Ayya nod.

I tried again, this time with Lakshman, pushing and pushing the god energy, spinning more of it from the cotton in my mind, and Roopa lay there, breath rasping inside her chest, not moving except for her eyes. She opened her mouth, and the room was silent. She mouthed something. I leaned forward to hear.

Still too quiet.

I pressed my ear against her lips.

"You look constipated," she said.

I didn't realize I'd laughed until I heard the bark of it echo back at me from the silent room. Some of the villagers traded looks. Heat prickled up through my head and narrowed my vision.

"It will take time to heal her," Ayya said, his voice booming across the room. "She needs to stay at the ashram until she's well."

People nodded. The girl's mother and father looked at each other for a long time, searching for something, the mother's eyes baggy and raw. The father turned to me and bowed, acknowledging his consent.

I clenched my hands into tight fists to keep them from trembling.

"Meditation time," Ayya said.

Roopa's father picked her up and put her in his lap. Everyone bent their heads for meditation. Lakshman still held my hand, his little fingers slippery in mine. I lowered my face too, grateful that the angle hid my tears.

The healing session took so long that the sun had almost set, and the village kids had finished a full game by the time Ayya allowed Lakshman and me to join. The boy with the bat showed it to me, and I ran my fingers along the flat edge. It wasn't new—the wood at the end was pocked from too many hits to the ball, dented from pounding wickets into dirt, the red grip frayed into many little threads. But it was the first bat I'd seen in real life.

"Let's play," Lakshman said.

I wished he hadn't said it. I wanted to play. I pictured the scene—me, the star of the game, running down the field with the bat held high in the air. As a god, they'd expect me to be good at everything. But I'd never played cricket, never touched a bat. Now that it was in front of me, I was sure I'd trip or miss the ball completely.

The village kids were dark and reedy, with thin legs sticking out of well-washed, now-dirty shorts—unlike Lakshman and me, both scrubbed clean and fed enough that our cheeks were plump.

"We're tired," the boy with the bat said. He was my age and had crooked teeth and hair parted fiercely in the middle of his head. "But for you we'll play one small game, Kalki Sami."

I didn't like his tone, which was both challenging and mocking, and I didn't like the way he made eye contact with me, which no one but my family did. He seemed like the leader of the group. He offered the bat to me handle-first, and I took it. The boys had already pounded in three sticks at the edge of the field to act as wickets. I walked to the spot in the faded din of the adults' conversations as they sat around socializing after the bhajan. Through the open door, the small, sick girl curled up in her father's lap like a kitten. I searched for Ayya, but he was busy taking donations from the villagers in a little box.

Lakshman followed me to the wickets. The bat was heavier than I expected, the grip of it sweaty from the boy's hand. I held it the best I could, but I didn't know if it was right, if the boys noticed my awkwardness.

The boy leader stood opposite me with the ball in his hand while everyone else scattered to the edges of the field.

"Lakshman," he said, "you have to come here to get ready to run. Kalki Sami is going to hit the ball. Maybe he'll get a sixer."

Lakshman started to walk away, and panic took my throat.

"Let Lakshman hit first," I said. I ran to him, pressed the bat into his waiting hands, and walked back to where the boy with the ball stood. I hoped I seemed gracious instead of scared.

Lakshman hefted the bat and held it the way we'd seen in photos in the newspapers Ayya and Kantha Chithappa bought from the village.

The boy with the ball ran forward, wound up, and threw. Lakshman swung and made contact. The ball rolled sideways between the two boys who were fielding.

"Run!" someone shouted. "Run to the other side!"

I ran and saw Lakshman do the same from the other end, the bat swinging wildly from his hand. We ran past each other and to the other side.

"Touch the ground! It doesn't count otherwise."

We both touched the ground where we stood. I turned and prepared to run back to my spot, but the boy leader had gotten the ball.

"One run!" he called out. "Your turn to hit, Kalki Sami."

Lakshman came to give me the bat. No going back. The boys watched me expectantly.

I took my place in front of the wickets, the bat in my hand. I'd sweated a sheen all over my body. I held the bat the way Lakshman had. Most of the adults in the ashram's meditation room watched us now. Even the sick girl, Roopa, watched from her father's lap. A small frown curled Ayya's mouth.

I imagined hitting the ball, how it would feel for me and Lakshman to run back and forth and score the most points, the way Ayya would smile at me from the veranda.

The boy with the ball took his place, and Lakshman stood near him, bending close to the ground, ready to run. The boy ran forward, wound up, and threw. The ball left his hand—I saw it there, hanging just so in the air, rolling from the tips of his fingers.

I swung upward in a scooping motion, the way I knew I should. But the impact of the ball never came.

"Out!" the boy cried. "Hit wicket."

I turned. Behind me, the right wicket had been hit. The stick lay half-toppled, and next to it, the ball.

The boys cheered.

"You bowled out Kalki Sami!" one of them said. They ran forward to clap the boy leader on the back. "You bowled out a god!"

A burn grew behind my nose, filling my sinuses. I looked toward the ashram building. Ayya's frown had deepened, and he turned away. Roopa's eyes were swollen and large in her withered face. Lakshman tugged at my arm, but I didn't turn around. If I saw his face, I was sure I would cry. I sniffed the clogged feeling out of my nose and took a deep breath to steady myself.

"Good job," I said. My voice cracked, but it was loud enough to reach the boy who had thrown the ball.

He grinned with missing teeth.

I wanted to disappear into the ashram's coconut grove and the creek that ran through it. I wanted to sit on the banks with my knees tucked under my chin and listen to the clattering of the water as it dragged rocks against the riverbed.

Lakshman pulled at my arm again, and I wrenched it out of his grasp. I strode deliberately back to building instead of running the way I wanted to. I ignored the stares of the rest of the adults, all except Ayya, who refused to look at me. I was so used to being watched by him that the absence of his gaze scorched my skin.

I sat next to Amma, who pulled me to her and patted my hair. I clamped my teeth so tight to keep from crying that my jaws hurt. Two failures in one night, and this was the day before my tenth birthday, the year Ayya told me I was supposed to come into my full god powers. The year I was supposed to prove myself.

3

Here are the facts of my life as a living god—I have blue skin. I grew up at the Kali Yuga ashram on the outskirts of Tamil Nadu, India. Ayya raised me believing that one day, I would travel all over the world to meet with my devotees, but only if I proved myself, if I passed the three trials. I was desperate to prove myself.

Here are the facts of my life as an Indian boy on his tenth birthday—I'd never been to school. Ayya taught me and Lakshman every day, and my whole sense of the world came from newspapers and his lessons. I'd never had a friend besides Lakshman, and I'd never interacted with anyone like Roopa.

Her family left her in our care. We put her in the smallest room, an eight-by-eight-foot square with a bed and a chair in the back of the ashram building. This was the first time anyone had stayed overnight at the ashram. This was the most serious illness we'd seen yet.

"It'll take all of your powers," Ayya said that first night, after the villagers went home. "You got distracted today."

He didn't frown, but his mouth twitched. A bad sign.

Everyone said I looked like him—our faces thin and long, our hair fluffy, our bodies soft and doughy. But his skin was the color of burnt sugar, and mine was blue. His hair was black and sleek and held in a bun at the back of his neck, and mine was a dark, curly brown that shone lighter in the sun. His eyes were inky, and mine were like smooth, sticky honey. We chalked up these color differences to our Brahminic lineage, which we traced to central Asia and to my godhood.

Ayya's angular face and hard, wet eyes gave him a stern look, made more severe by a scar that cut through his lower lip, leftover from a bicycle accident when he was in medical school. Like me, he wore cotton veshtis and a poonal diagonally across his body to signify his Brahmin caste. Traditionally, boys—and, as I'd learn later, girls in pre-modern times—would earn the thread when they started their formal education of the sacred texts. I'd gotten mine at six years old, and Lakshman had gotten his at five, when Ayya started teaching us. Every year during Avani Avittam, we changed our poonal.

Ayya linked his fingers above his head and stretched, the muscles of his hairy chest and arms pulled tight. He had a confidence that made people listen. The villagers came to me for healing, but they went to him for advice about everything from wayward sons to stubborn crops. Groups of elder village men would sometimes walk to the ashram and sit with Ayya and Kantha Chithappa out on the veranda, talking late into the evening. Lakshman and I liked to hide behind the open green doors of the meditation room and listen to them discuss temple-building fundraisers, petty village crimes, and scary new ideas youngsters brought back from urban universities. I liked to picture myself all grown up, surrounded by the village elders, all of whom would hang on to my words and ask me for advice. In the imagining, I always put Lakshman next to me, like Kantha Chithappa next to Ayya, listening and nodding.

"Your eagerness to play distracted you from healing Roopa

properly," Ayya said now, sitting with me in the courtyard of our home after the prayer meeting. "You know you were wrong. It's why you didn't hit the ball. You knew inside that you were wrong."

"Yes, Ayya," I said. The shame of my double failure bristled at my skin and climbed up my spine to my neck and face. I had been childish. Ayya told me that at ten, I was old enough to know right from wrong, to have the responsibility to choose. I chose wrong.

"If you can't heal her," he said, "people will doubt you, and you'll never get to go on your world healing tour. Everyone needs to believe. You can't fail."

Hindus, Ayya was fond of saying, were lost without our gurus and gods. We were a people that needed guidance, needed faith. We'd had our religion longer than most of the world—we'd kept it alive through thousands of years of Muslim and Christian rule—and it was up to me to guide us through the next epoch.

"Yes, Ayya," I said. Hindus—and the world—had no use for a god who couldn't heal. The villagers would stop coming.

When he was just a toddler, Krishna, one of my previous incarnations, showed his mother the entire universe held in his mouth. All I had done was heal some minor ailments. Roopa would be my first big miracle, and everyone was waiting.

That night, after the adults and Roopa had gone to bed, Lakshman shook me awake, standing over me and holding out a piece of candied jackfruit like an offering. Syrup glazed his wrists.

"Happy birthday," he said.

"What time is it?"

"Midnight."

I had turned ten years old. He was still nine. His eyes and teeth glowed white against the dark. Through the open shutters, the moon hurled mango leaf shadows against the wall. The air hung with humidity.

The jackfruit was slimy and fleshy in my hand, like a little heart, if hearts were cold to the touch. Lakshman watched me. I'd brushed my teeth before bed and I wasn't hungry, but he'd gone to the trouble—had sneaked it out of the kitchen and risked getting caught. I wanted to see his gap-toothed smile. So I bit into the fruit, the sweetness of it hurting my teeth.

Jackfruit grew on trees at the edge of the ashram property, and when they swelled and stank of rot and weighed as much as either one of us, our mothers harvested the fruit, broke them open, and canned handfuls in sugar water. Jackfruit in syrup was one of our favorite snacks, and it was the only thing Lakshman had to give me.

I pretended to eat the fruit like a monkey, slurping the juice from my hands. Lakshman laughed. I reached out to touch him with my sticky fingers, and he jumped away, squealing.

"Shhhh," I said. Ayya was a light sleeper.

Lakshman watched me eat. When I finished, I sucked the juice from my fingers and settled back into the blankets. He waited, blinking in the moonlight, until I raised my covers. He crawled in and shaped his body next to mine in the narrow bed. His breathing turned slow and drum-like, and I lay awake, listening to its rhythm in the swaying dark.

I took a walk in the cold dawn, leaving Lakshman snoring in my bed. Normally I went to the oxbow pond with Ayya in the mornings, but today I was ten, and like I'd planned, I'd woken up early enough to go on my own. I'd be back at the ashram by the time Ayya got up, and he'd look at me with pride and recognition of my grown-up responsibility. He'd forgive me for my failures the night before. He'd smile. He'd love me again.

The ashram in those days was small and isolated—one building ten kilometers outside a tiny village. Rice paddies bordered the east side, beyond which lay the oxbow pond, and beyond that, the village. I'd never been to the village, but several times a week, Ayya and my uncle Kantha Chithappa would go in the mornings to buy vegetables, and we had an old cleaning lady who came from the village every other day to sweep out the house.

Two kilometers to the oxbow pond. I walked slow, carrying a small stool and the materials I needed for the sandhyavandanam liturgy, a cleansing of my sins so that I could perform my healing.

Sunlight slingshot itself all over the rice paddies and the thatched roof of the ashram. Birds called. All around me, monkeys climbed high in the trees, cradling their young. Everyone was waking in their own cocoons before they faced the world. Soon, my mother, Amma, and her sister, Vasanthy Chithy, would be in the kitchen, boiling water for morning tea; Ayya would meditate out on the veranda; and Kantha Chithappa, Vasanthy Chithy's husband, would remain in bed, reading the newspaper.

The oxbow pond glistened under the new sun, cradled on all sides by wild reeds. When Ayya was my age, the oxbow was part of the outermost bend of the river that flowed by the village, but by the time I was born, the river had changed shape, leaving behind a pond shaped like a comma. All throughout my childhood, the river flooded the surrounding plain every few seasons, spilling into the oxbow and feeding it. Twenty-five years after my tenth birthday, I returned to this pond to find it a mere puddle among dried-up weeds, the river having neglected it for decades.

I dipped a copper pot into the piercing cold water. I set up my materials and sat on the small wooden stool. *Om bhuur bhuvah svah,* I chanted, *tat savitur varennyam, bhargo devasya dhiimahi, dhiyo yo nah pracodayaat* . . . I dripped water from the pot, poured it on my hand, and brought my palm to my mouth to drink, thinking about the importance of this tenth birthday.

Whenever the world needed him, Vishnu took human forms on earth—avatars, from the Sanskrit word *avatara*, which means "descent." So far, Vishnu had taken nine avatar forms on earth, beginning with Manu the fish and moving on up through Rama, the hero of the epic *Ramayana*, then Krishna, and finally—this depended on who you asked—either the Buddha or Jesus. I, Kalki, was the last incarnation before the world would start anew.

On my walk back, village farmers waded knee-deep in the flooded rice paddies, white turbans wrapped around their heads to protect them from the sun. They put their palms together in front of their chests and bowed to me as I passed.

Back at the ashram, Ayya would be leaving for the pond, a blue shawl around his torso to keep warm. I would try not to look too pleased when he saw me. I would keep my head down, and when I looked up, Ayya would have a small smile at the corner of his mouth, my failure forgiven because I was exhibiting good decision-making and responsibility. My chest expanded as I imagined it, and I drank in the air.

But as I walked toward the ashram, Ayya wasn't there. The balloon in my chest deflated, and the cold of my body returned.

I dried myself in my room, where Lakshman was still sleeping with his feet wound around the covers and his mouth drooling into my pillow. I went to find Amma, who would be making hot, sweet milk tea in the kitchen.

The ashram's one cement building had a square hole in the middle that formed a courtyard. The clay shingle roof leaked water during the monsoons. Terra-cotta plaster columns held up the ceiling like blank-faced soldiers. Out of four bedrooms, I had one all to myself. Lakshman slept in a room with his parents, though he often came to me in the middle of the night to squeeze himself into my bed. The last room, we reserved for guests—where Roopa slept now. The windows had no glass, just bars to keep the monkeys from sneaking in and curtains Amma stitched together from old podavais and veshtis. Even in the height of summer, a breeze filled the house.

Tucked away at the very back of the ashram, the kitchen had a clay stove which I liked tending when Amma let me, stoking the heat inside by blowing through a long iron tube, the cold metallic tang pressing against my lips.

Voices floated from the kitchen as I approached—Amma's and Ayya's. I paused to listen, hidden behind the door.

"He's just a boy," Amma was saying. "What's the harm?"

"He'll get spoiled," Ayya said. "Did you see him yesterday? All he cared about was playing that silly game. It's not good for him. He's distracted, and he failed."

"But it's the only thing he asked for."

My body, already dispirited that Ayya hadn't seen me go to the oxbow pond alone, leaked out all the air I had left. There would be no cricket bat for my birthday. And I'd been hopeful—I'd been on my best behavior.

"Publicly!" Ayya said. "He failed publicly. What do you think the villagers thought? They're all waiting to see if he'll fail the first test. He doesn't need more distractions."

Amma said nothing. I wondered if she had turned back to the stove, or if she was angry.

"Amma?" I said, trying to sound as if I was wandering toward the kitchen and not already here.

"Your tea's in here," she called, her voice choked.

I pushed open the door and went in. The room smelled like the clay pot of rice and lentils that Amma had left to ferment overnight, which she would soon steam into little idly cakes for breakfast.

Ayya stood awkwardly with a rolled-up newspaper in his hand while Amma crouched by the low stove, blowing air into the flames and moving around the wood inside. She'd already set up the steamer, and banana leaves sat on the counter, waiting to serve as plates.

When my parents stood together, Amma looked even younger, and Ayya even older. I didn't know exactly how far apart they were in age, but I would have guessed at least fifteen years. The closer they stood in proximity, the bigger the gap seemed.

"Happy birthday," Amma said. She wiped her hands on a dirty rag and hugged me. She smelled like sweat-infused cotton and jasmine from the flowers in her dark, oiled hair. I liked to think Amma looked like pictures of Yashodha, Krishna's mother, with heavy-lidded eyes, a thin button nose, and a dark mole on her cheek. The plump skin of her stomach spilled over the waistband of her podavai. She had golden brown skin, a beauty in her teenage years—and now still.

She handed me my tea in a warm silver cup.

"Happy birthday," Ayya said, his mouth pursed at the edges. He always looked like he was angry with me, but today he looked angrier than usual.

I'd hoped that since today was my birthday, we would be excused from lessons, and Lakshman and I could play all day until it was time for me to do my next healing session with Roopa. But with Ayya thinking I was afraid we might not get to play at all. I had to convince him.

I touched Ayya's feet for his blessings. When I stood up again, he asked, "Did you go to the pond?"

"Yes. I got up early."

He nodded but wouldn't look at me. He cleared his throat and left the kitchen. I'd thought my going to the pond would be enough compensation for my failure, but of course, with Ayya, nothing was enough. Nothing short of miracles. My shame calcified inside my stomach.

"You are my godsend," Amma said, kissing my cheek. The smell of her skin made me feel younger, like I had never turned ten and could go on sitting in her lap every day. She looked around to make sure Ayya had left and pushed a small bag of peanuts into my hand. "Be careful with these."

Peanuts weren't allowed on the ashram property because Ayya had a severe peanut allergy. Their rarity made me love them all that much more, since they had to be smuggled back from the village. I would enjoy the peanuts with Lakshman later, in my room, and we'd make sure to wash our hands and our mouths carefully so Ayya wouldn't know.

Amma pressed me tight to her. "I have your painting for you," she said. "Come get it later, okay?" She was a wonderful painter. She'd trained in the visual arts in college in Hyderabad, and now she painted as a hobby, though few of her paintings were ever hung at the ashram. I'd requested a painting of Krishna and Radha for my birthday.

Most of Amma's paintings told stories of gods and goddesses. A human-headed Ganesha standing guard for his mother as she bathed. Devaki, Krishna's birth mother, in her brother the king's prison. Vasudev, Krishna's birth father, delivering a newborn Krishna to safety through a miraculously parted river. Her paintings had a way of morphing before your eyes if you stared at them long enough, the colors saturated and thick.

When I finally got my requested painting, the canvas was the size of my face, a surreal riot of colors that looked like they were moving on their own. A blue Krishna stood under a tree playing his flute, and his lover, Radha, leaned her head against his shoulder. It was a pose I'd seen a million times, but in Amma's version, Krishna looked a lot like me.

After breakfast in the courtyard—a silent affair—Lakshman and I headed out to play in the coconut grove, which lay to the west of the ashram and was so deep and thick that I hadn't seen the other side. Giddy with our rare freedom, we raced each other through the grass to the trees. As we ran, Vasanthy Chithy, Lakshman's mother, followed behind us, carrying a blanket and a book. I tried to let the fun absorb me fully, but the guilt of not healing Roopa gnawed at the back of my mind.

When we reached the coconut grove, Lakshman and I played our favorite game—acting out scenes from the *Mahabharata.*

Vasanthy Chithy kept an eye on us from the blanket she spread out on the dirt. She sat with her legs folded underneath her, the pleats of her podavai flowing all around, and a ragged copy of a Tamil novel in her hand. Ayya didn't like us reading anything that wasn't religious. He thought it put strange ideas into our heads, poisoning our brains. But Vasanthy Chithy owned some books Ayya didn't know about, books with pictures of sad women on the covers. She hummed under her breath as she read. Like Amma, she was pliant and soft all over, except for her sharp elbows and collarbones. Unlike Amma, though, she had thin, slanted eyes and a pointed chin that Lakshman had inherited. She plaited her kinky black hair into a braid that ran down her spine, which she liked tossing this way and that over her shoulder as she read.

Lakshman and I acted out the crucial battle scene from the *Mahabharata,* in which the hero Arjuna despairs at the thought of killing his great-uncle on the battlefield; in response, the avatar Krishna, Arjuna's friend and charioteer, reveals his true god form as Vishnu, and begins narrating the text of the *Bhagavad Gita.*

Lakshman, playing Arjuna, kneeled in front of me, the pleats of his white cotton veshti pooling around his lap.

"I can't do this, Krishna." He blinked his glassy eyes. "He's my great-uncle. I can't kill him."

I stood on my tiptoes to pretend that I was swelling to my god size. "Arjuna." I used the best god voice I could muster, from deep inside my stomach. "This is your duty to your family, to your brother and king. You must fulfill your destiny."

Lakshman nodded at the ground. He prayed to me. I blessed him.

"You are weak, Arjuna," I said. "You are distracted."

Lakshman stood. This was the part where he strung his bow and, with tears running down his face, shot arrow after arrow into the coconut tree that we pretended was Arjuna's great-uncle Bhishma.

"I want to be Krishna," Lakshman said. "You're always Krishna." His thick eyebrows drew together. He put his fists on his hips. "I want to be Krishna."

The sun beat down, but he didn't seem to mind. My arms itched with sweat. He was acting this way because Ayya had scolded me. Because I hadn't healed Roopa yet. He, too, thought I was less of a god because I hadn't passed my first trial easily.

"Let me be Krishna," he said.

I shook my head. I was Kalki—even if I'd had a momentary struggle with healing Roopa—which meant I was all my previous lives, including Krishna. He couldn't change that by pretending.

He dropped his bow. "Let me be Krishna."

"*I'm* Krishna."

He put two hands on my chest and pushed me hard. I was slightly taller, but he had the muscle mass. I fell backward into the grass, the blades rubbing my back raw.

"Lakshman," his mother scolded. She rushed over and helped me to my feet.

My yellow panchakacham veshti was stained green. The full shame of Ayya's words—and the failures of the night before—hit me as I looked up at Lakshman.

"Lakshman, apologize," Vasanthy Chithy said.

I sat in the grass, trying to wipe my tears away without them seeing. Gods didn't cry, even when they were children, even if they were failures.

Lakshman watched me for a while, his face pinched. He dropped to his knees and threw his arms around my neck.

"I'm sorry, big brother," he said. "I'm sorry. I'm sorry. You're Krishna. I'm sorry."

Back at the ashram before lunch, Ayya called me to the courtyard, and I went, my face scrubbed clean of dried tears, my knees wobbly and nervous.

Our small square courtyard had no roof. A mango tree grew out of the concrete foundation and spread its leaves over us. In the middle of the open square, a tulsi plant flowered in a raised concrete pot. Tulsi was considered holy, an incarnation of Laxmi herself, and at every end of the Tamil month of Karthigai, we performed a wedding ritual where the tulsi plant was married off to Vishnu.

On most days, Amma and Vasanthy Chithy squatted in the courtyard, picking rocks out of rice on broad palm leaf sifters and laying out sheets of red chili peppers to dry in the sun. Now they brought out clay pots of rice and curries from the kitchen and set up our banana leaves, their backs hunched under the shade of the mango tree.

Ayya sat on the step that led down into the sunken courtyard, leaning against a plaster column with *The Hindu* open on his lap. He saw me and called me with a flick of his finger.

I sat at his feet to show utmost respect and didn't look him in the eye.

He tapped his knuckles once on the paper. "The birthday present I arranged for you is so much better for you than a cricket bat," he said. "There's a journalist coming this afternoon. He's going to do a story on you. Imagine." Ayya held out his arms wide. "You'll be in *The Hindu*. The world will know about you." He let his arms fall back down. "That is, of course, if you heal Roopa. He's coming today to see her, and he'll come back in a month. If you heal her, he'll write up a story."

I was still caught between renewed disappointment that I wouldn't be getting a bat and panic that someone would be checking my work with Roopa.

I had to heal her. I had no choice. Ayya had always helped me before, but this was my test, and I was on my own.

"You're going to have devotees all over the world," he said. "This is your destiny, but first you heal Roopa. After lunch, I want you in your prayer night outfit. You've had enough playing for today."

I knew how to tie my own veshti, but after lunch, Kantha Chithappa helped me so that it looked perfect. He fixed the Namam on my forehead, pulled my shoulder-length hair into a bun on one side of my head, and wrapped it in a string of pearls. I put on my gold earrings, necklace, waist chain, anklets, and armlets. My hands shook.

Lakshman wore his white silk veshti. Our hair matched. He had less jewelry than I did, and of course, his skin wasn't blue, but otherwise, we were a pair.

Kantha Chithappa led us to the meditation room. Our mothers and Ayya were already there.

The man who sat waiting for us looked too young to be a journalist. He wiped sweat off his forehead with a kerchief. His blue shirt had patches of sweat at the armpits and on his chest. He told us his name was Anton. He had a wide nose and too much space around his ears.

I nodded to him, trying to feign calm, and we took our seats. I sat with one leg tucked underneath me and my hand on my knee, mirroring the image of Krishna that hung behind me, our skins the same shade of blue.

"Do you want to hear a story?" Ayya asked.

"I'd like to ask him some questions," Anton said.

Ayya waved this aside. "First I'll tell you the story of how Kalki got his blue skin. Then you can ask your questions."

Ayya commanded the room, and Anton was quiet as Ayya began. I focused on my breathing, trying to get my heartbeat to slow down.

"I was young," Ayya said, "an immigrant doctor working in America. I didn't believe in gods, or in Vishnu. I thought science would solve everything. I was stupid. And that stupidity led to the death of my first wife. Then I married Kalki's mother, and she saved me. She taught me how to pray and the importance of believing. But we couldn't have children."

I knew the story. Ayya and Amma couldn't have children. They scoured the world looking for cures. Science let them down, and the treatments left Amma's body weak and ragged. One day, they found an old swami on his deathbed in Nepal.

"The dying swami sat up," Ayya said, "and told us we would have a beautiful little boy with blue skin, a boy who would be the next and last incarnation of Lord Vishnu."

A boy who would save the world. This part was my favorite. I wanted so badly to be the boy who would save the world. Anton sat listening to Ayya and not saying a word, but his face was clouded, not enraptured, as if he was doubtful.

"Kalki wasn't born with blue skin," Ayya said. "He was perfectly normal. Pale, even. Still, we were thrilled. I continued to work as a doctor in America. We didn't fully believe the swami."

When I was six months old, we all visited India, and a cobra snuck into my room. Amma saw it, but it had already climbed into my crib. With one strike, it bit my ankle and crawled out the window. Amma wept, thinking I would die.

I didn't. Instead, my skin turned blue.

"The swami had been right all along," Ayya said.

The Kali Yuga ashram was once owned by Ayya's father, who

was a respected priest and guru before his early death. He died right after Ayya left for America, and Ayya's greatest regret was not returning for the funeral. After I was bit by the cobra, Ayya and Amma renovated the ashram and moved us back to India, where they could raise me and teach me everything I needed to learn to realize my destiny as Vishnu's avatar. Vasanthy Chithy and Kantha Chithappa joined us soon after with young Lakshman, and none of us had ever left.

"Show him your scar," Ayya said.

I uncrossed my legs, lifted my veshti, and showed Anton the faded dots of the snake bite on my ankle. He looked at it closely, bending over and grazing the scar with his fingers.

"What are your questions?" Ayya asked.

Anton flipped open a notebook. "How old are you, Kalki?"

Ayya nodded to tell me it was okay to answer.

"I'm ten," I said, feigning calm.

"Do you believe yourself to be Sri Kalki, the last avatar of Vishnu?"

"Yes." I looked Anton straight in the eye, so he could see I wasn't lying. Ayya had made me practice this with him. I had to command respect. I puffed out my chest. "I am Sri Kalki Sami," I said.

Anton stared into my eyes for a few seconds before writing something down. "And are you going to heal this young girl, Kalki Sami?"

"Yes."

"I've seen her. She looks very sick. Do you really think you can heal her?"

Dampness grew in my armpits. I squeezed my arm to my side so that no one would see. "I will heal her," I said.

"And you think this is the first test, as prophesied by the *Sri Kalki Purana*?"

"Yes. And I will pass it." The confidence in my voice pleased me.

Anton wrote some more in his notebook. "Can I see your hand?"

I gave him my hand, hoping it wasn't shaking. Anton rubbed the blue skin with his cold fingers. He looked at his thumb, as if seeing if any of the color had transferred. "Can you get some water and wash your hands?" he asked.

I yanked my hand back. None of the villagers had ever asked me these kinds of questions. Their belief was easy, given freely. I didn't like this man and his questions, his skepticism.

Vasanthy Chithy got a bowl of water for me and some soap. I washed my hands. They remained blue.

He took my hand again, this time without asking. He rubbed the back of it some more.

"If you don't believe," Ayya said, his teeth pressed tight and a vein throbbing in his temple, "look in his mouth."

I opened my mouth. Anton peered inside. He looked afraid at what he saw. Most people did. I didn't have the whole universe inside my mouth like Krishna did, but my tongue and gums were purple. I was blue inside and out.

Anton didn't ask any more questions. When he left, he told me he'd be back in a month to see if Roopa was healed.

4

Twenty-five years after Roopa arrived at the ashram, I got a call in the middle of the night, informing me that Ayya had died of a heart attack. It was Gopi who called, Ayya's assistant, who had been hired when I was thirteen.

"Your Ayya," Gopi said. His usually unctuous voice had lost its whine. "Should I tell them to go ahead with the funeral?"

I sat up from my bed and rubbed the sleep out of my eyes. Outside, in the glow of streetlights, fat, white snowflakes fell steadily onto the Toronto streets. My nose was cold from the chill inside my studio apartment.

"No," I said. "Tell them to wait. I'm coming."

I booked a flight immediately—the fees exorbitant for my paltry lecturer salary—and took a cab to the airport, where I caught a red-eye and three flight transfers back home to Tamil Nadu. I hired a car to take me to the ashram, which, Gopi had told me, had passed in inheritance to me. I didn't want it. I didn't know what I would or should do with it.

For the past decade or so, Ayya and Gopi had run the ashram like a spiritual retreat for white foreigners wanting to find themselves. Newly divorced women and men in their midlife crises, young people taking gap years to travel the world and do yoga—they all wanted a backdrop of exotic color for their social media posts, and Ayya was happy to oblige. He even hosted destination weddings for Westerners, complete with hired dance performers, silk podavais, and food from all over India.

In my imagination, as I devoured movie after movie on my sleepless flights to India, the ashram—once the home of a living god—had been turned into little more than a theme park.

But the ashram I found looked the same as the one I remembered leaving. It was bigger, of course, than it had been when I was ten, but the expansions had all happened while I was still living there. The buildings had been maintained but not upgraded, and everything— even the trees in the coconut grove—were exactly as I'd left them.

I wanted to feel sad as I completed the last rites for Ayya, but all I felt was relief. Still, I was here, surrounded by a meager crowd, performing my final Hindu duty as his son. Ayya lay on a pyre, a garland of marigolds around his neck. His skin sagged more than the last time I'd seen him. The night hummed with humidity, the darkness pricked with stars. I touched the tip of a burning torch to Ayya's body and set his soul free.

5

Two days after the failed cricket game and the failed healing, Roopa didn't seem to be getting better. At least she wasn't getting worse, I told myself. It would take time, I told myself. I just had to believe.

But doubt still wrapped its hands around my neck when I laid down at night. So far, only the people from the village close to the ashram knew about me, and they believed. But the spine of their faith was unstable, like a string pulled too tight. If I failed any of the three trials as foretold by the prophecy, they would see me as a fraud, and my fame would never get to spread beyond the village. If I was going to go on a world healing tour like Ayya had promised, I needed that journalist to write about me.

I performed my healing prayer three times a day. Every morning, afternoon, and night, I went to Roopa's small room and stood by her small cot. I willed and willed her to get better, but for two days she didn't move, except for the cough that scraped itself out of her chest.

I redoubled my efforts. I did healing sessions on her every hour while she watched me with her big dark eyes. As I held my hands over her blanketed body, heat crept up from the small of my back to my neck, up my face, and to the top of my scalp. I had to concentrate to keep my hands steady. I wanted to touch her, to feel the papery thinness of her skin, which wilted over her like too-big clothing, but I didn't.

On the fourth day, Roopa stirred when I came to her room in the morning. She opened her mouth and whispered something. I pressed my ear to her lips, my body shivering at the closeness.

"Water," she said.

I helped her drink water from a cup next to the bed. She coughed and laid back down. I put my hands over her and closed my eyes, summoning up all the loose cotton from the edges of my mind, spinning it into light, and directing it outward through my fingers.

"This isn't working," she said, so softly that I leaned forward again to hear her. "They said you were a god."

"I am," I said. "It'll take time." I remembered what Ayya had said. "You have to believe in me, Roopa, or else you won't heal."

"I don't think that's how it works."

I laughed despite myself. She was talking, and that was a good sign—maybe even a sign that she was healing.

Lakshman thought that Roopa would get bored lying in her tiny sick room all day, so he started sitting by her bed in his free time and reading to her from Ayya's books. Before Roopa came, Lakshman and I rarely separated during the day—when I walked to the oxbow pond for my morning sandhyavadanam, when I had my bath at night—but otherwise we followed each other like shadows.

Now he took every second of free time to be with Roopa in her sick room. He read his favorite Arjuna story over and over until I was sure Roopa craved silence. I missed him, and I was jealous of Roopa for taking his attention.

On the sixth night of Roopa's stay, I went into the sick room to heal her, but also to spend time with Lakshman. I brought a copper jug of a potion I'd made myself with the leaves of the tulsi plant in our courtyard. I'd tried everything else. I'd tried singing, chanting. I'd tried rubbing sacred kumkumam and sandalwood paste on her forehead. I'd exhausted my imagination thinking of ways to heal her.

Lakshman, as expected, was already sitting on the wooden chair by the head of her bed, his thin legs sticking out from the seat and the illustrated *Mahabharata* open on his lap. He stopped reading as I gave Roopa the potion to drink. I tipped it to her lips and cupped her head in my other hand. My palm grew hot and sweaty where I touched her—electricity between our skins.

I'd given her a bead of tulsi bark made from the stem of the same plant, which hung on a thin chain around her neck. This, combined with the tulsi water, was sure to heal her.

I did my healing prayer, not making eye contact with Roopa and hoping the heat in my skin wasn't apparent.

"What if you can't heal her?" Lakshman asked.

"I can," I said, and tried to act like his question hadn't made my throat twist with worry. "It'll take time." I touched Roopa's forehead, schooling my face so Lakshman couldn't see how much I was straining to push my god energy into her.

"I'm serious." He hopped off the chair. "What if you can't?"

"Healing is what I do." I tried hard to keep the anger out of my voice, but I didn't know if I succeeded.

"Well, Rama didn't have most of his powers until he was an adult," Lakshman said, referring to an earlier incarnation of Vishnu.

"I'm more like Krishna," I said, though a what-if fear fluttered inside me. "I manifested my powers early."

Kantha Chithappa appeared at the door with a cup of water. He looked like an older version of Lakshman—they had the same broad shoulders and almond skin, their curly hair cut into the same fluffy shape above their flat foreheads. The thing that separated them was Kantha Chithappa's cleft chin, cut so sharply in half that he looked like a caricature from a newspaper cartoon. His body had a quiet ease to it that I often tried to mimic.

"Lakshman," he said, "you shouldn't doubt Kalki Sami. He can heal her." He came to Roopa's side and tipped up her chin. Her eyes rolled in her head. He put something small and white on her tongue, poured some water into her mouth, and held it closed until she swallowed.

"What's that?" Lakshman asked.

"It's vibhuthi," Kantha Chithappa said. "To help her heal."

We didn't use vibhuthi at the ashram, because it was associated with Shiva worship. I didn't know where Kantha Chithappa would've gotten vibhuthi from.

"But—" I said.

"Ayya has said we have to be unorthodox in her treatment," he said. "Don't worry. He approves."

Roopa closed her eyes tight, trying to swallow.

"You should do your healing prayer one more time." Kantha Chithappa cleared his throat and rubbed at his chin. "Now that the vibhuthi is inside her."

Before I was born, both he and Ayya had been doctors in America. If they said I could heal her, I could. I hurried to her side and prayed with everything I had.

When I returned that night to do my last healing session of the day, Roopa was sitting up in bed. It was the first time I'd seen her upright. Her shoulders drooped, and her head rested heavily on a propped-up pillow, but still—it lit a spark in my chest to see her with some energy. She felt well enough to talk freely, and as I worked, she told me stories of the mischief her brothers got up to, their spirited games of hopscotch and climbing the guava trees in their yard.

I started to wonder if I should give all my believers vibhuthi, if the vibhuthi had more healing power than I did. When I asked Ayya about it later, he said, "Without you, the vibhuthi is useless. Your devotees know that. *You* should know that."

I did know it. I tried to believe. But Roopa's shriveled body had shaken me. Before the vibhuthi, I was unsure she would heal.

When I didn't answer, Ayya said, "I think you should be the one giving her the vibhuthi from now on. We have some special vibhuthi we made for her."

The next time I went in for a healing session, Kantha Chithappa brought me a small bowl full of the special vibhuthi, white and grainy between my fingers.

"Make sure to use all of it," he said. "Don't waste any."

He stayed and watched as I put bits of it on her tongue and helped her swallow it down with water.

6

Roopa remained confined to her bed at the ashram, but after two weeks, her arms and legs filled with flesh. Her cheeks lost their hollow look, and her eyes seemed more normal-sized for her face.

Before I saw the effect the special vibhuthi was having on Roopa, the facts of my divinity seemed clear to me, even if I did doubt my abilities at times. My skin was blue, like Vishnu's. I saw myself in all the godly stories, and all the villagers and my parents and everyone I knew were true believers. So was I—a true believer.

But then I saw my healing powers outdone by that little ball of white something Kantha Chithappa put into Roopa's mouth, by the special vibhuthi that I was convinced was the reason Roopa was getting better. This doubt grew when I discovered the secret of my bathwater.

Every night at the ashram, my mother bathed me in our private bathroom. She filled the square stone tub with water from the well, rubbed me down with turmeric powder and sandalwood paste, and let me soak in the water for an hour while she told me stories. Krishna teasing the cow-herding girls. Stories of Rama's sons when they were young and uncontrollable.

Two weeks after Roopa came to the ashram, Ayya and Amma took a trip to Virudhunagar, the closest city. Ayya had been called to help bless the building of a new temple, and Amma went along to buy the things we couldn't easily get in the village or the nearby town—podavais, veshti fabric, and imported paintbrushes.

For the three days they were gone, Amma couldn't bathe me. I was going to do it by myself, but Lakshman insisted on helping that first night. If the adults had known, they might have stopped him. But he didn't ask anyone, just followed me to my bathroom. I'd spent such little time with him after Roopa came to the ashram, and I was happy for his company, so I didn't tell him to leave.

Vasanthy Chithy had hauled in water from the well and filled the tub so that when Lakshman and I came in from playing outside, it was waiting.

"Why is it so blue?" Lakshman asked that night. He walked around and around the stone tub.

I stripped down and took off my underwear. "It's always blue."

"Mine's not blue." He stood with his hand over the water.

"Your tub's not as big as mine," I said. "Plus, you don't have the sky." My favorite thing about my bathroom was the ceiling, where a window let in the darkening sky. While I soaked, I liked to watch the sky and tilt my head, trying to get the moon to fit inside the window frame.

Lakshman dipped a tumbler into a bucket of water and poured it on my head. Normally Amma warmed it up with water from a kettle, but Vasanthy Chithy had forgotten to. I yelped as the cold water shocked me all the way down.

Lakshman laughed and did it again.

"Stop it," I said.

He handed me a silver plate with turmeric powder. I rubbed myself down with it. He poured more water on me, laughing, and I playfully swatted at him. Lakshman was the only one who teased me ever, and it made me forget the pressure of being a god. He made me feel human. And with Roopa around, I was even more grateful for his company, for every moment he spent with me instead of her. While we laughed together, I rubbed sandalwood paste on my limbs and rinsed it off.

"You sure take a long time to bathe," he said. He looked around the room and finally sat on a wooden stool beside the tub.

I gripped the rough stone and climbed in.

"Now what?" he said.

"Now I soak. Amma tells me stories."

The water in the tub was cold too. I shivered as I sank into it. He sighed. He dipped a hand into the tub and swirled it around. "Look," he said. "My hand looks like yours."

Through the blurry water, he held his hand next to mine, and they both looked blue. He drew his out slowly and looked at it, his eyebrows pressing together. He wiped his hand on his veshti and looked at it again. The sky was darkening.

"It's still blue," he said.

I squinted. "It's not. It's too dark to see."

He held his hand up in front of his face, his eyes getting rounder and rounder. "I'm blue like you."

"You are not." His hand looked brown, like it always did.

He got up and flipped on the light. I blinked in the brightness from the one bare bulb. He spread his palms in front of me. One hand—the one he'd dipped into the water—had taken on a blue tinge.

"This is why your skin is blue," he said. "It's the water."

My skin was always blue, had been since as far back as I remembered. Because of the cobra that had bit me, because of the venom my body absorbed. Lakshman knew that. Everyone knew that.

"It's not the water." I put my palm next to his. "See? My body is blue everywhere, always. It's blue because I'm Kalki."

"If I bathed in that water, I'd be blue too."

I stood up. The water dripped cold down my body. "No you wouldn't."

"I would. Get out and I'll show you."

I wanted to push him down onto the tile. But gods didn't get angry at little outbursts. He was jealous. I got out and rinsed off with the bucket of clean water.

Lakshman took off his clothes and struggled to climb into the tub. When he finally got in, he sank neck-deep into the water.

"I'm going to soak," he said.

I toweled myself off and walked out of the bathroom.

I calmed myself by meticulously drawing a Namam on my forehead. I had to have one on at all times, even when I was sleeping. And when I woke up with it mussed and smeared, I was supposed to wipe it off and draw another. It was the mark of Vishnu for Vadakalai Iyengars—a red upward streak surrounded by a *U*-shaped white Srichurnam. I focused on getting the dip of the *U* just right in sandalwood paste.

Lakshman ran into my room, his whole body wrapped in a towel.

"Look, look!" He had a big, wild grin. He opened the towel to show me his body, its normal brown tinged bluish-green. "I'm blue like you."

I turned him toward the light of the kerosene lamp on my desk—we used lamps to save on electricity, which was expensive. In the lamp's yellow light, his skin looked green and dark. I put my arm out next to him.

"You're green, not blue," I said. "You're too dark to be blue."

He covered his body again with the towel.

"You're a fake, Kalki," he said. He ran from me.

I found him in my bathroom, scrubbing furiously at his skin with soap. The green was fading back to brown. After seeing his shoulders hunched in defeat, the anger drained from my body.

I spread the soap over his back and rubbed where he couldn't reach.

He hiccupped. "I'm sorry," he said.

"It's not your fault," I said. I spread soap from his shoulders down to his back and scrubbed, wondering what had just happened, and what it all meant.

"You're not a fake," he said.

But I wondered what would happen if I only bathed in clear water. The room tilted.

I held onto his shoulders and kept rubbing. I focused on that. His dark skin under my fingers kept me rooted to the ground. I wouldn't fall, even if the room was spiraling. All I had to do was focus on the soap frothing blue around my hands.

I didn't soak in the ink water for the three days that Amma wasn't there to bathe me, just to see what would happen. My skin stayed the same.

When Ayya and Amma got back, I went in for my bath and Amma was by the tub, stirring the water around and around with a stick. She held out her arms.

I walked into her embrace and she hugged me close. She hadn't touched me in four days. She smelled like talcum powder and the wilting jasmine flowers in her hair. I breathed her in and pressed my face into her faded podavai.

The only thing godlier than Hindu gods are the people who give birth to them. Ganesha and Murugan, the sons of the god Shiva and the goddess Parvati, once had a competition to see who could win a mango that was supposed to be sweeter than the nectar of the gods and would give anyone who ate it wisdom and learning. The challenge was to race around the world three times, and whoever was first would win the mango. Murugan immediately mounted his peacock and flew around the world. Ganesha, with a mouse as his steed, knew he couldn't beat Murugan. Instead, Ganesha asked his parents to stand together, and circled them three times. He won the mango because his parents were the whole world to him.

Amma ran her palm over my hair. "Hand me the turmeric," she said.

"How was the city?" I asked. "What's it like?"

"Dirty and crowded and smelly. You wouldn't like it."

Later, she would call me into her room and give me a bamboo reed flute that she'd bought in the city. A flute like the one Krishna played. She said she'd tried to convince Ayya to get me a cricket bat, but he'd refused, and they'd settled on this instead.

She tucked the end of her podavai around her waist and rubbed me down with turmeric powder.

"Roopa's going to live with us from now on," she said.

"What about her family?"

"They'll visit her on some festival days. But she owes her life to you, and they've decided to give her to the ashram." Amma washed the turmeric out of my skin with water. Yellow rivulets ran between the floor tiles. "She can help out with chores."

I noticed something missing—the four gold bangles Amma had always worn on her right wrist.

"What happened to your bangles?" I asked.

Amma looked stricken, but then she smiled and said, "I got tired of them, that's all."

She rubbed me down with sandalwood paste and washed it off. She waited for me to climb into the tub.

The blue water swirled. Now that I knew, I could see the little dots of indigo powder eddying on top, settling into snaking ripples.

Blood thudded in my fingertips. "Why is the water blue?" I asked. I turned around and looked into her eyes. "There's ink in there," I said.

Amma remained silent, her face pained, as if I'd told her I no longer loved her.

I sat on her lap, but she didn't hug me. My belly crushed itself from all sides.

"Amma?"

"Someday, Kalki, you'll figure this out. Some people need help believing." She looked off into the distance while she spoke, like she wasn't really seeing the tiled wall of the bathroom or the high slit window. "Everyone at the ashram believes in you. But the others need convincing. There's nothing wrong in that."

In the glare of the moonlight, my skin still shone blue, despite not soaking in the ink water for a few days. Lakshman's blue had come off with soap and scrubbing.

"Your skin is blue," she said. "With or without ink. The water helps it shine."

My body grew cold in the night air, my chest in knots. Amma was on my side. I was healing Roopa. That should've been proof enough, but I was still all jumbled up inside my head. My ears buzzed, and the noise overlaid everything else, including Amma's voice and the quiet sounds of the ashram as night fell.

Amma lifted up my chin. "Will you get into the tub?" she asked. "You'll catch a cold."

I climbed in. The water was warm this time as it enveloped my body. If my skin was blue anyway, there was nothing wrong with deepening the color.

Amma sat and told me the story of my birth for the millionth time. The details never changed, but I listened closely, trying to ignore the ringing in my ears.

"You aren't just a godsend," she said when she finished. "You are Vishnu himself. Don't ever doubt that."

But I did doubt. The feeling sat like a worm inside me, wriggling around and making me queasy. I wanted to keep it all in, to push it down, but I couldn't.

I tested myself by trying to bring a wilting mango leaf back to life, but it just wilted more until it fell off the tree. Maybe wilting leaves weren't meant to be healed. I kept my eyes peeled for any wounded animals that might be around, but I was also afraid of not being able to heal them. If Ayya had known, he would've said I was weak. And maybe I was. I wasn't strong or fast, and I couldn't talk to the birds or the beasts. I didn't have exceptional knowledge or wisdom. If I hadn't healed Roopa on my own, and if my skin was being dyed with indigo, it also meant that I would never be able to bring peace to the world, or travel to meet my followers. And if I did still manage to do those things, I'd be a fraud.

"Do you really think I'm a fake?" I asked Lakshman.

He cocked his head. I'd called him into my room and closed the door, which I never did, because Ayya didn't believe in closed doors for anyone but himself.

"No," Lakshman said, slower than I liked. "You're Kalki."

I gripped him by the shoulders. "But the bathwater—what about the bathwater?"

"But your skin is blue anyway. You're blue inside and out."

I sat down on my bed. "There has to be a way to know for sure. Know—you know." I couldn't think of how to articulate the writhing worm inside of me.

"To know if you're a god?" Lakshman asked.

I nodded.

"Do you feel like a god?"

I had my mind room full of cotton, waiting to be made into

light. I could meditate for hours. I had memorized large swaths of the Puranas. Was that all a god was?

"I don't know," I said.

"We can see if you can heal yourself," Lakshman said. "We could cut your hand."

A cut on my hand—that would be conspicuous. Ayya would see. And it would be painful, too.

"Somewhere else," I said.

That night, Lakshman waited until all the adults were asleep, stole a knife from the kitchen, and met me in my bathroom. It was the brightest place we knew, and the one bare bulb glowed in the darkness. We also had my kerosene lamp on hand, to add to the light.

"Ready?" Lakshman whispered. He held the knife over the skin of my right thigh. I'd stripped off my veshti and boxers and stood naked except for the poonal I wore diagonally across my chest.

I closed my eyes and held them shut with my hands. "Okay," I said. "Go." I waited, counting the seconds in my head. One. Two. Three.

The cold metal grazed my skin, and I jumped back.

"Sorry, sorry," I said.

"You have to keep still."

"Do it faster. Faster and press harder. One swoop."

Lakshman took his position again. I clenched my eyes and teeth and prepared myself not to move.

In the quiet, my heartbeat ricocheted in my skull.

Before I was ready, pain seared across my thigh, almost like a burn. I clapped my hand over my mouth to keep from screaming.

Lakshman dropped the knife with a clang. Blood dripped down my thigh, but it didn't look like blood. It was dark—almost black, like mud.

"Your blood," he said. "Your blood isn't red." He fell backward onto the floor, crawled toward the kerosene lamp, and brought it close to the cut, right up to the skin.

No matter how much light we put on the blood, it stayed dark. The pain traveled from the cut up to my hip. I hopped up and down, biting my hand to keep from crying out.

"Go get water," I said.

Lakshman ran to the corner where we had water in a pot and dragged it to me. He splashed water on the cut, which clanged with more pain. Dizzy, I sat on the edge of the tub. He washed the wound out with my veshti, but it kept bleeding.

"What are we going to do?" he said.

I tried to breathe through the pain. *Focus.* We needed to bind it. "Bring me a clean veshti," I said.

He went to my room and brought one back. I helped him tie it tight around my thigh, where it bled through slowly, the blackness blooming like a plague. He helped me stand up, and I limped back to my room.

"We have to clean up," I said. "Just let me sit for a while."

"I'll do it." He pushed me gently down onto the bed and drew the covers over me. "You sleep."

"But I—I have to try to heal myself."

Lakshman put his hands on his hips. "Your blood is *black.* That should be enough. I don't think regular humans have black blood and blue skin. You're a god. Now sleep."

7

On the night of Ayya's funeral, after the small crowd dispersed, after I got back to the ashram, and after I showered the remnants of death off my body, I turned down the servants' offer of dinner and settled into my old bedroom. The room was just as I'd left it, as if Ayya had been sure I'd come back.

For years I'd been telling my students that religion was in crisis. Between the Catholic church covering up decades of child molestation, Hindu swamis engulfed in sexual abuse scandals, honor killings in the Middle East, ruthless Israeli expansion, and Buddhist monks inciting genocide in Sri Lanka—this much, at least, was clear. Religion had been in crisis for a long time. And I'd participated in it. Even as I lectured at the university about the ills of religiosity, I'd kept the fact of my involvement with the ashram from my students. Every once in a while, a student would discover old videos on the Internet, or look up news stories. I dodged their questions instead of owning up to my part in the charade.

I took out a notebook that Lakshman had given me, in which I'd written snippets of lesson plans and grocery lists.

People had been asking me to write this book for years, the memoir of a childgod, but I didn't know what would happen to Ayya if I told the truth. At least now that he was dead, he wouldn't have to answer to any mortal authority.

I turned to a new page, and began: *The driver slammed the brakes, whipping my head forward and back . . .*

8

After Lakshman cut my thigh, for a few days I had to bind the wound tightly with fabric from a veshti I tore into strips, and take care how I sat. The binding kept me from bleeding onto my clothes. I cleaned out the wound with tulsi water and fed myself some of the special vibhuthi to heal. Lakshman helped me and had the idea of burying my black bloodstained wrappings in the coconut grove. I was careful not to show how much I was favoring my wounded leg, and no one noticed. I told Amma I was ready to take my baths by myself from now on, so that she wouldn't see me naked.

Over the next week, new raw skin knit itself in ridges over the cut. But even as I healed, a combination of confusion, depression, and guilt grew in my head—not just for cutting myself, but also because I couldn't instantly heal the wound like I was supposed to. In an unspoken agreement, Lakshman kept silent about our transgression.

Roopa was healing, and Ayya was in a jovial mood. We all knew what the second trial would be. According to the *Sri Kalki Purana*, I would need a white horse as my steed, and I needed to call this horse down from the sky.

A week after the incident with my leg, Ayya called Lakshman and me into the meditation room after breakfast and told us the horses were coming. Sunlight burst in from the glassless windows and shone off Ayya's balding, brown head.

"I've seen it," he said. "I've been told. They're coming."

Lakshman's face glowed with excitement. *Horses*—plural. Not only would I get a horse, but Lakshman would too. But I didn't know how I was supposed to call them down from the sky. And Ayya told me he couldn't help me, that I would have to figure this out on my own. If wild horses came to the ashram and fulfilled the second trial of the prophecy, it would mean I really was a god. The second step on my way to save the world.

After I left Ayya, I snuck back into my room and prayed. I prayed to the painting of Krishna Amma had made. I wanted the horses to come down from the sky. My hands jittered with the helplessness of not knowing what to do. All I could think to do was pray, so I did.

"Please," I said, staring up at Krishna's blue face. "I'll give you anything."

The next morning, Vasanthy Chithy went to get water from the well and screamed. We ran to her, all five of us from all sides, spilling out of the open doors to beyond the veranda and the cow's lean-to, where the stone well butted out from the grass.

"What is it? What is it?" we asked.

Vasanthy Chithy raised a crooked finger toward the well. Lakshman ran toward it to see for himself, but his father grabbed him and held him tight.

No one stopped me. I stepped forward and looked over the edge of the well wall and down into the murk. Something floated on the black water. It bobbed up and down in the ripples made by the metal pail Vasanthy Chithy had let fall.

The cat's body had swollen to twice its size. The fur moved on its own, slipping over the skin.

Bile rose up, and before I could stop myself, I threw up into the well. Amma patted my head and wiped my vomit with the edge of her podavai. She shot Ayya an angry look, as if it was his fault I'd thrown up.

"You two will have to get water from the other well," Ayya said. He gave Lakshman and me two small buckets each.

Lakshman kept trying to sneak a peek at the cat, but I seized his arm and we set off, the metal pails swinging at our shins. The other well was past the oxbow pond and rice paddies, halfway to the village proper. The farmers out tending their fields bowed as we passed.

"But just tell me a little," Lakshman said. "Was the cat dead?"

"Of course it was dead."

"*Dead* dead?"

"Yes."

"What did it look like?"

I kept quiet. It was the first large dead animal I'd seen besides bugs and lizards. I pictured it lying on top of the water, bloated and with only half its skin, too horrible to talk about. If Lakshman had seen it, he'd have understood.

He nudged my arm. "What did it look like?"

"Like a cat. Just dead."

Like most Hindus, we believed in samsara, the cycle of death and rebirth. That cat would soon be reborn, and it would live out the karma it collected in this life, paying for its bad deeds and reaping the benefits of its good service.

"The cat will be reborn," I told Lakshman.

Of course, as an avatar of Vishnu, I wasn't bound to this cycle. When I died, my soul would go back to manifest itself as a full god—ever-present, the lord and protector of the world. But sometimes I liked to wonder what my reincarnation might look like if I was human. Something beautiful, or something ugly and weak? It would depend on the karma I accumulated in this life.

"Do you think the horses are here yet?" Lakshman asked me.

"How can you think of the horses at a time like this?" I said it dismissively, as if I didn't care. But I was trying not to think of the horses, too—of how they hadn't shown up yet, of how this was my second test, of how my prayer was yet to be answered. I had asked for horses, and all I'd gotten was a dead cat in a well.

Lakshman shrugged his bony shoulders. "Ayya says something bad will always be balanced out by something good. It's the way of the world."

On the way back from getting the water, when we had passed the fields and the oxbow pond but hadn't yet neared within sight of the ashram building, Lakshman said, "Let's stop and play."

He pushed my elbow with his, and a slop of water spilled down my front. I put down the pail. Lakshman put his down and ran away, giggling and screaming as I chased him. Going back to the ashram meant facing the reality that the horses weren't coming, and I welcomed this distraction.

We ran and ran through the tall grass. When I couldn't breathe anymore, we laid down to watch the clouds pass by. The sun had turned the sky into a bright blue canopy, so clear and unblemished that it looked like a painting. Lakshman climbed on top of me. We wrestled the way we only did when no one was watching. We weren't supposed to wrestle. The adults said I might hurt him, but although he was shorter and younger than me, he was much stronger than I was, sinewy and tight like a drum.

He was holding me down and trying to lick my face when we heard it. A soft neigh from the direction of the ashram.

"The horses," he said. He got up and ran toward the sound.

I scrambled to my feet. Ayya was right. The horses were coming to find me. A white horse just for me. The second trial of the prophecy, and here it was.

I ran after Lakshman, and there, in between two palm trees, stood a white horse. It was small, still a baby. It gleamed in the patches of sunlight that fell through the leaves, as if its hair was made of bright liquid metal.

Lakshman took a step toward it. He raised a hand.

He was going to claim my horse. I had the urge to shout to him, but I didn't want to spook the young animal.

He stopped with his arm halfway extended, turned around, and said, "This is your horse, Kalki Sami."

I let out the breath I'd been holding. I put out a hand and walked toward the horse. I knew from the reading assignments Ayya gave us that horses could be dangerous, especially wild ones that weren't used to being around people. But Ayya had said that a white horse would find me. I was a god, and the horse wouldn't hurt me.

I walked near enough for it to sniff my hand. Its eyes reflected my blue skin. I touched it gently on the muzzle.

"Where's my horse?" Lakshman asked.

I looked around, but there were no other horses. I had prayed for horses—plural. I had no idea how I'd called this one down from the sky, and no idea how I could call more.

"You can pet this one," I said, stepping aside.

He looked up into its eyes and rubbed its cheeks.

Watching Lakshman with the horse, a revelation struck me. I had bartered in my prayer. I'd told the universe that I would give anything to call the horses. The cosmos had taken the cat and given me my horse. The cat's death stained my hands.

I let Lakshman lead the horse back to the ashram, grinning and lugging his pails of water. The horse followed us like it knew that was what it was supposed to do. When we could see our little building, Lakshman pointed to the ashram and said, "Look!"

I squinted against the sunlight. All around the ashram, little brown dots stood against the green. Horses. At least four.

Lakshman put down his pail and ran toward the ashram, my white horse forgotten. I wanted to run too, but I walked gently, leading the horse, the doubt in my belly forgotten.

The adults were outside, petting the horses. The pitches of their voices suggested excitement. Tire tracks lined the dirt road that led up to the ashram, all the way to the spot next to our old, slate-gray car that Ayya used to go to the city—bigger tires than I'd ever seen before, twice as large as the ones on the village jeep or our car.

Lakshman was petting one of the other horses, a brown one with a black tail, when I finally walked over, lugging my pails and his. My white horse stood behind me, pawing the ground with its hoof.

"Kalki," Amma said, her eyes bright. "You found your horse. It called you."

"Did a lorry come?" I asked.

Vasanthy Chithy was sweeping away the tire tracks.

"They took away the dead cat," Amma said. She kneeled so she was eye-height with me. "See? You made this miracle happen."

I had traded the life of a cat for that of many horses. It didn't seem like a miracle. I tried to push that guilt to the back of my mind. I'd passed the second test. The universe had listened to my prayer, had sent me my white steed. It was the cycle of nature. New life could not be born without sacrifice. The longer I stood looking at the horses, the more elated I became.

"What are you going to name your horse?" Amma asked.

I said the first name that came to mind. "Arjuna." A hero of the *Mahabharata*, Krishna's friend and Lakshman's favorite character— the beautiful warrior who could shoot anything with a bow and arrow. Krishna the god, and Arjuna the hero. In real life, I got to be the god, and that meant Lakshman would always get to be the hero. In that moment, I sensed the vastness of the path before me. The prophecy had begun, and when I was ready, I would travel the world, spreading peace and truth.

9

A month after Roopa came to the ashram and a month before Lakshman would leave, Anton the journalist returned, as sweaty as ever and mopping at his forehead with a handkerchief. The story of my two successful trials—Roopa's miraculous healing and the horses showing up at the ashram—had spread through the countryside. Until then, people had believed, but this was proof.

My family gathered in the main room of the ashram. Roopa sat in a bright new dress, looking radiant. Her skin had returned to a normal plumpness. She smiled to show too-big teeth mixed in with the baby teeth she still hadn't lost.

"How are you feeling?" Anton asked her, his notebook flipped open to a blank page.

"I feel good," she said. "I was sick, but Kalki Sami healed me." She had a flat, practiced tone to her voice. I wondered if Anton could hear it too.

"And what about you, Kalki Sami?" he asked me. "How do you feel now that Roopa is better?"

I snuck a glance at Ayya before answering. He was chewing on the inside of his cheeks.

"I'm happy Roopa isn't sick anymore," I said.

Sweat rolled in rivulets down my back. It would stain the silk, and Amma would have to wash it later.

"And did you heal her?" Anton asked.

Without warning, the image of my bathwater sprung up in my mind.

"Yes," I said, louder than I'd intended. "I healed her."

Anton looked me in the eye for a few seconds longer than was comfortable. He turned back to his notebook and scribbled something down.

"And," I added, "I called the horses down from the sky. That's two out of three trials."

Anton smiled. I couldn't tell if it was mocking or sincere. He asked for my birth certificate, and Amma laid it out in front of him.

"Madurai," he read. "Sri Kalki Visnuyasa."

I tried to read the birth certificate from where it lay on the floor. This was the first time I'd seen it. It had a seal that said "Meenakshi Mission Hospital."

Father: Visnuyasa Ramakrishnan. Mother: Sumathi Visnuyasa. Meenakshi Mission Hospital, Madurai, Tamil Nadu, India.

Anton didn't ask any more questions of Roopa and me, and the three of us kids were allowed to go while the adults stayed behind to talk more.

"Do you think he'll write about me too?" Lakshman asked when the two of us were back in my room, changing out of our formal outfits, mine soaked through with sweat.

"I think so," I said. "You're my Arjuna. You're Lakshman."

He smiled and poked my arm.

"You're my sweaty," he said, and giggled.

I wiped my hands all over my chest, gathering up the sweat, and lunged at him. He dodged, and I chased him around my room, threatening to smear my sweat on his body.

I hung Amma's painting of Krishna and Radha—her birthday present to me—above my desk at the ashram. I was struck by how much Radha looked like Roopa in the picture, though Amma had painted it before she knew her. For me, it was a sign. That same round face; the thick, upturned eyebrows; the lower lip that was twice as big as the upper lip—Radha was older than Roopa, but the resemblance was there.

Laxmi, as Vishnu's wife, would have taken a human form, would be waiting for me, our love transcending birth and death. If Roopa really was Laxmi, it would make sense that we found each other. And if she was, I wasn't going to lose her like Krishna lost Radha. I'd marry her, and we'd be together forever, soulmates as decreed by the universe.

Roopa joined us for most lessons. I snuck looks at her while Ayya lectured on Indian history and long division. I liked that when she smiled, her gums flushed with blood. I wanted to spend more time with her, and one day when she had a hard time with our math lesson, I took my chance.

"I can tutor you," I said. I barely heard my own voice. "If you like."

Roopa, Lakshman, and I sat out in the meditation room, our books open in front of us. Ayya had finished up for the day, but we were still studying for our upcoming math test. The shutters let in monkey laughs and the smell of mangos ripening on the tree outside.

Roopa shook her head, and her two braided pigtails swung around her. "I don't like studying."

"Kalki Sami's always so boring," Lakshman said. "Study, study, study. No one likes to study."

A stab of annoyance shivered in my chest.

Roopa frowned. "Fine. But I want to ride your horse."

"Arjuna?" If Roopa was Laxmi, it would be okay. In fact, if Arjuna liked her, that was a good sign that she was divine. "You can ride him," I said.

Roopa opened her notebook. "Let's do this quick."

Lakshman slammed his textbook shut and stood up. "I'm going to feed the horses," he said. Without another look, he left. I knew why he was acting so surly—his crush on Roopa was obvious, but I was older, a god, and if Roopa was Laxmi, she'd choose me. At least, that's what I told myself.

Questions of what life was like for Lakshman didn't trouble me at the time. Until he was gone from the ashram, I never bothered to think about what he must have felt. Always the other one—the one on the sidelines, in the shadows. Always the afterthought to the godchild. It couldn't have been easy, and his little aggressions now make sense to me.

I explained the lesson on ratios to Roopa, which became difficult as my mouth got drier and drier. She nodded as I explained, and my chest twinged every time her arm brushed mine, as if someone was shocking me with electrical wire applied directly to my sternum.

"Let's race," she said. She held her pencil above the paper on which I'd written all her practice problems. "You do them too."

I didn't know who I wanted to win more. Far from making me angry like I expected, the thought of Roopa being better than me at something excited me.

She counted to three and we started, the veins thrumming in my head.

"Done," Roopa said after a few minutes.

"How did you finish so fast?" I still had three problems to go, and I wasn't going slow on purpose. "Let me check your answers." I compared notes. She got everything right.

I could have run for miles; my legs held so much happy, springing energy.

She stood and smoothed down her skirt. "Let's go ride Arjuna."
Someone had spread chili peppers to dry on the veranda. We
stepped around sheets full of shiny red peppers that rustled like
worms. Clouds twisted open, spreading their petals to the sun. We
ran through the tall grass that surrounded the ashram, blades and
flowers scraping our knees.

We found Lakshman at the edge of the coconut grove, brushing
his horse. He pretended not to hear us as we got closer.

"I beat Kalki Sami in ratios," Roopa said, delighted.

Laksham laughed a little too loud. "Kalki Sami's not that good
at ratios."

"I'll go find Arjuna," Roopa said. She wandered into the grove,
toward the small creek that emptied into the village river. The horses
liked to amble near its banks.

When she was out of earshot, I asked, "Why are you mad at me?"

Lakshman didn't respond, just continued to brush his horse. He
took extra care with the black-tipped mane.

"I can't stand it when you're mad," I said.

He paused his brushing. "You can't have everything, Kalki Sami."

"I don't want everything."

"You like Roopa." He turned around, his eyes ready for a fight.
"You can't have her."

"I think she gets to decide." If she was really Laxmi, she'd
choose me. I tried to hold onto that conviction, but the longer
I looked at Lakshman, at his smooth brown skin and dimples,
at his hair that flopped over his ears, the more my confidence
slipped through me. If she was won over by his looks, if she was
repulsed by my blue skin, if she was afraid of being paired with
a god, I'd lose her.

"Let's ask her," he said.

But when Roopa came back leading Arjuna by the neck, neither
of us brought it up. Arjuna liked her. He was docile and calm, and

nudged her so that she could pet him, which was a good sign that Roopa might be Laxmi.

Lakshman helped me put the bridle on Arjuna, and Roopa climbed on behind me. He mounted his own horse, and we rode through the grove toward the open fields. He said nothing. He galloped out ahead and refused to look back.

Roopa's arms squeezed around my waist. Her chin tapped at my shoulder. She threw her laughter into the wind. I should've been happy, I knew that, but instead I wondered if she was watching Lakshman's back as he rode away.

The next time we played *Mahabharata*, I let Lakshman be Krishna. The day started hot, cloudless, and muggy. The sun battered our heads, and all I wanted to do was go swimming in the creek—the cool water would feel so good on my overheated shoulders—but Lakshman begged me to play the scene instead, so that he could be Krishna.

Vasanthy Chithy watched us from a blanket she had brought to the edge of the coconut grove. She hummed the same song I'd heard her sing before.

"Let's play Krishna's defeat of Kamsa," Lakshman said. "You be King Kamsa."

"He's evil." I hadn't agreed to play a villain, not even to keep Lakshman in a good mood.

Lakshman sighed loudly. "I play evil characters all the time." He made his eyes as round as they would go. As a toddler, he'd been irresistibly round-cheeked and mischievious. As a nine-year-old, he retained that same charm. I couldn't resist him for long. I relented, and his smile stretched all across his face.

Kamsa was Krishna's maternal uncle, who'd tried to kill him as a baby after hearing a prophecy that Krishna would defeat him. But the newborn was snuck away at night and raised in secret. As a teenager, Krishna returned to kill his uncle and free his imprisoned parents.

I brandished a wooden sword that Kantha Chithappa had built for us. Lakshman, playing Krishna, jumped out of the way. Kamsa was strong, but he couldn't bring down a god.

Lakshman put his fists on his hips and laughed at my feeble attempts to destroy him, but then he caught sight of something over my shoulder.

Roopa ran through the fields toward us, holding her dress over her knees.

"You shouldn't be running," I said when she came within earshot. "You're still healing."

She sat on the ground to catch her breath, and I was torn. Normally, I would've been glad to see her, but playing these scenes was something only Lakshman and I did. It was our special time. We let Vasanthy Chithy watch because she liked our performances. But I worried Roopa might think our play was childish.

It was too late. We couldn't kick Roopa out of our play without Vasanthy Chithy scolding us.

"Do you want to act with us?" Lakshman asked. "You can be Balram. Krishna's brother."

Roopa smiled with her new missing tooth. Lakshman helped her up before I thought of offering my hand.

I renewed my efforts with the sword, swinging it around while Lakshman danced out of the way. I was careful not to hit him, but I wanted Roopa to see how good I was with the sword. I overswung, and the weight of the sword pulled me forward. I tripped.

Lakshman laughed.

I wanted to punch him. He was showing off for Roopa. This wasn't how the afternoon was supposed to go. I was supposed to let him be Krishna, and we'd play, just the two of us, and Lakshman would be grateful to me.

"This isn't how it happened," I said. "Kamsa held a wrestling match and sent wrestlers to defeat Balram and Krishna. There was no sword."

"But it's more fun this way," Lakshman said.

Roopa stood the way he did, with her fists on her hips. "I have a better idea," she said.

But at that moment, Vasanthy Chithy's song, which had been a constant hum behind us, stopped. When we looked over to where she was sitting, she was slumped over on the blanket. I dropped the sword.

Lakshman ran to the blanket and shook her. "Amma!"

Her eyes stayed closed.

We needed to get help, but my legs wouldn't move.

"Amma. Amma. Amma," Lakshman said.

Roopa was the one who ran back toward the ashram while Lakshman and I waited with Vasanthy Chithy. I helped him hold her upright, her weight almost too much for our combined strength.

Kantha Chithappa and Ayya came back with Roopa, their faces held tight against the sunlight.

Ayya took my spot holding her up. Kantha Chithappa kneeled on the blanket. He opened her eyes with two fingers and peered into them. They both picked her up—Ayya holding her feet and Kantha Chithappa her shoulders—and carried her back to the ashram. Roopa followed them.

I started to walk, but Lakshman wasn't moving. He stood watching them carry his mother away. I held him as the grass swayed around us.

When we got back to the ashram, Vasanthy Chithy was awake, sitting up in her bed. Kantha Chithappa was giving her water. The adults congregated around her bed, talking in low murmurs.

They fell silent when we walked in.

Lakshman climbed onto the bed and into his mother's arms. The softness of her face hung down with its own weight, and one side of her mouth drooped, candy melting in the sun. She held Lakshman tight to her.

"Are you sick?" Lakshman asked. "Kalki Sami can heal you." He looked at me. "What are you waiting for?"

Vasanthy Chithy held out her hand, which shook as she held it in the air. "Come, Kalki. Do your healing prayer."

When none of the other adults stopped me, I climbed onto the bed. I closed my eyes against her shivering hand. I just had to push my energy into her. I held the cosmos in my body. I healed Roopa; I could heal Vasanthy Chithy. I prayed extra, repeating it inside my head over and over until I was sure it would work. I gathered every last bit of cotton in my mind room and spun it into god light. *Om Sri Ram Om Sri Ram Om Sri Ram*. I put a thumb on her forehead and willed the energy into her.

My bun had fallen loose. Vasanthy Chithy pushed the hair out of my eyes. "Thank you, Kalki. I'll be fine."

The day after she fainted, Vasanthy Chithy convinced us all she was okay. When I saw her in the courtyard after my morning meditation lessons, she was cutting boiled sugarcane with a string held taut between her fingers. One side of her mouth still drooped, but her hands weren't shaking anymore, and she seemed almost back to normal.

Ayya sat on the one step that separated the sunken courtyard from the rest of the house. He leaned back against one of the columns of the ashram building, his face hidden behind *The Hindu*. The front page showed a meeting of politicians, black microphones pressed into their faces. *President's concern over cult of violence. Attack on nun in Gujarat. Mastermind behind church blasts arrested.*

He noticed me reading the headlines and called me with a finger. "Your story's in here," he said.

He bent back the fold of the paper and pointed to a small write-up, crushed into the corner of an inner page. A photo of me in my Friday clothes, a clone of the Krishna picture that hung in the meditation room. *Blue-skinned boy believed to be Vishnu avatar.*

Excitement quivered inside my body. I was in the newspaper, and for some reason—though I was a god—this felt big. *I* felt big.

Ayya adjusted his reading glasses. "The world's going to know about you. Soon you'll be everywhere." He smiled at me, and that look in his eyes was one I wouldn't forget, because it was so rare. He was proud of me.

At lunch, Ayya talked excitedly about the article. We sat on bamboo mats in the courtyard, under the shade of the mango tree. The sun shone through the open roof and heated the cement floor.

I smiled into my food and tried not to look too pleased with myself.

"This is exactly the exposure we need," Ayya said. He leaned over his banana leaf to put a ball of rice and lentils into his mouth. A piece of rice clung to his lip.

Lakshman caught my eye and giggled into his food.

Amma and Vasanthy Chithy spooned more rice and curries onto our banana leaves. They'd eat with Roopa after the men and boys were done, after they cleared our banana leaves and bamboo mats.

"We'll need to expand the ashram, that's the next step," Ayya said. He crushed a fried chili pepper between his fingers and mixed it into his rice. "If we're going to have more visitors, we'll need the room. We'll take donations."

An expansion. More visitors. I tried to picture it—what it would be like with the ashram teeming with people like Roopa. Whole masses of them. I could heal them. They would love me.

Kantha Chithappa was quiet through Ayya's speech. When

Vasanthy Chithy poured rasam onto his rice, they held each other's gazes in silence. I knew something wasn't being said.

That evening, Lakshman didn't show up to get help with homework. I went looking for him, expecting him to be with Roopa, but instead I found him in the room he shared with his parents, sitting on their bed, the shutters pulled tight against the fading sunlight, the room dark as could be during the day.

"What are you doing in here?" I asked. I squinted, but I could only see his outline.

He didn't move, didn't look up.

I climbed onto the bed. "What's wrong?"

Up close, his body trembled.

"Amma had to go to the hospital," he said.

No one had told me. I hadn't noticed that our little gray car was missing from its parking spot at the ashram.

"She'll be okay," I said. I wanted to make him stop shuddering. My own throat was closing, and it was getting harder to breathe. "I'm Kalki. It's proven. That means I can heal her."

"Ayya didn't want her to go. He said you could heal her." Lakshman wiped the snot from his nose. "They got into a fight, Ayya and my Appa."

"They're brothers," I said. "Even if they had a fight, they'll be okay."

"You want my Amma to go to the hospital, right?"

"If she needs to," I said. "But I'll heal her."

He nodded at the floor.

I helped him wipe his nose, wrapped my arms around him, and pulled him to me. "I promise you," I told him. "I'll heal her."

10

One night after his mother got sick, I woke to Lakshman shaking me. The moon hung full outside my window, half hidden by the curtains. Lakshman's eyes glowed in the dim light.

"What is it?" I asked.

"Can I sleep here?"

I scooted over so he could climb in under the sheet. He lay down on one half of my pillow with a hand under his cheek. Moonlight filled his eyes.

"What?" I said. I brushed away a piece of hair from where it fell over his lip.

"She's really sick," he said.

Vasanthy Chithy had gotten back from the hospital earlier that night, weak and pained. I had already wondered if this was going to be my third trial according to the prophecy, but I grew more and more convinced. Vasanthy Chithy's illness was my third test, and if I healed her, the prophecy would be proven.

"She'll be okay," I said. "Get some sleep."

"You'll heal her?"

"Of course I will."

"Promise?" He held out his palm. "On your life? Sathiyam?"

"Sathiyam" in Tamil literally translated to "truth." If you made the vow, it was the truth and you had to keep it, or else someone close to you would die.

I put my hand on Lakshman's. "On my life, I promise. Sathiyam."

He turned so his back faced me. "Every time I try and sleep," he said, "I dream that all our horses die."

I drew the sheet over him and put my arm around his waist. He scooted back so that we fit like two crescents. I held him tighter and fell asleep with my cheek on his shoulder.

A few days after her hospital visit, Vasanthy Chithy had another fainting spell while cooking lentils for our lunch. I'd been doing regular healing sessions with her, but it was hard to focus my energy because I couldn't tell what was wrong.

One morning, we heard Roopa scream from the kitchen during our morning meditation.

Ayya sprang up like he was still a boy and rushed out of the room. Lakshman and I followed.

Vasanthy Chithy lay on her side in the fire-warmed kitchen, a wooden ladle still in her hand. Roopa kneeled next to her, trying to shake her awake.

Kantha Chithappa ran in.

Lakshman tried to push past me to get to her, but I gripped his arm and held him back. He didn't need to be close to this. He'd be in the way. I hugged him so he'd feel safe, but also to hold him in place. Kantha Chithappa plunged a tumbler into the water jar. He sprinkled the water on Vasanthy Chithy's face.

She stirred. Kantha Chithappa helped her sit up. Lakshman thrashed to break free of my hold.

"I'm fine," she said. She tried to smile, but it slipped off her lips. She sipped at the water that Kantha Chithappa held.

Lakshman stopped struggling. Ayya and Kantha Chithappa helped her stand. Together they limped out to the gray car outside. Ayya filled it with petrol from a metal can. The car's tires kicked up the dry dirt of the road as they left.

Lakshman held onto one of the terra-cotta columns on the veranda and watched the bumper of the car fade away. I knew I should say something. I'd promised to heal her. This was my third trial. But I couldn't think of anything to say, so I put my hand on Lakshman's shoulder and hoped that was enough, though I knew it wasn't.

The sun had nearly set when they got back from the hospital, and Amma, who hadn't been there to see her sister faint, had cried herself dry. Vasanthy Chithy looked drowsy when she got out of the car, but she walked on her own. Kantha Chithappa's lips were chewed and raw, and his broad shoulders slumped with fatigue.

They went straight to their room. He tucked her in. When Lakshman and I came in, he patted us on the head absently and walked out, his gaze far away.

Lakshman crawled onto the plaid sheets and climbed into his mother's arms. I hesitated. She smelled different, something foreign and artificial. She held out her hand to me, and it quivered more violently than before. I went to her, and despite the smell, I snuggled into her other side opposite Lakshman.

"Kalki Sami's going to heal you," Lakshman said.

In the window, the red sun melted into the coconut trees.

"He promised," Lakshman said.

Vasanthy Chithy looked at me, expectant. I put my palms together and prayed. I made deals with the universe; it had listened before. Lakshman needed his mother, and I needed Lakshman. If I could make her better, I'd study more. I'd go to bed on time instead of lying awake reading. I'd let Lakshman play whoever he wanted to play when we reenacted scenes. I'd help Roopa with her chores.

I put my thumb on Vasanthy Chithy's forehead and pushed the energy into her. *Om Sri Ram. Om Sri Ram.* She'd get better. *Om Sri Ram.* She'd be okay.

A hiccup. Vasanthy Chithy's head pressed harder against my thumb. At first I thought it was Lakshman crying, but when I opened my eyes, Vasanthy Chithy had her head bowed and her face clenched, like she was holding back sobs.

"Chithy?" I said.

The tightness in her face broke open. Her arms drew me close and held me so tight I couldn't breathe. She swayed back and forth, Lakshman in one arm and me in the other. A soft wail pulled itself from her mouth. Underneath the stench of the hospital, she smelled exactly like my mother.

That night, Lakshman came again to sleep with me. He woke me just as I'd started to fall asleep. He got under the sheets and lay on my pillow.

I didn't know what to say. I was failing my third test to heal his mother, but more importantly, I was failing my promise to him. I stared at the moon in his eyes until he fell asleep.

I woke again to voices. Loud. Amma, Ayya, and Kantha Chithappa. Lakshman was awake, too, lying in the same position as before, face-to-face with me. He put his finger to his lips. We listened.

The voices came from my parents' room, loud enough to drift across the courtyard and pierce the cement wall of my room.

"We have to get help," Kantha Chithappa said.

"People will talk," Ayya said.

Kantha Chithappa's voice cracked. "You're concerned about what people will say?"

Lakshman clutched the feeling out of my fingers.

"She needs more than your herbs and fake medicine."

"You can't," Ayya said.

A crash, like someone had fallen over the bed. Amma screamed. Lakshman's cold hand trembled in mine. I held it tight.

"You don't care," Kantha Chithappa said. "Goddamn you. You don't care about this family." He sounded strangled, choking on his words.

Lakshman shivered. His teeth clacked, drowning out the quieter voices. I pulled the sheet over him and rubbed my hand up and down his back in a steady rhythm, again and again until he fell asleep.

For a few seconds after I woke up, it felt like a normal day. A monkey sat by my window and ate a mango. It peeled off the skin, digging its face into the yellow flesh. I tried to be quiet, but as soon as I moved, it dropped the mango and ran.

Only then did I notice the quiet. I normally woke to sounds of prayer songs on Ayya's cassette player, hisses and clangs from the kitchen as Amma and Vasanthy Chithy made breakfast, Kantha Chithappa's snores from his room.

Lakshman was still fast asleep, drooling on my pillow.

I slipped out of bed without waking him. I was supposed to have gotten up hours ago to do my sandhyavandanam at the oxbow pond. Someone should've come to wake us—Amma, with a silver cup of sweet tea.

In the kitchen, I found Amma alone, grinding lentils and water to steam into idly for breakfast. She worked a large stone rolling pin against a flat piece of granite, cupping and scooping the lentil-water mixture before it ran off the edges.

"Your tea's on the counter." She wiped her nose with her forearm and pointed a white-coated hand to two silver cups.

"Where's Vasanthy Chithy?" I asked.

"She's resting," Amma said. "We do all this for you. I want you to remember that, no matter what happens."

I had no idea what she meant, and I didn't know what to say. As a god, I should've known exactly what to say. Krishna had always said the right things at the right times, even when he was a child. Wisdom far beyond his years. I tried to will the words into my mouth, but they wouldn't come—not in Tamil, not in Sanskrit, not in Hindi, not in English. No appropriate Purana verse or Vedic scripture. I sipped my tea in silence.

Lakshman was quiet all through our morning lessons with Ayya. He was the one always squirming during meditation or trying to pass notes to me during study time. But today he didn't even notice Roopa.

I caught him looking at me a couple of times out of the corner of his eye. When I looked back, he glanced away, frowning.

After lessons, Roopa left to help Amma with the cooking while Lakshman and I went to take care of the horses. We filled pails with water and hay and carried them to the edge of the coconut grove. Silence gnawed away at my ears.

The sky turned gray. Seasons changing. Soon the monsoons would come again. "It'll rain today," I said.

Lakshman huffed.

"Did you hear me? I said it'll rain today."

He looked at the ground. "Just because you say it doesn't make it true."

The edge in his voice made me stop. I'd heard that same tone the night we found out the adults were dyeing my water. I set the pails on the ground.

"Do you still think I'm a fake?" I asked.

He kept walking for a few steps, then turned around. His eyes squeezed under drawn brows. His jaw twitched where he ground his teeth. He slowly put down his pails.

I held out my hands. "You know my skin is real. I passed the first two trials. Why are you so jealous all the time?"

"It's always about you, isn't it? The great Kalki Sami," he said, his voice high and breathless, imitating the voice women in the village sometimes had when saying my name. "Kalki Sami, come to solve all our problems. Kalki Sami, come to save us from ourselves. Kalki Sami, the slayer of sin."

My cheeks burned, but I stood firm. I hadn't asked to be born blue. I hadn't asked for a prophecy. If he was jealous, that was his own problem.

He walked toward me. Each step shook the ground. A few raindrops plopped on my head.

"It's going to rain soon," I said. "We should go back."

He put a hand on my chest, his fingers cold, his eyes unblinking at the contrast of brown on blue.

"You said you'd heal her," he said.

I'd tried. Every morning, noon, and night for the past week. I'd tried everything. This was my third trial, but maybe it wasn't a test in the way I was thinking of it. Maybe the failing was part of the test, to see how I accepted failure.

"Maybe it's her time," I said. "Our fate is already written. Not even gods can change that."

Lakshman flinched as though I'd made a swipe at him. He held my gaze. The anger turned to pain in his eyes, but when he blinked, the fury flooded back. He pulled his hand away from my chest and punched me hard in the mouth.

I fell back, my knees weak from shock. I touched the place where he'd hit me. My jaw throbbed. The pain rang in my skull. No one had ever hit me like that.

I pushed down the urge to hit him back. It wasn't right. He was angry.

The sky spit water in steady drops.

Lakshman fell to his knees, hunching over his lap. The rain ran over his back and drenched his white cotton veshti.

I crawled forward and touched his arm. "We should go back to the ashram."

He shook his head. The tips of his hair threw droplets into the air.

"You'll get sick if you stay out in the rain," I said.

"Good. I can die before she does."

"Lakshman, please."

I touched his hand. He leaned forward. The top of his head pressed into my chest.

"We're leaving, Kalki Sami."

The words didn't make sense.

"We're leaving," he said again, to the ground. "We're going to America. To help Amma."

My lungs emptied. I no longer felt the bruise forming on my jaw. I breathed in the rain, drowning. Lakshman looked up at me. Water blurred his face.

"I don't think we're coming back," he said.

When we got back to the ashram, no one scolded us for going out in the rain. Kantha Chithappa quietly wrapped Lakshman in a towel and changed his veshti.

The car idled in front of the ashram, billowing a steady stream of black smoke into the air. In the rain, Kantha Chithappa dragged out three large suitcases and stuffed them into the trunk. Amma stood on the veranda, holding onto a column as if she couldn't stand her own weight. She pressed the end of her podavai to her mouth. Roopa stood at her elbow. Ayya was nowhere to be found.

I wasn't inside my skin. I was somewhere else, watching it all happen.

Vasanthy Chithy limped out of the ashram. She put a hand on Amma's cheek. She wasn't crying, but she looked weak. She hugged me hard. I wanted to apologize for not being able to heal her, but the words wouldn't come.

"Be good, Kalki." She lowered her voice so no one else could hear over the thud of steady rain. "When you grow up, if you want a different home, come find us."

I didn't know what she meant, but I nodded anyway.

Lakshman watched me as he got in the car. He turned around in the back seat so he could look at me. I thought about all the games we'd played, how he'd sometimes hold my hand during healing sessions, or how he'd squeeze himself into my bed at night. He was the only person I'd known from the time they were born. There's a picture of him as a newborn lying across my lap on a pillow, his little body swaddled in blankets so that only his face is visible—dark red skin and wispy, curly hair peeking out from under the fabric. In the picture, he's holding my face with his tiny arms, and we're looking at each other, the camera an intruder on our moment.

But now I wasn't sure if I would ever see him again. America was so far away.

We watched each other through the back car window, and I never broke eye contact, not once—not even when the car drove down the dirt path and away from the ashram.

Amma, Roopa, and I stood there long after the car had disappeared, watching the rain drum the tire tracks out of the road.

BOOK 2: AYYA

1

At ten years old, losing Lakshman felt to me like the world had ended. His absence settled inside me like an ache, an emptiness where joy used to be. Food didn't taste right. I stayed awake at night watching the moon fade away, and when I did sleep, I dreamed of awful things—of standing on small islands, facing tsunami waves, being swallowed up by the ocean.

Shame ate at me. It was my fault they'd had to leave. I couldn't heal Vasanthy Chithy, and worse, I'd been jealous and petty over Roopa's affection. I was so guilty that Roopa's presence made me sick with remembering.

I'd also failed my third trial, which meant the prophecy was broken. I hadn't proven my worth. Whenever I thought of asking Ayya, he huffed and dismissed me, saying it was too early to tell if my healing had worked. He told me it could work so slowly that we might not know for months.

Each morning, Amma waited for me to wake by myself and find her in the kitchen, where we drank our tea together. I tried to make conversation.

"Are you painting anything new?" I asked.

She shook her head. "I don't feel much like painting." Her hair wasn't as neatly plaited as it used to be. Two hairs grew out of the mole under her eye. I missed being so little that she'd pick me up and put me on her hip, or so little that I could crawl into her lap.

When I was five or six—the memory is hazy—I would go into her room, open the armoire in which she stored her clothes, and run my fingers over her cotton and silk podavais. Sometimes, I'd take out a podavai and unfold it just enough to wrap it around me. One day, Amma caught me, and I threw off the podavai and hid behind her bed, embarrassed.

Amma put her hand on her cheek and laughed softly. She closed the door and scooped me up from the floor, where I was trying to disappear.

"My mischievous little boy," she said, setting me down on the bed. "Hold up your arms."

She took the podavai, shook it out, and wrapped it around me the right way. She pleated and tucked and spun a pottu on my forehead with the red paste she used herself. She put two dots of the paste on my cheeks, rubbed it in, and turned me around to face the mirror, transformed into a convincing, blue-skinned little girl. I doubt Lakshman would've recognized me if not for the skin color, but I never told him, never shared this with him. It was just between Amma and me, and after that day, whenever I wanted to dress up, I'd go to her, and she'd help me. We'd pretend to be a mother and her daughter. She'd brush my hair and kiss me on my temples.

"Remember when I'd dress in your podavais?" I asked her in the kitchen.

A faint smile passed her lips as she raised her teacup. "You were such a pretty little thing," she said. "Why did you stop?"

"I can't remember," I said. I wondered if she wanted me to do it again. If I got caught this time by Ayya—who never seemed to have figured out back then what Amma and I were doing—it would mean severe punishment. There was plenty of cross-dressing in classical Hinduism—Arjuna spent a year of his life living as Brihannala at King Virata's palace of women, teaching song and dance to princesses, and Krishna cross-dressed as a woman to spend more time with his lover Radha—but Ayya would've thought it degrading.

"I called you Mohini," Amma said.

I'd forgotten that part. Mohini, the name of Vishnu's female form. Watching the wistful look on Amma's face, I wondered whether she'd ever wanted a daughter.

One morning, a week after Lakshman left, Amma looked less dreary when I found her in the kitchen. Against the greasy cement walls, which had darkened with all the cooking over the years, Amma sat on the grating stool, passing a coconut half over the serrated edges of the stool's blade as the white shavings fell into a bowl on the floor. I sipped my tea until she spoke.

"I want to go to the village," she said.

She and Vasanthy Chithy used to go to the village once a week, but I had never been allowed to go. Amma usually bought brushes and paper in the village for her paintings, and Vasanthy Chithy used to buy books.

"We're going to go to the village today," she said, firmly this time.

My gulp of tea burned down my throat. Sometimes, Lakshman had been allowed to go with Vasanthy Chithy, and he'd bring me back tales of what he saw—the delicious smells from street food vendors, how close the houses were to each other, stray dogs wandering the dirt paths—along with sweet tamarind candy, and once, a wooden snake that danced when I held it.

Amma held out her hand. "Help me up, Kalki. I need to get ready."

I gave her my hand, but she helped herself up.

"Don't tell anyone," she said before entering and shutting the door of the bedroom that used to belong to Lakshman and his parents. Since they'd left, Amma had taken to sleeping in their old bedroom.

I stood outside the door, not knowing what to do with myself, too stunned to feel excited. I'd never seen a village. The villagers had never had a god walk among them.

When Amma came out in a newly pressed cotton podavai, her hair neatly plaited and strung with a garland of jasmine buds, I started to speak, but she shushed me, and I followed her floral haze. Quietly, we avoided the meditation room where we knew Ayya would be. Roopa was still sleeping, or at least her door was still closed. The ashram was otherwise empty, and no one stopped us.

It was a long walk, longer than I'd expected. Amma answered my questions about the village with little information, saying, "It's not that impressive," and "You'll see for yourself," and "I think it's time for you to see the outside world." I might have swelled at the responsibility with which she was entrusting me, but as we passed the oxbow pond, guilt poked at me. I hadn't gone to do sandhyavandanam once since Lakshman left. I hadn't been able to get up early enough in the mornings, and Ayya hadn't even asked me about it. All the rules of my life had changed. I didn't know how to act or what to do.

"What if Ayya finds out?" I asked.

Some emotion rippled through Amma's face.

"Ayya is only a man," she said. "I'm your parent too."

She reached out and took my hand. We walked farther than I had ever walked in my life, following the path between the rice paddies for a long time before we saw signs of the village. Then, as if spun out of the clouds, smoke rose out of the horizon, houses smattered against the brilliant sky.

The people in the village noticed us immediately, as soon as we approached the edge of the rice paddies. The village was really just one strip of dirt stamped down to make a road. The houses were smaller than I'd expected, little whitewashed plaster-and-cement homes with thatched roofs and front porches.

Amma tugged on my hand to hurry. People watched from behind shutters and from the edges of roof railings. Amma didn't give any indication that she saw them.

I recognized people who came to healing sessions at the ashram. Bala, the milkman, tending to his cows. He had a bad back. Ananthy, the butcher's wife. She had a sadness she couldn't shake, one that made her ache all over. She was drawing a kolam with white rice powder in front of her doorway, though the sun was already high and the other wives had drawn their kolams at dawn. Everyone who noticed us looked shocked—Hindu lore told stories of gods visiting people's houses, but none of these people had ever had this fortune. They caught each other's gazes and smiled widely. A god walked on their street; prosperity would follow.

We passed the tea stand where a man cooked dosas on a circular flat griddle, filling the area with the sound of sizzling oil and the smell of salted urad beans and rice ground into a paste. My stomach grumbled. We hadn't eaten breakfast, and it had to be lunchtime. With Vasanthy Chithy gone, Amma was the only one who made food at the ashram. Roopa might be satisfied with a mango or two for her lunch, but Ayya would sit in the courtyard, waiting for a meal that wasn't coming. He would be furious.

Amma stopped at a small store under a bright yellow awning. The sign said LONG-DISTANCE CALLS in black letters. We had a phone in the ashram, but not one that could call outside India.

A man with puffy cheeks and crooked yellow teeth stood behind the wooden counter. "What can I do for you, Akka?" He used the formal term for "older sister" and spoke to the counter instead of looking at Amma, both signs of respect.

Amma produced a roll of money from the waistband of her podavai. "I need to make a call. To America."

He shook his head. "I can't accept money from you. Not from you, Akka."

Amma put the roll next to his hand and he ignored it.

We stepped up to the wooden counter. He slid a shell-pink plastic phone onto it. He punched in some numbers, waited, punched in some more, listened, and handed the phone to Amma.

Amma took the phone and dialed. It rung against her ear. I listened hard. The phone kept ringing. When the ringing stopped, she let her breath out in a hiss.

"Vasanthy, it's me." Amma smiled, whispering into the phone.

The man at the counter pretended not to listen as he flipped through a magazine, on the cover of which was a light-skinned woman in fewer clothes than I'd ever seen any woman wear.

I couldn't hear what Vasanthy Chithy said, but Amma listened without interrupting. She turned to me and held out the phone.

"Here," she said. "Talk to Lakshman." The long pink cable coiled around her arm. "Take it."

I held the cold receiver up to my ear. I'd never talked on the phone before, though I'd seen Ayya do it many times on the phone at the ashram, which only made local calls.

"Kalki Sami?" Lakshman's voice sounded higher than it normally did. Maybe it was the distance. I didn't know how far away America was, but I knew we were separated by at least one ocean. I didn't know whether or not to apologize for not healing his mother, for being the reason they had to leave. I was afraid he'd call me a fraud again, because I hadn't passed the third trial.

"How is America?" I asked. "When are you coming back?"

"I—I don't know." He paused, hesitating. "I start school tomorrow. They bought me shorts and T-shirts like the other kids wear."

School. I couldn't imagine Lakshman wearing anything but the white veshtis he wore at the ashram, Lakshman in shorts and T-shirts going to school with white kids in America.

"They cut my hair short," he said.

We'd both had long hair down to our backs since we were little.

"When are you going to visit?" he asked.

I didn't need to visit. He needed to come back home. I clutched the phone to my cheek.

"You're a god," he said. "You can visit whenever you want."

"Soon," I said. "But come back. Come back as fast as you can."

Amma held out her hand and I placed the phone in her palm.

Within a few minutes, we were walking back through the village, in the direction of the ashram.

I had to figure out a way to bring Lakshman back home. He sounded sad on the phone. He didn't want to be in America, so far away from his family and the ashram.

"Don't tell anyone about this, Kalki," Amma said. She didn't have to say it. I didn't know what Ayya would do if he found out Amma had taken me to the village, but I didn't want to give him any chances to stop Lakshman from coming home.

Ayya didn't give me homework for the first week after Lakshman left. I almost wished I did have it; it would've made the absence easier to bear. Lakshman hadn't been sure when he'd be back, but whenever I asked Amma, she avoided the question or pretended to be sleepy. Roopa treated me like I was made of glass, like if she spoke too loudly, I'd crack open and shatter. I spent most of that week by myself in my room, avoiding everyone but Amma.

On Friday, the villagers came as usual for the bhajan and healing sessions. I thought I was ready.

I wore my yellow silk panchakacham veshti and sat on a cushion in the corner of the meditation room. Roopa was told to sit next to me, where Lakshman usually sat. She wore two garlands of orange firecracker flowers woven into her braided pigtails. I tried my best to ignore her. If Lakshman had been taken from me because I'd had inappropriate thoughts about Roopa—if this was my punishment—I would learn my lesson.

She tried to get my attention by hissing at me out of the corner of her mouth.

"Ssssss," she said.

I trained my gaze straight ahead at the villagers gathering in the room.

"Ssssss."

The musicians removed their instruments from dusty velvet cases and tested them out.

"Ssssss."

"What?" I whispered, still not looking at her.

"Why are you not talking to me?"

I looked around to make sure Ayya couldn't hear or see us.

Ayya had set up the donation box near the green door that led to the veranda. It was the same box he passed around every Friday, but now it had a permanent place in the room, the top slit waiting for coins and folded-up bills. He stood next to it, greeting the visitors with a wide, fake smile. His presence made it awkward for them to not contribute anything to the box, so they put in colorful, rolled-up bills.

"Are you mad at me?" Roopa asked.

"No, I—" But I didn't know how to tell her. I'd have to confess to liking her, and then explain that I'd been punished for it.

"I miss Lakshman too," she said.

At the mention of his name, my body heated up.

"You're no match for Lakshman," I said, my heart a raucous drum. "He's *my* cousin, not yours. Leave me alone."

I refused to look at her, at what I was sure was a hurt look on her face. But I didn't need her company if she would rather have Lakshman, and I didn't want her pity.

Ayya took his place on the other side of me, and the bhajan started. I tried to concentrate on the songs, the music, letting the rest of the room and the world fade away. After the singing, as usual, we held a healing session.

An old woman came forward. I healed her every week, but each week she came with a new complaint. Her thin gray hair sat coiled on her head. Her neck wobbled when she spoke.

Ayya helped her sit closer to me. Her eyes raked around the room.

"Where is your Lakshman?" she asked.

I cleared the dryness in my throat. The rest of the villagers were also looking around, letting the absence soak in again—not only Lakshman, but also his parents. Ayya had told people that Lakshman and his parents had moved for Lakshman's education. I was supposed to hold up the lie.

"The important thing is that he healed his aunt," Ayya said. "They had to move for Lakshman's school, but she is healed thanks to Kalki Sami. He passed his third trial."

The room broke into applause.

I was stunned by this news. I had healed her. That meant the prophecy was true.

"Tell him what you need healed," Ayya said to the woman.

But the old woman seemed to have forgotten her illness.

"What is Rama without his Lakshman?" she asked me. In the old tales, Lakshman was Rama's younger brother, his most devoted friend, and the person my Lakshman was named for. "You need him," she said. "He makes you who you are."

Lakshman's voice on the phone had sounded so far away. Oceans away. He was starting school. He had cut his hair.

I tried to swallow it down, this feeling that my lungs were filling with water. I couldn't cry in front of all these people. But it was too late—the tears came anyway. I hid my face in my elbow. My voice came out high like a baby's. The tears wouldn't stop. I got up and ran out of the room before any of them could react.

I shut myself in my room, but I didn't dare lock the door. Ayya and Amma argued outside.

"Let me talk to him," Ayya said.

"He needs his mother right now."

"He needs some authority in his life. He's too spoiled. He needs to be told he can't act this way."

I waited in my bed, the sheet pulled up over my head. I knew a monkey was watching me through my window. I'd seen it when I first came in, eating another mango from the tree outside. The fruit squelched as the monkey turned the flesh in and out.

Ayya didn't knock. He opened the door, came in, and stood by the foot of my bed.

"Kalki." His voice was firm, the same voice he used when Lakshman didn't do his homework on time.

He waited. When it became clear that he wasn't going to say any more, I pulled the sheet slowly from my head.

"You know what you did was wrong," he said.

He might have been waiting for me to apologize. In his hand, he held a thin stick, plucked from the tulsi plant and stripped of its leaves. "You must know why you can't continue to do things like that."

I wanted to pull the sheet back over my head. During the fight with Lakshman's parents the night before they left, I'd heard the same sharpness in Ayya's voice that gave way a minute before the attack.

He reached down for the sheet over my legs. I lay there, unmoving.

He pulled back the sheet and pushed up my veshti so my shins were visible.

Ayya swung his arm back with the stick. I took a quick breath in and held it. He brought the tulsi down onto my naked legs, the stick flexing like a whip.

The first hit stung more than it hurt, like I'd touched an open flame. I bit down on the sheet to keep from crying out. Any noise would make him angrier. But more than that, I knew my cries were what he wanted. My hatred for him sprung up wild inside me, an animal instinct that I couldn't have predicted existed underneath my love and need for his approval, an invisible third rail.

Ayya hit me again, on the other shin. This time, a yelp escaped me, one I squelched as soon as I heard it. I closed my eyes tight, waiting for the next blow.

Instead, Ayya sighed. "I know you miss Lakshman."

The stinging on my shins deepened into a burning pain.

"I miss him too," he said. "I miss all of them. But change is a part of life, Kalki. You'll watch the humans you love die and be reborn. You'll see them suffer. It is too great a burden for a child." He put a hand on my shin and squeezed it, and I bit down another cry of pain. "But you must have hope. You'll see Lakshman again. When you're grown, you'll travel the world. You can find Lakshman. Come now, Kalki—you healed Vasanthy Chithy. That's what matters, right? You healed her, and she's better. You've proven yourself. You're the real deal. A god." Ayya stopped in the doorway with his hand on the frame. "Come now. Gods don't cry."

But gods did cry. Shiva cried when he lost his wife, Sati. Rama cried when Sita was kidnapped. Ayya either didn't remember this, or he was lying. Did he also not remember how those stories ended? When those gods were done crying, their sadness turned to anger, and they threatened to destroy all the worlds.

2

It was a month after Lakshman left that I first heard my past lives. Ayya had always told me that because I'd lived a thousand lifetimes, I had a thousand wisdoms inside me, if only I could learn how to listen. Losing Lakshman must have taught me something about this wise listening.

As an adult many years later, I watched an animated show about an avatar reincarnated over and over. In the cartoon, the current avatar would meditate in order to talk to their past lives, each of whom appeared to them as hazy, blue beings made of wispy smoke.

That's not how my past lives came back to me. But they did come back.

One day, a month after Lakshman left, I was doing chores. Roopa had offered to take over Lakshman's chores at the ashram, but I couldn't bear to let her. I did them all myself, from feeding the horses to fetching water from the well. I didn't get many hours to play, but without Lakshman, I didn't know what to play in the first place.

Roopa had tried to get me to race with her again, doing math problems. But at this point, it was no longer fun, as if Lakshman had taken my joy with him. Roopa had suggested we act out a scene from the *Mahabharata*, and I'd tried it—but she didn't know the stories well, and her improvisation annoyed me, like when she tried to hold a wedding for Krishna and Radha. Lakshman and I had everything memorized, down to quotes of dialogue. Roopa barely knew the names of the characters, and often got the five Pandavas—the heroes of the tale—mixed up. I invented excuses, mostly that I had no time because of Ayya's extra homework—which didn't exist—and Lakshman's extra chores.

After the phone call in the village, I had been so sure that Lakshman would come home, that I could figure out a way to get him back. But it had been a month, and whenever I asked Amma or Ayya about Lakshman, they pretended not to hear me.

I hauled out a brush and some hay in a pail to the coconut grove and looked for my horse Arjuna, whom I hadn't ridden in weeks. As I stomped over twigs and dried fallen fronds, I kept my eyes peeled for Arjuna's glittering white coat in between the trees. The grove was quieter than normal. I headed toward the river, wondering if the horses had gone there to drink instead.

But I didn't see any horses that day in the coconut grove. I didn't see anything out of the ordinary, except for a fuzziness at the corner of my vision, as though someone was hiding out of sight. When I turned my head, the blur kept eluding me.

"Hello?" I said. "Arjuna?"

I turned my head again to try to see more clearly. But whatever it was, it lurked beyond my line of sight.

A voice in my head whispered to me. "Kalki," it said. And somehow, I knew exactly who it was.

"Rama?" I said. "Is that you?"

The wind blew around me, and I knew that meant "yes." One of my past lives had come to offer me wisdom.

"What should I do?" I asked. "How can I get Lakshman back?" But the gust of wind died back down.

"Did I really pass the third test like Ayya said?" I asked.

The grove was quiet again. I listened and listened, but he made no reply. Rama had gone, but he'd shown himself, and I'd heard his voice.

As his seventh incarnation—and, as some would argue, his greatest one—Vishnu took the avatar of Rama, rightful king of Kosala. In human form as Rama, Vishnu's life was full of hardship. He was exiled with his wife Sita and his brother Lakshman for fourteen years. In pictures and temple statues, they're depicted as a threesome—Rama in the middle, Lakshman on his right side, and Sita on his left.

The *Ramayana*, the great epic that details Rama's adventures, tells how devoted Lakshman was to his older brother. Lakshman gave up his own royal title, left his wife, and followed Rama into the forest to live a hard and dangerous life.

One day in the forest, Sita saw a golden deer and asked Rama to get it for her. Rama, who suspected a trap, asked Lakshman to guard Sita while he pursued the deer. As they waited, Lakshman and Sita heard Rama's voice cry out in the forest.

"You must go after him," Sita said. "He's in danger."

"Rama is the manifestation of Vishnu," Lakshman said. "He is all-powerful."

But Sita, worried, ordered Lakshman to go after Rama. Lakshman couldn't disobey Sita. He drew a circle of protection around her.

"Please do not step outside this circle," he said. "In this circle, you are safe."

And off he ran to Rama's aid.

Sita waited, but before they could return, an old beggar arrived at Sita's house. He asked her for alms, and out of compassion, she stepped across Lakshman's line to give it to him.

The beggar revealed himself to be Ravana, the demon king, who abducted Sita and took her to his kingdom in Sri Lanka. Thus begins the climax of the *Ramayana*, the cause of the great war that Rama conducted against Ravana in order to rescue Sita and return home, always with the ever-faithful Lakshman at his side.

The only time the brothers fought was over Sita. When Sita was returned safely from the forest, Rama caved to public pressure and demanded that Sita take a purity test to prove her chastity in captivity. Lakshman became angry and opposed his beloved Rama for the first and only time in their lives. Rama may have been the god, but for Sita, Lakshman was the hero.

Now that Rama had visited me, even though he'd said nothing but my name, I felt that he was trying to tell me Lakshman wasn't far behind. Maybe Lakshman had returned to the ashram already. I hurried home through the grove, bursting with nervous energy.

Back at the ashram, there was no sign of Lakshman, but a woman sat in the meditation room. She rested on a bamboo mat with her eyes closed, leaning against the whitewashed wall. A battered leather suitcase sat beside her. She looked to be around the same age as Amma and Vasanthy Chithy. She had no gray in her curly black hair, which tumbled loose to her shoulders. Her skin was lighter than anyone in my family, and she had a long nose that took over most of her face. When she breathed in and out, the softness of her belly expanded and folded in on itself. She wasn't wearing a podavai—the first woman I'd ever seen in a skirt and blouse. Her legs, peppered with black hair, were visible under a pleated skirt.

She opened her eyes and caught me looking.

"What's your name?" she asked. She had a strange accent when she spoke Tamil.

No one had asked me my name before. Everyone just always knew. Her eyes roamed over my body, all over my skin. They were lighter than any eyes I'd seen except mine, a mango color. Amma used to say that people with light eyes had no soul, but this woman looked too beautiful for that to be true.

"I'm Sita," she said.

I'd thought Rama's presence in the woods meant that Lakshman was here, but now a woman named Sita was at the ashram instead. It had to mean something.

"Who runs this ashram?" she asked.

"My father." It was that time of day when Ayya should've been meditating, but he was nowhere I could see. "I can get him for you."

She scanned the room, her eyes settling on the picture of Krishna that hung above my corner. "You're Kalki Sami," she said. "The boy I read about in the news." She took a small notebook and pen out of the breast pocket of her shirt. "Are you happy here?" she asked, her pen tipped on the notebook and her keen eyes watching me.

"I—yes, I'm happy."

"Do you believe you're a god?"

"Yes."

I had a suspicion that her questions meant she was a journalist. Ayya would want to know about her before I answered.

I asked her to wait. She frowned as she put her notebook and pen back in her pocket.

I found Ayya in his room, spinning new wicks out of string for the lamps, one of Vasanthy Chithy's old chores at the ashram. He sat at his desk, the wood littered with wiggling pieces of what looked like white larvae.

"There's a woman here, Ayya," I said. "She wants to see you."

He put down the wick he was twisting and brushed off the pieces of string that clung to his veshti.

I followed him back to the meditation room. The woman sat exactly where I had left her, again with her eyes closed and her belly breathing in and out.

"Sita, yes?" Ayya said.

Sita opened her eyes. She held out her hand to Ayya. He hesitated before shaking it.

"Welcome to the ashram," Ayya said.

Ayya showed Sita the grounds around the building. I trailed after them, putting enough distance between us that they didn't seem to notice me.

"Where did the horses come from?" she asked. She wandered up to one standing near the well and rubbed its muzzle. "They're tame."

"They came because of Kalki Sami. He called them. It was his second trial, according to the *Sri Kalki Purana*."

She looked back at me, as if she'd always known I was following them.

"Have you met Kalki Sami?" Ayya called me with a flick of his wrist. "He's the star of this ashram."

She extended her hand out to me. It was soft and had hair clinging to it from the horse. I tried to grip her hand firmly, but my palm was already sweating and slippery.

"Of course, you've heard about our Kalki Sami, yes?" Ayya said.

"Of course," Sita said. Her eyes bored into me, like she was trying to catch me at something.

"The ashram will be going through renovations soon," Ayya said. "But don't worry, it shouldn't interrupt the daily functioning of the place. You'll have as much peace and quiet as you could wish for."

Ayya led her back into the building, where Sita peered into every room.

"Where are you from?" he asked her.

"I studied in America, in Boston," Sita said, looking curiously into my room.

I stood shocked at the mention of America. If she had been to America, she must know Lakshman, or at least would have met his parents. If only I could bring myself to ask her.

"What brings you here?" Ayya asked.

Sita ran her fingers through her hair, walking through the courtyard and watching the monkeys in the mango tree. "I went to Sri Lanka to teach with UNICEF, but with the war it got to be . . . too much. I'm at the ashram to relax. My boss thought I needed the time off."

"This will be your room." Ayya gestured to the sick room Roopa slept in.

Inside, Roopa was putting new sheets on the bed, stretching them tight over the mattress.

"Hello," Sita said. "And you are?"

Roopa turned shy, which was unusual for her. Her eyes fell from Sita's glance and she busied herself stuffing two fat pillows inside checkered cotton cases, her pigtails swinging wildly around her head.

"This is Roopa," Ayya said, placing Sita's leather suitcase inside the room. "Kalki healed her from a serious illness as his first trial. She's a servant here."

Ayya and Sita moved on, talking about the ashram expansion, but I stood rooted to my spot, dumbfounded. He'd called Roopa a servant. I hadn't thought of her that way, and I'd had no inkling that this was how Ayya saw her.

I tried to catch Roopa's eye to see what she thought of this, but she avoided my gaze, fluffing up the pillows and smoothing out the tiniest wrinkles in the bedsheet.

"Roopa," I said.

She lugged Sita's suitcase across the room and slid it under the bed. "Go away, Kalki."

Before I could say anything else, she marched to the door and shut it in my face. I listened at the door to the muffled sounds of her finishing getting the room ready, not knowing what to do or how to help.

When I prayed later, I asked for guidance on why Sita had come. I was sure my vision of Rama was connected to Sita's stay. It meant something. Maybe she knew Lakshman.

But Sita mostly kept to herself for the first couple of days. The door to her room stayed open, and whenever I walked by, I saw her sitting on her bed, her back resting against the headboard, a book open on her lap. I wanted to ask her about Lakshman, but I never dawdled. If she saw me hanging around, she'd ask me strange questions about my time at the ashram—how I got here, did I like it here, and what were my duties. I was afraid of talking to her, because if she did turn out to be a journalist, Ayya would be furious at me for giving her any information.

I wonder now if Sita was the universe's way of distracting me from Lakshman's absence—a pale replacement that should never have worked, but did, and for an unexpected reason. Sita brought my first real contact with the outside world, and though I didn't know it then, she would also be the one who would teach me not to trust anyone.

As she got more comfortable at the ashram, Sita wandered the grounds. One day, she snuck up on me when I was watering the horses.

"You seem sad," she said. It was the first time she'd addressed me directly since the day she arrived.

I dropped the pail of water I was holding. Cold well water splashed over my sandals.

She hugged a black clothbound book to her chest. I tried not to look at her legs, bare again under her skirt.

I righted the bucket and offered the rest of the water to Arjuna. Sita came closer. "Is he your horse?"

"His name's Arjuna." I stood steadier with my hand on his neck. She smelled spicy and sweaty and wholly unlike any of the women I'd been around before. "I'm not sad."

Lakshman's horse Draupadi watched me from behind a tree. She was more skittish than Arjuna and still hadn't gotten used to me feeding and brushing her. I pointed at Draupadi. "That one is Lakshman's horse."

"Who is Lakshman?"

This was my chance. The inside of my nose itched in anticipation. "My cousin," I said, as casually as I could. "You don't know him?"

She laughed gently. "I don't know any Lakshmans, I'm sorry. But where is your Lakshman now?"

"He's in America." I tried to hide my disappointment. "Do you know Vasanthy Chithy? Kantha Chithappa?"

She shook her head. I shifted my weight from one foot to the other, wondering if I'd revealed too much, if she'd jot down notes about this conversation.

"Have you been to America?" she asked. "To see Lakshman?" I shook my head as she settled herself at the base of a coconut tree and spread the book open on her lap. "Come, sit."

I sat next to her. On the book she held, gold lettering spelled out *Midnight's Children* in English.

"Can you read English?" She opened the book to the front page and asked me to read.

I read slowly. I was better at English than Lakshman and Roopa, but I still couldn't read it fast like I could Tamil. Sita waited patiently for me to decipher and stumble through the unfamiliar words. After a long paragraph, she asked me what the book was about.

"Somebody's birth?" I said. "A boy. A boy's birth."

Sita laughed. The sound curled her voice high and crested over the trees.

"Good, good. You're a good reader," she said.

She had me read a few more pages and walked with me back to the ashram. I followed her to her room. The bed had been made with the green plaid sheets that Lakshman used to sleep under. Dark blue blankets, woven thick and strong, lay folded across the sheets. Roopa had made the bed, and Ayya had called her a servant. He'd done it so dismissively, as if there was no question in his mind.

"Roopa is my friend," I blurted out.

Immediately, I was embarrassed at my bizarre outburst, but Sita nodded as if she accepted the fact. She pulled her leather suitcase from under the bed and heaved it on top of the blankets. She unlatched the suitcase with a snap, revealing a mound of clothbound books.

"This is my secret library," she said. "This is everything I own."

I ran my fingers along a spine that said *The Immoralist*.

"What is Gide?" I asked.

"Not what. Who." She waited for me to ask the question again.

"Who is Gide?"

"He was a French writer. And you say it with a soft *G*-sound, like *Zheed*."

The suitcase was crammed with books I'd never heard of, books I knew Ayya wouldn't allow in the ashram library, which was full of paperbacks covered in brown paper, on which Ayya had stenciled titles like *Understanding the Bhagavad Gita*, *Essential Hindu Prayers*, and *Karmic Destiny in the Kali Yuga* in his perfect, even writing. We only had one leatherbound book with gold lettering pressed into its spine, a Sanskrit copy of the *Sri Kalki Purana*, the book that prophesied my birth and life. I read from it many mornings before my other lessons.

"You pick," she said. "I'll lend you any book you want."

I looked through the suitcase and picked a thin, ragged book with a cover that showed a woman in a blue dress against a deep purple background, the color of the sky after the sun dips under the earth. *The Awakening*, I read. I turned the book over, feeling its coarse cover on my fingers. I wondered what it could be about, what awakening I would find. At the bottom, in neat black letters, was the name KATE CHOPIN.

"Kate Cho-pin," I read.

"Chopin," she corrected me, pronouncing the name without the *n*, ending in a nasally sound that hinted at the letter. "She's one of my favorite writers."

I'd never encountered a book written by a woman before.

"It's about a painter," Sita said.

A painter. Like Amma.

"Are you sure you want that one?" Sita asked. "It's not really for kids."

But the cover had caught me. I wanted to know what this painter woman would awaken from, or into. I wanted to know if she was like Amma.

"This one is fine," I said.

Sita shut the suitcase with a snap, heaved it off the blanket, and shoved it back under the bed.

I clutched the book to my chest and took it to my room. I didn't know why I accepted it from her, but I suspect now that I took it because it was what Lakshman would've done. He would've been thrilled by the idea of a secret library, full of stories we weren't supposed to read.

3

I'd never met a woman like Sita before. She did what she wanted. She wasn't cowed by Ayya at all, which made me like her more and trust that she wouldn't tell him anything she and I talked about.

Sita ate with the men at every meal. She offered her thoughts and opinions and didn't back down when Ayya disagreed with her. For me, she was a revelation—the first sign that the world held more than Ayya was letting me know. Sita wasn't married. She didn't have kids. Even Roopa seemed fascinated with her—she stared at Sita during her meals with us, looking away when I caught her eye or when Sita glanced back.

As Sita became more of a presence at the ashram, Amma kept to her room when she wasn't cooking, or she'd wander off to the village at odd times. She didn't ask me to go with her. I hadn't even seen her painting, not since Lakshman left.

It took me a full day to get through the first page of the book Sita gave me. The English wasn't as straightforward as the activity books Ayya used to teach us. I read sentences over and over, and still didn't know what was happening by the end of the page. Sita had told me to write questions in a notebook. I scribbled down, *What is Allez vous-en?*

In the story, Mr. Pontellier went about his day, smoking cigars and reading the newspaper. I was more interested in the parrot he kept. I wrote, *What is the parrot's name?* into my notebook. On the second day, I met Mrs. Pontellier in the story. And Robert. They swam under a hot morning sun. They leaned toward each other as they sat.

This book held no miracles. No gods, no heroes. It told of nothing but quiet human problems. Yet it was more exciting and more unrealistic to me than bloody battles or powerful demons. Every person and every situation in the first few pages were like nothing I'd ever seen or thought about before, but it also seemed just like the world where I lived.

I made sure to hide the book under my mattress when I slept, in case Ayya came into my room. Every time I opened the book, it was the most disobedient I'd ever been. If I was Vishnu, this was my teasing of the village girls and my godly mischief. I was filling my mind with all sorts of things that Ayya would say was distracting. Every word was a new distraction, every sentence. It wasn't just that I wanted so badly to know what came next, but that I was reading descriptions of all sorts of things—things I'd never seen but always wanted to see, like the ocean. And things I'd always seen but never seen descriptions of before, like people's faces.

I thought of Lakshman and how he would've loved to read this story. As I read of Mrs. Pontellier and her affair with Robert, I knew he would've thought it was exciting, and when I thought that, I found it exciting too. It must have been easy for Lakshman to find this kind of book in America, perhaps this exact same book. I imagined that he was also reading *The Awakening* at the very same moment. I imagined that we were reading to each other. And that was the most exciting thought of all.

I frequently read lying by the trunk of a coconut tree after history class, during the time Lakshman and I used to act out scenes from the *Mahabharata*. Sometimes, Roopa followed me out to the grove.

"Do you want to play?" she'd ask.

I'd lie on the grass and squint at the vacant sky until she got bored and left to go do her chores at the ashram. I still thought she was beautiful, still wanted her to want me, but something between us felt sour. She was tied in with the shame embedded deep in my body. I didn't know what Ayya's pronouncement that she was a servant meant. He'd never told me not to play with her, but she seemed far away from me, the label sitting in between us like a fence. Laxmi wouldn't be born in this world as a servant.

But other times, I was so lonely that I gave in. We'd play tag out in the coconut grove, chasing each other around and hiding behind the trees. Afterward, we'd sit by the banks of the creek and skip rocks across the water.

"Do you think Lakshman is coming back?" she asked me once. She threw a rock, and it skipped twice on the water before landing with a *plomp* sound.

I took a deep breath to calm myself. I didn't understand why I was getting so annoyed.

"I hope so," I said.

I wondered if my anger at Roopa was because even when she got to hang out with me, she was still thinking about Lakshman. I threw a rock into the water, and it plopped without skipping.

In the last few weeks, I'd been trying to look for Rama everywhere, hoping that he was hiding just beyond my vision, but he didn't show up. I wanted him to answer the question I'd asked: *How could I get Lakshman back?*

Roopa skipped another rock—three bounces this time—and bent to look for more.

I picked out a flat rock and gave it to her.

She pushed me playfully, and I fell onto my side, exaggerating my fall. We giggled, and the sound of my own laugher lifted me.

"What's that?" Roopa asked. She picked up the book I'd been reading. "*The Awakening*," she read. "What's it about?"

I had the urge to snatch the book back.

"It's about a woman," I said instead, sitting up on my heels. "She's a painter."

"Like your mother." Roopa adjusted her dress over her crossed legs. "Will you read to me?"

I flipped to the page I'd been on and started reading. Roopa listened, and every once in a while, skipped a rock on the water.

A few days later, Sita found me in the coconut grove as I started the eighth chapter.

"Are you enjoying the book?" she asked. She settled herself by the trunk of my favorite tree and tucked her legs underneath herself.

"Mrs. Pontellier loves Robert," I said.

She cocked her head. "How did you figure that out?"

I filed through the pages. It was all in the words. I wasn't understanding all of it, but it was there. Mrs. Pontellier's love for Robert was the most basic part of the story, woven into the letters.

"But that's wrong," I said. It was an automatic interjection. It occurred to me that maybe this whole thing was a test. Maybe Ayya had arranged this, arranged for her to test my beliefs. Maybe this reading that I thought was so roguish was really part of my planned lessons.

"You think her love for Robert is wrong?" she asked.

I hesitated. I wasn't sure what she wanted to hear. I knew the proper answer for Ayya, but he wouldn't have let me read this book in the first place. And if there was a different answer, if Mrs. Pontellier's love for a man who wasn't her husband could be moral, it meant that Ayya wasn't always right. My head ran around on a wheel.

"You think love is wrong?" Sita asked.

"Love isn't wrong, but she's married," I said.

"Draupadi had five husbands. Krishna had many lovers."

"Yes, but—"

"Murugan married twice."

I tried to remember what Ayya had said about this. You're asking the wrong questions, Ayya would've said.

"You're asking the wrong questions," I said.

"Am I? What are the right questions?"

She waited. Lakshman was always the one who'd questioned, who'd tried to find loopholes. I was always the one who accepted what Ayya would teach. But Lakshman was inside my head now, like I had to be both of us now that he wasn't here.

"This was a bad idea," she said. She frowned and reached for the book in my hands.

I held it away. I wanted to know what happened to Robert and Edna Pontellier. I wanted to keep escaping to this strange place between the tattered covers. I wanted to imagine the conversations I could've had with Lakshman about the story. Maybe Amma would take me back to the village, so I could speak to him again. Maybe he could teach me how to find the loopholes between this book's world and my own.

Sita sat back on her heels. "When you finish," she said, "I have more for you."

Sita challenged me on everything I believed. She and her books did their best to upend my so-far-firm sense of right and wrong. Every day my brain got resized, and it was exhausting.

I fell asleep at night wondering if Edna could've been with Robert if she'd lived in another time and place, if she could've been Draupadi, married to five men at the same time. I wondered, too, about Edna's resemblance to my own Amma, who was a painter—if Amma dreamt of a life away from her family, away from me.

Ayya had given me a month off of prayer meetings, but soon I was back sitting in full costume in the meditation room, ready for healing, on a bhajan night. Sita wore one of Amma's borrowed podavais. Ayya stood by the door to the veranda instead of taking his normal place on the floor beside me, greeting people as they came in. Each person stopped, talked to him in a low voice, and dropped something into the donation box before stepping over the threshold and sitting in their usual spots on new bamboo mats in the meditation room. Most people brought envelopes of cash or checks. Some dug into their pockets for money. Women slipped gold bangles off their wrists and dropped them in.

I missed Lakshman's voice. I automatically looked for him in the room before I remembered. Roopa sat to my right side, trying to be a comforting presence. We weren't allowed to talk when visitors were around, so we sat together, and that's how I liked us best—silent and supportive, two lonely kids living half-grown-up lives, friends by proximity and our isolation from everyone else our age.

The village boys laughed and ran around in the field beyond the veranda. I might have been able to talk Ayya into letting me play with them after the healing session, but I hated the thought of playing without Lakshman. I ignored them. I wondered what Lakshman was doing right now, with his new haircut and American clothes.

One woman's song drew me back to the room. She hit a high note and held it, sounding exactly like Lakshman's voice.

The world stilled. And I felt it again—Rama's presence in the room. So familiar, though this was only the second time. The hair on my body tickled, and the noise of the room fell away. I sensed he was listening, and I knew I didn't have much time.

"Rama," I whispered. "How do I get Lakshman back?"

I held my breath. Rama's presence wavered at the corner of my vision. I turned my head sharply, hoping I'd be quick enough to catch a glance, but all I saw were more villagers, more wall space.

I felt the answer more than I heard it—like a breath on my ear. "He's gone," Rama said.

"Will I see him again?" I asked, keeping my voice as quiet as I could.

"If you do, it won't be for a long, long time."

The villager ended her song, and Rama was gone.

Outside, the boys continued to play. Other people sang other songs. The world continued, oblivious to my devastation.

As the villagers left that night, Ayya watched them from the veranda, his fingers drumming against the donation box. I wanted to finish my homework in my room and read more. I had to distract myself from Rama's latest visit and the confusion he'd brought me.

"I have great news," Ayya said to the four of us left in the room— Amma, Sita, Roopa, and me. "We've made enough in donations to expand the ashram."

"In one day?" I asked. This Friday was the first time I'd seen people consistently giving to the donation box.

"I've been canvassing all month in the village and the town," Ayya said. "People are hearing about you. They're eager to help a god's shrine. We got a big donation from the village elder. And several more from powerful people in Virudhunagar and Madurai who've heard about your gifts." I'd rarely seen Ayya smile this big. "We'll start renovations next week."

Ayya hired some boys from the village to help clear the area around the ashram, boys not much older than I was. I watched them through the window while I sat in my room to read. Dark brown backs hunched against the sun, throwing weeds and sticks into baskets to be hauled away.

I wanted to go read in the coconut grove, but I was too embarrassed to pass the boys. More of them worked near the paddies, and on the edge of the grove. If Lakshman had been here, he would've insisted on clearing the brush with them, or else, if he wasn't allowed, he would've sat by the paddies with coconut juice, making fun of the boys' ratty clothes or the way they always had mud in their hair.

An architect came and walked all over the fields around the ashram, a group of assistants following him like a line of ducklings. They stooped over the tall grasses. Ayya pointed out the herd of horses. The architect wrote in a notebook. Sita came out to talk to them. They chatted and Ayya laughed at something she said. I watched them from my room as I read *Wuthering Heights*, as Heathcliff slid into tortured misery over not being able to be with Catherine. As much as the ashram was changing, the world inside my head was starting to change even more.

Roopa had more chores to do, and most days after our lessons, Ayya called her to bring water and food to the workers, a never-ending task. Secretly, I was glad it was she who was being called for these chores and not me.

As the expansion went on, a group of thirunangaigal came and set up camp near the oxbow pond. I'd seen them before—the same troupe came during the festivals we hosted at the ashram, and I'd gotten used to their faces and bright podavais. Ayya called them "aravanis," and so did I back then, before the transgender movement in Tamil Nadu gained momentum and they finally named themselves. Elsewhere in India, they would have been called "hijra."

Ayya warned me to stay away from them. He regarded them with distaste and never spoke to any of them except for Muniamma, their stocky leader, with whom he negotiated fees. The blessing of the thirunangaigal was necessary to begin the new expansion auspiciously. Assigned male at birth and presenting as women, thirunangaigal clung to an unsteady place in Indian society, but they held a special connection with me. When Rama was exiled to the forest, large groups of his supporters followed him. Rama beseeched them, saying, "All the men and women must return to their homes and families," and everyone departed, except for the thirunangaigal. Pleased with their devotion, Rama blessed them.

After I resumed my daily morning walks past the workers to the oxbow pond to do sandhyavandanam, I passed the thirunangai camp every day. Around twenty of them lived in colorful tents made of old podavais and tarp. When I passed, the younger ones would be outside, bent over the rice flour kolams they were making in front of their tents. They put their palms together and bowed to me, and I bowed back.

Some of them were teenagers who stood in groups and gossiped and giggled, but only one was my age. I saw her every day as I passed, usually sitting by herself at the edge of the camp, watching me with doelike eyes. She wore flowers in her shiny, shoulder-length hair, and she was always dressed in one of two sets of clothes—a skirt that fell to the grass, either flower-printed or olive green, and a blouse with puffy sleeves, either in black or a faded blue that could have once been cobalt. She was usually mending one of the older thirunangaigal's clothes, the bright fabrics spread all over her lap. Something about the pointed cup of her chin reminded me of Vasanthy Chithy. She watched me as I passed, and I had to keep my eyes on the horizon to hide my interest.

In the midst of the chaotic expansion project, Amma and I slipped out one afternoon and went to the village. This was the first time she'd asked me to go with her since I'd spoken to Lakshman on the phone.

She was in a good mood, humming under her breath for most of our walk. Unlike Ayya, when we passed the thirunangai camp, Amma greeted them with a smile. The girl watched me again. She was mending a sun-bright yellow skirt, attaching a string of fake pearls to the golden hem.

When we got closer to the village, I asked Amma if Vasanthy Chithy was feeling better.

"Last time I talked to them, she was getting treatment." Amma smiled. "I think she's going to be okay."

I nodded. Inside me churned the guilt of not being able to heal my aunt, no matter how many times Ayya claimed I'd passed my third trial.

"Do you think she would've gotten better if she'd stayed?" I asked.

Amma took my hand and kissed it. "Your powers are strong, Kalki, but sometimes people need a different kind of healing."

That wasn't what she'd told me when Roopa was sick. Roopa's sickness couldn't be healed by the clinics.

"What is Vasanthy Chithy's sickness?" I asked.

"She has cancer," Amma said. "Do you know what that is?"

I shook my head. Ayya's teachings hadn't mentioned anything by that name, which Amma said in English. Reading Sita's books, I had already started to realize how much Ayya hadn't taught me. The vastness of what I didn't know stretched before me, frustrating and never-ending.

"Cancer is when your body fights against you," she said. "Gods can heal a lot of things, but gods can't heal cancer."

It didn't make a lot of sense. I healed people's back pain and made barren wombs fruitful, but I couldn't heal cancer. As I tried to wrap my head around it, Amma fell back into a contemplative silence.

In the village, we found the same store from before and called from the same pink phone. Amma didn't give me the receiver this time, but I heard Kantha Chithappa's muffled voice on the other line.

"Can I talk to Lakshman?" I asked.

Rama had told me he was gone, that I might never see him again. And if I did see him, it wouldn't be for a while. But that only made me want to talk to him more. I wanted to at least ask Lakshman when he was coming back.

I pulled on Amma's hand to ask again.

She shushed me. Her eyebrows drew a harsh line across her face. Her eyes, nose, and mouth were all held tight by some invisible string. And then the string broke, and her face melted into her palm. Her quaking hand gave the phone back to the man.

"What is it?" I asked. "What did they say?"

She shook her head and wiped her eyes with the heel of her palm. She said nothing on the walk back home, despite my repeated questioning. Something was wrong. She'd said that Vasanthy Chithy was healing, but maybe her health had worsened. Maybe it was something else. Maybe it was that they had to stay in America forever. Maybe Amma had realized she might never get her sister back.

That night as I laid in my bed, I heard Ayya and Amma fighting in his room.

"You did this," Amma said. Her words came out stifled and slurred, and I imagined her hands over her face. "You did this."

"Suma," Ayya said. He usually referred to her as "your Amma." I could count on one hand the number of times I'd heard him say her name. "Please, Suma. You know it was no one's fault."

"You didn't let them leave."

"I was faithful," he hissed. "It was your doubt that caused this. You should've believed."

"I believed," Amma said, crying softly. "I still believe."

I heard a crack ring in the air. Instinctively, I knew what it was. Ayya had slapped Amma. A startled sob escaped me, and I held very still.

"It was your painting," he said, his voice full of poison. "Your neglect. A good mother isn't concerned with selfish pursuits. If you had been pious, he might have been able to heal her."

Amma's words melted into wordless sobbing.

If Vasanthy Chithy was still sick in America, it was my fault, not Amma's.

"Rama," I whispered. "Rama? Please, tell me what to do."

No answer.

I wanted to run out and go to Amma, to soothe her and push Ayya away, but I remembered the way my shins had stung when Ayya hit me with the stick from the tulsi plant, and I stayed where I was. I wrapped myself tight in the covers. Through my window, the limbs of the mango tree splintered moonlight into countless dots. Amma's cries abated, and finally stopped.

The next morning, Amma made thayir saadam—yogurt rice—for breakfast. She made more for lunch. Ayya regarded the glop of white on his banana leaf. He hated thayir saadam, which was why we almost never had it at the ashram.

Amma slammed down a jar of pickled chili limes next to him.

Thayir saadam was a favorite of mine, but never in all my memory had we eaten it more than once a week. Ayya didn't say a word all through lunch. When I caught Roopa's eye, she gestured that she didn't know what was going on either. Sita kept quiet, too, and I took her lead in eating my meal quietly so as not to disturb the thin layer of ice that had formed between Amma and Ayya. I didn't know what would happen if that ice cracked. I didn't know what was underneath.

Dinner that night was more thayir saadam, this time in a giant pot to feed the architect and the workers. They passed around jars of lime and mango pickle. Ayya said nothing and avoided eye contact with everyone.

The next day, Amma made more thayir saadam for breakfast, lunch, and dinner—and the next day, and the day after that. Roopa complained to me all during lessons in little whispers thrown out of the side of her mouth when she thought Ayya wasn't paying attention.

At night, I wrapped myself in my covers and waited for the sounds of fighting, but instead, the ashram was covered in an oppressive silence, broken by the rustling of monkeys in the trees and the occasional whinny of horses in the distance. In the daytime, when Ayya came into a room, Amma would leave. She said nothing to him for a week. When I asked her about it, Amma said, "I've cooked for your father for fourteen years. I'm tired."

I couldn't think of a response. It was her duty to cook for her family, but if she wanted to feed us the same thing every day, that was her prerogative. The dharma of a wife and mother never talked about variety.

"Your Ayya needs to be taught a lesson," she said.

She'd never spoken of Ayya like that before, like a petulant child. As a woman and as a mother, Amma was close to godliness. But as a man and as a father, Ayya was close to godliness, too, and I didn't know if punishing him was the right thing to do. Still, a part of me—the part that remembered all the times Ayya had punished me with no playtime or more homework, and that time when he hit me with the stick—that part of me relished this moment.

After a week of eating the same meal, when the chili limes had burned the top of my mouth, Ayya brought an old lady from the village to cook for us, and we had no more thayir saadam.

On her first day, the old lady received a slap from Ayya for cooking with peanut oil that she'd brought. He put dosa in his mouth, only to gasp and choke. I ran to his room and found his EpiPen, which I plunged into his thigh the way he'd taught me. He recovered, and as soon as his strength returned, he slapped the old woman right across her face, right in front of all of us during breakfast.

"I could have died," he said.

She bowed and apologized over and over. Ayya sat with his arms crossed while she recooked breakfast, and then we ate.

Amma started coming to me at night—showing up like Lakshman used to, when I was teetering on the edge of sleep. She'd wake me with a gentle shake. I'd scoot over so she could climb in and fold her body around mine.

Sometimes I couldn't sleep. Her body was too warm, and I woke up sweating. Sometimes she cried softly, and I lay awake, holding her like she was a baby, stroking her hair and kissing her forehead.

"What's wrong?" I'd ask.

She'd shake her head and hold me tighter.

"Is it Ayya?" I asked once.

She held her face with her hand. "I was so young when I married him," she said.

4

Daily lessons with Ayya got harder and harder. Workers shouted to each other. Tractors brought rocks and bricks. Trucks with spinning barrels poured cement where the workers dug.

We tried our best to ignore the sounds, but Roopa and I got so distracted during lessons that we usually watched out the window until Ayya scolded us. Between the construction and all the stories in my head, I barely paid attention. Often Ayya got frustrated, his teeth grinding and his thigh bobbing up and down. He let us out before lunch, assigning us double the homework.

After lunch, I usually slipped away to the coconut grove, saying I was going to feed the horses. I brought my secret books and read under the shade of my favorite tree, the one that grew horizontal, like a man bending at the waist. Roopa was too busy to play, running around at all hours when we weren't having lessons, getting the workers tea and snacks, helping the old cook make the workers' meals in large cauldrons in the kitchen, setting up their banana leaves for their meals, and walking down the line of seated workers during mealtimes, filling their banana leaves with more rice and curry. And at the end of the day when the workers went home, she was so tired that she shut herself in the room she now shared with Amma, saying she had to do homework or sleep. I was lonelier than ever without Roopa's company.

One day, a few weeks after the construction started in earnest, I was sitting at the base of my favorite tree, reading the end of *Wuthering Heights*. I'd thought I was alone until I heard a rustle.

The thirunangai who was my age, the one with the piercing eyes and pointy chin that made me think of Vasanthy Chithy, stepped out from around a tree, looking as startled to see me as I was to see her. She had her flowered skirt balled up in her hands, the hem dirty and torn. She wore a brown tulsi bead on a string around her thin, long neck.

"Hi," I said. I put my book aside on the low trunk of a tree.

She looked at the ground, her hands shaking where they held her skirt. Ayya had said that thirunangaigal were dirty and immoral and that I should never, under any circumstances, talk to them. But this girl looked so innocent and so pretty. Besides, Rama had called thirunangaigal his most devoted followers.

"Do you want to sit?" I asked, moving over to offer her the most comfortable spot, where I'd created a cushion out of a pile of fallen fronds.

She stood for a minute, staring at the ground, but then she came over, her steps tinkling from the bells on her anklets. She arranged her skirt over her knees and sat next to me.

"What's your name?" I asked. Up close, little circular indents marked her cheeks. She'd lined her eyes with black kajal.

"Kalyani," she said in a whisper.

Around her obvious shyness, I felt brave and generous. I showed her the book I was reading and told her the story as best as I could summarize in Tamil. She listened, her fingers picking at the hem of her skirt, a small smile on her lips. She proved to be a great audience, her face making the right emotions at the right times.

Kalyani didn't talk much that first day, but the next day when she came to the coconut grove during my reading time, she started opening up. She told me about how when she was born, no one could tell if she was a boy or a girl—how her family had hated her for it, and how her mother had taken her and fled their home, fearing for both their lives.

I was so curious to know more, but I knew by her hesitant demeanor that it was a touchy subject.

I asked her what being a thirunangai meant.

She thought about the question for a long time, so long that I worried I'd offended her. But eventually, she answered in a small, quiet voice.

"It means something different to everyone," she said. "But for me, it means everyone thinks I'm a boy, or that I should be. My family does. My body does. But—I'm not. I'm a girl, I think. But I'm different, because of this body."

I sort of understood. Gods transcended their sexes and genders all the time. Vishnu became Mohini, the enchantress.

"My body and soul are in misalignment," she said. "I stand in the middle somewhere."

I wanted to tell her I stood in the middle, too, somewhere between god and not-god.

"What happened to your mother?" I asked. She'd mentioned her mother several times, but always in the past tense.

She held her hands tightly in her lap. "She got sick. We didn't have any money to get her treatment, so she died."

In the silence after her statement, I put my hand over hers without thinking about it. She snapped her head up and looked me in the eye for the first time. My heart shook itself like a wet dog. I wondered if Kalyani's mother had had cancer, like Vasanthy Chithy, or if it was something else I could have cured if I'd known—or if they would have been allowed to see me.

I made sure we were well-hidden in the depths of the grove when we talked. I couldn't imagine the punishment Ayya would give me if he knew I was talking to Kalyani. In the mornings, when I passed the thirunangai camp on my way to the oxbow pond and back, I would catch Kalyani's eye and we'd smile at each other, content in our secret. When I read in the afternoon or brushed down the horses, Kalyani would find me in the grove.

We chased each other around the trees, playing tag. We hopscotched on the banks of the creek. We skipped rocks on the water. We told each other stories. She taught me how to dance, away from everyone else's prying eyes. I read to her, and because she didn't know English, I translated each sentence as I read. I loved hearing her laugh because it was so rare. When she laughed, it came startled and spilling out of her, as if she hadn't expected it and had surprised herself. She hid her face in her hands and bent forward with the force of her laughter. I tried to make her laugh as much as I could. When I was around her, I didn't think of Lakshman or how much I missed him.

Eventually, Kalyani told me more stories about her life, how her troupe of thirunangaigal traveled around and performed all over Tamil Nadu at festivals and weddings, how people often cheated them out of money, how no one would hire them even though some of the thirunangaigal were educated and had degrees, how they were so poor that sometimes the older thirunangaigal had to take men to bed to buy rice. She told me about Shyama, the thirunangai who had first taken Kalyani in after the death of her mother, and how Shyama had fallen in love with a police officer's son, and how she'd been so distraught after finding out he was already married that she'd walked off one day and never came back. I learned also of Kalyani's friends, Vijjy and Kiran. They had all entered the troupe together under the mentorship of Muniamma, who was like a mother to them.

"Kiran got homesick," Kalyani said. Whenever she told me these stories, she always shook like a scared rabbit, and I held her hands, hoping to bring her some ease. "She went back home to her family and pretended to be a boy again. And Vijjy, when she started to grow a mustache, she—she thought she was ugly. She thought she'd never look like a girl. And she—she tried to—"

I realized I was squeezing Kalyani's hand so tightly that I was hurting her. I couldn't sit with this pain. I didn't know what to do. My limbs felt swollen and too much. I was supposed to be saving the world, healing people, but here was proof that the world was eviller and crueler than I'd ever imagined, if it would subject a girl like Kalyani to this kind of hardship.

When I got back to my room, I climbed into bed. I couldn't move under the weight of all of this new knowledge, all of Kalyani's pain. I lay on my side, staring at the wall, until Ayya came angrily to my door to call me to dinner.

"What's the matter with you?" he said, annoyed.

I couldn't explain it to him, and I had a feeling that even if I could, he wouldn't understand. These days, he was so excited about the expansion. He wouldn't stand for me feeling any emotion other than glee. But I was distanced from myself; I wondered what would've happened if I'd been a thirunangai, or if Lakshman had been—if Ayya would have disowned us, if we would have worn dirty, torn clothing and been forced to perform for money, if we would have faced a future of taking men to bed in order to buy rice.

I started to love Kalyani for showing me more of the real world, and I wanted desperately to protect her. Sita gave me books where I read about life outside the ashram, but Kalyani told me stories that showed me the cruelty of the world directly. I knew Ayya would never allow her to stay at the ashram, but I also knew I should do something for her besides offer my prayers and blessings. When I asked Kalyani, she said, "Be my friend."

I felt guilty about my feelings for Roopa, but Kalyani was different. Kalyani had seen true suffering. I had to be a strong, invincible god around Roopa, and around Kalyani I could be myself, safe in the knowledge that she wouldn't judge me for anything.

A month after the construction started in earnest, I walked to the woods with Sita's latest book under one arm and a pail of water and a horse brush in the other. I gave Arjuna water and brushed him down. Kalyani joined me, and I showed her how to brush down Draupadi, who liked her. As we picked horsehair from the brushes, I heard Sita's voice, high and whispering. It came from the direction of the creek that ran through the grove.

I put down the brush and took a few steps toward the creek, making a shushing motion so Kalyani would stay silent. A man's voice cut under Sita's laugh. Ayya's voice, his chuckle like gravel.

I walked faster, Kalyani right behind me. Some instinct told me we shouldn't go, but my feet carried me all the same.

Near the creek, we hid behind a coconut tree. Sita sat with Ayya next to the water, her skirt spread out on the grass. Ayya's face and chest tilted toward her. He threw rocks into the water. I'd never seen him laugh like that, or do something so idle and silly. They talked in a low murmur I couldn't make out, but their laughter spiraled wild over the rustling water. Wind blew the hair out of Sita's ponytail. Ayya tucked a piece of it back behind her ear.

The hissing in my head muted the world. Ayya and Sita looked at each other. I clung to the trunk of the tree, my fingers digging into bark. I was barely aware of Kalyani's hand on my arm, trying to pull me away.

Ayya kissed Sita right on the mouth.

One time, Lakshman had shown me what adults kiss like, which he claimed to have learned from one of the village kids. "Tamil kisses are closed-mouth," he'd said. He'd pursed his lips into closed circle. "But English people kiss like this," he'd said, opening his lips so they fit into mine, his tongue pressing on my teeth. I'd gotten dizzy and pushed him away.

But Sita didn't seem dizzy at all. She pulled Ayya closer by his collar and they continued to fit their mouths into one another.

My grip on the coconut tree slipped, and I fell forward a step, crunching the leaves in the underbrush. Sita and Ayya broke apart, looking around in our direction.

"Who's there?"

"Is somebody there?"

We turned and ran. We kept running until I couldn't hear the sound of their panicked voices.

Anger inflated inside me. My chest heaved up and down. Kalyani tried to pat me on the back to calm me, but I walked out of the coconut grove in shock, away from her, lightheaded from not enough air.

Alone in my room at the ashram, I sat at my desk and prayed to the Krishna painting that hung above it. I hoped Rama would come and tell me what to do, but there was nothing—no breeze on which I sensed his voice, no hair-raising feeling that he was nearby. And I'd left Kalyani walking back to the thirunangai camp. I was alone with this.

The image of Ayya and Sita wouldn't leave my head. I wanted to scrub my brain clean with soap. I thought of telling Amma, but I couldn't bear to see her cry more than she already did most nights, curled around my body. I could keep this locked up in my heart. I could bear this secret for her, so she didn't have to. Gods held secrets all the time. They bore that which others could not.

That afternoon, while I lay on my bed staring at the ceiling and trying to motivate myself to do homework, Sita came into my room, holding the book I'd left in the coconut grove. She set it silently on my bed and sat down, not looking at me.

"Sometimes," she said, "adults do things that are wrong. Like Edna Pontellier and Robert. It doesn't mean they're bad people."

I bunched my fists in my veshti. I hated her, and I hated the way her skin was so smooth under the light of my kerosene lamp.

"You can't tell anyone what you saw," she said. "No one."

I'd already buried the secret underneath my ribcage, where it sat spasming. Inside me grew a rage I didn't know how to feel, a rage I'd only witnessed before from outside, a rage that always existed in Lakshman a few inches deeper than his skin, ready to break and boil over. I wanted to push Sita off my bed, hit her, and tell her to leave the ashram.

"I saw you," I said.

She sat, letting the words hang, her face set like stone.

"I saw you," I said again, unable to stop myself. "I saw you both."

She stood up. "Do you like meeting the villagers every Friday?"

The question took me by surprise, like she'd asked it in a language I couldn't understand. I stammered, "I—I like helping people." I didn't try to keep the bitterness out of my voice.

"But do you *believe* you're helping them?" she asked, dragging out the word *believe* like it was an accusation.

Far from distracting me, her questions stoked my anger.

"Why are you asking this?"

"I know you think you're happy," she said. "But sometimes what we think is true, isn't. What do you really think a little boy can offer to someone like me, someone who has been through war?"

The question hit me like a strike across the face. I stepped back from the force of it.

Immediately, her face softened. "I didn't mean that," she said.

Those books I'd been reading—this was what she'd been trying to show me. That the world was too wide for me to help it. Hindu philosophy talked about *maya*, the concept of illusion. The world itself, all of reality, was an illusion that kept us from searching for our greater purpose. I was the maya for the people who believed in me. *I* was the illusion. That was what Sita wanted me to think.

"Kalki, I don't know what you think you saw," she said, "but you have to forget it. Ayya doesn't know that you saw us. I didn't tell him I found your book. This is our secret, yours and mine. And you can't tell anyone. It was a mistake."

I tried to think of what my god self would say. Gods were supposed to be kind and forgiving. Unlike the Christian concept of eternal damnation, Hindus believed in paying for the sins you commit to absolve yourself of them. Sita would pay for this sin—the universe and the wheel of karma would make sure of it—regardless of whether or not I could forgive her.

A part of me—the part that sounded like Lakshman's voice in my head—crossed its arms and turned its back on her. That little-boy part of me wanted to see her suffer. And the god part of me wanted to reach out and touch her hand in pity. I stood in the pull of these two voices.

Sita said, "I know you've been spending time with that—that *girl*." She turned her face so it was half in shadow, hidden from me. "I've seen you. Ayya would be furious if he found out, but I won't tell him if you don't tell anyone about what you saw."

I waited for my thoughts to catch up with me. As surprised as I was at her attempt at blackmail, it was something I could understand.

"You need to promise me two things," I said after a pause. "Promise me that you won't do it again." I held out my hand, palm-up. "Sathiyam. Make a vow."

She ground her teeth, but she put her palm on mine and said, "Sathiyam."

"And promise me that you won't tell Ayya about Kalyani." I held out my hand again. "Sathiyam."

"Sathiyam," she said again, touching her palm to mine. "I promise."

5

Seeing Sita with Ayya was one of those things that didn't fit into my ten-year-old narrative of the world. All the stories of the gods, of Rama and Krishna, were filled with men and women who had many lovers and sometimes many spouses. But they always loved others openly, with the acceptance and permission of their wives and husbands. Amma hadn't permitted this. Ayya was making a fool of her.

Meanwhile, the ashram expansion bloomed as if growing from a seed. Pillars rose from the dirt, blossomed into walls, and spread over themselves to make roofs. Unlike the thatched roof of the existing hut, the new expansion had a smooth domed roof surrounded by baked clay shingles. Ayya wouldn't let any of us inside, saying it was a surprise.

Ayya's enthusiasm permeated any conversation about the ashram. The expansion would allow more visitors, more exposure, and would lead to fame, which would lead to more devotees, which would lead to me bettering their lives, which would lead to a spiritual world tour. I nodded along to these conversations, but deep down I wondered: If the rest of the world was as wild and different from us as Sita's books and Kalyani's stories led me to believe, could I really better the lives of people who lived so wildly and differently? What could I offer to an American who owned more than one car and went to work in a glass office building? What could I offer to a soldier? What could I offer to someone who had no spiritual beliefs? What could I offer to a person whose body and soul were in profound disagreement, a person the world hated despite their beauty?

When Sita wasn't alone in her room, she was out talking to Ayya and the workers. She kept her promises, or at least it seemed that way to me. Physically, she stood at a distance from Ayya. She avoided his eyes and avoided being left alone in a room with him, like Amma. And Ayya didn't suspect my friendship with Kalyani.

Roopa, when she wasn't busy with chores, spent more and more time with the village kids who came to help build the extension. Every Friday, she dressed up in silk clothes and gold jewelry and Ayya sat her next to me, the living proof of my healing powers. I never introduced her to Kalyani because I was afraid she wouldn't like her, or would be mean to her, or would tell someone about me being friends with her. I didn't know how Roopa felt about thirunangaigal, but I didn't want to take the chance.

My life had torn. I wasn't the same person I had been when Lakshman was here, or the same person I had been when I first made friends with Roopa. To me, the only people who saw me exactly as I was now—the people who saw my sadness and isolation—were Kalyani and Sita.

As the ashram expanded, Amma's body shrank. I noticed it when I hugged her one morning, how her cheeks sagged, the bags under her eyes. Amma ate less and less and painted not at all. The days of me watching her paint and her laughing as she answered my questions were over. At first I thought she was sick, but nothing else seemed to be wrong with her, and she kept telling me she was fine. I sat with Amma while she and Roopa took their meals, but even my prodding couldn't make her eat any more than a handful per meal.

I kept reading the books Sita gave me. Even though I couldn't stand her company anymore, I'd come to need her books. Each one filled my mind with worlds and teachings beyond anything I thought I could know. I hid them well—until I didn't.

One day, Ayya found me in my room, curled against the edge of the plaster wall, reading by the light of the sunset outside. I slammed the book closed and shoved it under my pillow.

He narrowed his eyes at the pillow. "What have you been doing in here?" he asked. He stood at the edge of my bed, towering over me.

"I'm just—" I stopped. My voice sounded small and lost. "I was taking a break from homework."

He held out his hand. He looked at the pillow.

I slid the book out and placed it in his outstretched palm. I only had a few more pages left.

Ayya squinted at the cover. He opened the book and flipped through.

"It's a story," I said. "A—a novel."

He stopped flipping. He read a few lines on the page, his eyes roving downward. "Who is David Copperfield?" His voice threatened pain.

"It's just a story."

"Who gave this to you?"

I considered lying, but there was no one else to blame it on.

"Was it those aravanis?"

I couldn't let them take the blame. He'd send them away, and I panicked at the idea of not seeing Kalyani again. Part of me—the part that wanted Sita gone, the part that still had nightmares about seeing them kiss in the grove—knew this was my opportunity.

"Sita Aunty," I said. "I borrowed it from her."

He clutched the book hard. "I'll take care of this." He paused in the doorway. "Finish your homework. If you have time for nonsense stories, you have time for more homework."

I waited until he left, then tiptoed down the hall, following him to the meditation room. I hid around a corner.

Sita stood with her back against the sunset in the meditation room, her arms folded over her chest. She was the one facing the door, and her eyes flickered toward me like she noticed me standing just out of view, but she didn't say anything. Ayya stood in front of her, holding the book out so she could read the title.

Her body was a statue backlit by the dying sun.

"You can't give him these books to read," Ayya said.

"Why not? He's a little boy. He's bored. Stories can be good for him."

Ayya's back tensed. "I know what's good for him. His *parents* know what's good for him." He shook the book at her. "These nonsense stories will fill his head with the wrong ideas."

"You're saying he shouldn't learn ideas that aren't yours? I'm a teacher," she said. "I like teaching him."

"Teaching him is *my* job."

She unfolded her arms and shifted her weight from one foot to another.

Ayya lowered his voice. "You've rested at the ashram long enough."

Her face drew closed, like a curtain had fallen. She took the book from him. "I'll leave if you want to get rid of me." Sita's eyes again flicked to where I stood, hidden in the shadow of the door. "I'll stop giving him any more books."

I ran quietly back to my room, my body a colony of ants puttering in all directions.

The new prayer center held an office for Ayya, rooms for visitors, a modern kitchen that took up the entire back of the building, and a banquet hall Ayya told me was to be used for weddings. Ayya and the architect gave us all a tour when it was done. The building's smooth plaster walls had been painted bright white, its wood floors buffed and shined until they gleamed. Workers from the village had lined the edges of every wall with string lights. Dark beams crisscrossed the ceiling. Embroidered silk hung in place of pictures on the walls.

During the tour, Ayya ignored Sita, and she pretended not to see him. He led us to the round main room. Inside the domed ceiling, someone had painted a mural of all my avatars. I knew without having to ask why Amma hadn't been asked to paint these—Ayya thought her paintings were too wild, too unruly.

Paintings of my past lives lined the curving ceiling so that when I stood in the middle of the room, gods surrounded me. The painting of me looked nothing like me in the face, or in the blueness of the skin. It looked more like the paintings of Krishna that hung all over the old ashram building.

Roopa watched me watch myself on the ceiling. Each avatar stood alone. Their wives, their consorts, their children, their brothers—nowhere to be found. Rama without his Sita, without Lakshman. Krishna without Radha, without Balram. And me, all alone in my yellow panchakacham veshti, a flower garland around my neck, gold-leafed jewelry all over my body.

"It looks good," Roopa said. She gazed at the ceiling, and then at me. "It looks just like you."

The celebration pooja for the expansion took place early in the morning on a Friday. The whole village swarmed to the ashram.

Ayya threw open the doors of the main hall in the new building and people spilled onto the grass outside, dressed in their very best. Some had had new clothes made for the occasion, judging by the pristine hems on the girls' skirts and the unsoiled underarms of the women's podavai blouses.

The thirunangaigal, including Kalyani, stood at the edge of the crowd. After the pooja, the older ones performed in a circle while Muniamma beat a riotous beat on a double-skinned kachhi dhol drum. Each wore short blouses that exposed their stomachs, anklets full of brass bells that jangled with every step, and bright satin skirts that twirled rippling circles around them as they spun. Kalyani didn't dance with them, but she was dressed in a new pink blouse and a skirt with a gold hem, and she had a crown of flowers around her head. I couldn't stop looking at her, and once or twice, she caught my eye and smiled.

I knew this was the last day they'd be here, but I didn't know then that this was the last time the troupe would come to the ashram. When the next festival came around, Muniamma turned Ayya down, and though he wouldn't tell me why, I learned years later that it was because Muniamma and most of the thirunangaigal under her wing had become politically active, pushing for social justice in employment, housing, healthcare, and education for the transgender community in Tamil Nadu. As an adult, a decade after I met her, Kalyani made the front page of *The Times of India*, leading a sit-in strike in front of the Parliament House in New Delhi.

Around mid-afternoon, when the third set of villagers were eating in the shiny new banquet hall, I snuck out with Kalyani. Ayya had disappeared, Amma was busy overseeing the banquet, and Roopa was still serving. The village kids had all been wrangled into eating by their parents.

We went back to my room to take off my gold jewelry. The sight of Kalyani standing in my bedroom filled me with a combination of dread and excitement that I only got when reading Sita's books, but this time it was so intense that my teeth clattered. Kalyani helped me remove my jewelry, and I stood immobile, the hairs on my arms and neck standing straight up in little bumps. I was acutely aware of every time her fingers brushed my skin. Once or twice, as she struggled with a clasp, I suppressed the electric bolts that ran up my body.

"Will you visit?" I asked.

"I'll try," she said.

When she was done helping me, we tucked the jewelry into red-lined boxes, and Kalyani ran her fingers over them softly, longingly. It struck me that she might have never owned gold jewelry before. I put the boxes away in the lockbox in my armoire and dug around in the back for an old, tattered box I knew was there, one that held my baby jewelry. I pulled it out and showed it to Kalyani—small, flower-shaped earrings, two thick bangles big enough for a toddler, tiny anklets, and a chain that used to hang to my naval.

"You were so small," she said, touching the jewelry lightly, her face full of wonder. I wondered if she would ever want a baby when she grew up, and how she would get one, if she wanted.

I put the earrings and chain into her palms.

"You keep that," I said. "They're small, but you can still wear them."

She looked terrified as she tried to press them back into my hands. "If anyone found out, they'll think I stole these."

I shook my head, again feeling brave. "If anyone finds out, I'll tell the truth. Keep it."

I helped her wrap up the chain and earrings in a soft washcloth, and she slipped them into the waistband of her skirt. When she was done arranging herself again, she stepped up to me, put her hands on either side of my face, and kissed me on the lips.

She had warm, soft lips, and up close I smelled the powder she'd put on her face. Her eyes were closed, and I marveled at how even and beautiful the lines of black on her eyelids were. Inside me, a thunderstorm broke, and lightning shot everywhere, to the tips of my fingers and into my chest.

Kalyani and I were walking on the veranda when we saw Sita coming out of her room with something hidden in the end of her podavai. She looked both ways and down the path toward the new expansion before heading off to the coconut grove.

I knew we had to follow. Sita took my normal path toward the creek, past where Arjuna liked to graze. She walked around a corner.

Kalyani and I hid behind a tree.

Ayya was waiting for her, alone. He had his hands in the pockets of his kurta. She stopped in front of him and showed him what she had hidden in her podavai—a bottle I'd seen in her suitcase earlier, its cut glass filled with a dirty brown liquid. She lifted the stopper from the bottle, tipped back her head, and drank from it. She offered it to him, wiping her mouth with the back of her hand.

Ayya shook his head. She drank a few more times, and he watched her. She put the bottle on the ground. They stepped toward each other.

Sita had promised. This was supposed to be over.

He put his hand on her waist, inside her podavai.

Even as the anger rose up in me, and even as Kalyani pulled at my arm, I stood with my hands glued to the tree.

"We should go," Kalyani said. "You don't want to see this."

But I couldn't move, and Kalyani wasn't strong enough to make me, so we stood there, hidden.

Ayya kissed Sita. Sita laid down on the ground. He laid down on top of her, kissed her neck, pushed up her podavai around her hips. When she writhed, he held her wrists above her head and kissed her some more.

I felt every pulse of blood in my body, in my skin, and on my skull. And when I couldn't stand it anymore, I floated away from myself, leaving my body to boil up in rage and disgust.

Ayya kneeled in front of Sita's spread legs, partially hidden by Amma's borrowed podavai draping across her knees. He laid down on top of her and pushed his hips forward, again and again. Sita made a sound from deep inside her stomach that sounded like an animal in pain.

My mouth dried up, my palms turned sweaty, and the rest of my body emptied of thought. Wind spiraled around us. The hairs on my arm stood up, and I felt it—Rama, there with me in the grove. His fury bolstered mine. He laid a firm hand on my shoulder, letting me know I was right.

"She has to go," he whispered to me, and he was gone again. But I had heard him, and I had understood.

When they were done, Sita took another sip from the bottle and repinned her podavai. The two of them gathered themselves and left the grove. I stood there for what felt like another hour, stunned, until Kalyani gently pried my fingers from the bark of the tree and led me back to the ashram. On the way back, she spoke to me, her voice soft and soothing.

"Adults do all kinds of things," she said. "Especially men. Men want this. All men, even your Ayya."

All men. I didn't want it. I thought it was ugly and revolting.

I opened my mouth to say so, but Kalyani interrupted me, as if she knew what my objection would be.

"All men," she said. "Even you."

That night when I closed my eyes, I saw Ayya and Sita, him kneeling between her bare legs. I oscillated between being furious for Amma and wanting to keep thinking of Sita and her podavai pushed up like that, her writhing. I pictured Kalyani with her body spread out before me, her skirt hiked up to her thighs. My body stirred. I turned over in the bed and pushed myself into the mattress, thrusting and thrusting until something exploded and wetness seeped into the fabric of my veshti.

I cleaned myself up and laid back down on my bed, hollow, as if someone had scooped out my organs. In the absence of my depleted desire, shame and anger filled me. I knew Kalyani was on the bus to Madurai. Before she'd gone back to camp, she'd kissed me again, though I'd been too terrified of anyone seeing that I hadn't enjoyed it like I had in my room. Now I was heartsick.

I didn't want to think any more about Kalyani or the possibility I wouldn't see her again, so I focused on Sita. She had promised to stay away from Ayya. And Amma—the more my mind drifted to Amma, the more my heart broke for her, and the more I wanted someone to suffer for it.

Eventually, I gave up trying to sleep and went to Sita's room. It was late, but not so late that she would be asleep. She'd broken her promise. I held my quivering hands pressed against the side of my thighs.

The lights were off in her room. Sita sat at the small desk she'd had moved into the space. Usually she'd be reading a book, but it was too dark to read. In front of her sat the bottle of cut glass, its liquid turned silver by the moonlight. She sat at the desk and stared at it.

"You promised me," I said. "You broke your promise."

She nodded like she understood. She looked back at the bottle, and I saw it in the black of her eyes, like it was staring back into her.

My rage about Ayya was caught inside my want to see what she would do with the bottle, what it would do with her. The first time I'd seen her and Ayya kissing, my anger had almost swallowed me. Now it sat humming like a dangerous animal underneath the surface, waiting to swallow something else. I could handle this the right way. I could be an adult—a god—about this.

Eventually, she asked, "Do you want more books?"

I knotted up my hands in my veshti. She was offering me books for my silence. I didn't care. I wanted more books.

She asked, "Do you want to read a book about gods? Or a book about no gods?"

I said the thing I should've said, as if Ayya was listening. It was automatic. "About gods."

She pushed her chair back and stood up. She closed the door, not bothering to turn on the lights. The edges of her body glowed in the moonlight. She stopped and took out the suitcase. She reached inside. She pulled out a book. I couldn't read the title, but the letters glinted in the dim light.

"I want you to keep this book," she said. She left the suitcase open. "It's yours." She picked up the bottle and tipped it to her lips. The blue-lit liquid dripped down her tongue. She shuddered like it had burnt her, tilted her head back again, and drank some more.

I clutched the book to my chest. She drank until the bottle was empty and her eyes turned cloudy, like she couldn't see the shapes of things anymore.

"You know why I came here?" she said. She slurred her words, and it was hard to follow her accented Tamil. "I can tell the world what's really going on."

I wasn't sure what she thought was going on, didn't know if she was talking about her and Ayya.

"Do you want me to?" she asked. "I can set you free. You'll be free of him."

But I didn't feel caged. I couldn't imagine a life without Ayya to guide me on my god journey. And Amma—if everyone found out about Ayya and Sita, it would destroy her.

"Don't tell anyone," I said. "But—" I gathered my breath. I

needed to do this. I closed my eyes, tried to feel Rama there with me, and for a second I sensed his presence in the room, a gentle pressure on my skin. "You need to leave," I said. "You need to leave this ashram. And never come back."

"Maybe you're a god after all," she said. She chuckled and wiped her mouth. "Promise me you'll read this book."

"Yes," I said. "And I'd ask you to promise me that you'll go, but your promises are worthless."

Her eyes were glassy and sad. "Would me leaving make you happy?"

I didn't know if it would make me happy, her absence. Her presence had been a distraction from my grief about Lakshman. And the books had been a gift beyond measure. But now that I knew the whole picture—that Lakshman wasn't coming back anytime soon, that Ayya and Sita's relationship couldn't be allowed to continue, and that Sita might have come to the ashram with ulterior motives—I had to do it. My body drooped as if I'd been awake for a hundred lifetimes.

"You'll go?" I asked.

She shrugged. "I don't know. I like it here," she said. "And you don't have any room to judge me." Spite seeped into her voice. "You and your little girlfriend, running around in secret. What if I told Ayya about that? What do you think would happen?"

I walked out of the room, slamming the door behind me.

Back in my bed, I examined the book Sita had given me. A book different from the others. Its cover broke apart, crumbling as I touched it. A thin film of dust clung to my fingers. On the front, a title written in Sanskrit: *Sarva Darsana Samgraha*, by Madhava Acharya. It looked like all the other religion books Ayya assigned me to read; it was laid out the same in neat Sanskrit letters on the inside. But unlike the other religion books, which started with an invocation of Ganesha or Vishnu, this one started with a prayer to

Shiva. That itself made the book dangerous. We were Vaishnavites who worshipped Vishnu as the supreme god, and an invocation to Shiva meant that this book was written by a Shaivite who worshipped Shiva. Historically, there had been a lot of bloodshed between Vaishnavites and Shaivites.

I made sure my door was closed and read the first few pages under the faded dawn light that broke through my windows. Amma wouldn't come back in to wake me for at least another hour.

There were Sanskrit words I hadn't encountered much before—*nastika*, which referred to someone who didn't believe in the supremacy of the Vedic texts. Ayya had gotten mad about the other books, but if he knew about this, he would burn it.

In the very first chapter, Madhava Acharya took back his prayer to Shiva, calling it useless. I slanted the book toward the growing yellow orb of the sun and read on. This author didn't believe in anything Hindu. Reincarnation. Rebirth. Souls. Dharma. Karma. Afterlife. Gods. Nothing. He believed only in what he could see with his eyes, touch with his hands, perceive with his body. He didn't believe in sin, or judgment, or paying for the decisions of a past life. He didn't believe in prayer.

I wanted to eat the book whole to quiet my heartbeat. The man was delusional, a lunatic. I had hoped for a story, and instead here was a man calling my whole life a lie.

I snapped the book shut and tried to work myself up to the thing I knew I had to do. The adrenaline of confronting Sita sat like syrup all over my chest, and I had a quiet, ominous feeling, like I was doing something wrong.

I went in search of Amma making tea in the kitchen. She'd be hunched over the wood stove, blowing the hot wood redder with a silver flute. But Amma wasn't in the kitchen. The old lady cook looked up at me from the stove, where she was stirring a clay pot of rice.

"Where's Amma?" I asked.

She kept nodding her head and bowing. "I don't know, Kalki Sami. Forgive me. She might be in her room."

When I found her, Amma was bent over a suitcase open on her bed, fitting neatly folded podavais inside. Roopa sat cross-legged on Lakshman's old bed, watching.

"Amma?" I said.

She looked up, startled. Her eyes were puffy and red, rubbed raw.

"What are you doing, Amma?"

She caught her face in her hand, walked to the window, sat on the bed. I climbed onto the bed and stroked her back. Roopa joined me, and together we tried to rub solace into Amma.

Her body trembled. She clutched me so tight I couldn't breathe, but I didn't complain. She held me, and I was enveloped in her skin and podavai and smell, and I knew.

"Please don't go," I said.

She rocked me back and forth and held me tight. Roopa started crying, the silence broken by her high-pitched sobs.

"Please," I said.

Amma stroked my hair.

"Please."

She kissed my forehead and rocked harder. "It's me or her," Amma said. "Go get Ayya. It's me or her."

Amma had known. She'd known the whole time.

"I'll take care of this," I said. The god energy rose within me. "She will leave the ashram. She'll never come back."

Roopa's sobs went silent. She looked at me like she'd never seen me before.

I clasped Amma's hands and rubbed my face on hers. "Please," I said. "Unpack your suitcase. Roopa, help her. Help her unpack."

I went to Ayya's room with the book and found him awake, balancing a complicated-looking spreadsheet in a notebook at his desk.

"I'm busy," he said, not glancing up.

I shut the door behind me. He sighed, marked his place in his notebook, and looked up, his eyebrows raised.

I took a deep breath. "Sita Aunty gave me this," I said. Saliva gathered at the back of my throat. I held out the book to him, hoping Sita hadn't gotten to him first or told him about Kalyani.

He took it and flipped through. "But this is—"

"Yes," I said. "I think she's trying to convince me I'm not a real god."

He jumped up from his chair, his face twisted in what I hoped was fury. I saw it like a burning flame. I stoked it.

"She's been giving me a lot of inappropriate books."

He tapped the book against his open palm. I waited to see if he would come to the conclusion on his own, but he looked around the room as if he wasn't sure. I took my chance to push him over the edge.

"I don't think she should stay here anymore," I said. "She might put doubt into the minds of future visitors."

Later, Ayya came to my room in a rage, a belt held in his hand. He didn't bother to knock. He pushed open the door and closed it behind him.

I'd been staring at the same passage of the *Upanishads* for ten minutes, the words blurring before me.

"You filthy dog," he said.

I stood up from my desk, backing away from my father.

He breathed like an animal, the way a lion would as it advanced on its prey.

"You've been spending time with those aravanis," he said. "Sita told me."

I looked at the belt he held in his hand. It was the one good belt he owned—goat leather dyed a dark brown. He wore it when he wore Western clothes, which was almost never.

"I wasn't," I said. "Sita Aunty is putting flowers in your ears. I wasn't."

"Don't you lie to me!"

The sheer volume of his voice shocked me into silence. My whole body stood frozen. I knew running would make this worse.

Ayya took a deep breath, as if to steady himself. "You know what you did was wrong. Take your punishment like a man." He gestured with his eyes at the floor in front of him.

I knew I needed to walk to him, to kneel at his feet. It was the only way. I couldn't prove I hadn't talked to the thirunangaigal if he already believed Sita, and they weren't here anymore to lie for me. But my body refused to move forward, my hands stuck to the back of my desk chair, my legs bolted to the floor.

Move, I told my legs. But they held still.

Ayya took the three steps he needed to cross the distance. He loomed over me, the belt raised.

I closed my eyes for a moment, before I winced at the slicing sting of the belt on my leg. It burned a streak into my left calf, and the shock of it made me fall to my knees. I cried out.

Ayya stooped over me, the belt whipping back and forth, cutting sharp welts into my legs. My body folded itself into a fetal position, shivering and crying. Tears and snot fell out of my face and pooled onto the floor where I lay. Ayya shouted with every word.

"Don't. You. Ever. Disobey. Me."

I was being hit everywhere, my legs, my back, my arms. Burning, stinging pain everywhere. I wished to be numb, to float away in my mind, but every hit shocked me back to my body.

I stayed in my bedroom for hours, massaging a numbing, sharp-smelling herbal balm into every reachable spot on my skin. Ayya had locked me inside. Roopa snuck me food through the window, but I didn't have an appetite, and the full plate still sat on my desk, uneaten when Amma came by that evening with the key Ayya had given her to open the door.

I got up and went out to the courtyard in a daze. On her knees, Amma hugged me, apologizing for what Ayya had done. But I couldn't feel anything inside me, only the burning pain in my legs and the glossy wax of the balm coating me.

"I'm sorry, I'm sorry," Amma said, her face pressed into my waist.

The door to Sita's room was open. Her things had disappeared—her wooden comb and the box of face powder she kept on the desk, her notebook. I shushed Amma and helped her stand up. I went out to the veranda.

Tire tracks led away from the front of the old house.

Amma and Roopa found me standing on the veranda, staring in the direction of the village. Roopa took my hand and held it. Amma's face was swollen and red.

"I think she'll miss you," Roopa said.

I had an awful feeling inside my ribs. It felt a lot like guilt, thick and viscous and unmovable. I did the right thing, I said to myself. Sita needed to go. Rama said so himself.

I'd avoided disaster. Ayya, Amma, Roopa, and I were paper dolls held together with glue, and it was my responsibility to protect us. I'd saved Amma from misery, the ashram from disrepute, and Ayya from himself. Wrapped in my bittersweet victory, I didn't understand then that no one can save paper dolls from the fire or the sea or the wind. Eventually, paper will tear, or fly away, or be eaten up by the dirt.

BOOK 3: AMMA

1

As a teenager, I fell in love. By then, the ashram had grown into a sprawling estate, and my own divinity had turned into a tedious, plodding burden. It was all ceremony now, all pomp and performance, every day a chore and a costume. Ayya created a litany of rules—so many rules—that governed my waking hours, my days so scheduled that they passed in a haze. I led yoga and meditation every morning after sandhyavandanam at the oxbow pond, followed by English and Sanskrit lessons, healing sessions, lunch, math and history, horse riding and feeding, more healing sessions, meditation, bath, dinner, homework, and bed.

After the initial expansion of the ashram, Ayya bought up the surrounding land from village farmers. We built three more buildings and Amma, Ayya, and I moved into the newest one. The others lodged visitors who came to relax and find god under the shade of our coconut grove. The old building housed the staff Ayya hired for the daily running of the ashram: a burly-faced cook; an old woman who crouched over the floors, sweeping with brooms she made of palm fronds; a livestock keeper with teeth like broken glass; Roopa; and a secretary by the name of Gopi—a sycophantic, fidgety, reedy man with thick-rimmed glasses and hair slicked back with coconut oil. Gopi served as Ayya's right-hand man. Devoutly and fundamentally religious, he never stepped out of his room without a red-and-white Namam on his forehead. We all called him the Deputy, and it was unclear to me whether he knew about the nickname or not, or if he cared. The servants avoided him as much as possible. Roopa said he was creepy. Amma pretended he didn't exist, and I tried to minimize my contact with him.

Over the years, ashram visitors came and left. Some stayed for years in the new building, which essentially served as a religious hotel—up to twenty visitors at a time, and always with a long waiting list. A few visitors came from Western countries, but most came from New Delhi and Pune, Indians with money to spare and kids they'd left with nannies back home. I had healing sessions with the ones who were old or needed extra care. Some people with serious illnesses had come—autoimmune diseases, far-gone infections, cancer—and many had healed after their visits. Others were healed from the brass mandalas we'd started to make, blessed by me, without them ever setting foot in the ashram. Mail-order god—that was Roopa's joke.

One of the visitors, a woman named Priya, had quickly become Amma's best friend. Priya had been at the ashram for two years. Within a few months of her arrival, Amma and Priya started sleeping in the same room, in the same bed, and were rarely seen without each other.

Priya had come to the ashram troubled. She couldn't bring herself to love her husband or her two twin children, and she wanted me to help her rid herself of this hate. To take this on in addition to my normal coursework, Ayya coached me from a psychology textbook.

"Most people just want to talk, even Priya," he told me. "They're lonely, especially the foreigners and white people. Their religions and cultures have let them down. They want a friend in their god. That's what you need to be for them. A friendly god."

For the most part, Ayya's strategy worked. Many visitors came to me with questions, and Ayya taught me how to direct the questions back. "I'm just a blind man," I'd tell them. "You tell me. What is your purpose? What ails you?" I taught them how to breathe properly, advised them on being mindful about their bodies and souls. I sat with them, chanting *om* and mantras until they reached peace. And they would bow and touch my feet—even the foreigners—and trip over themselves to tell me how devoted they were to me. "Kalki Sami, Kalki Sami," they'd say, while bending over.

Every prayer meeting, one of the visitors received the honor of washing my feet. People who stayed at the ashram had a good chance of being picked by the Deputy, who made all such selections, but if you were one of the hundreds who showed up only for prayer meetings, your chances of being picked depended on the size of your contribution to Ayya's donation box. The lucky person also got to speak to me directly while I stepped onto a gold tray and they poured water on my feet.

I'd like to think the level of adulation I received from devotees never changed—it was always uncomfortably high—but while I found it flattering when I was young, the fawning bored me more and more as I got older.

Unbeknownst to the visitors, Ayya and I kept copious notes on them, their backgrounds, their comings and goings, their likes and dislikes, their psychological profiles. Part of my homework was to memorize what people said and write it all down. We had a file on every person at the ashram. It was all so organized, so much a part of my daily life, that I learned to tune it out into a backdrop of rotating faces and menial sufferings.

But Priya was utterly unlike most visitors. She never let me redirect questions, and she didn't fall for the basic psychology techniques from the textbook. As a young mother, her face remained smooth and shiny and dark, with a nose piercing that glittered every time she moved and buggy eyes too round for her sharp, angular features. During our healing sessions, while I hovered my hands over her body, she'd stare straight at the ceiling, as if she didn't care whether or not I was there. Any other visitor would've been reverent, and just having me next to them would've produced some sort of change.

"Is this working?" I'd ask Priya.

"Keep going," she'd say.

I tried to concentrate, but it was hard not to look at the drape of her podavai across her chest, the way her flesh flattened out when she lay down. It was hard not to picture it at night. I wished my costume didn't reveal so much skin. I itched all over with sweat.

One day, she told me, "I think I'm being punished." Her hair curled in tiny coils around her ears. "I'm being punished by my children."

Ayya's training kicked in. "Why would they punish you?" I asked.

"Because I hate them."

I took my fingers away from her body. She folded her hands above her stomach and continued. "I hate them. I hate their little toenails and their tiny bodies."

"You don't hate them," I said. "They're your children."

"So they say." She turned her head. "But most of all, I hate *him*. I hate him."

"Who?"

"My husband."

In the middle of all this, when I was fifteen, during a whole year that saw a global recession, the ashram entertained fewer visitors than normal. Oftentimes that year, Priya was the only permanent visitor we had. I held one short healing session a day instead of the usual three hours, and there was no need to lead yoga and meditation classes in the mornings and evenings. I spent a lot of time with Amma, watching her paint, trying and failing to learn from her. But her time was split between me and Priya, for which I tried my hardest not to resent anyone. Amma liked Priya's company, and after Vasanthy Chithy's leaving, Amma must have been so lonely. I tried to remind myself of that every time I saw the two of them walking in the grounds or sitting in the garden, laughing and talking.

To stave off my boredom, I read. But the Deputy seemed to believe—with or without Ayya's direct order—that being busy was the only way to live right. If he saw me lounging, he'd give me speeches to prepare for upcoming prayer meetings, or letters to write to devotees who lived far away. He never went so far as to order me around—his devotion wouldn't let him cross that line—but he would insist in a tone that betrayed a threat to tell Ayya if I didn't obey. "Ayya would be very happy if these speeches were finished today," he'd say, or, "Ayya is so busy these days. Maybe you should write these letters to take some of the work off him?"

To get away from the Deputy and his busywork, I hid in the dark corners of the old building where I used to live. I was tempted to go back to my old room, but Roopa lived there now. Instead, I sat near the mango tree and the tulsi plant that looked toward her room from the courtyard and read the books that visitors sometimes gave me without Ayya knowing. These were books with magic, evil masterminds, scary villains, car chases, and forbidden love.

One day, Roopa found me sitting at the base of the mango tree outside her window. She pushed the shutters open further.

"What are you doing down there?" she asked. "Will you fetch me a mango?"

I hadn't climbed a tree in so long. I hiked up my veshti and heaved my way up, hoping I wouldn't slip. The bark scratched my hands. The mangoes were still young and green, their firm skins not yet leaking the sweetness that would waft around when they got ripe. I twisted two mangoes off their stalks and wrapped them carefully in the pleats of my veshti.

Back in Roopa's room, we hid in a corner where we couldn't be seen through the windows. Being caught in a girl's room would mean punishment.

The room—my old room—had changed only a little since I'd lived there. Roopa's clothes were neatly folded into the old bookcase where I used to keep my notebooks. My desk still had that same picture of Krishna and Radha hanging above it.

When I was fourteen, Roopa had bled for the first time, and Ayya, in a show of magnanimity, had offered to host a puberty ceremony for her. Only girls received this honor, because it meant that they were able to bring forth life to this world, and that was something worth celebrating. I'll never forget seeing Roopa at her ceremony, draped in a podavai for the first time, marking her step from childhood to womanhood. Priya, who had been a sought-after makeup artist before she got married, had helped dress and decorate Roopa.

Roopa had worn a dark magenta podavai with her hair plaited in the back and decorated with jasmine and firecracker flowers, my mother's gold jewelry stacked on her chest and pinned into her hair, her eyes darkened with kajal and her lips painted red. She'd looked utterly unlike herself, and I'd been entranced.

I wondered if Ayya had seen me looking at her in a new way, because soon after, he declared me and Roopa spending any time together inappropriate. She was a young woman, and proper decorum had to be followed. I had dutifully avoided being alone with her, though I had watched from afar as her body softened and changed.

I didn't know what had made her want to invite me into her

room, or why had she asked for a mango. Somewhere in the back of my mind, I still remembered my childhood conviction that Roopa was Laxmi incarnate, and how she had finally looked the part at her puberty ceremony. Maybe my waiting was over. Maybe it was time.

Roopa peeled and cut the mangoes with a small knife she had smuggled from the kitchen, sprinkled the pieces with salt and chili powder, and offered them to me on an old piece of newspaper. We ate in silence, sucking the juices from stringy flesh. Roopa was fifteen, too, and time had flattened out her face. Her nose had become wide and round, her cheeks marked with tiny red pimples. Her eyebrows looked like someone had smoothed out their thumbs on top of her eyes. Her body was plumper and rounder than before.

"It's rude to stare," she said. A bit of pepper clung to the corner of her mouth.

I coughed on my mango pieces. She thumped my head with the flat heel of her palm, and I drank the water she held out to me.

The room no longer smelled like the crumbling books I had studied for schoolwork. Now it smelled like the camphor that Roopa used to dry her hair and the talcum powder she sprinkled all over her body. It was the same kind that Amma used—Pond's powder in jasmine. We could now afford luxuries like that for the ashram, and Roopa had told me more than once that she liked living at the ashram for these small extravagances, like air-conditioning and showers in the new buildings, which her parents and brothers didn't have. She visited them every few months, but for no more than a few days at a time. What I hadn't understood as a child, and what I did now, was that Roopa was getting paid for everything she did around the ashram, and that money went back to her family.

Roopa sat back down and popped a few more cubes of mango into her mouth. The silence thudded against my chest, but she continued to eat her mango, not bothering to hide the suggestive way she lapped juice off her fingertips.

We shared stories of when we were kids and of Lakshman's obvious crush on her.

"When I first got here," she said, "I thought I'd marry him."

The mango cube burned a chili powder streak down my throat. Lakshman was fourteen. I hadn't heard from him in years, and my parents never spoke of him or his family. Amma had never taken me back to the village when she went.

"You should try and find Lakshman," Roopa said. "You can go to the Internet café. No one would stop you."

The thought had obsessed me years ago, but by now the drive had faded into a dull ache. I'd begged Ayya to get a computer at the ashram, but he said it would be a distraction for the visitors, who came to get away from the world. Sometimes they brought their own computers, but we didn't have Internet. I knew all about the Web from what visitors told me, but I wasn't allowed to go to the new Internet café in the village. Ayya said I wasn't ready to see how much the world loved its own vices.

"Ayya would never allow that," I said.

"You don't have to tell him."

The thought of Ayya's possible reaction if he found out made my palms sweaty.

"Why don't you go?" I asked.

"Come with me."

If Ayya didn't have to know, if we could be back before he missed me . . . but the thought was still terrifying.

"I can't," I said.

Her eyes showed no reflection. Deep like wells, and as dark. "Tomorrow. Pretend you're going to feed the horses." She waited for me to respond. "There's a library now at the village."

A library. I wanted to read new stories again, instead of rereading the few books I owned. I missed Sita's secret library. I could be back before Ayya noticed me gone. There weren't many healing sessions with so few people, and my regimented schedule had gaping holes of time.

"Tomorrow," she said. "After our history lessons."

The day after the mangos in her room, around the time I would've normally gone to feed the horses and when I knew both Ayya and the Deputy would be shut up in Ayya's office on a phone meeting with a temple in Chennai that was helping recruit visitors to the ashram, Roopa and I snuck away in the direction of the village. Again we were alone for what felt like the second time in years. I wiped my sweaty hands on my veshti. We walked on the ridges between the flooded rice paddies. Roopa held up her floor-length skirt, but the gathering darkness at the hem revealed it was getting wet anyway.

She glanced at me out of the corner of her eye and kept walking. "What will you do if one of the villagers tells Ayya? Or the Deputy?" She had a smiling, mocking tone to her voice. "All it takes is one."

I stopped walking, jarred by her words. She was right. There was no way to do this without Ayya finding out. I hadn't thought it through. I'd jumped at the chance, enamored with the idea of a library and the possibility of finding Lakshman again. Of course the villagers might tell Ayya.

"I can't go," I said.

The wind blew Roopa's skirt around the curved outlines of her calves. She gathered the skirt and tucked it into her waistband to free her ankles. She wore scalloped silver anklets and black plastic flip-flops.

"You can't live in fear of Ayya your whole life," she said. "I'm going to the café and the library." She started walking again. "You can come if you like."

I followed her. I couldn't go to the village. I wouldn't. Fear of Ayya's reaction made me dizzy. But I could walk with her as far as the edge of the houses. We strode side by side down the raised ridges of the paddies, Roopa humming absently with the wind at her skirt, the sound of her anklets keeping time to our steps.

Somewhere near the oxbow pond, Roopa reached out and took my hand. I tried to breathe, but my lungs wouldn't expand the way I wanted them to. My breath came in little gasps that I tried to keep silent. Roopa's hand was soft and slippery with heat, but I held on. We laced our fingers through each other. My body burned, but my fingers and toes turned so, so cold. We walked like that until we saw the first of the village houses in the distance.

"You wait here," Roopa said, dropping my hand. "Or come with me. Your choice."

She walked away. Long green blades peppered the rice paddies. No farmers to see me. The sun hammered against my head and shoulders as I waited.

"I think I disappointed her," I said to the air, pretending Rama stood beside me, ready to tell me the wisdom I needed to know about love. I didn't sense Rama's presence anymore, like I had when I was younger—he'd disappeared, but I had developed the habit of pretending he was with me always, staving off the loneliness that creeped around my consciousness.

But what did Rama know about love? It was Krishna I needed, Krishna who loved the cow-herding girls. Rama had married Sita, sure, but theirs hadn't been a love story for the ages. Theirs was a story of duty and piety.

"Never mind," I said. "You wouldn't understand."

Roopa returned faster than I expected, holding a small stack of books under her arm.

"Did you find Lakshman?" I asked.

She shook her head with a sad smile. "I ran a search for his name, but I didn't find anything. But I got these at the library." She held out the books to me.

On top of the stack was *Wuthering Heights*, and underneath, two other Tamil books I didn't recognize. A hook tugged at my chest. I'd loved reading *Wuthering Heights*.

"Will you read these to me?" she asked.

"Let's read to each other," I said. Amma had read to me as a child from a big book of stories about Krishna's youth and all the pranks he used to pull and his love of fresh churned butter. Sometimes now, I read to Amma while she painted in her room or outside—usually religious stories, but sometimes from my psychology or history textbooks, because she said that she was curious.

I pictured Roopa and me in my mind, cuddled together in her room at sunset, away from the bustle of the ashram and the prying eyes of visitors, away from Ayya. My face grew warm with the image. I didn't know what cuddling would feel like, but the visual was enough to send a shiver up my neck.

I tried to find Roopa to read the next day. During our morning lessons, I tried to speak to her and make eye contact, but she ignored me. After our language lessons, I followed her to her room, but she shut the door behind her. I sat by the mango tree outside her window, but she didn't open the shutters. Every time I tried to get her alone at the ashram, she remembered some chore she'd forgotten to do.

When I showed up at her door in the morning after my single healing session with Priya, Roopa told me she had to go help cook lunch. When I came again in the afternoon, she said she had to catch up on homework. After dinner, I brought my homework and offered to help, but she said she was tired and needed to sleep. Each time I tried, my hope leaped and crashed.

I didn't understand why she was avoiding me. Maybe it was

because I'd held her hand; maybe she was embarrassed. Or maybe it was less innocent than that, like a boy from the village that she liked. These thoughts made my feet itch.

Every day after breakfast and before our English and Sanskrit class, I knew Roopa picked flowers in the gardens behind the main building, which had been added during one of Ayya's fevered expansion projects. Filled with pink bougainvillea, red roses, and plump marigolds, the garden was a popular place with visitors, who used it for relaxation, reading, and socializing.

Two days after we went to the village, I sat on one of the stone garden benches and waited, pretending to read a book Ayya had assigned for Hindi class.

Most visitors didn't come here until the afternoon or evening, and that month we only had Priya, so the place was almost always empty. Roopa's anklets tinkled with each step. I put down my book and stood behind her as she crouched over rose bushes, balancing a wicker basket on her hip.

"I want to read to you," I said.

She pinched off the roses with her fingers, her short, round nails cutting off the stalks.

"If Ayya notices us talking too much, we'll get in trouble," she said. She dropped a handful of roses into her basket. "We have to be strategic."

My thorn-filled chest pricked me with each breath. I'd only started talking to her in earnest two days ago, and already I couldn't stand the distance between us. I wanted to reach for her hand.

Roopa's back tensed. The band of her bra cut across her skin. I'd noticed it on countless women before, but I couldn't look away from Roopa's, the way the cotton of her blouse was translucent enough that the white of her bra straps showed through.

"I don't know if this is a good thing," she said, continuing to drop more roses into her basket. "If you're not brave enough to go to the village, you won't be brave enough to stand up to Ayya if he finds out about us."

Us. She'd said *us.* There was an *us,* but it was fragile, a newborn that needed coddling. I needed to say something. I needed to convince her I wasn't a coward, that I would dare to be alone with her.

"Let me help," I said.

Her back tensed further, but she didn't try to stop me. I bent down into the fog of her talcum powder. I pinched the rose stalks like she did and tried to twist them off, but they wouldn't break. The threads held on, and the roses drooped on their stalks. I tried again farther down the stalk. A thorn pierced my finger.

"Ayyoo," Roopa said. She took my finger and sucked the red end of it.

My chest clamped so tight I thought it would burst. Out of the corner of my eye, I saw movement, a person standing there. I snatched the finger away.

Priya stood watching us from the path that the visitors often walked on. I stayed very still. If she'd seen us, she could report to Ayya.

But Priya smiled at us, winked, and kept walking.

Roopa turned back to the rose bush like nothing had happened. "Like this," she said, and showed me how to pinch the stalk between my fingernails without touching the thorns, how to twist with my wrist, making a half-moon jerk at the end, and then I was picking almost as fast as she was.

When the basket was full, she took me back to the servants' quarters, to the courtyard where we separated the flowers into piles based on size, color, and type. She measured out cotton string and showed me how to tie the flowers into garlands, two at a time, laid stalk to stalk. She worked fast, her garland woven thick, the flowers close together and held tight. My garland turned out ragged, the petals stripped off where I pulled the string too tight, the tension elsewhere loose.

Roopa laughed at my failed garland. I laughed with her.

If I could point to the moment I fell for her, it was then, when she tilted back her head and opened her mouth wide and laughed like no one could hear. I should've known by the vertigo in my head, the way my body scorched hot in my torso and freezing in my extremities. But all I knew at the time was that I'd give up being a god if I could make that minute last forever.

2

Over the next three years, Roopa and I grew closer and closer, until her love for me and my love for her became so much a part of my life that I couldn't imagine who I would be without her. We kept ourselves a secret from Ayya and even from Amma, because Indian cultural custom required it—though Krishna and Radha's love was the stuff of legend, Ayya had made it perfectly clear to me that I wasn't allowed to date anyone or fall in love. It would be, according to him, a weakness of character, and a straying from my duties as a god.

In those three years, Amma found peace too. Almost every single day since Priya came to live with us, I saw them together. They'd walk hand in hand through the coconut grove, or sit by the banks of the river sipping mango lassis and laughing, or cook together after sending the servants away from the kitchen, before they'd both go to sleep in the room they shared. It seemed that Priya was a requirement for Amma's happiness.

But when I was eighteen, Priya's husband came to the ashram

looking for her. I was teaching a yoga class, standing in tree pose. He was a tall, intimidating man with a thick neck that melted into his chin, and short hair around the perimeter of his skull. He barged into the classroom and weaved his way through the visitors as they all stood in the best tree poses they could muster. When he made it to the front, the smells of his vinegary sweat and the old food in his teeth swirled around me. I stood my ground.

"My wife is here," he said. He spoke with a grating voice, as if he'd smoked most of his life.

"Kalki Sami?" some of the visitors asked. They weren't used to hearing anyone address me as gruffly as this man had.

"My wife is here," the man said again.

The Deputy appeared at the door, looking anxious and harassed. He made his way to the front and said to the man, "Sir, what do you need?" He wiped his hands nervously on his short-sleeved plaid shirt. "Please, there's a class in session. Tell me what you need."

The man ignored the Deputy as if he were an annoying fly.

"Priya," the man said to me. "My wife. I need her."

Priya was always so put-together, her hair always combed and plaited back, her jewelry polished, her cotton podavais ironed into crisp pleats. This man was balding, sweaty, and had bloodshot eyes, like he hadn't had any sleep. I couldn't picture them together.

I stayed in tree pose.

"Gopi can show you to her," I said.

The Deputy snapped himself up to his full, thin height. "I cannot go to the women's private quarters. It would be most inappropriate."

Priya and Amma stayed in our family building. The Deputy entered Ayya's office by way of the front door and never went to the rest of the house.

"If you'll wait," I said to the man, "I can go find Priya Aunty when the class is over."

"No, no." The man shook his head in agitation. "I need to see her now. Her mother is sick."

I put my foot, which had been balanced on my inner thigh, on the ground, and released my arms to my sides. Brad, a white Canadian visitor, held a perfect tree pose at the front of the class. I asked him to take over and led Priya's husband toward the residential house. The Deputy stayed behind, saying he would make sure Brad didn't do anything unsuitable, which, knowing Brad, was a definite possibility.

In the residential house, Priya and Amma sat in the courtyard under the shade of the awning. Ayya had built our new family house to resemble the old one. An open courtyard took up the middle of the house, and all the rooms faced out into it. Unroofed, sunlight flooded in and warmed the mosaic floor, which showed a flowering sun on a blue background. Unlike the old house, where a mango tree grew out of the concrete floor, this courtyard was pristine, with nothing to attract monkeys or other wildlife except a potted tulsi plant in the very middle of the space.

Priya was braiding Amma's hair. She had a couple of bobby pins held in her teeth and smiled through them. When she saw us, the smile slipped off her face. She stood and took the bobby pins out of her mouth.

"You need to come with me," her husband said. His demeanor had shifted. Before he'd seemed respectful, if hurried, but now he spit the sentence like an order. "Your mother is sick."

Priya stared at him as if she didn't understand. Amma had stood up, too, holding her half-plaited hair and looking from Priya to the man.

"Your mother is sick," the man said again. He smoothed down his mustache, as if punctuating the sentence.

"I don't believe you," Priya said. I'd never heard her use that tone before with anyone. And all at once, I understood that her hate for her husband was very real, and not just in her head as Ayya had suspected. Her voice told me she felt the hatred down in her bones.

"What's going on here?"

We all turned around at Ayya's voice. He stood in the doorway to his office, which faced the courtyard.

Priya's husband, looking relieved, went to shake Ayya's hand and introduce himself. He again put on the tone he'd used with me.

"It's very important I take Priya back right away," he said, ignoring us altogether and talking to Ayya.

"I'm not going," Priya said. "I don't believe you."

Amma put a hand on Priya's arm, but Priya's whole body was wound tight, ready to snap.

The man dug in the pocket of his brown pants and produced what looked like a thin box that fit into the palm of his hand.

"Look, here," he said, his face full of disgust. "I'll call."

"Mobile phones aren't allowed at the ashram," Ayya said.

But the man had already dialed and raised the phone to his ear, and didn't seem to hear Ayya, or didn't care.

"Sir," Ayya said. "You need to take that away right now."

"Listen," the man said to Priya. He crossed the courtyard, raised the phone to Priya's ear—she flinched at his touch—and held it with a triumphant look on his face.

"Appa?" Priya said into the phone, her voice softer, uncertain. "Okay, okay. Tell Amma I'm coming. I'm coming. Don't worry."

The man took the phone away and put it in his pocket with the attitude of someone who'd won a big battle.

Priya grabbed Amma's hands and pulled her toward their room. I knew it wasn't proper for me to follow them, but I wanted to. Anything not to be left alone with Ayya and this man. I fidgeted while Ayya crossed his arms over his chest, and the man rocked back and forth on the balls of his feet.

"I have the driver waiting," the man said to no one in particular.

We waited in silence until Amma and Priya emerged from their room, each with a suitcase, and each with noses rubbed red. The man took the suitcase that Amma carried.

Amma wiped away her tears, biting her lip hard. She kissed Priya on each cheek. Priya cried, too, and my eyes and nose burned with the effort of not crying with them. I wasn't that close to Priya, but seeing Amma distressed was too much for me.

Priya followed the man out, but she kept looking back at us—at Amma—and her face showed a sadness I hadn't felt myself since the day Lakshman left for America.

After Priya left, Amma barely came out of her room. Most days, she refused to get out of bed. Every morning, I woke up expecting her to be normal again. Every night, I went to sleep with hope beating like a pair of little wings in my chest. I prayed and prayed, but Amma continued to lock herself away. Often, I told the visitors that she was sick, and in between my duties I brought her tea and food that she never touched. Sometimes I sat by the edge of the bed as she pretended to sleep. Sometimes she spoke. More than once, she squeezed my hand and said, "You're the most important person in the world to me." I wished I was little again so I could curl up in her lap and fidget with the border of her podavai.

Other times, when she wasn't catatonic, she painted—madly, feverishly, with a desperation I'd never seen in her before. She made painting after painting, and when she ran out of canvas, she either bullied the Deputy into going into the village for more, or she painted over her old pictures. She abandoned her old content of gods and their stories in favor of bold, colorful abstracts that approximated the faces of women. She painted a few realistic pictures of Priya based off of old sketches she had done. Priya getting water from the well. Priya sitting in thought by the river. Priya walking through a rice paddy. In the paintings, Amma captured Priya's face

163

and body perfectly, as if they were photographs, but the backgrounds distorted into surreal spirals.

For a month, Priya called the ashram phone every week to talk to Amma, and these calls were the only time Amma came out of her room. For a few hours after each call, Amma would smile again, but then her shoulders started to hunch, and her face lost its glow, and she retreated back into her room and the sadness of her bed. After a month, Priya stopped calling, and no matter how many times Amma called her, or asked me to call, there was no answer except for a pleasant automated voice telling us that the number was no longer in service. Amma begged Ayya to let her go find Priya, but Ayya refused.

I didn't know why Priya had stopped calling, or why she was refusing Amma's calls. What I did know was that I was fast losing the Amma I knew.

Most days, Amma lay in the middle of her bed, staring at the ceiling with the sheet pulled up to her chin and her hair splayed all over the pillow, or else she painted in a frenzied trance. Her room had absorbed the stink of her sweat, since she now bathed once a week, or not at all. Still, I sat by her, sometimes stroking her graying, knotted hair if she were laying down, and other times just talking to her. I told her about the visitors and their latest problems. I told her about my horse, Arjuna, and what we'd done on our rides, or rumors about the servants, or Ayya's latest plan to get fame, or the Deputy's most absurd rules for the staff. I said I understood her sadness about Priya leaving.

I hadn't yet told Amma about Roopa and me, about how we'd kissed more than once, about how we held hands when no one was looking and hid our love from everyone. But I read her passages from the books I had. And I told her I loved her. Usually, she lay quiet, her eyes open but seeming to see nothing. Ayya said that it was gloom deep inside her, and that sometimes, no one could do anything about it.

"She needs to pray harder," he said. "It's her doubt—and your doubt—that's causing this."

I tried not to doubt at all. I tried to fully believe, to accept my godliness, to accept Ayya's teachings—and I knew by now that my healing powers didn't always work if the universe was in play, if fate had written some other destiny. Even without doubt, I still felt helpless sitting next to Amma, wishing and willing for her to get better.

"Why are you sad?" I'd ask, and I'd wait for the answer—*Priya's absence*—but Amma rarely spoke anymore. Whatever the source of Amma's sadness, I couldn't fix it. I lost faith in ever summoning Rama again to my side for wisdom, but I tried to think of what he might say. He would want me to do what I could, so I continued to sit with Amma so that she knew she was loved, so that she knew she was missed. And I did miss her, even when I was sitting there touching her arm. She was fading from my life, and I didn't know how to stop it.

During this time, my love for Roopa turned into a sharp, painful thing that prodded me from the inside. My stomach folded itself into pieces. This is what love is, I thought. Sometimes you can't eat; other times you want to eat the world. I couldn't focus enough to read or do homework, and when I wasn't worrying over Amma, I thought about Roopa.

For three years, Roopa and I met alone a few times a week, when both Ayya and the Deputy were busy. But I wished to see her all the time. I had the urge to write down every little thing about her, so I could have those details with me always. I kept sheets of paper tucked under my mattress on which I'd write notes to myself—the way her fingertips smelled like cloves after helping to cook lunch, the way she'd throw her hair over one side of her shoulder, the way the armpits of her blouse stained a darker color after she drew water from the well, the way she ran her toes back and forth over my calf when we cuddled on her bed kissing. I wanted to memorize it all.

Roopa came by my room more often at night, after the ashram had gone to bed. Sometimes we kissed on the veranda. Sometimes she pulled me by the hand all the way to the mango tree outside her room that used to be my room, and we'd kiss under its trunk. One night, she took my hands and put them on her chest, moaning when I rubbed her nipples over her blouse. I held her by the waist, scratched the skin of her back, played with the bones of her ankles. She touched me over my veshti, let me rock against her hand until I shuddered, and when the world fell apart and broke into piercing light behind my eyelids, she held the night together with the moonlight in her hair.

Whenever Roopa was busy, as she was most days, and I wanted to disappear from all of my responsibilities at the ashram, I hid in Brad's room. Brad the Canadian yogi was the only visitor who treated me more like a person than a god. He'd been visiting the ashram for some time and had become my new window to the outside world.

He had a tattoo of his ex-girlfriend's name written right above his heart—the Indian way, he said. He said he'd gotten it done in a village near Pondicherry by a man who had no ears. He told me about backpacking across Southeast Asia, about the kathoey he met in Thailand, about living on a fishing boat in Vietnam. He talked about his job as a short-order cook in Queens. I hounded him for details about New York City—I loved the idea of a city that never slept, of lights surrounding me until they seeped into my skin. He taught me about Incubus and No Doubt. My brain expanded every time I talked with him, and it wasn't long before he became my trusted friend.

Brad draped batik sheets over all his windows, so no one could see inside his coveted corner room. We played Rush albums on an old record player that he claimed once belonged to an American president. He smoked his hookah, which wasn't allowed. I didn't know how Ayya didn't recognize the smell that hung around the walls of Brad's room, but as long as he didn't catch me in there, Ayya turned the other cheek.

When we hung out, Brad puffed at his hookah until his eyes glazed, then jumped around, gesticulating to the music. "Join me," he'd say. He'd hold out a hand. He always wore a collection of colorful woven bracelets on his wrist that I admired. When I shook my head, he'd crouch-walk around the room, pretending to play guitar and drums alternatively. "Air-drum with me," he'd say, pumping his arms up and down, his long, dirty blond hair following the movement.

It took me months to warm up to this play. One day when Brad held out his hand, I took it. He pulled me up, and we air-drummed to the Rush song "Hemispheres." It felt awkward, but I'd spent months rehearsing these moves in my head, and in my bathroom.

"Not bad, little man," Brad said. "You know what this song's about? It's about Apollo and Dionysus fighting over a man's soul. Gods fighting."

He played the song again, so I could write down the lyrics. Unguided people and a divided universe. It was beautiful. We listened to the song again, air-guitaring and singing along.

"I'm impressed," Brad said. He took a puff of the hookah and pulled his sweaty shirt away from his body. "I thought you'd never explore your other hemisphere." He winked and held out the hookah to me.

I shook my head.

"Well, how about this," he said. He took one of the bracelets off his arm, a turquoise and red one with diamond patterns, and tied it around my wrist. "It's a friendship bracelet," he said. "You're never supposed to take it off. It's supposed to stay on for as long as the friendship lasts."

Ayya asked about the bracelet that very night at dinner, which he and I—along with the Deputy—took together, with Amma, too, if she was feeling up to it. These days, she'd been joining us about once a week. She still hadn't remade contact with Priya, even though she'd sent letters and emails from the Internet café in the village. The more time that passed without Priya returning, the more it seemed like Priya wouldn't ever be coming back.

"You can't wear that thing around," Ayya said, pointing to my friendship bracelet. "It's not sacred. It's silly. You're a god."

The Deputy snorted into his pittu and sambol. "It is very silly, sir," he said.

Amma was with us that night, and she said, "I think it's nice for Kalki to have a friend here."

Ayya shook his head but went back to his food. The Deputy opened his mouth to say something but fell silent at Ayya's look. As an unspoken rule between Ayya and me, we didn't dare contradict Amma. She was fragile but getting better, and neither of us wanted to ruin any upward swing in her health, even if we all knew—though we hoped and prayed for the opposite—that it wouldn't last.

3

Roopa grew tired of keeping our relationship a secret. Traditional Hindu culture held no space for dating—we wouldn't have known the concept if it weren't for English literature books and the foreign visitors who came to the ashram. According to Ayya, dating took place after the wedding.

"Let's get married," Roopa said one night as we laid on her bed, still mostly clothed. We hadn't yet had sex—Hindu traditions forbid it, but we'd kissed and rubbed each other half-naked, and after three years, I'd stopped feeling guilty about it afterward.

I hugged Roopa tighter. If we got married, Roopa and I wouldn't have to hide our love anymore. At this point, we'd hosted plenty of weddings at the ashram, and I knew all the rituals. I'd even officiated some celebrity weddings. I pictured it—Roopa wearing a red wedding podavai and a garland of flowers. Her father would come, and she would sit on his lap when I tied the golden thali around her neck to signify our marriage.

But Roopa wasn't a Brahmin, so caste would be an issue. And

there was still the matter of our age. Amma had been my age when she married Ayya, but men were supposed to marry later in life. Ayya hadn't brought the subject up to me, not even a hint, which meant that he thought I wasn't ready. But I could take care of Roopa. Nothing much would have to change. She and I would move into a room together, that was all, and we could love each other openly.

"What are you thinking about right now?" Roopa asked me. She caressed my cheek. She was lying on her side, facing me, her head on her hand. The sun blazed in through the window, hot and sweltering, coaxing little beads of sweat onto her upper lip.

"I'm going to talk to Amma about it," I said. That, at least, I was ready for. I'd been thinking about it for a while. The news might jolt her out of her catatonic state—a shock to the system, good or bad.

I had to first get Amma on my side before broaching the subject with Ayya. She was sick and tired and slept a lot, but she would understand. She would be happy for me, and she would take my side when it came to Ayya.

"Are you sure?" Roopa asked. "She's fragile."

But Amma loved Roopa. They still ate breakfast and lunch together when Amma felt up to eating. Roopa took tea and food to Amma's room on a tray and sat with her to make sure she ate. Amma already regarded her as a daughter.

"She'll be happy for us," I said, though I wasn't sure. Love marriages had been increasing in India, but parents still panicked at their kids basing the most important relationship of their adult lives on what could be a fleeting emotion. The village elders brought news of upsetting new marriages across caste and religious lines happening all over Tamil Nadu. And Ayya, sensing their distress, took their side, and assured them they had every reason to be troubled.

I had no idea what Amma thought. But I would find out soon. I just had to wait until a day when she felt better.

A week later, when I went for tea after my morning sandhyavandanam at the oxbow pond, I found Amma in the kitchen, directing the servants as they made breakfast. Her voice sounded tired and she was thinner than ever, but she was up, and she had combed her hair. I ran to hug her. It had been so long since we'd stood side by side like that. I'd grown at least a foot taller than her in the last year, and my arms fit around her easily.

"Are you going to paint today?" I asked. "It's a good day for painting." It was also a good day to tell her about Roopa.

"It's nice outside," she said. The sun dried up the dew on the grasses, and from the chilliness at dawn, I knew it wouldn't get too hot.

"Come for a walk with me," I said. "I'm going out to the coconut grove."

Amma hadn't walked outside of the ashram compound in months, even to the coconut grove or the rice paddies. We needed privacy to have my planned conversation, but I also wanted to get her out in the fresh air.

"I don't know," she said. She looked out the kitchen window toward the grove, but her eyes stared at something more distant.

"I'll help you with the easel," I said, seized by inspiration. "Why don't you paint the coconut trees, with me sitting underneath them?" She chuckled, which gave me hope. "The light is great today. I'll take you to my favorite place."

She sighed but smiled faintly, and didn't stop me when I turned her away from the kitchen. I didn't want her to change her mind, so I immediately led her in the direction of the living quarters. Ayya had moved her painting equipment into her new room's armoire. All her paintings stood stacked up against the walls, sometimes five deep.

Someone had been in to clean, and the room was tidier than I'd seen it last. The newly made bed looked strange with its corners tucked in and no Amma hunched in the middle of the blankets.

I opened the armoire, which was once full of her podavais. Chaos. Jars of pigments lay scattered all over the place, some half-closed and spilling their contents out onto the wood. Brushes wormed their way through the disorder, their bristles stained and crusty with old paint. I gathered some brushes that looked clean and a basket full of pigment jars, and gave them to Amma, who watched me as if in a daze. Behind her, her newest painting stood propped on her bed like a headboard—a giant red slash swirling on a gold background.

I carried a bedsheet and a canvas out for her, stopping by the yoga and meditation class to ask Brad to take over. His blue eyes quickly took in Amma's half-vacant expression, the tools we carried, and my nervous face, and he said, "No problem, little man. You go have fun."

"If the Deputy comes along—" I started to say.

Brad snorted. "I'll handle him. You go."

Amma and I ambled into the coconut grove, making our way around the thick trunks of the trees and the old coconuts they'd littered on the ground. The sun shone through the canopy of fronds, turning the ground into a maze of stripes. Even though I strolled slowly so Amma wouldn't tire herself out, she panted, as if the weeks shut in her room had drained her of her strength. Arjuna grazed by the edge of the grove, and when he saw Amma, he came up to her and presented his muzzle for her to pet. This gave Amma more energy, and we pressed on, past the place where I liked to read, all the way to the creek. The light on the water was dazzling.

"I used to paint here," Amma said. She sounded startled, like she had woken up from a deep sleep. "When you were little. I'd strap you to my back and carry my basket and easel all the way to this spot."

"Well, let's stay here," I said, seeing how the place spoke to her. "This is better light than what I was thinking, anyway." I laid out the bedsheet next to the bank of the creek. She kneeled on it and unscrewed jars of pigment. The early-morning light softened her face, but she looked so much older than she did in my mind. The skin of her elbows had become ashen and stretchy. Her face had acquired new lines and a sunken, papery look. The mole on her cheek hung lower. Her face now held the weight of her sadness. I could see all the people she'd lost, all of her despair, right in the new lines in her skin. I wanted to hold her, to comfort her, but I just stood there staring as the real, flesh version of her erased the decade-old image I still had in my mind.

"Do you want to paint with me?" she asked without looking up. "Get some leaves, will you?"

I swallowed, my mouth dry. "I'll watch," I said, as I plucked leaves off of a hibiscus bush and laid them out for her to use as a palette. I sat on the far end of the bedsheet.

She positioned the paper in front of her, pinched little bits of pigment with her fingers, and put each color on a different leaf. She dipped her brush into the river water and mixed the water with the pigments on the leaves.

"What are you going to paint?" I asked.

"My little god, of course," she said. "Though you're a grown-up god now."

She mixed indigo powder with water, and I wondered if she already knew what I was about to tell her about Roopa and me. She'd always been empathetic, had always known more than she let on, had intuited secrets she wasn't supposed to figure out. I kept silent, more worried than excited.

"Sit over there," she said, pointing at a spot by the bank.

My head thrummed as I sat, trying to position myself exactly how she wanted me. I didn't want her to see how all the blood had rushed into my face in anticipation of the conversation I knew I needed to have. I turned sideways. "Like this?"

Amma began to paint. I waited, gathering my courage. Every second slithered by like an eternity.

"Rama, give me strength," I whispered under my breath. My skin tingled everywhere. I imagined Rama's cosmic hand like a warm weight on my shoulder, steadying me. "There's—there's something I want to ask you," I said. "Tell you. Something I want to tell you."

She continued to paint, dabbing her brush into the pools of pigment on the leaves. The outlines of the figure she drew rendered me much younger, like a toddler, sitting by a river.

"Amma?"

"I'm listening."

"I—" I'd practiced this, but I'd forgotten everything. "I think—" No. Be more firm, I told myself. I don't *think*. I *know*. "Amma," I said, "I'm in love with someone."

Amma's hand dragged itself to a stop on the paper. She looked up at me. Her mouth formed words, but nothing came out.

"I'm in love with Roopa," I said, before I could lose my nerve.

She was silent for a long, nauseating minute.

"You're in love with Roopa," she said, her face slack, as if she didn't understand.

I broke my pose, went over to her, and took her hands. She was still holding the paintbrush, and as soon as I touched her, she dropped it onto the canvas, where it splattered a blue streak all over my baby self.

"How could you?" she whispered.

"I didn't mean to. It just happened. Like it was meant to."

She pulled her hands free from my grasp and lowered her face onto them. "No, kutti, no." She shook her head. "This isn't meant to happen. He'll be so angry." She looked up at me, fast and purposeful. "Don't tell him. Don't ever tell him." And she seemed so genuinely terrified that I had to stop and think about what to say.

"I need to tell him," I said finally. "I want to marry Roopa."

She shook her head faster. "You can't. You can't. She's not a Brahmin."

"You know her. You like her. She's lived here for a long time. She knows our life, this ashram. We'll be happy here."

Amma closed her eyes, took a deep, rattling breath, and opened them again. The fear that was threatening to consume her receded from her face, but she still looked concerned.

"I'm going to tell Ayya," I said. "Will you support me?"

She took another deep breath.

"Please, Amma?"

I couldn't read the look on her face at all. But slowly, she nodded.

I found Ayya in his room, putting away folded clothes from a laundry bag propped open on his bed. The man who usually washed our clothes had gone to a family function, which meant that he didn't have time to put away our clothes, only to drop them off in our rooms. Ayya hated laundry.

"Ayya, can I talk to you?" I asked. I shut the door behind me.

"Come, help me with these."

I picked up some of his clothes and put them away in his armoire. He sat on the bed and watched me. I used the excuse of laundry to not have to look at him.

"I need to tell you something," I said, hedging.

Ayya waited, crossing one leg over the other. His bare brown skin was stained with gray hairs. He looked out the window and frowned slightly. I gathered up a stack of his veshtis and turned back to the armoire.

"I'm in love." I said it so quietly I couldn't tell if I'd said it out loud at all. I dared not repeat it.

Ayya laughed, a loud bark that boomed into the room.

I turned around. "I'm in love with Roopa."

His laugher cut off. Sharp sunlight sliced his face in two. "You're not little kids anymore," he said. "She's a big girl."

"I know that." Something flared in my chest—fear or anger, I couldn't tell which. "We want to get married."

Ayya leaped up off the bed. My ears filled with buzzing. I wondered if he'd go search for his belt.

He exhaled sharply, his breath stinking like old food. "When the time comes," he said, his voice wavering, barely under his control, "I will choose someone for you. Someone from a good family. Someone who is a Brahmin. Someone who is destined to marry an avatar of Vishnu."

I stood straighter, realizing we were the same height now. I looked him right in the eye. "I want to marry Roopa."

Ayya took a few steps forward so we stood nose to nose. When he spoke, he did it through his teeth, each word wrenched from his mouth. I tried not to flinch at the odor of his breath.

"You can want it all you want," he said, "but it's not going to happen." He turned away before I could say anything and took a veshti from the nearest pile on his bed. He shook it out, the cotton snapping over and over again. "You need to think about how this might look to the people who visit the ashram."

"Nothing has to change," I said. "Everything can stay the same, and we'll just be married."

"You're eighteen," he said, whirling around. "That's not even legal marrying age in India."

"It can be a religious marriage."

He poked his finger into my chest, punctuating each word. "You. Are. Too. Young."

"Amma said—"

"Amma is sick! She's barely out of her room, and you think this will make her feel better? It'll destroy her health to see you married so below your status."

"I don't care about status."

"We do. Your family does. The villagers do. The visitors to the ashram do. You have to do what's best for everyone. Don't think so selfishly, Kalki. You're a god. Do you want to kill your mother? Do you want the visitors to stop coming? Do you want the villagers to laugh at us? Do you want this ashram to be destroyed by your selfish lust? Do you want to shame your family?"

I struggled to process everything. I was in love. I wasn't backing down from my father.

"You'll bring the word of god to the world," he said. "That's what's important. Not some silly crush."

"It's not—" I began, but Ayya cut me off.

"You'll never be able to see her again," he said. "I'll be arranging for her to go somewhere else before the day is out. She can go back to her family, finally."

My stomach compressed so tight I thought I would vomit.

"No," I said. "Please."

He turned his back on me. The full fear of losing Roopa hit me all at once, all over my body.

"Please, Ayya. Let her stay." I cast around for a reason. "She's the only one Amma lets take care of her. Amma trusts her. You can't send her away."

He looked at me again, his face closed and hard. "If I let her stay, you must keep away from her," he said. "That's the deal. I'll be watching you both very closely. Gopi will change her schedule. If I catch you even thinking about meeting her, I'll send her away for good, I promise you that." His wide eyes and raised finger made him look dangerous. "But I'm also going to need you to promise me, Kalki. You must promise me that you'll stay away."

I'd never said no to Ayya before.

"Kalki. Promise. Think of Amma. It's your disobedience that's making her sick."

My insides were a churning mess.

"I promise," I said.

Roopa was furious when I told her.

"And you promised?" she asked. "Just like that? You caved in and promised like a coward?"

I hung my head. "I'm not going to keep the promise. We can still be together." I tried to reach for her hand, but she jerked it away. I'd left Ayya talking to businessmen in the main building, and he hadn't yet had the opportunity to implement his new watchful measures. We sat in Roopa's room with the curtains drawn, speaking in whispers in case any of the other servants heard us.

She shook her head, a grimace on her mouth. "I was right, you know. I was right when I said you wouldn't have the guts to stand up to your father."

I took her hand, and this time I didn't let go, though she tried to pull it out of my grasp. I brought her fingers up to my lips and kissed her knuckles one by one.

"It won't be for long," I said. "We'll figure something out."

But I was out of ideas. I couldn't see a way that this would happen any time soon. Ayya's heart would take years to thaw, if it ever did.

"We could leave," Roopa said.

"Leave the ashram?" I asked. Inconceivable.

"We could go back to my family." She drew little circles on the floor with the tips of her fingers. "My parents wouldn't be happy, but my brothers would take us in. We could live with them while we figured out the rest." She talked herself into a smile. She touched my cheek, her eyes alive with new energy. "We could be together. We could get married."

A little fire erupted inside my chest, beating out of sync with my organs. Images flitted in my head of all the lives I could have out there in the world, outside the ashram. I would be done listening to Ayya like a puppy.

But there was so much wrong with this plan.

I opened my mouth to answer, but Roopa put her finger on my lips to shush me.

"Think about it," she said. "Think about it for a week at least before you answer."

The more I thought about it, the wilder the idea seemed. I imagined working at an office, in a suit. It made no sense. I was only ever taught to be a god and a guru, guiding people in their spiritual journeys. People with serious illnesses had reported miracle cures after visiting the ashram. But that wasn't something companies hired you for. Ayya controlled all the money, so I had no savings. And the issue of Amma—I wouldn't leave her. She'd already suffered enough loss. I wondered if she would leave Ayya behind and come with us.

Ayya had already started planning the world tour. It would happen in a year. If Roopa and I were going to leave and take Amma with us, we had a deadline.

4

Now that Ayya had his eye on us, Roopa and I had to be even more careful, even more secretive. The Deputy watched me all hours of the day. He never followed me into our family quarters, or into healing sessions with the visitors, and he never made it obvious what he was doing, but wherever I was, he was close by, pretending to be busy with some task or other and acting like he didn't see me. Roopa's schedule of cleaning the visitors' rooms had been changed from the timetable I'd memorized, so it was hard for me to predict where she'd be at any moment. At night, Ayya locked Roopa and me inside our rooms—we had doors that locked from both sides, from the inside with a key we each had for our own rooms, and from the outside with a master key that only Ayya had. Short of stealing his master key, I had no way to meet Roopa at night.

Every time Ayya and the Deputy disappeared into Ayya's office for meetings with foreign investors and planning the world tour, I ran from building to building, searching for Roopa.

When I told Brad of my predicament, he provided us with a safe haven in his quarters when Ayya and the Deputy were busy. Brad even left the room sometimes to give us privacy. Bringing Roopa into the fold of my friendship with Brad brought me a joy I hadn't expected. I found it so liberating to hold Roopa's hand in front of another human.

Brad loved the idea of us running away.

"Sometimes you have to do you," he said. He put the song "Entre Nous" by Rush on his turntable, because he said it was the most romantic song he owned. He sang along like he was serenading us. The lyrics were about leaving room to grow.

The three of us sat on a bamboo rug in Brad's room. Brad lit a joint, and Roopa's eyes flickered to it as we spoke.

"You guys should totally run away," Brad said, taking a drag and holding his breath. He let the smoke out in a cloud. "Elopement is the most romantic gesture."

I looked at Roopa, hopeful, and lifted my arm a bit. She scooted closer but didn't snuggle. I put my arm around her anyway, and drew her to me, but she resisted, sitting upright like one of the columns of the building.

"What do you say, youngblood?" Brad asked. "You think you'll do it?"

"Yeah," Roopa said in her accented English, with a smirk. "Are you going to run away with me, youngblood?"

Geddy Lee continued crooning in the background about how we're all just islands to each other.

"I'm still thinking about it," I said, not meeting their eyes. It wasn't that simple—they both seemed to think the idea was marvelous, but the bigger picture was complicated and scary. And there was the question of Amma, still unanswered. But I wanted to make Roopa happy. "Leaving might be the best long-term option," I said. "But in the meantime, we can figure something else out, here at the ashram."

Brad stood up from the rug, stretching loudly. "I think I'm going to take a walk," he said, winking at me. "You guys have fun." He took a book from his shelf and left the room.

Roopa waited until the door closed behind him, then launched herself on me, knocking me to the floor. She squeezed my wrists and pinned them above my head. She straddled me, grinding her hips into mine.

"Are you really still thinking about it?" she asked. She thrust her hips forward again and pushed me closer to unraveling. "We could . . ." She trailed off, and her fingers drifted down into my veshti. "Let's see what marriage would feel like."

It turned out that marriage felt amazing. But as soon as I climaxed, my stomach began to hurt. I rolled off Roopa, my hair plastered to my head with sweat, and lay next to her on the rug. Guilt roiled inside me, whipping itself into shame. I had taken something from Roopa that I could never give back. She could never be made whole again. She was fallen, and I had dragged her.

"I'm so sorry," I said. I stared at the ceiling, where Brad had hung up a batik tapestry with white elephants all over it.

Roopa rolled over to face me, propped up on her elbow. "What are you sorry for?"

"I'll marry you, I swear. I'll marry you."

"Oh, Kalki." She put a hand on my cheek and rubbed my earlobes between her fingers. "My beautiful Kalki. It's okay. I wanted this."

"But—"

"I chose this."

Roopa rolled back over onto her back, and we both watched the elephants on the ceiling for a while as I fought my nausea. Whatever she said, I knew how everyone else would look at her if they knew. She was spoiled—deflowered—and I had been the one to do it. I had to marry her, not just because I loved her, but also to protect her from the horrid things people would say if they knew.

Roopa sighed, and said, "If we have a baby, do you think it'll be blue?"

A baby. In all my imaginings of marrying Roopa, I'd never once pictured a baby. But it was there now, in my head, a little blue baby that Roopa would hold and nurse, that would sleep in a podavai slung from the rafters. But that baby wouldn't be blue.

"No," I said. "None of Rama or Krishna's kids were blue. The baby would look like you."

Roopa was still naked, her clothes in a pile next to her, her breasts flattened against her chest, her dark brown nipples puckered. She put a tender hand on her belly.

"A couple of months ago," she said, "Ayya called me to his room." She watched the sun through the curtains with her eyes scrunched up. She took a breath that filled up her whole body and let it out. "Don't be mad at me."

"Mad at you about what? I could never be mad at you."

When she spoke next, after a long silence, her voice broke softly. In between her words, I counted my heartbeats.

"I went," she said. "I couldn't say no. I went, and I was scared. Everyone was asleep. He asked me to come when the moon came up. It was after midnight."

I pictured it as she told the story. Roopa, timid and scared. The ashram asleep. Not even the servants were awake. A clear night with a waxing moon. She walked to the new building, past my room, to Ayya's room in the back. She stood in his doorway alone, with only the moonlight to see by.

"He told me to close the door. So I closed it. Then he told me to come closer."

She turned her back to me, curled in on herself, brought her knees up to her chest, and hugged them. I put my hand on her shoulder. I wanted to feel close to her—she felt so far away. I wrapped myself around her, my blue skin to her brown.

"He made me lie down on the bed," she said. Her voice was so soft it was hard to hear her over my grinding teeth. "He covered me up with the blankets. Then he climbed into bed next to me and fell asleep. He didn't touch me, but I was too scared to sleep." She turned around and looked at me. The sun lit her face in flame. In the light, her eyes glowed brown instead of their usual black. "I think he was testing his vow of chastity, making sure he could resist the temptation."

She was crying now, something that would've normally made me reach out to her, but my body kept itself still. I didn't pull myself away, but I didn't hug her tighter, either, which I should've done. The scene of her getting into Ayya's bed played itself over and over in my mind. When she laid down, her dhavani would have moved to reveal her waist, fleshy and curved. Ayya had resisted that. I wanted to burn the vision out of my brain.

Roopa waited for me to make a move. All I could picture was her little body lying next to Ayya's, together under the covers.

"He didn't touch me," she said, pleading.

My hand was covered with our combined sweat. The anger took me, climbed up from my belly and into my fingers, down into my toes.

Ayya.

I jumped up and paced across the room. My body filled with energy, the springs of my muscles coiled too tight, ready to release their violence.

"I've made a decision, Kalki." She sat up and wiped her face. "Come. Sit."

My stomach writhed and spat like a cobra that knew it was going to be killed. I walked over to her, my head dizzy and my eyes unable to see much beyond the pools of brightness in her face. She had her head down and her hands clasped in her lap.

She reached out and cupped the side of my face, ran her fingers down to my shoulders, my chest.

"That wasn't the only time," she said. "It keeps happening. Ayya keeps calling me to his room. At least once or twice a week."

I imagined it again in my mind, Ayya and Roopa lying in bed together. This had been happening for months.

"Why didn't you tell me sooner?" I asked, surprised by the tone of accusation in my voice.

"He's never touched me," she said. "Never. I didn't know what to make of it. And I didn't want to hurt you or make you mad. But I can't do this anymore."

"I'll talk to him," I said. I sounded more confident in the air than in my head.

"That's not what I meant." She cupped both of my cheeks with her hands. I finally saw her face fully, the whiteness of her eyes and teeth. "I'm leaving."

She waited for a reaction, but my brain couldn't make the leap she'd asked for with her last word.

"I'm going to my parents, Kalki. I already talked with them. I'm going with or without you."

With or without. My ears hummed, and it was hard to make out her words.

"Say something," she said.

"You can't go," I said. "You can't—I'll talk to Ayya. I'll make him stop."

She shook her head. "I'm going, Kalki. Will you come with me?"

I could make this stop. I could marry her. Leaving wasn't the answer. I couldn't breathe, couldn't pull the air into my lungs.

"I can't," I said. "I can't leave Amma. She's not well. I—I can't. Please don't go. Let's get married."

"Everyone does seem to leave you, don't they," she said. "Oh, Kalki. My Kalki."

She pulled me to her and held me as I sobbed into her naked chest.

Roopa decided to leave after Holi, our biggest annual festival. In Tamil Nadu, we didn't normally celebrate Holi—we celebrated Masi Magam, Pongal, Karthigai Deepam, and Thai Poosam—but a few years earlier, Ayya had implemented a Holi festival to attract North Indians and foreigners to the ashram.

Nothing I said could sway Roopa from her decision to leave.

"Let's get married," I'd say.

She'd remind me that without Ayya and Amma's permission, we couldn't get married. I was too young under Indian law, and if I secretly married Roopa, the whole ashram would be engulfed in scandal. My reputation would never recover. We'd lose everything.

I pleaded with Amma to leave, but she refused. And I couldn't—*wouldn't*—leave Amma, not even for Roopa.

Roopa's decision set me simmering with a fury that threatened to boil over every time Ayya was around. I tried to figure out in the lines of his face and the way he moved his body if he felt responsible for driving her away. But he smiled for the visitors, acted stern for me and the servants, and disapproving but kind for Amma and her sadness that kept her in bed most of the time. I wanted to ask him why he'd called her to his room, but Roopa made me promise to wait until after she was gone. Every time I thought about her leaving, I drowned.

On the day of Holi, we dressed in white. Ayya had brightly colored dyes and water guns brought in from outside Tamil Nadu. We filled hundreds of balloons with colored water in the morning. Afterward, and before the color fights started, Brad invited Roopa and me back to his room.

"I have a surprise for you," he said. "Ta-da!" He held out a silver cup full of white liquid.

"Milk?" I asked.

"No, bhang."

I looked closer at the milk, its green tinge, topped with ground-up cashews and cardamom.

"It's your tradition." He took a swig of bhang from another cup. "The traditional drink of Holi."

Roopa and I took the cups he offered and sipped the sweet bhang. "It has ganja in it," he said, sounding like a naughty child. "I guess you should know that."

The cup seemed so innocent. Ayya had never held forth on his opinions about bhang. Many ancient texts refer to the drink as something that helped focus energies inward when meditating, or else would steel nerves when going to war. Brad was right—this was part of my history, and different than smoking ganja out of a pipe or joint.

I took several large gulps of the milk. I was going to be running around throwing colored dye at people anyway. I didn't care what Ayya thought or what his punishment would be.

Roopa chugged half her drink in one go and wiped the milk mustache off her upper lip. She grinned, getting into the revelry, but each of my organs had little weights attached, pulling them down.

"I don't feel anything," I said. I'd hoped I'd feel lighter, so I could enjoy the festival with Roopa one last time.

"It'll sneak up on you," Brad said.

We swallowed the rest of our drinks. While we waited for whatever was going to sneak up on us, Brad lit a joint and passed it to me. I'd already drunk the bhang, so I took a few puffs.

"Hold it in," Brad said.

I tried to hold in my breath but started coughing. Brad laughed and said that was supposed to happen.

Brad, Roopa, and I lounged on pillows thrown all over the bamboo rug on the floor. Roopa held my hand, rubbing her thumb back and forth over my knuckles. On the blue batik sarong hanging over the ceiling, a line of elephants paraded around our heads.

"Did you know that blue was the last color our ancestors evolved to see?" Brad said. "I read it in an article once. We couldn't see the color blue until a couple thousand years ago."

The elephants moved in my vision. *A couple thousand years ago* didn't make sense. Some of the gods had been blue since time began. But maybe we couldn't see that then. Maybe it took us thousands of years of evolution to see godliness.

My skin tingled all over, the feeling spreading up from my fingertips toward my core.

And then I felt it—that warm presence I hadn't sensed since my childhood. Rama. He was here with me. The energy was unmistakable, like electricity all over my body.

"Rama?" I whispered.

"What color do you think Kalki is?" Brad asked. "Cerulean? Royal blue?"

"Those are both darker," Roopa said. She gave me a piercing look, like I was blurry and she couldn't see me. But it was she who was blurring in my vision. She was blurring, and Rama's presence was getting stronger.

"Rama?" I mouthed again.

"He's more periwinkle, I think."

"Isn't that purplish?"

"He's the color of those flowers. Those blue flowers. You know what I'm talking about?"

We were all silent while we thought about it.

As the room distorted and everyone faded from my vision, a shadow of a person emerged and became clearer. The elephants continued to march in the sky. Rama came into focus. There he was, a deep blue—darker than me, more indigo than my light blue—dressed the way I'd always imagined him, in a white silk dhoti and gold jewelry piled on his chest, his face aquiline and majestic, the thin face of royalty.

"Have you met Krishna yet?" Rama asked. He turned his head to the side, and another shape clarified into being.

Krishna was more my skin color, a bright, unblemished blue sky. He was younger than Rama, closer to my age, and he held a bamboo flute in his hand. They both sat on the floor cross-legged between Brad and me.

"Forget-me-nots," Brad said after a while. "He's the color of forget-me-nots. It's a type of flower."

I didn't know what forget-me-nots were, but I imagined a whole field of flowers the color of me. If I got some of those flowers for Amma, she could grind them up and make paint in my color. I studied my arm. I wasn't just blue. I was forget-me-not blue. The color of the sky on a spring morning.

The elephants marched around the ceiling. Rama and Krishna sat with me, not saying anything, watching the elephants too. The sky, I'd learned from my thin science book, wasn't blue. It looked blue to us because of the way the light broke apart in the dusty air. And Krishna, I'd learn years later, wasn't blue either. Not like me. He was so dark—his skin so black—that he was described as the color of a rain-dark cloud. And Indians had just been so obsessed with light skin that they took their dark-skinned gods and turned them blue.

Sitting on Brad's rug, I loved the idea that even though everyone thought blue was a cold color, the color of water and relaxing, there was still blue inside a flame—at its very center, where it was hottest. Blue. Some stars burned blue, little blue dots in the sky that burned brighter and hotter than the others around. Blue flowers and blue water that reflected the blue sky, vast oceans and oceans of it, holding blue fish and blue crabs that walked on the sandy floor. A whole world of blue, right where no human could see it.

But blue was also a feeling, the color of sadness and peace. And Brad played us a music called "The Blues," full of minor chords on the guitar and gravelly voices singing sad songs about loss and pain.

What did my lungs look like? My stomach? My heart? Were they all blue? Were they sad? Were they godly?

"My eyes aren't blue," Brad said, getting up close to me so I could see how blue his eyes looked. In his movement, he stepped right through where Krishna sat, and Krishna gave him a dirty look. "They're very light brown," Brad said, "and they look blue because of the way light scatters around the iris."

Was I really blue? Were Rama and Krishna blue? Or did we just look it? Maybe our skins refracted light around and made us look blue. Maybe we were no color. Maybe we were translucent, reflecting everything around us like human mirrors.

Holi was the one time of the year when no one seemed to care that I was a god. It wasn't so much a religious celebration as a fun one, and I was glad Ayya had introduced it to the ashram. Heaps of colored dye sat on little platters at the edge of a large clearing behind the ashram. People came from all the villages around and even from town to participate. The horses had been corralled into the coconut grove so they wouldn't be spooked by all the activity. Arjuna hated this, tossing his head and tail and whinnying to make a point.

I wore a plain white cotton veshti with no jewelry. We locked all the doors to the ashram so nothing could be stolen. Amma came out of her room, put on one of her best podavais, and pretended to laugh with the rest of us. She had dark circles under her eyes and smiled with only her mouth.

Ayya hired a band to play music—at least ten drummers in a semi-circle with tavils and kanjiras, and two nadaswaram players on either end, blasting out their nasally instruments.

Rama and Krishna followed me out to the field with Brad and Roopa. When the band started, people rushed to grab handfuls of colored powder. We chased each other around. Some of the village boys had water guns filled with colored water they pumped at us. I jumped and avoided them. I had a handful of magenta powder. Roopa rushed away from me, and I chased her.

At some point, I realized I was dizzy. I couldn't breathe. The music faded out, and it was as if I was set apart from everyone, floating in my own body, watching them all. So much happiness. Hands on my back, sweeping across my skin. Roopa. Her face bloomed in front of me, one side of it colored yellow with some cobalt in her hair.

"I marked you!" she shouted through the noise.

"What are you waiting for?" Krishna asked. He'd grabbed ahold of a water gun and was running next to me. "Let's go get her."

Red streaks on my back in the shape of her hands. Her soft hands. I grasped at them. Soft soft soft. I kissed them.

"What are you doing?" She pulled away, pushed me back with a hand on my chest. "Everyone can see."

"You're a god," Krishna said, gesturing with his water gun. "It's you who decides."

Rama stood next to him, too dignified for colored dye or water guns, and nodded.

I put my hand over Roopa's.

"Someone will see," she said. She pulled her hand away and disappeared into the crowd.

I chased her, colored dye forgotten. The drums beat louder, more frantic. The world spiraled around me, around and around until I couldn't tell which direction was up. I folded over my knees and vomited. Hands, hands grabbing me all over, dragging me away.

"Quickly, quickly," someone said, "before anyone sees."

"Is he sick?"

"Shhhh, someone might hear you."

They dragged me into the coconut grove, and it was Ayya, Brad, and Amma. We walked and walked. We sat by the creek. Amma dipped the end of her podavai into the cold water and pressed it to my head. Rama and Krishna had dissolved into the air.

Up through the canopy, blue sky. Green fronds. Empty space. Wind.

"How could he have gotten sick?" Amma said. "We were so careful."

"It might be the bhang." Brad's voice.

"What?"

"It's no big deal—I mean, it's your tradition."

Ayya was shouting, his voice wobbling into focus. "What were you thinking? This is your fault."

Brad, backing away, the scene blurring again. "We were just having fun."

"You leave this place. I won't have you corrupting him anymore."

"My money keeps this place afloat."

So loud so loud.

"We don't need your money anymore," Ayya said. "You and your bad influences can get out."

Amma floating into the space between them, holding out her arms. Ayya lurching toward Brad, but Amma holding him back.

He pushed her, swung back his hand, and in a flash, slapped her across the face. Amma fell. A sound sharp, like a rock cracking open. I tried to push myself up to go to her, but my legs tipped me too far and I fell. Amma held her cheek, curled up on the ground.

Ayya knelt, tried to hug her. She pushed him away, pushed and pushed herself away. She ran through the woods until the colors of her podavai disappeared in the trunks of the coconut trees.

"That was messed up," Brad said.

"Don't you tell me what's messed up." Ayya's voice roared through the space. "What's messed up is you giving a kid bhang. Get out of my sight! Get out of my ashram!"

Brad walked back toward the Holi festival, leaving me alone with Ayya. This was the last I'd ever see of Brad, I thought, lying there. The canopy spun above us. Spinning and spinning itself into darkness.

5

I woke up in my own bed, my head too dense to move from the pillow, my room empty. Two small monkeys watched me through an open window, concern and curiosity in their faces. On my desk sat Amma's half-finished painting of me as a toddler in the woods. The setting sun blazed through the curtains.

As the buzzing in my ears subsided, voices filled in. Amma and Ayya. Amma yelled at the top of her voice, but the words muddled together, and I couldn't make them out.

I heaved myself out of bed and walked to my door, holding my head. I opened the door to a scene I'd never expected.

Roopa leaned on a column in the courtyard, sobbing. Amma stood in front of her, facing Ayya, who motioned with his hands as if to get Amma to be quieter.

"Everyone will hear," he said. He was speaking loudly, too, but through his teeth to mute the sound. His shoulders were thrown back and stiff.

Amma was still in her Holi podavai, its crisp pleats softened and wilting.

"Let everyone hear," she yelled. "Let this place go to ruin. But you don't ever touch her. Ever, you hear me?"

No one had noticed me yet. My head throbbed like a spring someone had pulled and let go.

"That slut can't be in the ashram anymore," Ayya said. "She's leading our son astray. She's going to destroy everything we've built."

"Everything *you've* built, you mean. I've raised her like a daughter. She's not going anywhere."

Roopa continued to cry, her face pressed into the column. As if pulled by her tears, I went to her.

Amma and Ayya fell silent, watching me as I crossed the courtyard. I put my arm around Roopa, and she turned to press her face into my chest.

"Don't you touch that whore," Ayya said. He took a step toward me as if he was going to wrench Roopa away, but Amma placed herself in between us.

Ayya's face warped with anger. He shoved Amma to the floor.

I ran to Amma, panicked, but as I squatted next to her, helping her sit up, Ayya took hold of Roopa's elbow and dragged her to the door of his room that faced onto the courtyard.

I leaped up, but it was too late. He pushed Roopa into his room, closed the door, took his master key from his pocket, and locked her in.

I jiggled the doorknob. Roopa banged on the door from the other side.

"Let her out," I said. I pulled and pulled at the door. "Let her out!"

"I'll let her out right into a car that'll take her home," Ayya said. He tapped the key against his cheek and put it in the waistband of his veshti.

From across the courtyard, Amma ran at him, hitting her fists against his chest—hard, from the way that Ayya backed up and flinched. She swung and swung her fists.

Ayya pushed her backward. He slapped her again across the face.

I jumped in between them, and his hand, raised for another strike, made contact with the side of my head instead. Pain buzzed all across my skull, ringing in my brain.

Amma pulled me backward through the courtyard, away from Ayya and his room door, in front of which he stood guard. She held her cheek, where a large red spot bloomed. Together we went into her room, and she locked the door from the inside.

We stayed in Amma's room for an hour. Amma lay facedown on the bed, silent and still. I paced, trying to think of how to get the key from Ayya and let Roopa out.

"Amma, do you want to go away from here? We could run away, you and me and Roopa. We could go somewhere, to Roopa's family. We could get away from Ayya."

She rolled over, and I saw how the tears had streaked down and smeared all over her face.

"You want to run away?" she asked.

"I—yes, I think it would be—it's the best option we have."

She sat up slowly, shaking her head. "I can't, kutti. But you go. You go with Roopa."

I took her hands and kissed them, sitting by her on the bed. "Come with us. We can all go."

She shook her head more vigorously. "I can't. Maybe I should've, years ago. I should've taken you far away from here." She caressed my face. "I'm sorry, kutti. I was so stupid. I was faithful that things would get better. But I've failed you."

"You haven't," I said, my chest a piece of wrung-out cloth. "It's okay. We can fix it."

"I can't come with you, kutti. I—I'm too broken. I want to be done."

Her voice was a soft whisper, as if she was saying something meant only for herself. "I thought if I kept painting, it would go away." She gestured to the side of her room, where canvases were stacked five-deep, all painted or painted over in the last few weeks. Abstracts with bold, violent colors, pictures of Priya and some of me, curving lines that looked vaguely like women. Amma shook her head. "It's not working. I want it to end. I'm tired."

I didn't know how to help her. I hugged her, and she was soft and pliable in my arms. I should've spent more time in her room, more time telling her stories or reading to her, more effort in trying to pull her out of bed. If I'd tried harder, she wouldn't have felt so much pain, all alone.

But I also thought of Roopa in Ayya's room, locked away.

"Amma," I said, "we have to get Roopa out of that room. We'll figure out the rest later. But right now, that's what's important."

"Yes, yes, of course."

She pushed herself off the bed and wiped her eyes. She stood up. I caught her as she swayed and led her to the door, where she turned the key in the lock with trembling fingers.

The courtyard was deserted, and Ayya's bedroom was still locked, but blue light glowed under the door to his office. I escorted Amma, who leaned heavily on me. We knocked and waited.

When Ayya came out of his office, I stepped up to him, blocking Amma from his reach.

"Let Roopa out," I said.

He bared his teeth. "One of the servants is packing up her things. The driver will take her home."

My throat threatened to squeeze shut.

"Please," I said. "Let her stay."

But Ayya was pitiless, his face unbreakable. "You didn't keep your promise."

I fell at his feet. "Please."

I begged and begged, but he didn't relent. A half hour later, one of the servants showed up with a suitcase, which she loaded into Ayya's new car as his driver stood by.

Ayya unlocked the door to his bedroom, and Roopa rushed out, her eyes wide and red. She threw herself onto me, and as I held her, her body shook and shivered all over.

"That's enough," Ayya said. He dragged her by the arm away from me and into the car.

The car drove away. I should have chased it down, thrown myself into the car, left Ayya forever. I should have eloped when I had the chance.

6

By evening, Amma still hadn't come out of her room. I knocked and knocked, but nothing. I asked a servant if she had eaten anything, but no one had heard from her. I went to Ayya's office.

He opened the door a crack to show a slit of his face. Behind him, some bright white light reflected off numerous calendars and clocks. Whatever the source was, he'd hidden it from view.

"Amma hasn't eaten today," I said. I was still reeling and furious from earlier, and hoarse from crying in my room. But Ayya had the master key to Amma's room. I tried to control the pitch and volume of my voice to make it as neutral as I could. "Can you go check on her?"

"I've already brought her dinner. She's eaten." He made as if to close the door again.

"Are you sure? I knocked and didn't hear anything."

"Let her rest. She needs rest. Don't disturb her. And I told you not to knock on this door unless it's an emergency. Go do your healing rounds."

He slammed the door in my face.

What pulled me out of bed was Amma screaming outside my window. I rushed out of my room into scorching heat. Under the midnight sky, a bonfire blazed in the middle of the courtyard, sending plumes of gray smoke up through the open roof. On a bed of hay, Amma's paintings burned, the canvases curling and tearing. Molten coils of painted canvas bits floated in the air, caught in the currents of the fire.

Ayya held Amma back from running into the flames, one hand clamped firmly over her mouth. She pulled and yelled, her words muffled but her voice still strong. Her hair swung, unclipped and wild, and she wore nothing but her nightgown.

"What's going on?" I asked.

"Go back to your room!" Ayya shouted. "Go."

Instead, I ran to Amma, who collapsed into my arms.

"He burned everything," she said. "Every last painting." She shook her head, her hands hiding her face. "Every paintbrush and all the paints."

Amma crumpled into my chest like a piece of tissue paper. She shivered against me, and I felt like I would shake apart too. I held her as best I could, ignoring Ayya. When neither I nor Amma responded for a few minutes, he walked back to his office and shut himself inside.

I peered into the flames to see if I could save any paintings, any brushes, anything. But everything glowed red, coming apart into smoke and ashes. One of the paintings, which showed Krishna driving Arjuna's chariot in the climactic battle of the *Mahabharata*, lay half-charred—Arjuna's face gone and only Krishna's hands intact, holding the reigns of blackened horses.

I squeezed Amma in my arms as the fire burned itself out.

Later that night or early the next morning, Amma woke me from a deep sleep. She stroked my hair and sat by the head of my bed. I sat up and hugged her. She rocked us both back and forth while crickets sang outside my window.

"Amma?"

"Shhhh," she said. "Sleep. I love you. You are the most precious thing to me."

"Amma, are you okay?"

"I'm sorry." She kissed my cheeks, my eyes, all over my face. "I'm sorry I failed you. We should've left when you wanted." She stroked my hair. "But you're a man now. You're grown up, and you don't need your mother anymore."

I held her tight. I was still not fully awake, and I didn't know what she was talking about.

"I still need you."

She shook her head. "You find your way out of here, Kalki. I'm tired. But you're still young. You find your way out. Promise me?"

"I—I promise," I said. "Come with me. We can run away."

"There's nowhere in India we can go that he won't find us. And Ayya burnt my passport a long time ago. But it doesn't matter. I'm tired, Kalki. You go. Find Lakshman."

I had no way to reach Lakshman halfway across the world.

She laid me back down like I was still a baby. She pet my hair.

"Sleep," she said. "And remember that I love you. Always, I love you."

She shuffled toward the door, and I laid there, confused and groggy until I slipped into sleep.

Looking back, I wish I'd dreamed something that would've prepared me for the morning. Some sign. Some omen. But I didn't dream at all. I woke up, and Amma was gone.

After all the events of the last night, I didn't feel like going to the oxbow pond. Instead, I made tea in the kitchen. I steeped enough for Amma, but when I went to her room to give it to her, she wasn't there. Her bed was made, and her room was clean.

I searched for her in Ayya's bedroom, in the courtyard, in the garden, all over the ashram. I walked to the oxbow pond, the clearing where we held Holi, the rice paddies, the coconut grove, the river. She was nowhere.

By the time I came back, I'd missed my yoga class, and Ayya was furious. I found him in the sunlit yoga room as the class ended. He had led it himself. We drifted to a corner while the visitors packed up their bamboo mats.

"You think you can wander off and neglect your responsibilities?" he said, his anger stifled within a whisper the others couldn't hear.

"But Amma," I said, not bothering to keep my voice down. Everyone deserved to know, so they could look too. "Amma's missing."

Ayya's lips twitched, but he held his rage in check because visitors were watching. They were all wealthy older Indians and Europeans whom I didn't talk to on a regular basis.

"I'll worry about Amma," Ayya said, his voice a grumbling volcano. "You fulfill your responsibilities."

The fire in my chest grew, and I wanted to yell. Ayya didn't care about my mother. I had to find her.

"You do your job," he said. "Don't worry about Amma."

The meditation students filtered in, and some of the yoga students who stayed for meditation had already taken up their positions.

"I'm going to find her," I said.

Ayya grabbed my arm before I could walk away, squeezed it so hard I was sure I'd have a bruise.

"You will"—he measured out each word one whisper at a time—"finish this class."

I tried to pull away, but he gripped my arm too tight. I raised my voice so the whole room could hear.

"Ayya is going to lead you in meditation today," I said. "I have an emergency healing session."

Ayya growled, but he forced his face into a smile. I tugged at my arm, and he let go. As I left, he took my place at the head of the class, cross-legged with his wrists on his knees.

I walked out to the oxbow pond in a roundabout route, past the horses and the edge of the coconut grove and back, but still no Amma. I stayed out all day, walking all over the property. When it got too dark to see, I came back hungry and tired, my feet aching. The light was on in Ayya's office. I avoided that side of the building altogether. Instead, I went to the kitchen to beg some dinner off the servants, went to my room, and fell asleep without undressing.

The next morning, Ayya caved. He organized a large search party. People came from the village. We moved in a sweeping motion across the entire property of the ashram—me, Ayya, the visitors, the villagers. We searched all night, and all day the next day. The search spread out beyond the ashram and all the way through the nearest villages in every direction. It was hard for me to breathe, hard to eat, hard to sleep. For two days, men came back shaking their heads. No sign of her. But on the third day—

The man who found Amma's body had brought his dog with him, and the dog had sniffed it out.

Three men carried her limp form all the way back to the ashram. I couldn't look, but I couldn't look away, either. Her podavai was dirty and torn. She looked ashen and bloated, and had smears of red foam on her mouth, eyes, and nose. They laid her on her bed.

"Rat poison," the man who found her said. "Looks like she drank rat poison."

Her face looked nothing like her.

Someone screamed, wailing like a wounded animal. And then I was holding her, wrapping my body around her on the bed, and I was howling, too, and maybe I was the only one howling. Everything blurred in front of my eyes, even Amma's bloated, cold body. If I hadn't felt it heavy and rigid, I wouldn't have believed it was her.

I remember flashes. I remember holding Amma on her bed. I remember how the dog that found her sat next to his owner's heels, looking pleased with itself. I remember the men from the village prying my hands off Amma, wrenching her away from me. I remember the village barber who came to shave my head. I remember the funeral that same evening, where I threw myself on Amma's body, which had been washed and dressed in a new podavai and flower garlands with turmeric on her forehead. I remember Ayya and me clutching Amma's body and weeping.

I remember the rage building beneath the sadness as I carried Amma's funeral palanquin on my shoulder, as I performed the last rites before her body was burnt at the pyre, as I laid down trying to sleep that night. The building fury was all for Ayya—Ayya, who was responsible for all of this. It was he who had pushed Amma to such unhappiness.

I remember someone handing me the torch at the funeral pyre, where Amma rested on a bed of wood chips. I remember touching the flame to the wood and letting Amma burn like her precious paintings, all of them lost to the heat.

That night, as I closed my eyes, I saw Amma's body in the fire. My body weighed a thousand pounds, my limbs dragging me to the floor. It was like I'd overdosed on bhang again. In my sleepless dreams, the fire that held Amma's body turned into the bonfire Ayya had built in our courtyard with her paintings, Amma and her paintings all together in one, burning in the night.

It was all Ayya's fault. Ayya. Ayya. Ayya. I hated him. That feeling woke me fully from my tortured sleep. I was furious, as if the dream visions had focused my anger like a lens.

I jumped out of bed, ran across the building, and pounded my fist on the door to Ayya's bedroom. "Ayya!" I called. The soon-to-be-rising sun drew a thin pink line in the dark sky.

No response, so I knocked again, louder. "Ayya! You bloody dog, open up!"

Ayya opened the door, his eyes bloodshot, his graying hair mussed. He looked like he'd gotten less sleep than I had. But I didn't care. I barged in past him and paced in front of his unmade bed.

"Go back to bed, Kalki," he said. He sat on the bed and rubbed his eyes.

I clenched and unclenched my shaking hands.

"Kalki," he said, his voice softer. "Kalki, come here." He spread his arms, as if he wanted to give me a hug. "Kalki, life is full of good and bad. And we have to move on."

I rushed at him, not knowing or caring what my plan was. I wanted him to suffer like Amma had—for him to know a tiny drop of the pain he'd caused her all these years. His expression didn't change as I approached. It was delayed, like he hadn't thought I would ever hurt him.

At once, I was on top of him, knocking him back onto the bed. I wrapped my hands around his neck. Fear grew in his face as he realized what was happening.

I squeezed tighter.

He pulled at my fingers, but I was stronger than he was, which surprised both of us. I tightened my hands around his neck. He sputtered and gurgled, gasping for air.

"You—you," I kept saying. It was all I managed. My hands around his neck told him everything I need to say.

"Kalki," he wheezed. His eyes bulged. "Please."

I controlled his tiny, fragile life, every bit of it. I held his fate between the palms of my hands, but it didn't make me feel powerful. I felt less like a god than ever before.

I loosened my grip. Ayya gasped hungrily at the air.

"Kalki," he said.

I let go and pushed myself away from him. We both stared at each other, breathing heavily, realizing the same thing. I had almost killed him. For once, I was stronger than he was, and something had shifted forever between us.

In the days afterward, Ayya demanded less of me. He acted like a punished child, not meeting my gaze, watching my face when I looked away. It was a week before he tried to talk to me about anything other than ashram-related issues.

I still had Amma's last rites to perform. For eleven days after the funeral, as Amma's soul made its way from Earth back to the far shore of Death's realm, we made daily offerings of rice balls. On the eleventh day, the village barber came again to shave my head. On the twelfth day, we fed another Brahmin priest who came from the nearest temple. On the thirteenth day, we fed thirteen Brahmin priests from Madurai.

On the fourteenth day, Ayya and I sat in silence in our empty courtyard.

Ayya said, "Kalki, you know I loved your mother." He seemed pitiful, resting against one of the plaster columns. The courtyard had been scrubbed clean of the residue from the bonfire, but burn marks had scorched the soot-streaked tiles.

Purplish bruises peeked above Ayya's shirt collar. "She's happier now," he said. "She's been depressed for years. It's better this way."

Amma's voice sounded inside my head, saying that she was done, that she was tired, that she wanted it all to end.

Ayya reached out and clutched my hands to his chest, looking into my face. An old man with the earnestness of a toddler.

"The village elders want me to marry again."

I was too disgusted to look at him.

"They've found someone for me."

I tried to pull my hands out of his grasp, but he held onto them. He kissed them and wouldn't let go.

"My son. I told them no," he said. "I told them no, because I will never leave you. I promise you; I will be all the parents you need, Kalki." He looked deep into my eyes, and I couldn't tell whether he believed himself or not. "I won't ever remarry, not ever. I will be your father and your mother. For you, Kalki. All for you."

BOOK 4: KALKI

1

A fault line runs through my life, a rift that creates for me a *before* and an *after*. The fissure wasn't Lakshman's leaving, or Roopa's, or even Amma's, though all three did shatter me. The fracture that broke my life into two separate lives was New York City.

I was twenty-two, on my world tour with Ayya, four years later than he'd wanted. When I'd imagined it as a teen, I'd pictured traveling with an entourage, like a king. I'd have sycophantic followers, a security detail, people to take care of my wardrobe and jewelry, speechwriters, journalists. But when the tour finally came around, it turned out to be just Ayya and me, traveling economy on airplanes and trains, sharing cheap hotel rooms.

"We might be rich in rupees," Ayya told me, "but they don't convert to many dollars."

We left the ashram and its daily running to the Deputy, who seemed delighted at his new power—overseeing the weddings that people had booked in our great hall; supervising the tending of gardens, horses, and buildings; and running meditation and yoga classes for the visitors who wanted to stay even without my presence.

I hadn't been out of the ashram since my parents had brought me there as a toddler. In the weeks leading up to the Sri Kalki World Tour, the idea of traveling made my body quiver. My knees refused to bend like they used to, falling and springing so easily, as if I had forgotten how to walk. I kept a copy of our two-month travel schedule above my desk—New Delhi, New York City, Toronto, Orlando, San Jose, Kuala Lampur, Bangkok. We prepared for months, writing and memorizing speeches, getting measured for new clothes, learning history about the places we were to visit. The tailor came from the village to make me jeans and button shirts for travel. The jeans were tight and stiff, hard to walk in. The shirts clung uncomfortably to my armpits. Ayya had the village jeweler copy my gold jewelry in gold-plated brass so we wouldn't have to worry about it getting stolen.

In New Delhi, the first big city I'd ever seen, we settled into a routine of bhajan, pooja, and meeting devotees. So much noise, so many smells, so much motion, too many people. Even the air in Delhi was oppressive, and the masses of bodies endless.

The three-day train ride had already blown my mind. I'd seen more people on the train than I had in my life, and every platform we stopped at bustled with more people: women selling tasty vadas and spiced peanuts out of reed baskets, valets pestering people about their luggage, parents screaming at their disobedient kids, families crying as they said their goodbyes.

But that was nothing compared to the city itself. One afternoon in Delhi offered more for me to look at than all my days and nights at our tiny ashram—streets crammed full of cars and auto rickshaws that honked incessantly, huge crowds surging around every corner, giant billboards advertising everything from jewelry to shiny new cars to skin-lightening products.

We went to half a dozen temples, each one dwarfing our prayer center back home, and every time, more than a hundred devotees sang bhajans and asked for healing. So many people came to me seeking the secrets of faith. I got used to the noisiness, the neediness, and the routine, but it was all very tiring, and by the end of the first week, I was ready to go home. Thoughts of Amma and Roopa followed me like ghosts, though they'd been gone for years. They had joined Rama and Krishna in tormenting my rare quiet moments, wheedling their way into my dreams.

I'd tried in the last few years to contact Roopa, but like Priya had done with Amma, she hadn't responded. I didn't know if it was because she was scared of Ayya or because she had stopped loving me, but I loved her still.

Two days before Ayya and I were to leave Delhi for New York, we took a rented car back from the temple after the last pooja. The night was muggy, the lights of the city fuzzy in the brown haze. Yellow-topped autos honked through traffic. The smell of rot and smog pressed at our faces.

Ayya argued with his cousin, with whose family we were staying, about the feasibility of a bigger world tour after this one.

"People really want to see him," Ayya said. "We're going to do a few countries easily, but we need to expand after that."

"You don't have that kind of money, yaar," his cousin said.

I pretended to look out the window so I wouldn't be expected to answer or participate in their discussion. I was doing this world tour because it was Ayya's vision—and because every time I'd pictured something else to do with my life, my own dreams had been dashed. I hadn't followed Lakshman to America; I hadn't run away with Roopa and Amma. I didn't know what I wanted for my life anymore, and following Ayya's dream seemed as good an option as any.

"There are rich people in Australia who need to see him," Ayya said. "Russia. Europe. We have to spread the message far and wide."

"But you know the risks. You can't use your connections."

The driver slammed the breaks, and I threw out my arm to keep myself in my seat. I rolled down my window. The sound of car honks flooded in.

We idled close to an intersection where an auto rickshaw had run into a small blue car, smashing its front end. The auto lay on its side with its wheels spinning in the air. Sharp pieces of glass littered the road, reflecting the streetlights around us.

People gathered at the scene. Ayya opened the car doors and we pushed our way into the crowd. Ayya's cousin called after us, but I didn't look back.

As we came closer, I saw that an older woman and an auto driver lay on the ground near the wreckage. The driver's eyes were open, and blood was everywhere, as if someone had painted red in large swirls all over the scene.

People yelled at each other to call the police, the ambulance. The woman took deep, rasping breaths. Two men tried to lift her.

"Stop," Ayya said. "Stop! You could make her injuries worse if you move her." He pushed his way into the clearing. "I'm a doctor," he said. "Let me look."

The men put her back down, and Ayya examined her. He hadn't worked as a doctor for two decades, since before we'd moved to the ashram. He opened the woman's eyes and checked her pulse.

"She's losing a lot of blood," he said. "She needs help, or she won't last."

"Look," someone said, pointing at me. "Kalki Sami can heal her." Everyone looked at me.

"Yes, Kalki Sami," someone else said. "You can heal her."

I knelt in the smell of iron and urine. Blood pooled near the woman's head. I put my quivering hands over her body. I chanted, my voice cracking. *Om Sri Ram Om Sri Ram Om Sri Ram.* Some people in the crowd bowed their heads and prayed with me.

I closed my eyes. I chanted and chanted until the woman stopped breathing.

I woke up sprawled in the backseat as our car pulled into Ayya's cousin's gated house. Ayya got out of the car without a word and went inside.

Sleep had clogged my memories, but they came back with the light of the front stoop. The woman, the red, the glass like glitter, the way the life had run out of her as I held her. *Kalki Sami can heal her!* But no, I couldn't.

I stepped out of the car, and my knees wouldn't hold my weight. I stumbled, following Ayya into the house. Servants appeared around us with plates of food, water in flowered glasses. Ayya waved them away and headed for our room. I went after him. The night had carved me out, emptied me of everything.

Ayya tried to close the door of our room behind him, but I kept it open with my foot and stepped inside. He laid down on his bed over the covers and shaded his eyes with his forearm.

"Turn off the lights," he said. "I'm tired."

I had no idea what I was standing there for. I hovered over his bed.

He took his arm from his eyes. "Turn off the lights."

"I couldn't heal her," I said. "I should've healed her."

"It was her time." He put the arm back over his face. "No one can control a fate that's written. Not even you."

Someone knocked on the door. I locked it.

"I should've been able to heal her."

"It was written." He turned over on his side and curled up like a baby. "Go to sleep."

"I won't—" I didn't know how to finish the sentence.

Ayya sighed. "Don't be a child, Kalki."

"I won't do the pooja tomorrow. I can't pretend anymore."

"You're not pretending." He kept his face hidden, the important parts of him all curled up out of sight. "You helped people today."

"I can't heal anyone."

"You healed Roopa."

The named doused me. I sat on my bed. I remembered the frail little girl looking like a skeleton laid out before me.

"What about the white stuff you and Kantha Chithappa put on her tongue every day? Was it medicine?"

"It was vibhuthi."

"It was medicine."

"Go to bed," Ayya said. He sounded tired, his breathing shallow. He closed his eyes. "One more day, and we can go away from this awful city."

I laid on top of the covers. I hadn't brushed my teeth, hadn't had dinner. But my body was lethargic, and I didn't know what else to do. I stayed there until sleep came.

2

Our second stop on the world tour was New York City. From my vantage point on the plane, the whole Earth seemed to slide beneath me, small and bright. It jangled in my brain to not feel like a god anymore, but to be able to see things like a god because I was sitting inside a flying machine. I was further away from myself than I was from the rest of the world.

New York City traffic rivaled Delhi. Instead of auto rickshaws, yellow cars flirted at the curbs. Buildings climbed impossibly high. With my face pressed to the glass of the car we took from the airport, I couldn't see where the buildings ended near the clouds. Garbage crusted every sidewalk. There were more types of people here than I'd ever seen, in all colors and shapes. You couldn't tell a person's religion by what they wore or how they groomed themselves. They were a mangled mass of bodies, passing each other under the low gray sky.

We held a pooja in Queens, on a street lined by identical white houses with identical patches of brown grass in front. In a tent attached to the side of a small marble temple, I sat on a raised dais. It was late spring in the US, but the tent sweltered with the heat of a hundred people crammed inside.

Ayya began by telling my devotees how I'd passed all three of my trials according to the *Sri Kalki Purana* when I was ten. People came up to seek my blessings. They told me their complaints. If these were small requests, I did quick healing sessions or prayers. Some people wanted to take their pictures with me; others wanted to touch my feet. I handed out kumkumam, turmeric, sandalwood powder from the ashram to each of the devotees, blessed them, and listened to their stories. Ayya gave each person five minutes, after which he ushered them away. Every hour, I took a ten-minute break while a music group played bhajan songs.

It had been four days since the car crash in Delhi, and doubt had grown like a weed in my brain. I'd believed so earnestly in my healing prayer when I was young. But after seeing the woman die in Delhi, I was sure that I was giving people nothing more than false hope.

When I returned to the dais, a man turned the corner into my vision, a few spots behind the front of the line. He was a young Indian man—tall, well-muscled, beautiful, curly-haired. He kept grinning at me. I tried to focus on my tasks, on the devotees in front of me, but I couldn't stop thinking that this young man looked familiar.

When he came to the front, he stood gaping at me for a few seconds before he spoke. His hair was long on the top of his head, with the sides shaved close. His broad shoulders strained at the seams of his yellow plaid shirt. He looked astonished, but not in an awed way like the other devotees who sought my blessings. Something about his smile, crooked at one corner, was so, so familiar.

"Kalki." He said my name without the respectful "Sami" at the end, as though he was a friend of mine. His voice woke something in my brain. "Do you recognize me?" He said it in English, with an American accent.

If he'd stayed at the ashram, I wouldn't have forgotten him.

"It's me," he said, still in English. He looked to where Ayya was talking with the next person in line and whispered, "It's me, Lakshman."

The name sank through my consciousness, and the voice—his father's voice, grating and raspy.

Lakshman kept smiling that same smile with one side of his face, and I recognized that, too, that impish look he always had when he was little, like he had something to hide.

I stood up, wanting to hug him but wondering if I should. The people at the front of the line looked up. The music group gathered their instruments. They all thought I was about to take a break. Lakshman gestured for me to sit.

I wanted to jump out of my bones. I wanted to hug him tight and grab him by the hand and run right out of the temple and into the new world of the city. Instead, I sat.

"I don't want to deal with Ayya," he whispered. "When I heard you'd be here, I wanted to see you."

"I'm glad you came," I said in English. I hadn't noticed my accent before this. My vowels sounded so warped next to his, my consonants so hard.

"I have so much to tell you. Can you come to my apartment? Will Ayya let you?"

"If I tell him, we can both come."

"No," he said. "Just you."

"I'm not allowed."

Ayya moved in. I saw him out of the corner of my vision. Lakshman's five minutes were up.

"Here," Lakshman said. He watched Ayya, too, stepping away slowly before he was asked to leave. He held out a folded piece of paper. "Read this. And come find me. There's so much I have to tell you."

I took the paper, and Ayya ushered Lakshman away with no note of recognition. Near the exit, Lakshman turned back and gave me his familiar crooked smile.

I tucked the paper under my knee as I sat. I had to see three more people before I could take a break, so I tried to focus to not arouse Ayya's suspicion. I tried to concentrate on what each person was saying. I did my healing prayer for them while my brain did cartwheels on the ceiling.

On my break, I read the paper in the bathroom. It was a copy of a newspaper article, an old one not more than a paragraph long.

CHARLESTON GAZETTE-MAIL NEWS BRIEFS: LOCAL WOMAN GIVES BIRTH TO BLUE-SKINNED BABY BOY
by Geoff Bouvier, Staff Reporter

CHARLESTON – A local mom expected a boy, but nothing like this: deep blue skin, from his tiny head to his tiny toes. Elizabeth Adcock gave birth on Saturday to what her doctors at Beth Israel called "the most unusual newborn they've ever seen," a healthy son whose skin is the color of a mountain lake. Due to a recessive genetic condition called methemoglobinemia, the little guy is one baby who'll be easy to find in any maternity ward. "It's the strangest thing," said one nurse, who asked to have her name withheld. "He sounds and acts perfectly normal, but then you look at him, and it's chilling, really. He seems otherworldly." In fact, there is only one other documented case of this rare genetic phenomenon in US history, from thirty years ago in Kentucky. This blue, otherworldly infant will be living a very different life soon, since his young, unwed mother has given him up for adoption, and an East Indian doctor and his wife from Trenton, New Jersey have chosen to love him as one of their own.

Underneath the article, someone had written, *2409 Clarendon Rd., Apt. 3C, Brooklyn. Beverly Rd stop on 2.*

My hands shook so much, I couldn't fold the paper back along its crease. I was adopted. I balled it up and stuck it in the waistband of my veshti, where the tailor had sewed in a small pocket. I had no question this story was about me. How many blue babies were born into this world and adopted by Indian doctors?

Amma, Ayya, Lakshman, the bond I'd always felt with them—I wasn't their son or brother. I wasn't Indian. I was the son of a teenage white lady who had given me away.

I went back to the temple to finish my healing, but I was no longer present. My head whirled in dizzying circles, picturing the newspaper clipping again and again. A blue baby. Born in West Virginia. Born here, in the United States. I spun faster and faster, and when I held my head still in the hopes that I wouldn't pass out, the world started spinning instead. My blue skin was the result of a genetic disorder. I was adopted. Ayya had lied, and Amma had lied too. I didn't know how to deal with that last part—Amma's lying. She had looked me in the face and lied I didn't know how many times. She'd propped up Ayya's absurd theory about me being a god. This meant that, by extension, I'd tricked and lied to hundreds if not thousands of people. And now, Lakshman, whom I'd thought I'd never see again, was back, and he knew all about the lies. He was going to tell me the truth. I knew I had to hear it, no matter what.

I read the newspaper article that Lakshman had given me again and again that evening in the hotel room I shared with Ayya. My stomach, a solid mass, pulled me down to the ground.

Once Ayya fell asleep, I rose in the hotel-room dark, snuck his black canvas bag into the bathroom, and looked through its many pockets. I found two passports held together with a rubber band. The first one was mine, the pages empty except for Canadian and

American visas pasted into it and stamps showing when we arrived in the US. I also found my birth certificate from the Madurai hospital, which I'd seen before. But folded up inside that was another piece of paper. I smoothed it out on the toilet seat cover. It was a thick, yellowed paper pressed with a raised seal. Another birth certificate.

Office of Vital Records, Charleston, West Virginia. I held it side by side with Lakshman's article.

NAME: JOSEPH ROBERT PRATT. MOTHER: ELIZABETH ADCOCK. FATHER: JOSEPH CHARLES PRATT.

My fingertips were so numb and cold, I couldn't feel the paper I was holding. Sweat rolled from my armpits. My real name was Joseph. Nothing made sense anymore.

I put everything back the way I'd found it inside Ayya's bag, except for the real birth certificate and fifteen hundred dollars of American money I took from his wallet, half of the roll I found. I put the birth certificate and stolen money into a small satchel that I carried around, which already held my sandalwood and turmeric and other things I needed for minor healing prayers—Ayya had made me pack the satchel in case anyone asked me for healing on the street.

I returned Ayya's bag to its place on the table. Tomorrow after temple, Ayya would be taking me to see the city. But I had to find Lakshman now. I'd been given half of a map that led to a place I hadn't realized I needed to go. Lakshman had more secrets for me; I was sure.

I could get back to the hotel before Ayya woke in the morning, or not. Maybe I wouldn't try to return. I didn't care anymore. I could sense my own young self coming back around to meet me, a hopeful blue boy with a laughing Lakshman by his side, two young boys trying to tell me . . . something. As I snuck out into the hallway of the hotel, I almost saw them both—my young self and little Lakshman, standing at the foot of Ayya's bed, pointing at me and whispering.

I shut the door behind me and walked alone into the night.

3

In the years since that day in New York City, since my life broke in two, I've learned about more childgods than I could've ever imagined from my little mango tree courtyard room. They all have one thing in common: the adults in their lives get to them young, so they don't know any better. No more than three or four years old. That's the secret. You have to take them before they can learn to disagree, before their brains have been hardened by the world. Get them while they're soft, and you can make them into gods.

A village in Nepal chooses a new girl every generation to be their living goddess—a Kumari—until she reaches puberty. I met one of these girls, now a woman, a month after I got to New York City, and she told me about all the trials she had to endure to qualify, and how when she started puberty, they stripped her of her godly title, as was tradition.

After I met the Kumari in New York, I reached out to other childgods. Most of them liked to brag, or their keepers did. In Nebraska, I talked to a little boy of seven who told me he had been to heaven.

He recited it like a story he'd learned. All the while, he turned his curious eyes away from my blue skin. I could tell he wanted to ask me about it, but his mother sat next to us, hawklike, and the boy kept silent, gears turning in that soft little brain. That had been me, years ago. Whenever journalists would interview me, Ayya was always present, watching.

A teenage boy in Indonesia had convinced the locals that he could anticipate the weather. He lived in a village in the mountains where they didn't have TV. The boy's family demanded a share of all the farmers' crops as payment for their protection.

In Nigeria, a girl's parents had died in a mysterious fire, which she had survived under unknown circumstances. She was believed to have the power of prophecy, thanks to her parents' lingering ghostly presence inside her skull.

Recently, I read an article about a young girl in India, the only one of a pair of ischiopagus conjoined twins who survived, who had four arms and four legs. Because she had a parasitic twin fused with her body, some organs in her body turned necrotic, and she suffered from frequent fevers and illnesses. Thirty-one physicians collaborated on the first stage of an operation to separate her twin from her body. But before they could operate, the villagers of her community insisted that she was the goddess incarnate, and some said that to operate would be heresy.

I didn't doubt that some of these children believed in their own divinity. I had certainly believed, back in those days with Ayya at the ashram. But, like me, these childgods were scams. The boy in Nebraska recanted his story after five years, two book deals, and a movie. The teen from Indonesia stopped answering my emails after I probed into his methods of telling the weather. Science could explain all of their weird stories and strange beliefs.

For years, I had such inordinate rage inside me. I felt guilty about it, too, because I had been one of the ones doing the conning. I had been lying to people my whole life. But I was also a victim, since the adults in my life had brainwashed me into believing I was a god. I was mad at Amma and furious at Ayya. But I wasn't just angry at those who tried to con children into conning the world. I was also angry at the world for believing it.

4

That night in New York City, when I was alone—really alone—for the first time in my life, I was vulnerable, scared, excited, confused, and angry all at once. But I was free. I had no direction, no schedule, no one to answer to. In the late-night, early-morning streets of New York, I could've gone anywhere.

At first, I walked quickly through the cool air, as though Ayya might have woken up and come to find me. I had no idea where I was or where I was headed, but something about the uniformity of the buildings and how high they were all around me made me feel protected. It was like the city was holding me in its arms. At this hour, there were only the giant street sweeper machines scraping noisily by the traffic lights that changed colors for no one, the stray homeless person or two sleeping in heaps under awnings, the garbage truck, and windows and concrete everywhere.

I walked in an emotional haze for over an hour before I realized I didn't know where I was going. My feet hurt from walking on all the pavement. The city was still lit up—streetlights, windows, fronts of buildings, the lone car or two that passed. And in the sky, the faintest morning light started to peek out from between the buildings.

I stopped and took out the address Lakshman had given me. I had no idea where Beverly Road was, or Brooklyn, and I had no clue how to read the subway maps. I found a park with benches, and I sat down, and before I knew it, I was asleep.

When I woke up, the city woke up all around me. Cars honked, people walked, and the night chill burned out of the air.

A man sold fruit at a stand on the sidewalk. He looked Indian, old and balding in a dark blue Yankees ballcap and matching windbreaker. Comforted by a familiar face, I walked over to him with the hope of hearing a familiar language.

"Can you tell me how to get here?" I asked in English.

"You want some mangoes?" he asked. "Best mangoes in New York."

I repeated the question in Hindi. His face changed. He looked me up and down and held out his hand for the address. I handed him the piece of paper.

"Why are you blue?" he asked me in Hindi. He scanned the headline of the newspaper article. "Is this you?"

"Do you know the address?"

He adjusted his Yankees hat. "Take the F to Manhattan, then back into Brooklyn. Then I think you need to take the B and then . . . the 2? Or get off the F at Lexington and take the Q. Or I guess the M could take you there, too, to the Q. Any way you cut it, you'll have to go through Manhattan, unless you want to chance the buses."

"Can you say that again?"

"Take the F," he said slowly, pointing down the street. "I'll write it down." He scribbled down directions in Hindi below Lakshman's handwriting and handed me back the paper.

I got lost on the subway and rode the trains for hours. People mostly ignored me, but some noticed my skin. I asked for directions from a young woman who, in return, asked if she could touch my face.

"Are you blushing?" she asked as she trailed her fingers over my cheeks. "Your cheeks are turning bluer."

Lakshman lived in a brown brick building with an old, faded oak tree out front, growing out of the sidewalk. I pressed the doorbell for apartment 3C and waited.

He opened the door. I still couldn't believe how much older he'd gotten. I hadn't yet grown accustomed to his adult face, which looked both familiar and new. The round cheeks of his childhood were gone, leaving his face angular. He was handsome, framed by a bush of curly black hair. I'd only known him with long hair like mine. He had grown taller than me, and much more muscular.

"You came," he said in English. Again I noticed his American accent, and again it surprised me to hear it.

When we hugged, I could barely wrap my arms around his wide, muscled shoulders. He smelled like soap and something astringent.

"Ayya would never let me come," I said. "So I ran away." The words felt new and wrong. "I ran away."

"Slow down," he said in English. "I can't understand Tamil so well."

"What?"

"I forgot most of it."

My quell of panic trickled away, replaced by awkward confusion. In his presence, my mouth wouldn't form English words easily, though I was fluent. I twisted my tongue to ask, "You forgot Tamil?" in English.

He shrugged and led me up a set of old black-and-white marble stairs. The building had been grand once, but was now in disrepair.

The scratched fleur-de-lis wallpaper peeled along the edges of walls, and the wooden doors of the apartments had thickened with many layers of paint accrued over decades of tenants.

"I share with my girlfriend and her ex," he said. "You can crash on the couch, if you're staying. Are you staying?"

"I can stay tonight. If you're free." I didn't have a plan. I didn't know what I'd been thinking. I'd just wanted so badly to get away. And now I was here, with no prospects for the future.

"We've got a gig tonight," Lakshman said, "but you can come."

I heard shouting behind a door on the third floor—a man's voice, and a woman's. The strings of a guitar floated above the yelling.

"How are your parents?" I asked.

Lakshman avoided my eyes. "Fine," he said. "In New Jersey."

He opened the door next to the one where the shouting was coming from, and I got a whiff of ganja smoke. I knew the smell from Brad's room, where it had permeated every piece of fabric he owned.

The apartment was small. A weathered couch and table had been squeezed into the tiny front room. Large band posters hung on the walls, unframed and held on with nails. In a corner, a closed door; a small, olive-colored kitchen; a black-and-white-tiled bathroom; and a set of old French doors that opened into a bedroom crowded with a desk and chair and clothes all over the floor.

The first person I saw was an androgynous-looking East Asian person, with a square jaw and short black hair gelled into spikes. Next to them on the blue, overstuffed plaid couch sat a dark-skinned Indian woman with a guitar across her lap, her facial features small and dainty. She had tattoos all over her arms and purple hair cut asymmetrically to fall over one side of her face. Her thick bottom lip was pierced twice with black metal rings.

"This is M," Lakshman said. "Meera. My girlfriend."

The Indian woman stood up, walked around the table, and

hugged me. "Just M, please." She kissed both my cheeks. I blinked in the fog of her smell, which, unlike the women I was used to, was unadorned by anything floral or fake. She smiled showing all her teeth.

"That's Han," Lakshman said.

The East Asian person smiled and said, "Well, aren't you a sight?" She stood up and hugged me, too, the roughness of her plaid shirt rubbing against my skin. Her stocky body held more muscle than I'd expected. If I'd seen her on the street, I might have assumed she was a teenage boy, but up close I found her handsome, even attractive.

"I use both she and they pronouns," Han said. "Whatever's easiest."

"I'll explain it to you later," Lakshman said.

Han winked at me. "Just don't ever call me a woman and we'll be golden."

"And this, of course," Lakshman said, "is Kalki, my cousin from India."

"The blue-skinned god," M said. "Do you want a beer?"

Something about the way she held herself, leaning on her hip, reminded me of Roopa.

"Kalki doesn't drink," Lakshman said. He turned to me. "Do you?"

"No." But I was curious. I wished he'd ask again. I wasn't a god. Now that I knew the truth, a whole world of possibilities opened up for me.

"Come sit," Han said. She patted the space next to her on the sofa.

M sat on the other side of me, and I hoped I wouldn't sweat, flanked by the two of them.

"Tell me about India," M said. "Tell me about the ashram."

"Aren't you from India?" I asked.

"My parents are," she said. "I've never been."

"You should go."

She gave a quick glance in the direction of the kitchen, where Lakshman puttered around. "I don't think so." She wrinkled her nose like she'd smelled something bad. "I don't think it's for me."

I'd never met anyone who didn't like India before. All the visitors at the ashram raved about their travels across the country.

"Why don't you think it's for you?" I asked.

Lakshman came with two dark glass bottles of what I assumed was beer. M cracked one open and took a deep swig.

"My parents hated it there," she said. "It's still home for them, but they haven't been back, either, since they left, and that was thirty years ago."

Lakshman fell heavily into a couch seat and leaned forward. "She's Dalit," he said. "You know, caste-wise."

Like a knee-jerk, I remembered her kissing me on the cheeks, and immediately felt ashamed of myself for not kissing her back. Upper-caste Hindus, especially Brahmins, thought that Dalits, the lowest caste on the ladder they'd invented, shouldn't be touched by members of any caste, in any situation. No Dalits had ever come to the ashram, nor did any live in the village, as far as I knew.

M twisted her face as if she tasted something bitter. "My parents were educated, but it was hard for them. You should hear some of the stories they tell about school—being asked to clean the cafeteria, being ignored by their peers, having to sit in a separate section from their classmates, sometimes even on the classroom floor. And *their* parents—my grandparents—cleaned shit from the Chennai rail station." She looked into my eyes. "Would you go back to a country that thinks the only job you deserve is picking up human shit?"

"No," I said. I'd never thought much about caste. I'd never had to, as someone at the top of the heap. But Lakshman—a Brahmin, my own cousin—was dating a Dalit woman. The enormity of that was hard to grasp. I wondered what his parents thought. And Ayya . . . he'd be beyond livid that our pure Brahmin blood was mixing with that of Dalits. But then again, I reminded myself, I wasn't a Brahmin. I was adopted. I was white.

Lakshman, to ease the tension and change the subject, I was sure, told the story of the horses that magically appeared at the ashram, while M and Han listened with interest.

"It had to be those jeep tracks," he said. "They delivered the horses while we went to get water."

"That many horses?" Han said. "That seems improbable. How do you know they didn't come to him like everyone believed?"

Lakshman laughed into a beer. "So you're saying you think he's divine?"

I tried to figure whether there was something mean under that laugh of his, but this new Lakshman was someone I didn't know, and it was hard to gauge his intentions.

Maybe, said a voice in my head, *maybe it all meant nothing. Maybe there was no grand plan.* Not having a plan—after twenty-two years of my life being planned out to the smallest detail—was terrifying.

"I'm just saying there's a hole in your theory," Han said. "Tell me more, Kalki."

I found it easy to talk about the ashram, feeling more and more aware of my thick Indian accent as I continued. The stories helped me push out of my mind any thoughts of Ayya waking up in the hotel without me, and the wickedness of the decision I'd made. This now, I told myself, think later. It wasn't like I couldn't go back. Ayya would be furious, but I could always go back.

I told Han and M stories that I knew Lakshman would remember, stories about playing scenes from the *Mahabharata* and about that time we'd played cricket with the boys from the village. I talked about the Deputy, and Brad, and the expansion of the ashram.

And I told them, in a flat, emotionless voice that surprised me, that Amma had died.

At that, Lakshman put his face in his hands.

M touched my arm, and her face told me this touch was a test. I tried not to flinch or pull away. The knowledge that she was Dalit sat deep in me somewhere, waking up a prejudice Ayya had instilled a long time ago. But if Lakshman hadn't told me, I wouldn't have known. I reminded myself it didn't matter.

"Tell me you're coming to the show tonight," she said. "Do you want to come? They'll love you. Lakshman's told you about the band, right?" At my headshake, she pursed her lips. "The three of us are in a band with this other dude named Jason. We're playing a show tonight at Zoo Bar. It's a pretty big deal. You'll come, right?"

"Don't force him." Lakshman rubbed his nose with the back of his hand. "He might have other plans."

Lakshman had outshined me at music back at the ashram. I missed his bhajan songs, the way he could hit the high notes as a kid, how the ragas sounded in his voice.

"I want to hear you play," I said. "I'll come."

Han took the guitar from M, and we listened as she played complicated note progressions and chords while Lakshman sang melodies over the strings.

A few hours later, after a nap and a shower and a lunch of something Lakshman made called "stir-fry," I sat on his bed while he tried on shirts in front of a mirror he'd propped up against the wall. He'd told me he was a student at NYU, studying urban planning. His walls were covered with maps, old and new—escalation maps of the city, maps showing the island in the 1700s, some showing the rivers, others the subway system.

He held up a black tie in front of a black T-shirt with artful rips on the sleeves. He scowled and threw it back down on the bed.

If I didn't diligently steer my mind away from such thoughts, Ayya loomed in my brain around every corner. I had run away. I had disrespected him and screwed up the world tour. The longer I stayed away from him, the more there would be no going back.

But I didn't want to think about that. I clicked my mind back to Lakshman and the utter mystery of what would happen tonight.

I watched his graceful limbs and toned body. I was used to being shirtless because that was part of my outfit at the ashram, but my body was soft, pliant—not like Lakshman's, where the skin sat close to the muscle, tripping over every shape. I was glad I was covered up and that it was Lakshman who was walking around shirtless, trying on different tops over his torn jeans. I wondered if he knew how defined his abs were.

"So how are you feeling?" he asked. "About everything?"

Everything covered a lot of ground. I was having trouble holding anything in my head at this point. I tried to find the right English word for it. "Numb," I said.

He stopped pulling a shirt off a hanger and smirked at me. Behind him, his small closet was messier than any I'd ever seen— shirts and pants spilling from white plastic drawers and piled on the floor.

"You didn't really believe it, did you?" he asked.

"Believe?"

"You didn't really believe you were a god, right? I always thought you'd have figured it out by now."

It was getting hard to think. I didn't know if Ayya had truly believed, or if Amma had—if they'd adopted me to love me, or if they'd planned from the start to use me to make money. Ayya might have been a monster all along, but I couldn't think that way of Amma.

"I bet Ayya's having a fit," Lakshman said. He looked overjoyed at the thought. "He deserves it. He deserves to be alone and angry."

Lakshman turned back to his closet and stood with his hands on his hips, looking a lot like Kantha Chithappa, his father. I wished I could turn back time and have the little boy I knew who would climb into my bed again, not this stranger I half-recognized.

"You read the newspaper clipping, right?" he asked. "What did you think?"

It was still in my pocket, but I didn't take it out. I'd read it so many times, I had it memorized. "I wish I'd known about it earlier," I said. "When did you find out?"

He shrugged. "Appa told me you were adopted a few years ago. And he said you were adopted from here. I looked around, checked out old archives. It's not hard to find a blue-skinned baby."

Lakshman, still shirtless, stood in front of me. From my angle on the bed, he looked gigantic.

"I'm glad you came, Kalki. It's really good to see you." He grinned, and for a minute, a ghost of the old Lakshman lived in his face. He ruffled my hair. "We can cut your hair if you want. It's not like you're a real Brahmin priest." He sighed at the floor covered in little balls of shirts he'd tried and discarded. "I think I'll skip the shirt tonight."

Cutting my hair felt like a step too far, and if I did decide to go back, Ayya would be even angrier. *But on the other hand*, said a voice in my head, *it's just hair*. It would grow back.

"What's your band called?" I asked.

Lakshman rubbed his neck. "Well, that's the thing you need to know. It's—the thing is, there are so many bands in the city, and we needed a way to stand out, be memorable to our fans, you know." He grabbed a few shirts from the floor and stuffed them into a drawer in his closet. "We're called the Blue-Skinned Gods."

My heart jumped. Warmth spread all over my chest and up my neck.

"We started out—well, we started out all painting ourselves blue, but it got weird with Han and Jason doing it. Seemed offensive, you know? So now me and M are the only ones who do it, since we're Indian. And M only when she feels like it."

"You paint yourself blue?"

"Are you angry? I won't do it tonight. Will it make you mad?"

"Don't change your performance because of me."

He sat heavily on the bed. "I didn't really think about it much when I first did it." He leaned his elbows on his knees. "And then it was too late. Everyone expects it. It's why they come."

"Can I see?" I forced my tongue around the dryness in my mouth. "Can I see how you paint your skin?"

He rubbed the back of his neck again, avoiding eye contact. "You can help if you want." He walked to the bathroom door. "Usually M helps me."

I followed him. In the living room, M and Han were sharing a joint and reading the same thick book I couldn't see the title of, held open in between them. The bathroom was small and cramped. M's muffled laughter reached us through the old wooden door.

Lakshman opened the cabinet under the sink and grabbed a bottle of bright blue liquid. He pulled out a small white machine with a tube and an end that looked like a futuristic pen. He put the blue bottle into an opening in the machine, plugged it in, and stepped into the bathtub.

He stripped down to his underwear. I folded the clothes he handed to me. He showed me how to use the machine to spray the blue paint onto his skin.

"Small, even strokes," he said. "Two layers should do it."

I sprayed his back first. The machine was temperamental, laying down too thick in some places and too thin in others. I tried to spray even, quick strokes two layers thick all over his skin.

"Appa will want to see you," he said.

I paused my work on the backs of his arms.

"Kantha Chithappa's here?"

"He lives in Jersey, but we could take the train over."

He turned, and I started painting his chest. He was half a head taller than me, more because of the added height of the bathtub. The air thickened. We were so close. I tried to think of him as the young boy I knew, but he wasn't, not anymore. He was a familiar stranger standing so close that his smell made me lightheaded.

"Where's Vasanthy Chithy?" I asked.

He was silent for a few seconds. "She's dead." His skin smelled like the beer he'd drank earlier and the ganja from the living room. "Didn't you know?"

I blinked fast. "When?"

"A few months after we left India. The cancer was too advanced by the time we got her treatment." His voice was even, practiced.

I waited to see if he'd mention the healing sessions at the ashram, but he didn't say anything. I clamped my mouth shut and continued to paint his chest, the front of his arms, down his abdomen, up his neck, and onto his face. I gripped the sprayer with both hands. The color was a brighter blue than my skin had ever been, the sort of blue that Krishna's skin appears in paintings.

When I was done, Lakshman held out his hand next to mine and said, "We finally look like cousins."

After we cleaned up the blue paint—M declared she wasn't going to paint herself that night—I sat in the tub while Lakshman cut my hair. He clipped off my ponytail and handed it to me. I clutched it tight to my chest while he did the rest. This seemed like a monumental change. Little curls of brown hair fell around me onto the white glaze of the tub. I reminded myself that hair would grow back, but it felt like I was stepping off a cliff.

For the show at Zoo Bar, Lakshman had me dress in his clothes, claiming that mine would make me stand out. The city was sticky and hot, but he gave me jeans and a long-sleeved shirt to wear.

"To cover your skin," he said.

Lakshman, M, Han, and I made our way to the train and rolled across town, and in the sudden glare of the fluorescent train car, I was grateful for the clothes and the way the others huddled around me.

Outside, the night hid my skin color. There were still people everywhere—on the streets, on the subway platform, on the train itself.

"What if Ayya finds me?" I said at one point, fear twisting my lungs into balls of string.

"You're in New York." Lakshman spread out his arms, like he was taking the whole city into a great big hug. "He's not going to find you out of millions of people."

At Zoo Bar, the door was blocked by dusty velvet rope. A crowd of people stood in a line that stretched around the block. Some of the women in line wore pottus, large sparkly ones they'd stuck right in the middle of their foreheads. They yelled as we passed them. Lakshman and Han high-fived some people as they walked.

At the door, a surly woman in a black shirt let us in.

"They're out early tonight," M said. "We should get in costume."

Lakshman carried a bag he'd packed earlier in his room with the kinds of things I normally wore when I met devotees.

"Do you need help?" I asked.

He shook his head and disappeared into a room behind the stage.

Backstage, I met Jason, a Black, thick-set, bearded man who thought my skin color was the greatest thing he'd ever seen.

"Holy shit! Look at you. Our band's come to life!" he said. He wore thick black eyeliner. "I'm a hugger. Can I hug you?"

We listened to the opening band play a few terrible, loud songs as the crowd swelled in size. The band wasn't very good, but Jason, a clear music lover, kept finding nice things to say. He called it "grunge" music. It was heavy on guitar and screaming, and I couldn't really tell what any of the lyrics were.

After the opening band finished playing, a few big men from the club set up the equipment Jason had brought in his van. I stood backstage, not knowing what to do, sipping a club soda, which tasted salty and bubbly and like it was burning my tongue. M appeared next to me and put her hand on my arm. She wore Indian jewelry and a loose tank top that revealed an outline of the tattoo she had on her chest—a semicircle of letters that spelled out *untouchable*.

"Are you ready?" she asked. A wide, sideways grin brightened her face.

The crowd had begun stamping and chanting, "Blue-Skinned Gods! Blue-Skinned Gods!"

The lights dimmed. The stage glowed. I found a seat at the bar behind the crowd as Lakshman emerged onto the stage, his skin electric-blue, his chest bare over torn jeans. The crowd went wild. He wore jewelry—a thick gold bangle on each of his wrists, earrings, and a collection of thin chains around his neck. People kept on cheering as M, Han, and Jason entered. M sat at the drum set. Han and Jason strapped on guitars.

"Thanks for coming out tonight," Lakshman said into the microphone. His voice filled up the room. "We are the Blue-Skinned Gods!"

The room erupted in more noise.

They played the kind of music that I'd heard from white visitors at the ashram, music that Brad would've liked. Lots of drums battling electric guitar and bass, and a raspy, energetic, and simultaneously crooning melody. Later, I would understand this music was called post-punk. I sat at the bar and hoped no one could notice my skin. I needn't have worried at all. In the radiance from the stage, everyone's skin looked blue.

Lakshman's voice was beautiful, though he made it hoarse and low for the music they played. While he sang, he jumped around onstage. M banged her head as she drummed, Han stood in a wide-legged stance and held the guitar up high, and Jason did a two-step dance and spun around so much I was worried the cord of his bass guitar would trip him. In between songs, Lakshman smiled and winked at the fans, asked them how they were, and told them charming little stories about the band's adventures.

The songs were bizarre, irreverence their entire point. One song had two lyrical lines repeated over and over: "Two pigs in a bucket! Fuck it!" Another song was called "Hairy Krishna," which made me laugh, and another included the phrase "taking a poop in an abandoned mine."

"You're with the band, right?" the bartender asked. He set a glass of beer in front of me. "On the house."

I took it and held it without drinking. At least it helped me blend in. Somewhere during the third song, I got curious and sipped the beer. It tasted like cool, fizzing, liquid bread that had gone bad. I kept sipping, and the more the bubbles numbed my tongue, the easier it was to drink. Guilt tried to sneak in, but I kept drinking.

Most of the world believes, and has always believed, in some sort of divine being or beings, whether that's a single, omniscient God, or many gods in complicated pantheons, or localized nature deities. But the number of people who had grown up believing they were divine beings themselves was very few. Later in life, when I told people about my upbringing, they often wondered what it does to a person to believe themselves a god.

Sitting in the bar drinking my first beer, I didn't know what I believed. We'd talked about it backstage before the show. Lakshman alleged that gods don't exist, that science is all we have. M said she didn't know, that there is no way to know or prove the existence or nonexistence of a god or gods, and Han agreed with her. Jason thought it didn't matter whether there is a god or not, because to be good human beings, we should always act like a benevolent god is watching. He told me this is known as Pascal's wager, named after the philosopher and mathematician Blaise Pascal, who believed that the best cost-benefit analysis pointed to us living our lives as if a god exists, because if god exists, we're in the clear, and if god doesn't exist, we don't lose much by being good people.

I didn't know anymore if I believed in a god or gods, but Hinduism is more than the existence of divine beings. Hindu philosophy is also about karma, reincarnation, dharma, maya, and moksha—all forces within the universe that exist independently of our large pantheon of gods. Karma, the sum total of the good and bad choices we make in life. Reincarnation, the cycle of birth and rebirth, where we live out the rewards and punishments for our karma. Dharma, the righteous path. Maya, the illusions of the world that tempt us into veering off our dharma. Moksha, the self-actualization that leads to the final release from our reincarnation cycle.

In Hinduism, these concepts are laws of the universe, like gravity or thermodynamics. Some believe the gods created those laws, and some believe the laws created the gods. What they agree on is that gods, by nature of being gods, are exempt from many of these laws—they don't reincarnate except when they want to, they can see through the illusionary temptations of the universe, they don't accumulate karma, and they always behave righteously.

But I wasn't a god, and I didn't know what that meant for me and these laws. And now that I knew M, I could no longer ignore caste—as much as I tried, I couldn't account for the positive points of a religion like Hinduism that would condemn an entire set of people because of their spot on an imaginary ladder.

For me, everything about religion was connected to Ayya and his teachings. And if he'd lied about me being a god, maybe he'd also lied about the existence of gods in general, and if he'd lied about that, maybe he'd also lied about the laws of the universe. What I did trust was the feeling I had deep inside me that said I wished to break free from him. I decided, sitting in the pounding half-darkness of the bar with my eardrums jumping, that it was time for me to start trying everything.

After the band's set, half the people in the bar filtered outside to smoke. Lakshman came and bumped me with his elbow.

"How many have you had?" he asked.

I couldn't feel my fingers from the cold of the glass.

"Three," I said in Tamil, and held up fingers to help him. I wobbled on my feet. "It tastes like burps."

Lakshman took the glass out of my hand and gulped down the rest of the beer. He was starting to sweat out the blue paint. In between splotches on his jaw and neck, his own tawny skin showed through. He put the glass back on the bar.

"Two more, please," he said to the bartender.

The bartender slid over two full glasses, and Lakshman handed me one.

"Should we toast to something?" he said.

My thoughts traveled through the sludge of beer in my head. I struggled to put the words together in English.

"Fuck it," he said. "Here's to being blue." He clinked my glass with his and drank.

Two beers later, the room swayed so hard I had to lean my arms on the bar to keep myself steady. Lakshman had done shots, saying he wanted to catch up. People kept coming up to him to talk about his music. Finally, he was telling M and Han that same horse story about the ashram, and I was overcome by sadness as I thought about my horse Arjuna—who I might never see again—and the times when Lakshman and I were children. A thousand sensations crowded themselves into my brain. The room continued tilting this way and that.

"He got the white horse," Lakshman was saying. He bumped me with his elbow. "Wait, shit. Did Ayya kill that cat on purpose to distract us?"

My head, too full to hold up, dropped onto the bar.

"Hey, what was the name of the girl who came to the ashram?" Lakshman asked. "The one you healed?"

"Roopa," I said.

"Roopa, yeah. My first love. I was ready to fight him for her."

"Women aren't prizes," M said.

The world was a vibrating, trembling mass holding off my sadness. Lakshman poked me. "Whatever happened to Roopa?"

"Roopa," I said. The word came out slurry and slow. I tried to say more, but my mouth didn't move.

"Did you ever get with her?"

I nodded into the wooden bar.

Lakshman laughed. "Nice. Was she hot?"

"Fuck the both of you," M said.

Han frowned, her arms crossed over her chest.

"What?" he said. "I just want to know if she was hot."

"Don't be a shithead," M said.

"I love her," I said. The rest of the thought came out in Tamil. "I'm going to marry her."

"Seriously?" he said. He clinked his glass against mine, which was sitting on the bar, still full. "Cheers, machan."

His word startled me. Machan. Cousin. I hadn't realized how weird it was, not speaking Tamil with Lakshman, until this word.

Han wound her arms around mine. "Let's get you home. Help me."

Lakshman downed his glass, and then mine. He and Han supported me on either side, and together they helped me walk out with M to Jason's van parked in the alley behind the bar.

I woke up in Lakshman's bed, my shoes off and the blankets wrapped around me. It was well past noon, judging by the light clamoring into the room. Someone was tapping my shoulder.

"You need a shower," M said. Her face swam into focus.

I sat up, and the minute I moved, I felt the wetness on my chest.

"You puked in your sleep," she said.

I smelled it, that acrid, tangy mixture of beer and bile and Lakshman's leftover stir-fry that I'd had after the bar. It was still wet, spewed all over the blanket.

"I brought you some aspirin and water." She pointed at a bottle and a glass on the upside-down crate by the bed.

My head clanged. The whole world was too bright. I tried to open the bottle of pills, but the cap wouldn't come undone. M helped me. I'd never taken pills before. At the ashram, everything was cured with chanting and my healing powers.

"I—I don't know how to swallow them," I said. I was pathetic, a grown man in front of a woman I barely knew, asking for help like a child.

M sat on the bed next to me, shook two pills out of the bottle, and held them out to me. She looked different. She'd pinned back her hair and replaced her nose and lip piercings with clear studs that weren't noticeable at first glance. A white shirt and long black pants covered up her tattoos.

"Open your mouth," she said.

I opened as wide as I could.

"Tilt your head back. I'm going to drop the pills into your throat, and you swallow. Okay?"

I angled my head back, and without warning, she dropped the pills. I choked and spit them back up. They tasted like nothing I'd ever had before, sour and bitter.

We tried again three more times before M held my mouth closed through my violent gagging. I finally swallowed and washed it down with water.

She got up and rummaged in the open closet. "Lakshman will be back soon, and he can show you where to wash the sheets." She took a black belt out of the closet and put it on. "You should clean up."

I wadded up the dirty sheets in a ball and stumbled to the

bathroom to wash myself off in the shower. The hot water started to make me feel better. When I came out in a towel, M was gone, and Han was sitting with her feet up on the table in the living room, drinking coffee from a clear jar. She was dressed in a fitted man's suit with her hair slicked back, and I hardly recognized her.

When she caught me staring, she said, "I have to fly out on Mondays. Tech work. You know, business analyst bullshit."

I didn't know what any of that meant, but I nodded like I understood. I was starving, but it was like my stomach was being punched from multiple directions. I drank more water and started to feel like I was inside my skin again.

Han patted the space next to her on the couch. "Come, sit."

I held the towel closed and sat. She leaned over and ran her fingers up my arm, over my chest. I tried to breathe normally.

She whisked my chest hair this way and that. "So," she said. Her hand traveled down, trailing along my abdomen. My body started to respond.

I stood up in a panic, my hand tight on the knot of the towel.

"I'm going to be sick again," I lied. I closed the door to Lakshman's room behind me and sat on the bed next to the wadded-up sheets. The smell of vomit in the room made me dry heave, but I stayed in there until I heard Han leave for her flight. I had that guilty lump in my stomach again, though I didn't know why. I tried to remind myself that Ayya wasn't here, that he wouldn't find me, and even if he did, he wouldn't know what I'd been up to.

By the time Lakshman came home from class, I had stripped the bed and washed off most of the vomit in the bathroom sink.

"It stinks in here," he said. He dropped his backpack on the floor, next to a bookcase made of wood held between stone bricks.

"I vomited on your bedsheets," I said.

He stopped himself from sitting on the bed and instead plopped down on the one chair in the room. He uncapped a bottle of Sunkist sitting on the drafting table, sniffed it, and drank.

"I forgot I put vodka in here," he said. He held out the bottle to me. "It'll take the edge off the hangover."

I took it and drank. The warm soda burned with an aftertaste that made my head shake.

"Is that the first time you've had alcohol?" he asked. "You were a mess."

I sat on the edge of the bed and drank some more of the soda. I could still feel Han's fingers on me. She was bold in a way that Roopa usually hadn't been. I missed Roopa like a constant ache around my lungs.

"Han, she—" I didn't know how to finish. "She—well, she—"

"Did they come onto you?" He reached for the bottle and gulped the rest of it. He laughed. "I should warn you. Han's polyamorous." At my confused look, he explained. "Han has multiple partners. She travels a lot for work, she's gone during most of the week, and she has casual hookup partners in every city. Don't get involved if you can't handle that." He tossed the empty bottle into a bin and wiped his mouth with the back of his hand. "Do you want to fuck Han?"

The translation came too slow to me, and he kept going.

"If you do, you should," he said.

"What?"

"You should let Han fuck you."

The thought of it made me hard. I turned to hide myself.

Laughing at my discomfort, Lakshman spun his chair back around toward the drafting table, where a half-drawn map of an alleyway park was clipped to the wood. He picked up a pencil and shaded in the foliage of a tree.

I napped and rested all day, and Han came onto me again that night when she flew back from Boston, which I had hoped would happen.

I sat in the living room watching TV while Lakshman worked on his maps in his room. Han walked in and dropped a leather briefcase on the coffee table. She wore cologne I'd only ever smelled on rich men who came to the ashram. The collar of her white shirt had a small yellow stain.

She sank into the seat next to me, too close. At Lakshman's recommendation, I was watching a documentary about an atheist man who, for an experiment, had convinced a bunch of Americans that he was a spiritual guru. He faked a thick Indian accent, wrapped himself in orange cotton, and made up all kinds of yoga poses. The Americans ate it up.

Han leaned over and whispered hot air into my ear. "I want to see how far the blue goes."

I thought of Roopa, of her head on my shoulder the night before she left the ashram, but Han slid a hand up my thigh and I couldn't hold Roopa in the broken teabag of my brain. Han pulled me up and led me toward Lakshman's bedroom.

She leaned on the doorframe. Lakshman glanced up from his drafting table, the bright light of the desk lamp lighting up the edges of his shaggy hair.

"Can we borrow the room for a bit?" she said. "Your bed's bigger."

"I'm in the middle of a map." He gestured toward the map that he had almost all colored in.

"I'll make you bibimbap," she said. "Omma's recipe."

Lakshman gathered up his supplies and his map, walked to the living room, and spread them out on the coffee table. On the TV, the fake guru gave a sermon to his followers.

"You can close the door," Han said to me.

I tried to catch Lakshman's eye, but his head was bent over his map. I shut the door slowly. I tried to wrap my head around all this, but it was happening too fast. I'd had sex with Roopa, but I was in love, and to me that hadn't felt wrong. I barely knew Han. Still, nothing in Hinduism expressly forbade this. Brad, the Canadian visitor at the ashram, had showed me the original text of the *Kama Sutra* in Sanskrit. There were rules, but none of them forbade this.

Han walked toward the bed, which was still bare without the sheets and blanket I'd stripped from it earlier that day. Her white shirt dropped off her shoulders, revealing a tattoo of a banyan tree on her back, the lines intricate like henna. She slid her pants to the floor and stepped out of them. She sat on the edge of the bed in green boxer briefs and stripped off one sock at a time. She pulled her bra up over her head. Whereas Roopa had full breasts that spilled through her bra, Han's could fit into the cup of my palm. The dark pink coins of her nipples puckered in the empty air.

"Are you just going to stand there?" Han asked. She sat back on the bed and spread her legs.

I walked to her, and only then did I notice the ridges all over her body. Little pink lines that ran like hatch marks from her hips down to her knees. She noticed me looking.

"I wanted to see myself heal," she said. "Touch them."

I touched the scars raised up from her skin—a patchwork of squares on her hips, her inner thigh. Her skin smelled like cologne and laundry.

Sex with Han was different than sex with Roopa. With Roopa, we'd done it out of love. Everything, the nervous fumbling, the knocking of teeth as we kissed, the stab of sharp elbows as we moved—it was all done with a ferocious passion that numbed any embarrassment I may have felt. With Roopa, I wanted to swallow the whole of her; that's how much I needed her closeness.

But with Han, sex was suddenly a distanced thing, something I could pick up and examine when I was in the middle of it. Halfway through our first time, I zoomed far away in my head and watched myself having fun. I thought of Sita, lying by the river with her legs spread open, Ayya grunting on top of her. Lakshman, sitting in the living room, coloring his map. Roopa, the way we'd had sex right before she'd left. I thought of what Ayya would say if he knew I was making love to a nonbinary stranger. I had to pull myself back to my body before Han noticed I was gone.

Han was carefree and confident in a way I hadn't encountered before. She was in possession of her body, and her lack of embarrassment helped me get over my own insecurities. I tried to not worry about how my nakedness looked, or if I smelled good, or if I was doing it right. Han guided me with verbal directions, taught me how to touch her, how to put on a condom.

She tasted stronger than Roopa had, a tang that clung to the inside of my nostrils when I wasn't kneeling by the bed with her in my mouth, when I was kissing her, when she pulled me inside of her with her legs hooked around my waist. I held Han by the scars on her hips and felt that I was being made new again.

Afterward, as I was overcome with that familiar guilt, Han held me against her chest.

"Have you ever read the *Kama Sutra*?" she asked while we lay together in the bed, cuddling. She didn't wait for my answer. "It says that when you have a lot of sexual partners, your body absorbs all their energies and gets confused. But I think that's bullshit. I don't feel confused. Do you?"

I shook my head, even as I wondered if she knew she was only the second person I'd ever slept with. I tried to remind myself that this was okay, that we had done nothing wrong, but the shame continued to roil inside me.

"Does it ever go away?" I asked.

Han lifted an eyebrow.

"I feel strange," I said, "like I did something wrong."

Han chuckled. "Yeah, it goes away. You have to do it more."

$$\begin{array}{c} \bullet \\ \bullet \\ \bullet \end{array}$$

5

In 1964, hematologist Madison Cawein III and nurse Ruth Pendergrass published a study of the Fugate family in the *Archives of Internal Medicine*. According to Cawein and Pendergrass, the Fugates of Kentucky showed in some of their offspring a most unusual genetic anomaly: blue skin. The Fugates had settled in such a rural area that their isolation drove them to marry their family members. After generations of inbreeding, the recessive methemoglobinemia allele showed itself.

The congenital form of methemoglobinemia has two types. I have Type 1, which means that my red blood cells lack the enzyme cytochrome b5 reductase. This condition is called erythrocyte reductase deficiency, and results in bluish skin. Type 2 methemoglobinemia, also called generalized reductase deficiency, could have been deadly. Cytochrome b5 reductase regulates the amount of iron in red blood cells, and without enough of it, people with methemoglobinemia can develop iron deficiencies.

At the ashram, my diet consisted of parboiled red matta rice, spinach, and different types of lentils—all known for being rich in iron. I have to wonder if this was on purpose. There's this, too: Ayya heavily restricted my physical activity. Sometimes if I pushed myself too hard, my lungs shrank, and I wouldn't be able to breathe. This is a symptom of anemia, which is one result of iron deficiency.

Methemoglobinemia can also be acquired if a person is exposed to large amounts of anesthetics such as benzene, which occurs naturally in crude oil, gasoline, and cigarette smoke; certain antibiotics like dapsone and chloroquine; and nitrites, which are used as preservatives for meat.

After I moved to the US permanently, a doctor prescribed me ascorbic acid for my methemoglobinemia. She said it would turn my skin normal and reduce the likelihood of seizures. I take them every day and have never had a seizure in my life, but still my color remains.

As rural travel became easier in the US in the 1960s and '70s, the Fugates spread out to neighboring states, and their trademark Type 1 methemoglobinemia disappeared. Until me. That is, until Fugate descendants Elizabeth Adcock and Joey Pratt unwittingly got pregnant, and gave birth to a little boy they didn't want to raise.

6

As I spent more time in New York City, right and wrong—starkly defined for me by Ayya's teaching—blurred together. My ethical vision degraded, or perhaps I'd been wearing the wrong moral prescription for so long that my mind's eyes had adjusted, and now without those scriptural glasses, I couldn't tell where good and bad ended and began. Drinking, smoking weed, sex, partying—decadence of any sort, by dharmic standards, was categorically wrong, but I was doing all that and more. In New York, away from Ayya for the first time in my life, I started the long process of figuring out who I really was, and who I was going to be. I wasn't divine; that much I'd figured out was a lie. But maybe I was still wise. I could still help people. I could make the world better, even incrementally.

But I'd left the ashram. Without the infrastructure Ayya had built and still controlled, I was a nobody. I'd been walking around on the streets of New York for over two weeks, and no one had recognized me. No one had come up to me at the shows for Lakshman's band. For the first time in my life, I was anonymous—and it was simultaneously freeing and terrifying.

Lakshman, who had learned about my event in Queens through social media, followed my presence there. I had never been allowed to touch a computer, but Ayya had made me social media profiles. Apparently, he'd been advertising the world tour online for over a year. The ashram had its own website, recruiting visitors to stay—some of the visitors, like Brad, had told me that this was how they found me. But now that I knew Ayya was using social media, I also had a suspicion it was he, and not an outside hire like he'd claimed, who ran the website.

According to Lakshman, Ayya had blasted my disappearance on social media. He'd called off our trip to Toronto, which was supposed to be next after New York City.

"He's trying to sound like you got kidnapped or something," Lakshman said, laughing. "He doesn't want anyone to know you ran away."

Lakshman thought the answer was to erase my anonymity, to vault me into the spotlight again, but this time in a different way— this time without lies. If I were to take control of my own narrative, he said, Ayya wouldn't be able to touch me.

"It's a matter of time before he finds you," Lakshman said. "You have to make yourself a presence. Take it out of his control."

The video was Lakshman's idea. I needed a new sense of my own identity, and since the band was releasing a new single, they needed a promotional video.

"Why can't *you* be on the video with your face paint?" I asked when he told me. I'd gotten comfortable with the band—I'd been to three of their gigs—but I didn't want to be a part of it. I didn't know what it would mean for me with my blue skin to be attached to them. I didn't want to be a mascot.

Lakshman put aside the guitar he'd been fiddling with and stood up.

"I'm old news." He squeezed my shoulders. "Clearly a fake. But you—you're the real deal."

I shrugged off his hands. "Stop it. You know I'm not real."

I couldn't figure out how he felt about the whole god thing. Sometimes I suspected I was a joke to him. I didn't know if I was imagining the smirk he had when he talked about my godliness, but every time he mentioned it, shame glowed hot inside me.

"Your skin is real, Kalki. We can fudge the rest. Come on. It's time you lugged your own weight."

I'd been staying with him for days and days, and my money was slowly running out from buying booze and takeout for the band after shows. I had thrown up in Lakshman's bed, and I was regularly sleeping with his housemate. I spent most of my time lounging around in the apartment, watching TV while Lakshman was at school and M and Han were at work. I took walks around the neighborhood to people-watch, or went to the corner store to refill the fridge with milk and bread since I was eating their food. I still had eleven of the fifteen hundred dollars I'd taken from Ayya, but it wasn't much. I needed to contribute more.

"Please?" Lakshman said. He gave me that look, the same one he used when he was little—a look somewhere between anger and affection, a look he used to make people give him what he wanted.

"Fine," I said. "But only this once."

We filmed the video on Lakshman's phone. There was no music. Just Lakshman and me. We filmed it like he found me on a side street in Brooklyn. Lakshman made me open my mouth and filmed my dark purple gums.

"It's too much to ask people to believe you can heal them," he said, "so let's say you're a spiritual leader. A guru. Yeah, that's good—Kalki the guru." My face must have seemed skeptical, because he added, "It's not like that's a lie, Kalki. You've been trained all your life to be a guru."

He called the video *the Blue-Skinned Gods meet blue-skinned guru.*

None of us expected the video to go viral, but it did. Two days after we shot it, I went shopping for groceries with M. At the corner bodega, the pockmarked young man at the cash register watched us from behind the strings of lottery scratch-offs that hung above the counter.

When we checked out, he said, "You that guy? The blue one from the video?" He pulled it up on his phone and played the opening of the video for us.

At my nod, he smiled with many yellow teeth.

"Take a picture with me?" He gave the phone to M, and we posed for a picture with his arm around my shoulder. "Now like you're buying something." I posed with money in my hand, leaning on the counter. "Can you bless me?"

"Sure." I did my short blessing ritual for him. It felt odd, doing it in a bodega in the middle of New York City. And I wondered if I was crossing a line, making him believe that a blessing from me was worth anything, or that I could affect his circumstances by praying for him.

The young man bowed us out of the store.

When we got back to Lakshman's apartment and told him what had happened, M pulled up the video before I could express my discomfort with the blessing the man had requested.

"Four hundred thousand views," Lakshman said. "Dude!"

Emails flooded in through the band's website, which crashed four days after we uploaded the video. People asked to be healed, to be shown The Way. Half of them believed I was a god.

"How is this any different from before?" I asked Lakshman.

"Relax," he said. "People will believe what they want. But we're not lying to them. That's what's important. We're not claiming you're a god. We're not lying. They choose what to believe, and if it helps them to think you're a god—if it makes them happy—who are you to take that away?"

He had a point. But my stomach kept churning and churning, like it was trying to separate out the good from the bad.

A couple of emails came in from Ayya, too, mixed in with the rest. He wanted to know where I was, when I was coming back. He'd seen the video. There was anger to his tone, and disapproval at my harming my reputation, but also a pathetic pleading. These emails made that sick taste return to the back of my mouth. Lakshman and I decided it was best to ignore them.

"What if he finds us?" I asked.

"He can't find where I live," Lakshman said. "While you're here, you're safe. And where does he get off, anyway, ordering you around like that? He's an absolute ass."

"I didn't realize you hated him so much," I said.

Lakshman looked me square in the face, his eyes earnest. "Don't you?"

Ayya had done so many terrible things, but I'd always been taught that hate wasn't an emotion gods should have. Then again, I wasn't a god, and the person who had taught me was Ayya. My mind couldn't stretch itself around the complications of this belief I held. Maybe I did hate him.

A week later, we made another video, and this time Lakshman put ads on it to make money. This one was a bigger success and featured me meeting a bunch of people on the street and giving them advice. "A guru they can relate to," Lakshman said. Requests came in for interviews, cultural interest pieces, one photographer who suggested doing a nude photo shoot with me. Lakshman wanted all of it.

"I'm not posing naked," I said.

"Of course. Of course. But the rest."

A few days after the second video, on the one-month anniversary of my walking out on Ayya, Lakshman burst into his apartment one afternoon while I was napping, thrilled because the Blue-Skinned Gods had been invited to play at a prestigious upstate music festival in a few weeks.

"Do you know how big that festival is?" He jumped up and down in front of his computer. "This'll put us on the map!"

M, it turned out, was well-versed in Hindu scripture, and wanted to debate it with me. How cruel, she said, that Krishna was switched at birth with a baby girl to keep his uncle from murdering him, and how awful that his uncle killed the baby girl.

"But the baby girl was a spirit," I said, "an illusion. She wasn't real."

M looked like she pitied me. "That doesn't matter. What matters is that they believed Krishna's life was more important than the girl's."

I almost opened my mouth to tell her that as a god, Krishna's life *was* more important, but a small inner voice stopped me. M could read the thought on my face, and though we were sharing the same giant blanket on the couch, she extricated herself from it and stood up.

"I suppose you think Pootana's murder was fine too," she said.

In the scene from the *Mahabharata*, Krishna murders the demon Pootana, who comes to kill him. When she takes baby Krishna and tries to suckle him from her poison-filled breast, Krishna suckles the life force out of her.

"What a gruesome way to kill," M said, walking away to the kitchen.

I disliked having these discussions, but Hinduism was what M most wanted to talk about when we were alone together, and I was eager for her to like me. She was so sweet if I agreed and cold if I argued, so I learned to stay quiet when she complained about the misogyny in Hindu myths. She was Lakshman's girlfriend, and on occasion, when it was just the two of us cousins, he'd told me that she was The One. I didn't want to say the wrong thing to her.

But sometimes I couldn't help myself.

"My best friend grew up as a girl," I said. "She didn't complain."

M raised an eyebrow. "Was your friend upper-caste? Was she light-skinned?"

I opened and shut my mouth. Roopa wasn't a Brahmin, but she was from an upper-caste family. She was brown-skinned but not dark.

M said, "Hinduism is a set of ladders, and the higher up you are, the better it all seems."

In New York, I missed Roopa so much that my body seemed to ache all over. To feel better, I reached out to Han, though she wasn't in town as much as I'd hoped. When she was, I held her close. I wished to see Roopa again and tell her what I'd learned. I wanted Roopa to know I saw the truth that our religion had done its share of violence against women like her, and even more against women like M.

I knew this wish was a fantasy. I couldn't get back to India. I couldn't find Roopa. And if I did, I couldn't explain to her that I'd slept with Han and a handful of band groupies since I'd last seen her. Even if Roopa did forgive me, we wouldn't be able to go back to our old love. My world had been blown wide open, but I wasn't sure if Roopa wanted this big a world, and that knowledge, more than anything else, sat inside me like needles on my bones.

And what was worse, I was doing violence to the presence of Han because I was thinking of Roopa. Perhaps I, too, thought of them as interchangeable, that I could hold one and think of another. I wasn't any different than these stories.

The popularity of the second viral video spiraled out of our control in a matter of days. People in the street and at the bars where I hung out with the band confronted me with the kinds of questions Ayya had trained me to answer. I snapped back into my robot self. I did healing sessions while people filmed me, because they asked. I didn't know how to say no.

It turned out that people did want to believe I could heal them, which might have been the most powerful part of the whole once-a-god-now-a-guru thing. I rubbed indigo powder on my skin again, so that it would look bluer on camera instead of the pallid gray it had faded into. I felt guilty about it, but only slightly, because the ashiness of my skin color without the indigo looked on camera like I was sick or dead.

The Blue-Skinned Gods were invited to play at Pianos to replace a popular band that had cancelled their show at the last minute—the biggest gig they'd had yet. Lakshman said it would be a great way to practice for the music fest in a few weeks. Pianos was large compared to the dives they'd played in before, and it was lit in an eerie red glow. Some band named the Lesbian Brotherhood opened for them. Their front man, a tattooed hippie named Toe Head who reminded me of Brad from the ashram, took pictures with me and offered me weed.

I helped the four of them set up and sat at the bar while they were backstage, waiting for patrons to fill the club. Lakshman had told me to take it easy, to drink glasses of water in between my beers. The Blue-Skinned Gods finally began playing, and the crowd sang along while I sat alone at the bar.

I was so busy watching the stage that I jumped when someone put a rough hand on my shoulder and spun me around.

"Ayya," was all I could think of to say.

His face cycled through surprise, anger, indignation, and back to surprise. If there'd been more light, I would've seen the flush of anger in his skin.

"I thought—" he said in Tamil. But the rest of the sentence seemed to have failed him. Silence stretched.

Before this moment, if you'd asked me what I'd say to Ayya if I saw him after running away, I wouldn't have known. But my brain knew, and it blurted out sentences.

"I found my birth certificate," I said. "The real one." I stood up from my seat and faced him.

Ayya's face turned unsure. He hadn't been expecting me to put up a fight.

"Why did you do this to me?" I yelled over the music. "Roopa, Amma, Sita, Lakshman—you sent them all away. Why did you do it?" Anger crested inside me. "Why did you turn my life into a lie? You've lied to me millions of times."

A new feeling wrinkled my nose and mouth: disgust.

His lips quivered before he spoke.

"It was all for your own good," he said. "Amma and I always knew you were a god. You were given to us by the universe by whatever means were necessary. But convincing others—convincing *you*— took a lot of vigilance and hard work."

"People aren't pieces in a game for you to maneuver. And I'm not a god, either. But you always knew that, didn't you?"

He stepped closer to me, the lights from the stage splashing over his skin. We stood eye to eye. I balled up my fists. I couldn't bear the thought of returning to the ashram with him. It was easier to see myself punching him in the face right there in the bar.

"I've always believed in you, Kalki." His voice softened, beseeching. "You *are* a god. You need to come back."

He reached out, but I stepped away.

"You should go back to the ashram," I said. "I thought you would've gone already."

"Some of the devotees have been hosting me at their homes. They still believe." He stepped toward me again. "You can still make this right. We'll come up with an explanation. Come home."

"No."

"Are you drinking?" he asked. His eyes flicked to the half-empty beer glass on the bar. "You've been drinking."

Shame flooded my gut and worked its way up to my face. I almost hung my head before I remembered that I had no reason to.

"You need to come home," he said. He made as if to grab my arm, but I yanked it away.

"I'm not coming home. Ever."

"You will listen to me. Think of what your Amma would've said."

I turned back toward the crowd. His mention of Amma was carefully calculated, but it wouldn't work this time. I pushed down the surge of sadness that rose in me.

"I've seen this—this nonsense on the Internet," he said. "If you continue with this behavior, your reputation will be ruined."

Other people near the bar started to take notice of us.

"You need to leave," I said. "Or else I'll have the bouncer throw you out."

"The what?"

"The guard at the door."

He looked back at the large man who was watching us carefully with crossed arms.

"You threaten me?" Ayya said.

"Go away," I said. I burned electric. I wanted to cackle or howl. "And don't ever speak of Amma." To prove the point, I gulped the last dregs of beer from my glass, put it down on the bar, and walked into the crowd near the stage. I didn't know if he'd follow me. As I tried to figure out what to do next, the band stopped playing and Lakshman spoke.

"I have a special treat for you tonight," he said into the microphone. "Some of you remember the video we posted a couple of weeks ago." Massive cheers. "Well, tonight he's here with us—the blue-skinned, real-life guru, Kalki!"

From the stage, Lakshman pointed at me, standing at the edge of the throng. Everyone turned to look. He motioned for me to join him onstage. He hadn't told me he was going to do this. But of course he was. Of course he'd planned it all along.

Invisible hands helped me toward the band. I left Ayya standing at the bar. The cheering made me feel lighter. The crowd pushed me up onto the stage. Lakshman slung his arm around my shoulder. Phones out everywhere, clicking clicking away, pictures being taken, statuses being updated, tweets being composed. Lakshman knelt in front of me, in all his blue get-up, and I remembered us playing the scene from *Mahabharata* when we were young, how he'd pretend to be Arjuna, and he'd kneel and ask for advice from me, Krishna, how I'd reveal myself to be a god. Except now we were onstage at a crowded club in New York, and this was all for show.

When the phones were done clicking, and I finally made my way back to the bar, Ayya was gone.

The night after Pianos, Lakshman asked me to go with him to a party in Brooklyn, claiming it would be good for publicity.

"You keep this up and you won't have to start paying rent," he half-joked.

New York was so far proving to be unpredictable and exactly the education I needed. How people really lived, not cloistered inside an isolated ashram, but here, partying and fighting and fucking and living with millions of other people in a crowded, overwhelming city.

"I can look for work," I said, although I had no idea what that meant. I wasn't trained for anything except for living the lie of being a god or guru.

"You don't know how visas work, do you?" Lakshman said. "You becoming our mascot is more than job enough. Thanks to you, we're starting to make some real money, and a part of that is yours. But you need to come with me to parties like this, so more people get to know you."

I wasn't sure how I felt about this new role as a publicity mascot, but a party sounded interesting. I'd heard of these kinds of get-togethers from Brad and other visitors to the ashram—all the drinking and rowdiness. M was working, Han was out of town, and Jason was only ever around when the band played, so it would just be Lakshman and me, brothers like we used to be.

Whatever I had imagined—strobe lights, pumping music, sweaty bodies—this party was mild by comparison. It took place in a Brooklyn brownstone with exposed ceilings and brick walls. The place was roomy, and the party's hosts kept telling everyone that it was only because five of them lived there that they could afford it. Jazz music played from small speakers all over the apartment, and young people lounged on leather couches and leaned against walls.

Lakshman knew everyone, and everyone knew him. In the dim light, no one paid attention to my blue skin. I lagged behind him, a beer in my hand. At first, he introduced me to people as his cousin, but after a few beers, he started telling people I was the guru from the viral video.

"Oh, wow," people said. Their once-dismissive tones switched into high gasps of admiration. "You're magical, aren't you?" one man asked. Another woman trailed her fingers up and down my arms. "You should wear your traditional clothes," she said. A cloud of ganja hung above all our heads.

Across the room, a young woman watched me. She held a wine glass, but I hadn't yet seen her take a sip. Her hair was straight, long, and black, around a round brown face with thin eyes that slanted up at the corners.

I stuck to Lakshman's side, getting introduced and whisked away.

"Do you see that girl?" I asked him. I nodded toward her. She was still looking at me.

"She's hot. Go talk to her." He pushed me in her direction.

She had seen it, that small stumble of mine as Lakshman pushed. I had no choice, so I walked across the room to her. She smiled with purple-painted lips. Her shirt was cut so high I could see her abdomen.

"You're Kalki," she said. "The *guru* from the Internet."

"Yes."

The emphasis she'd put on the word *guru* threw me. I couldn't tell if she was mocking me. She had a slight accent when she spoke English—not Indian, but close. She held out her hand for me to shake.

"From one childgod to another," she said.

Confused, I shook her hand. She took a gulp of her wine.

"I used to be a Kumari in Nepal," she said.

I'd heard of Kumaris before, young girls taken from their families and raised in sacred temples. Kumaris are revered until they reach puberty, when they're returned back to their families. While they live in the temples, they're believed to be the living vessels for the feminine energy of the universe, the goddess herself.

"My name is Sunita." I could see why she had been chosen—the process is rigorous, with the candidate required to possess both beauty and fearlessness. She leaned toward me ever so slightly and whispered, "I think we should talk."

Sunita pulled me away from the rest of the party. I was too intrigued to resist, and Lakshman had disappeared. We ended up outside, sitting on the front steps of the building, facing out into the darkened street. Light spilled from open windows across the street, and through them we watched silhouettes of people going about their lives—getting ready for a night out, going to bed, arguing, making love.

She told me how her village had chosen her, how they'd made her sleep in a room of severed goat heads to prove her worthiness.

"I'll never forget the smell," she said. "What did they make you do?"

I tried to think of something equally horrifying. "I had to pass three trials," I said. "It's predicted in the *Sri Kalki Purana*. I healed a sick girl and called wild horses to the ashram. And—" I hesitated. "That's it."

She laughed. "I bet you weren't thrown out when you started to mature."

"No," I said. "Most people still seem to want to believe."

"Do *you*?"

I couldn't meet her eyes.

"Do you still believe you're a god?" she asked.

"No." The air around us crushed me. Once, I'd wanted to be the god who could save the world from itself. Now I wasn't sure what I wanted.

"They believe that when a girl bleeds," she said, "the goddess leaves her body."

She waited for my reaction.

"That's not fair," I said. People like Ayya believed the same thing. Amma, Roopa, and the rest of the women at the ashram weren't allowed to attend poojas or bhajans when they were bleeding. They weren't even allowed to enter the kitchen or prayer center.

Sunita leaned her head on my shoulder. I held very still, like she was an animal I didn't want to startle. My body filled with a distant but strong longing for Roopa.

"So what are we to do now that we're mere mortals?" Sunita said.

"Fuck, drink, and party," I said, quoting a phrase that Lakshman liked to say.

Sunita laughed and shook her hair away from her neck.

"You seem to be on a plan to have your old life back, though," she said. "What with all those videos. People worshipping you."

I tried to come up with a response, to tell her that I wasn't trying to recreate my old life.

"Not that it's bad," she said. She drummed her fingers on my knee. Her face was open, earnest. "You're not hurting anyone. You're giving them what they want. This is what we were trained to do all our lives. Have faith."

My godhood was so central to my life for so long that I didn't think of it as faith. To me, my divinity had been as real as flowers, or the sun, or my own skin. And when that godhood broke—or rather, when that godhood was shown irrevocably to be foolish and misguided—reality itself had shattered to pieces around me. My worldview had been blown of precious glass, and Lakshman had come along and smashed it with a hammer.

For some reason, I felt like I could be honest with Sunita. She'd built trust between us in just a few minutes. After all, she better than anyone else knew my story. She'd lived it.

"I don't know," I said. "Isn't it still wrong? I'm tricking all these people."

She put her head back on my shoulder. "You can't trick someone who wants to be tricked."

Thanks to the viral videos, the band had a lot of new last-minute gigs. Lakshman posted details on the band's website. I was too busy to think much about this—busy becoming friends with M, busy discovering Han's many scars, busy meeting fans on the street as a publicity mascot, busy shooting a music video with the band, busy getting to know adult Lakshman. The videos had given me new purpose. I couldn't save the world, and I wasn't a god, but at least I could make people happy. And I could help the band become famous. That was something.

I didn't think, in all of this whirlwind, that we had made it so much easier for Ayya to find me. I assumed that he would've gone home by now, dejected after I told him I was never coming back. I'd missed almost all my stops on the world tour. Whenever I did think of Ayya, which I tried not to do, I imagined him back home at the ashram, or completing the tour without me.

But find me he did, again and again.

Sunita came to a Blue-Skinned Gods show with her girlfriend, a Tamil lesbian named Lucky who had short hair and the most muscular shoulders I'd seen on a woman. She held Sunita close around the waist and kept shooting glances at me, like she was daring me to say anything.

While the band played, Sunita, Lucky, and I sat at the bar, getting drunk for free. The schedule was the same. Soon Lakshman would call me up to the stage, and I'd do my part of posing with the band for the sea of phones in the crowd. Every time we did this, the Blue-Skinned Gods got dozens—sometimes hundreds—more followers on social media.

"You know, they say only ten percent of healing is due to medicine," Sunita said. She was telling Lucky how both she and I had been "village healers" when we were young. She didn't say the word *gods*. "The other ninety percent of healing is belief."

Lucky made a skeptical face. "Belief can't heal people."

"The human mind can do amazing things when it believes something. We were giving people healing through faith."

"Healing through faith." Lucky didn't look convinced.

"It's why the placebo effect works," Sunita said. "Belief. People need that. Back me up, Kalki. Don't you think the people you healed got better because they believed they would?"

Before I form a coherent thought about this, in the middle of a raucous song about a depressed swami who decides to try psychedelics, someone swiveled me around in my seat.

And there stood Ayya, looking murderous, breathing heavily, his eyes red and raw.

"You will come back home," he said.

I wrenched my shoulder out of his hold.

"Why are you hanging around these heretics?"

I was surprised he couldn't put together the fact that it was Lakshman onstage.

"You must come back," Ayya said. "You have to come back."

I shook my head, my ears full of my own heartbeat. I strode past him to the door where the bouncer stood, and Ayya followed me.

"Listen to me," he shouted.

The bouncer was a large white man named Gary who worked a bunch of the bars in the area. I'd met him at a couple of other shows. He had a mean face, but he'd always been very nice to me. His blond hair was cropped close to his head, and he had a long beard that he braided and dyed green.

Gary nodded at me as I approached and stooped down so I could talk to him.

"This man needs to be thrown out," I yelled in Gary's ear. Ayya's presence sat like a layer of slime on my skin I wanted to wash off.

"He bothering you?" Gary asked. He turned his glare on Ayya.

"He's screaming and shouting at me," I said.

Ayya watched the exchange with growing fury that I could read plainly on his face. But before he could yell at me, Gary grabbed him by the arm and pulled him out through the door like he was a doll. Next to Gary's bulk, Ayya was nothing, and it gave me satisfaction to see him dragged out like that.

Through the window, Ayya screamed at Gary, who stood mute

with his arms crossed in front of his chest. Gary took out his phone, and I assumed he threatened to call the police, because Ayya soon left, still in a rage by the way he marched away with his arms swinging wildly at his sides.

For the next show, and all the ones after, we gave a picture of Ayya to the bouncer as soon as we got to the venue, and asked them not to let him in. The bouncers were all friends with Lakshman, M, Han, or Jason, or else fans of the band, or fans of me, so no one refused our request. Still, Ayya hung around outside before and sometimes after the shows. He'd shout at me as I passed, raging about my selfishness, how I was like Amma, how I was destined for the same fate, how I was throwing my life away. Sometimes, instead of shouting, he'd beg me to come back to the ashram.

Jason or Lakshman usually kept him away physically, using nothing but their large statures. In the dimness of the bars, Ayya didn't seem to give Lakshman enough time or attention to recognize him. Ayya reserved his hate for me alone. Getting to and from the venues became a hassle. The band played bodyguard for me, and after the shows, Jason drove around in circles before taking a circuitous route back to Lakshman's place, in case Ayya followed us.

7

Ayya wasn't the only one who found me as a result of the videos. One day, Lakshman called me into his room and told me to shut the door.

I sat down on the bed. The room was flooded with light. Lakshman's maps littered his desk and the floor. One map, the one of the Brooklyn subways that he'd been working on all week, lay partially curled on top of his laptop. He brushed it aside and opened his computer.

"Look at this email I got," he said. "I think it's from your mom."

My hands went cold, my thoughts full of Amma and the night we burned her body.

He opened the email and we both read it in silence.

> *Dear Kalki,*
> *I found you! Finally, after so much searching, you're here!*
> *I should introduce myself. My name's Lizzy. Elizabeth, actually. Elizabeth Adcock. I'm your mother.*

What you need to understand was that I was young and scared, and I didn't know what to do when that sweet-talking doctor and his beautiful wife came calling, and, well, you know the rest.

I thought back then that I'd never see you again. But then I saw this video and I knew. I KNEW it was you. Call it mother's intuition.

Anyways, I'd love to meet you. Email me back, ok?

Your mother,
Lizzy

I sat back on the bed, dazed. The floor had dropped from under me with the thought of Amma, but now I was freefalling. A hard sadness waited below me, like cement.

"Well?" Lakshman said. "What are you going to do?"

I shook my head.

"You have to respond to her, at least," he said. "I'll send her an email for you. *Dear Mom.* Dear Mom? Do you want to call her Mom?"

His words took a long time to process, like they were traveling to me through a thick fog.

"You found your mother, dude!" Lakshman said, spinning around in his chair to face me. "Your birth mom. Aren't you curious?"

"Of course I am."

"Let me write this reply, then." He spun back to his computer. "Dear Mom—"

"No, don't use *Mom*." The English word *mom* had little real meaning for me, but I still felt uncomfortable using it.

"Lizzy?"

"Sure."

"Okay, *Dear Lizzy*."

It took us over an hour to write a one-paragraph response. We hashed over the simplest words, where to put articles, whether to incorporate the fact that English wasn't my first language. I thanked her for writing. I said I wanted to meet her, that I had so many things to say.

Ten minutes after we sent the email, a response came. It was short.

I live in Charleston, West Virginia. Take a Greyhound. I'll pick you up from the station. Send details. Love, Mom.

"Tell me you're going to go," Lakshman said.

"I should, shouldn't I? I have to, don't I?" It all felt so surreal. I wondered how long it would take to sink in, the idea of seeing my birth mother.

"It's three different buses." He was already looking up ticket prices. "I'll spring for the tickets, since I'm kind of your employer now." He winked. "Greyhound's cheap going out that way."

Everything was happening so fast. I missed the slowness of the ashram, the routine of my life, the way everything was scripted. I'd stepped off the edge of the known Earth into an abyss.

It took a few minutes for Lakshman to buy the tickets, and before I knew it, we were both at Port Authority and Lakshman was ushering me onto a bus.

Even though it was now summer in the US, he gave me his hoodie to wear on the ride.

"You're going into redneck territory," he said. "Better to hide your skin."

I didn't know what *redneck* meant, but I gathered from his sneer that he didn't think much of where Lizzy lived. I'd been trying to call her *Mom* in my head, but it wasn't working very well. At least I didn't have to call her *Amma*. That would've been impossible.

Lakshman reached over to pull the hood over my head.

"Keep it that way," he said.

He hugged me hard and long, and it reminded me of when he'd climb into my bed to sleep back at the ashram, how he'd curl his body next to mine and I'd fall asleep to the *tha-thump* of his heart. When I was young, when I thought I was a god, I wanted to know what people needed before they knew it themselves. But Lakshman had always been better at that than I was, had always known intuitively and without study what people needed. And right now, I knew he knew I needed to feel safe in his hold.

"I love you, Kalki," he said when he pulled away. "Those years after we left the ashram, I never got over it. Losing you."

I pulled him back to me, like we were living one of those over-the-top romantic comedies Lakshman liked to watch late at night when he couldn't sleep. I'd joined him sometimes, when I was sleeping badly, which happened a lot during my first two months in New York City. But as silly as it felt, I was grateful for the steadiness of Lakshman's body, for the abstract and foreign smell of his deodorant, and for the small patch of our faces that touched during the embrace.

The air-conditioning on the bus was turned up so high that I shivered even with all the skin-covering clothing I wore. I kept my hood up and sat in the back, where people left me alone. Each bus I transferred to had fewer and fewer people on it, until it was just me and three others on the fifty-seater to Charleston in the dead of night.

When I wondered what Lizzy would be like, I pictured a tall, slender white woman with light brown hair that was straight and slick, like the women I'd seen in New York. She'd wear stylish clothes and she might have other kids—my brothers and sisters. A new family. I wondered what kind of house she'd live in. Lakshman had told me that Charleston was close to the mountains, and that many people had houses tucked into the slopes. He'd shown me houses with windows reaching from the floor to the roof.

I wondered again whether I should call her *Mom*. That word for me was empty of feeling, of consequence. *Amma* opened something deep and painful inside me, but *Mom* seemed like just another word. Scholars say most Indian and European languages have the same root, some common, ancestral tongue that originated in Central Asia. That means that Greek, Latin, and Sanskrit are sibling languages, more similar than different. Tamil, on the other hand, is utterly unlike the Indo-European language cluster. Tamil and its handful of siblings—Malayalam, Kannada, Telugu, and others—share a mysterious past that scholars can't identify. Even though Sanskrit was supposed to be the end-all-be-all language of gods and scripture, Tamil, my native tongue, felt closer to my heart than any of the others.

As an adult, many years after this story, I lecture in both Sanskrit and Tamil. My students can't tell the difference between the languages as I speak them. They also don't know how to pronounce the words when they see them written. One young poet once described the melody of Tamil as sounding like the first syllable of a bunch of English words mashed together. But when written, Tamil words are long, and each one sets up the stage grammatically for the next. Even more than Sanskrit, Tamil is the hardest language my students, many of whom are working on graduate studies in linguistics, have encountered.

Take the word for *love*—only, there is no word for love. The word *love* in its Western concept cannot be translated simply into Tamil, because in Tamil, each type of love has its own name. *Anbu* means compassion and caring. *Natpu* means friendship. *Kadhal* means romance. But though all these different versions of love felt distinct for me, the loss of them felt exactly the same—Lakshman's natpu, Roopa's kadhal, Amma's anbu. The grief at losing each one occupied the same space in my heart.

I pressed my forehead to the cool window of the bus and watched the darkened world outside. The moon waxed full and eerie as the landscape grew tall mountains and the road curved snakelike through them. I'd spent so many nights watching the moon rise and set outside my bedroom window at the ashram, the mango tree throwing shadows on the wall to sway me to sleep. My old life felt so far away, and increasingly, it seemed like I'd never get it back.

When I ran away, I hadn't thought enough about the fact that I was losing my people, my language. Once, I'd been a god at the center of so many people's lives, and now I was a young man, alone.

We arrived in Charleston at seven in the morning, though I didn't know it until I opened the black curtains on the bus windows and the sunlight forced its way in. I covered my eyes against the intrusion. The other bus riders around me stirred, yawning, stretching, getting their bags from the top storage compartments.

"You don't look so good," one of them said to me. A white man, my age with a wooden septum piercing. "You all right?"

"I'm fine," I said. I tried to turn my head away so he couldn't see my face. It struck me that I'd never tried to hide myself when I was young. Back then, the ways in which I was different from everyone else had been a source of strength and power, but now, those differences were dangerous. Now, I was aware of every inch of my skin in a way I'd never felt before.

The man moved on. When I stepped off the bus after him, he saw my face in the new morning light.

"Dude, you should go see a doctor," he said, and walked away.

We stood on the side of a dirty river enveloped in fog. On one side of the road, the ground fell swiftly into the water. On the other side, it climbed taller than the bus station and rounded away. Past spindly trees and brick buildings, the blue valleys spit up smoke among the mountains that merged into clouds overhead.

"Joe?"

Someone touched me on the shoulder—a too-thin white woman with a long, drooping face, stringy blond hair cut into a bob, and sharp, bony shoulders.

"Joe! It's me."

"Lizzy," I said.

She encased me in a hug, chuckling and smelling of powder and flowery perfume.

"My, your skin really is unsettling, ain't it?" she said. It didn't seem to be a question. She stroked the side of my face, rubbed the skin with her thumb. "As blue as the day you were born."

I was hungry and nauseated at the same time.

"It's good to meet you," I said. Being polite was the easiest way to get through this. I had twisted my brain into knots, and part of me wished I hadn't come. I was also aware of my Indian accent when I spoke English, which was much stronger in those days—eventually, it would drop away, bit by bit, with every year I spent outside of India, like sand rolling down a mound until there was no hill left.

Lizzy's accent was different from the one Lakshman and the other New Yorkers had, a pull to her words where she flattened out her vowels and drew them longer.

"Come on," she said, leading me to a beige SUV. "I'll make you some breakfast at home. You like eggs?"

The total unfamiliarity of this woman unnerved me. I'd expected to feel at least a little recognition—some inner, primordial pull toward my birth mother, like the way Krishna felt when he finally met his biological mother after being raised by Yashodha. But Lizzy felt as much a stranger to me as the people on the bus. I couldn't see the similarities between us in her body or her face.

We rode in awkward silence on the city roads, which gave way to wider streets and houses. I tensed up my muscles so I wouldn't shake. Lizzy turned on the radio to country music—the stuff Lakshman hated.

I wanted to ask her why she gave me up, but I didn't know how to phrase it without making her defensive. I thought it was best to wait with that question until we knew each other better. But I couldn't think of what else I wanted to say to her. I tried to imagine what my life would have been like if I'd grown up here, with her.

Finally, she spoke. "You probably want to hear about my life."

I couldn't tell by her tone if she wanted me to tell her about my life too. She lit a cigarette and started talking, and between sentences, she blew smoke out of a narrow opening at the top of her driver's side window.

West Virginia terrain rose and fell beautifully—pale mountains in the background, little cottage-like businesses built into the side of the roads, fog lifting off every surface.

"I grew up in the mountains all my life, just about. A dying town you never heard of—ha!"

Her hacking sound made me jump in my seat.

"You're a nervous young man, ain't ya?" She reached across and slapped my knee. "Nothing for me there, so I moved out to Charleston. That's where I learned my calling."

She wiggled her fingers above the steering wheel. The cigarette dropped a fleck of ash as it smoked. "I got great hands, son. I became a dealer."

I met her quick gaze with a blank look. All I could think about was how she'd called me *son*.

"A dealer. A card dealer," she said. "In a casino. Jeez, you really don't know much about the world, do you, son?"

She called me *son* again. I tried to like the sound of the word in her mouth.

"Ha!" She hacked a second time, and I flinched. "I learned my calling at Mardi Gras Casino in Charleston. I'd already given you up by then. Met your father in high school. He was such a tall, strapping jerk."

With every sentence, my imagination blasted into thousands of questions. What did a "tall, strapping jerk" look like? What did he act like? Where was he? Between the cigarette smoke, talk of my American family, and the twisting mountain road, I thought I might be sick.

"Can we pull over, please?" I said, gripping my stomach.

I threw up bile beside the car while Lizzy sat in the driver's seat and asked if I was okay. My head and belly were full of flashing lights. Everything was wrong. The thin, cool air; this strange woman whose blood I supposedly shared; the way she was talking; the fact that I had no idea what I wanted from her. Or what she wanted from me.

I climbed back into the SUV beside her, and she said we better get home for breakfast before we talked about anything else. I stared out the window and tried to keep my head and my sanity from floating away.

"I was so young. I was so, so young. Imagine having a kid at eighteen. What would you have done?"

We sat at a small square table in Lizzy's kitchen with two empty, yolk-stained plates between us. I had never eaten eggs before, but I didn't know how to explain to her why Hindu Brahmins didn't eat eggs—it seemed like too much of a conversation than I wanted to have—so I ate them. They were delicious, and I felt guilty for enjoying them.

"I wouldn't have had a kid at seventeen," I said.

I was feeling more like myself, although I was starting to know less and less who that really was. I was talking to my mother, my birth mother, in a kitchen in the mountains of America, and she was telling me why my life had turned out the way it had. I had to keep saying it to myself over and over, trying to get my mind around it.

"Well," she said, "you can't control everything."

As we talked, her orange cat curled up and fell asleep around my ankles.

"She normally doesn't like strangers," Lizzy said. "You must be all right."

I didn't feel all right. My world was cracking apart around me. My father had been a popular baseball player, Joey Pratt, who died of alcohol poisoning the very same month he won a baseball scholarship to a big university. Before that, still in high school, they found out Lizzy was pregnant with me. I tried to wrap my head around the words *mom* and *dad* and *son*. I was grateful these were so different from the Tamil words *Amma* and *Appa* and *maghan*. The English words felt distant and cold, which was fine with me.

"He didn't drink that much normally," Lizzy said, shaking her head sadly. "And then you came along, and I couldn't take care of you alone."

But she also said how it was difficult to be different in her hometown in those days, how hard it would have been for me growing up there, because of the way the local people treated each other in small towns like hers, no matter that Charleston was close by.

"I guess I turned out more or less happy," she said. "I'm a happy person."

"I'm happy for you."

"Well, isn't that sweet?" Lizzy reached across the table and pinched my cheek. "You don't mind if I do this, right? I never got to do it before."

For all of her telling me about her life, Lizzy hardly asked me about my life at all. In the hour after breakfast, talking at her table, I mentioned one or two things about the ashram and about my childhood, but each time, Lizzy would interrupt me to talk about herself or the cat or some chore or other that she had to do.

But then she turned very curious, very quickly.

"Them viral videos you're making," she said, staring me in the eye. I still could see no flicker of sameness between us. Nothing in our facial expressions. But looking back at her like that, eye to eye, I felt a tinge of connection. "You have over three million views. That must mean you're making a lot of money. Fame and fortune for my only son. Ha!" She hacked.

"Not really."

"Why so modest?" She held my gaze. "How much are you making?"

"I'm not making anything. I need a job."

"Not making any money?" And just like that, Lizzy's attention drifted. She stood up and gathered the dishes.

Whatever else I thought about Lizzy, I realized with every passing hour that she was no substitute for Amma. I hadn't really wanted a replacement, but meeting Lizzy, talking to her, seeing how she was and how she treated me—I knew it was an insult to Amma to try to replace her.

I couldn't replace anything from my old life. All I could do was mourn it. But what I really mourned, more than the life I'd had, was the future life I'd imagined for myself. I'd only ever pictured myself in Tamil Nadu, in the ashram, healing people, married to a beautiful woman—Roopa—with adoring children and followers at my feet. All of that was gone, and there was nothing to replace it. My new life was an empty void, and I was falling aimlessly through it.

8

When I got back to the city, exhausted from three buses, overnight travel, and too much time with my own thoughts, I found the band practicing a new song at the apartment, all except Han, who was out of town. The chorus floated out to me through the door—"I love you, even though you're a little bit crazy."

"Kalki, finally," Lakshman said when I walked through the door. "How did it go? What was she like?"

"She was fine," I said.

Lakshman put his guitar on the sofa.

"Tell us, really. How was Lizzy?"

"She was fine. Nice."

A whole day on a bus hadn't helped me process much from my trip. If anything, I was more jumbled up than before.

"But?"

When I hesitated, he answered his own question.

"But she's not your Amma," he said, enclosing me in another warm hug. And before I could feel awkward, M and Jason joined in on the embrace. Jason started humming, and the other two harmonized until the whole world vibrated around me.

I deflated in their arms like a popped balloon. "She's not Amma, no. And I think she only reached out to me because she thought I was making a ton of money with the band."

As we emerged from the hug and peeled ourselves out of it like an onion, Lakshman's face brightened.

"Well," he said. "We might be making a ton of money sooner than you think."

He grabbed beers for everyone, and I accepted mine gratefully. I was learning to live in a perpetual state of drunkenness, and it helped deal with the nagging memories of Ayya shouting at me at shows, the ache of missing Amma and Roopa, and the anxiety of not knowing what was next.

"So here's my new idea," Lakshman said. "First thing, you're going to sing backup on our new song. Good?"

I had never liked my voice that much, growing up. But after all these times being onstage with the band in the past few weeks, I had started to wonder what it would be like to perform with them.

"Okay," I said.

"Don't sound so excited," Jason said, punching me lightly on the arm.

"We've got the whole part written out for you," M said. "It won't be hard to learn. Though I still don't think we should be using the word 'crazy.' It's ableist."

"But none of the substitutions rhyme," Lakshman said.

Jason slapped his palm against his forehead. "Lazy! What about 'lazy'?"

"Of course! Why did it take us this long to come up with 'lazy'?" Lakshman poked me with his elbow. "Are you on board, Kalki?"

They all seemed excited to have me sing with them. It felt good to be wanted that way.

"Okay!" I sang the word, sounding much happier than I felt. Everyone laughed.

"It's settled," Lakshman said. "You have to hear our other big idea. Jason, tell him. It's your idea."

Jason turned his whole body toward me, pushing his new box braids out of his eyes. "You ever heard of a prayer concert?"

I hadn't.

"So they've got a religious thing some people do here," he said. "Baptists, they're called. I grew up as a Baptist down South. And some Baptists have church outdoors with giant congregations. And they play music and preach all day, and they rake in a ton of money."

"A prayer concert," I said, feeling the new phrase in my mouth.

"There you go, sounding all excited again."

"A prayer concert!" I sang, taking a long swig of beer.

"I don't know," M said. "It's fine and all when we're doing the irreverent stuff—even the music video was pushing it—but courting a serious religious crowd? I don't know if it's a good idea."

"They're not seriously religious," Laksman said. "They're, you know, spiritual. And they'll mostly be white, I think."

M looked skeptical, but said, "I want to be on the record that this is a bad idea. But I'm outnumbered, so I'll go along."

"It's perfect," Lakshman said, undeterred. "We can make our set at the music festival into a prayer concert. And you can sing with me on one of the songs. This band is going to start going places very soon, my friends."

We all drank to that.

That night after Han got home, Jason and Lakshman cooked us all dinner—chicken, my first time trying any meat. Lakshman picked out boneless pieces for me because he said that I might be disturbed by small bones and cartilage if I encountered them on my first try. The curry they'd made was spicy and delicious, scooped up with flat white roti. The chicken had a texture and taste I could only describe as deep. Sitting in the cramped apartment with the band, Jason piling my plate with food, Han's hand on my knee, Lakshman and M attached to each other at the shoulders—I was truly happy for the first time in years.

After dinner, Lakshman and I went out for a walk. We wandered through the streets of Brooklyn, passing back and forth a bottle of Gatorade and vodka, my head already dizzy with singing and beer and a night's sleep in a bus seat. I kept tipping up the bottle to my mouth and letting the liquid burn into my throat.

We stopped outside a Korean market. Its white glow spilled out onto the streets, onto the young people who passed it. Inside the window, a hunched woman rang up goods at a register.

"Let's go to Manhattan," Lakshman said.

"Manhattan," I said blankly.

He put an arm around my shoulders and wove me toward the steps of a subway stop. He was drunk, and when he was like this, there was no way to get an idea out of his head after it had lodged itself.

"I want you to see Manhattan," he said. It didn't matter that I'd already seen Manhattan plenty of times.

I let him lead me away from the market and toward the subway. Lakshman was quiet on the train, his body swaying with the movement, the bottle traveling up to his mouth and down again. We changed trains once, and then he led me up a stone staircase that smelled like urine. Everything was whiteness.

Fog had descended on the New York night, slithering in between the buildings, silently taking the city. The lights jumped off the fog and back at the streets, magnifying so it looked bright as day.

I shielded my eyes with my hands. The fog clung to us as we walked.

Lakshman spread out his arms and looked up at the blank whiteness above us, laughing to himself. "*This* is god."

The city spun around me, the lights passing through me like ghosts. I was drunk, and I walked arm in arm with Lakshman through the streets, singing parts of the new song he had written.

I don't know why at that moment I thought of my real birth certificate, but it all seemed funny in the new blankness of the city, the hard edges of the truth warped around my head. Joseph Robert Pratt. My real name. I laughed. I bent over my knees and kept laughing.

Lakshman watched me, the fog seeping into his clothes and skin.

"You should come see Appa," he said.

The laughter continued to push its way through me.

"Kalki, you okay?"

"That's not my name," I said between laughs. "No one knows my name. It's—get this—my name's Joseph. It's not even Hindu. *Joseph.*"

"Lizzy told you that?"

"Yes. And I have a second birth certificate. You were right. There are two." I wiped my eyes and straightened up. "Joseph Pratt."

He cocked his head, a smile stretching his mouth. "You're not Indian. Not even in name. Dude, you're white!"

We broke into fresh new laugher and started walking again. I didn't care where we were going. We walked into the fog.

"Do you remember the indigo they dyed your skin with?" Lakshman asked. "Appa told me some of the other things they did too."

I was unprepared for this turn in the conversation. The laughter abandoned me. My body became quiet. I wanted to disappear into the fog. I didn't want to hear the words, afraid that hearing them said out loud would make them real, and therefore consequential.

"They'd secretly feed people antibiotics so everyone thought you were healing them when they got better. That's how Roopa got better. Your dad gave her medicine."

"Stop. I don't want to know."

"You should know. This is your lie, too."

"No, stop." I held my head and tried to steady the swirling of fog around me. It wasn't that I didn't believe him, but I didn't want to hear it. Even if he didn't mean to blame me, his words seemed full of accusation.

"You need to hear it from the source," he said. "Let's go see my dad."

I was too weak to resist as Lakshman took me by the elbow and walked me down into the subway.

Compared to the city, New Jersey's darkness caught me by surprise. We had arrived on a train as clean and nice as the airplane I'd flown in to get to New York, completely unlike the dirtiness of the city's subways. The night stood still. Stars winked above me for the first time in weeks. We walked through sidewalks held in by manicured grass.

Lakshman led me up the stairs of a small old house with red awnings and a slightly tilted look about it, as if it was so old it sagged. Lights were on in a back room, filtered hazily through the thick curtains of a bay window.

"I didn't tell him we were coming," Lakshman said. "We haven't talked in months."

"Why?"

"I told him about M and me. He didn't react well. I mean, what does he care that she's Dalit? I thought he'd be over it, since we've been away from India so long. But we had a huge fight, and I haven't talked to him since." Lakshman rang the doorbell.

Footsteps. The light turned on in the front room, flooding the windows. The red door scraped open.

I didn't recognize the man that stood in the doorway. I remembered Kantha Chithappa as a handsome man with his curly hair parted meticulously on one side. The man that stood in the doorway was old; crumpled; his skin riddled with folds, like he'd shrunk in it; his hair gray and clinging to the sides of his head around a patch of shiny bald skin.

"Lakshman," he said. His voice grated with an intensity it never used to, a hushed, scraping whisper. His eyes were glassy with tears. "And—"

"Hello, Kantha Chithappa," I said.

He blinked. It took him a few seconds, but then, slowly, he smiled. It looked like something he wasn't used to doing. The grin transformed his face, and I saw a hint of the old Kantha Chithappa I used to know.

We followed him into a narrow corridor paneled in white wood. Photos hung everywhere—photos of Lakshman as a kid, Vasanthy Chithy, their wedding. Everything once hidden in photo albums back at the ashram was now displayed on every inch of wall and surface.

We settled in at a circular kitchen table. A large photo hung above it, featuring the three of them and me. Lakshman, six years old, huddled on Vasanthy Chithy's lap. Her hair fanned out over his small shoulders. In the picture, I sat on Kantha Chithappa's lap, smiling at the camera.

It had been more than two months since Ayya and I left the ashram, and it jarred me to see reminders and pictures of it everywhere.

"When did you come to New York?" Kantha Chithappa asked.

"A few weeks ago," I said in Tamil. It felt good to speak my native language again, and it came out all rushed and fluid, like I'd built up a backlog of words I'd wanted to say. The train ride had sobered me up a little, but I was still tipsy. I focused hard on Kantha Chithappa's words and tried to act steady.

"What have you been doing?"

"I toured the city." I didn't know how much Lakshman had told him about my running away. "I saw Lakshman sing."

"Sing what?"

"It's nothing," Lakshman said. "I sang for him in my apartment." Lakshman gave me a look, and I understood that Kantha Chithappa didn't know about the band or our upturn in fortune thanks to the video. I wondered how long Lakshman's claim of not talking for a few months had actually lasted—how I could fix their relationship.

"How's the ashram?" Kantha Chithappa asked. He kept staring at me, like he couldn't believe I was there. "How are you?"

I told him about the ashram expansions, how many buildings we had now, how many visitors stayed at any one time—still trying hard to act and talk soberly.

"You're the spitting image of Krishna," he said. He looked me up and down with awe. "My god, I forgot what the blue looked like."

His eyes were glazed. He kept taking sips out of a porcelain cup, something brown-tinged but clear. Whiskey.

"What am I doing?" he said, standing up. "Let me make you tea."

"We can't stay, Appa," Lakshman said. "We have to get back." He stood up too.

"Stay for a bit." Kantha Chithappa seemed anxious and twitchy. I took that to mean that he missed Lakshman, and that he felt lonely. "Kalki hasn't told me about his Ayya yet."

"Appa—" Lakshman said with warning.

"How is the old brute? Your Ayya?" Kantha Chithappa sat again, as if he'd forgotten about the tea. His face was eager, though there was a demonic glee to it at the mention of Ayya. He'd shifted positions, revealing the painting behind him—one of Amma's, a lush piece depicting Krishna's mother Yashodha scolding him for stealing ghee. Amma had used Vasanthy Chithy as the model for Yashodha, and me as the model for Krishna.

"Ayya is fine," I said. I couldn't look away from Vasanthy Chithy's painted face.

Lakshman sighed and sat back down.

"He doesn't know you're here," Kantha Chithappa said. It wasn't a question. "If he did, he'd be knocking down my door." Kantha Chithappa leaned forward over his teacup full of whiskey. "Don't trust him, Kalki."

All the pictures of Vasanthy Chithy stared at me from the wall. Her eyes were everywhere, leaning up against every piece of furniture, nailed onto every inch of wall. Dead, just like Amma.

"Do you trust him?" Kantha Chithappa asked.

I hadn't trusted Ayya since his affair with Sita, hadn't liked him since Roopa left. "I don't."

"Good." He took a big gulp from his teacup. "Your Ayya is wrong. He's wrong about so much."

I nodded. My heart was balled up tight. Kantha Chithappa could confirm all my doubts about Ayya. How they healed Roopa. How the horses arrived at the ashram. How much money Ayya made off me over the years.

Before I could jump into it, Kantha Chithappa asked, "How's your Amma?"

Lakshman grabbed my hand and squeezed it.

I waited a beat to make sure I wasn't going to cry. "Amma died." I was surprised I could say the words without emotion. It had been a long time, longer than I realized. Or maybe it was Lakshman's support, or Kantha Chithappa's presence, that gave me the urge to tell the truth about Amma. This was more than I'd shared with even Lakshman. I'd told him she'd died, but not how.

"She drank rat poison," I said.

Lakshman's fingers crushed mine.

Kantha Chithappa slammed his fist down on the table. "Goddammit." He reached across and took my other hand into his. He pushed his face into my palm. "I'm so sorry." He shook his head. His tears soaked my fingers. "I'm so sorry. I didn't know. I—I should've been there for you. I shouldn't have left you two with him."

The world flanged away from itself, dizzying. But I breathed slowly. "Chithappa, it's okay," I said. I got up, went around the table, and hugged him. He cried against my shoulder. "It's okay, it's okay." I kept saying it, because it wasn't okay and I didn't have anything else to say, and the tears were climbing up inside me. We both cried together as Lakshman watched us.

Before we left, Kantha Chithappa clung to Lakshman's shoulders and said, "I want to meet Meera. And her parents. Please." He put his hands on each of Lakshman's cheeks and kissed his forehead. "Please. I want to meet the woman who makes my Lakshman so happy."

Lakshman sat silent on the train ride back to the city, staring at his knees, his head nodding as he fell asleep and woke up. Thin strips of light sliced us open. I couldn't take it anymore. I closed my eyes and pictured Amma's painting on the wall of Kantha Chithappa's kitchen. After we'd cried about Amma, Kantha Chithappa had told me as much as he remembered—how they'd secretly fed Roopa antibiotics; how the horses had been brought in on a trailer with everyone involved paid off to keep quiet; how Ayya had had a deal with the local medical clinic, where he would pay off the doctors and nurses if they would refer patients to the ashram instead of healing them.

These stories swirled in the vortex of my mind, creating a pressure cooker inside my skull.

When we reached our stop, Lakshman slipped out of the train and walked up the subway steps without a word. He kept his hands in his pockets, his eyes on the sidewalk.

"I'm sorry about your mother," he said. He walked so fast, I had to jog to keep up. His body slunk into a downward slope at his shoulders, everything tipped downward and morose. I'd thought he'd be happy his father finally wanted to meet M, but he was shaken and grieving. "I hope you're sorry about my mother."

"I'm sorry," I said. "Of course I'm sorry."

"Fuck you."

I kept quiet. His demeanor was different than I'd ever seen it. Maybe it was seeing his dad so lonely, or the house with pictures of his dead mother everywhere. I was an intruder on his grief. He felt far away again, a stranger once more.

"You can't heal anyone, you know," he said.

"I know." He wasn't really talking to me. He was talking through his sadness, addressing the world.

"You can't," he said. "You're not a fucking god." His eyes were shiny under the lights. "My mom was sick. She needed real doctors, and all she got was you."

I remembered the woman in Delhi, her breathing growing faint as she lay on the road and the car lights pierced into both of us, melding us into each other and carving us from our shadows.

I reached out for Lakshman. The alcohol had drained from my body, but I was dizzy all the same.

He shook his head at the ground and shrugged off my hand.

"I hate being in that house," he said.

"I'm sorry."

"You killed her," he said, and kept walking.

9

For the next few nights, Kantha Chithappa's face haunted my dreams. I kept waking up to visions of Amma and Vasanthy Chithy at the ashram, and as the days went by, my body unraveled. My belly always hurt. My joints ached. I woke up feeling like I hadn't slept at all. To avoid facing these new, scary realities, I took any excuse to drink and wander alone in the city. The noise was jarring on the best days. I was used to birdsong at the ashram, but here there were people everywhere. Everything smelled, even the air, which hung muggy and thick. I didn't walk through it as much as I waded through. I spent a lot of time riding the subway, but my favorite place was the Cathedral Church of Saint John the Divine in the Bronx.

Inside the giant, cavernous church, the noise of the city all but died away. I went on weekday mornings when men in black shirts and cargo shorts set up chairs, each thud ringing in the stone building like a small stampede. I liked to sit facing the high altar in front of the roped-off area, trying to get everything to line up in my vision—the white marble altar, the cross hanging above it, the stained-glass window behind the buttresses arching up to the domed ceiling, the large frankincense holder hanging above the pulpit. I didn't know a whole lot about Christianity besides that its history was too bloody for me to be drawn to it. But I missed the quiet of the meditations at the ashram, and in New York City this was as close as I could get to calming my mind. I didn't dare go to any Hindu temples for fear of Ayya and his loyal followers.

Sometimes other people would come in to pray as I sat in the pews. I watched them, both entranced and sickened. I no longer understood the nature of faith. I hadn't had faith or belief. I hadn't needed to. I had known god. I had *been* god. It was other people who had had faith in me. But now that I knew they were all lied to, that they believed in something that didn't exist, I wondered what even *was* faith—what use it had if all it meant was belief in a lie.

After another Blue-Skinned Gods gig, Lakshman, M, Han, Jason, and I went out drinking at a bar, where we met Sunita and Lucky and a group of three girls who laughed at all of Han's jokes. She sat in the middle of two girls with her hands all over them, buying them drinks and asking them to come back to the apartment. Sunita and Lucky made out in a dark corner of the bar. M snoozed with her head thrown back on a couch, and Lakshman watched her with such devotion on his face that it made me feel deeply lonely. Jason took shots with a mountainous friend of his, the two of them racing to gulp up the group of shots lined up in front of them. After each shot, they smiled at each other, and every once in a while, they kissed.

Another boy we'd met, Julian, leaned on me as he talked. Julian was lithe and bony, with a dark beard and dark hair and dark clothes that stood out against his pale skin. His heavily ringed hand rested so close to mine on the table that I kept finding myself focusing on it. At the end of the night, he invited me back to his apartment in Queens.

I looked to Lakshman. I didn't know how to ask for clarity on the situation.

Lakshman leaned close and whispered in my ear. "You're free now. Try everything at least once."

"But—"

"M and Han are bi. Jason's gay. And trans! It's no big deal. Go explore." He held my gaze for a second to show me he meant it, then turned his adoring attention back onto M, who'd started to snore.

In Hindu mythology, Vishnu sometimes takes the form of a woman named Mohini, who is so beautiful and perfect that she weaves a spell over all the men who see her. Even Shiva was so moved by her beauty that he spilled his seed just from a glimpse of her form. He begged Vishnu to become Mohini again so he could chase her and make love to her. One story tells of a time when, halfway through sex, Mohini became Vishnu again, but the lovemaking continued. The *Linga Purana* tells another story of Shiva and Mohini making love, but this time they merged into one being, Harihara, who is depicted as half-Shiva and half-Vishnu in his male form. At the ashram, I learned of these stories mostly from Western visitors like Brad. Ayya never talked about sex at all, and definitely never about same-sex attraction.

But when I'd believed I was a god, that godhood had formed most of my identity. My gender and sexuality were always ancillary to my divinity. Most gods and goddesses could shift in and out of their genders and attractions. Going home with Julian didn't seem like a stretch to me. He was good-looking and smelled nice. I said okay, and he took my hand and led me out of the bar.

We were both still tipsy when we reached Julian's apartment, and he struggled with his keys outside a scratched-up, olive-colored door two floors above a 24-hour Curry in a Hurry. The smell of cumin wafted up and turned sour on the walls of the empty hallway.

"Here we are," he said, finally getting the key turned. "Roommates are out for the night."

He giggled, leading me into a cramped living room with mismatched furniture, and further into a tinier bedroom squeezed with a bed and a strange luminescence. It took me a minute to realize the extra light was coming from crystals that hung from the drop ceiling on string and fishing line. Crystals covered the nightstand. A bowl of crystals in a hanging planter. Crystals blue and pink and white scattered multicolored light and threw it over the walls.

Julian sat on the bed and zipped off his boots. I toed off the shoes I'd borrowed from Lakshman. He laid down and looked up at me expectantly. His long, dark hair snaked over the tie-dyed quilt on the bed. In the refracted light from all the crystals, he looked otherworldly.

"What are all the crystals for?" I asked.

He offered me his hand and pulled me down on top of him. "Shhhh," he said. "Later."

Sex with Julian wasn't very different than sex with Han or any of the women. He waited for me to take the lead, but when I kissed him, he kissed back, aggressive and hungry.

Part of me wished I was sober, so that I could later remember clearly what he looked like with his head against the pillow. His white, translucent skin glowed under the reflected light of the crystals, and if I hadn't been distracted by his pink lips around me, I would've thought the scene beautiful.

Later, when we lay all tangled up under his covers, he said, "The crystals are for my health." He held my hand, his fingers twitching. "They charge better that way, hanging."

"Charge?"

"Their energies get charged by the sunlight."

Some of the visitors at the ashram had believed in crystals too.

They had given me a few to use in my healing rituals. I never did, and Ayya had told me it was all nonsense. Another fictional story that people believed and lived by.

"They're healing crystals, mostly." He pointed to a light purple one hanging directly above us. "That amethyst is the violet flame embodied. It cleanses negative vibrations from the body and turns negativity into light." He pointed to the others and listed them. "Petalite. Moonstone. Sugilite. Kernite. Lapis lazuli. My psychic told me to avoid red and green stones because they'll spread the cancer."

The word jolted me into movement. I tried to sit up.

"I have leukemia," he said. "But the crystals are curing it."

I looked into his eyes, which were spotted with little brown dots on the white of the iris. Ayya had taught me to use that as a way to recognize a person's health.

I pushed Julian's arms away, unable to take the contact. The room trembled.

"You have cancer?" Vasanthy Chithy had let me try to heal her cancer. She had to have known it wouldn't work. "Are you getting treatment?"

If Vasanthy Chithy had gone to the hospital earlier, she might have lived. Lakshman believed so. His voice floated up out of my memory, his body hunched over in the slate-gray New York night. *You killed her*, he'd said.

Technically, my methemoglobinemia is a disease. It's a genetic deviation from what my biology is supposed to do. But compared to diseases like the infection that Roopa had come to the ashram with, or the cancer that had killed Vasanthy Chithy, or Julian's leukemia, or Amma's severe depression—compared to all that, my disease is anything but. I never suffered.

Julian sat up and gathered his hair into a bun at the top of his head. He avoided my eyes. "I don't need their treatment. I have the crystals."

"But you do. You need treatment."

"They caught it early. As long as I use the crystals regularly, it'll help. Plus"—he smiled at me—"my psychic said I'd meet a guru. She said his love would heal me."

I jumped up from the bed, my head full of birds trying to escape. The crystals hung above us, watching, swaying without a breeze.

"They're reacting to your energy," he said. "You have a powerful aura."

"I have to go." I pulled on my clothes and shoes in a hurry. I couldn't be in this room any longer, with the crystals and this beautiful boy who was dying because he believed in them.

At the door, I turned around. Julian was still sitting on his bed, still topless, his soft white chest hunched under the crystal light.

"You need to get treatment," I said.

He gazed up at the crystals, their light falling on his face, the weight of his faith making them move.

Back at the apartment, Laksman was still up, fiddling on a guitar. He sat on the floor of the living room next to a passed-out Jason on the couch, who snored loudly and didn't seem to be bothered by the music. Through the open door to Lakshman's bedroom, Han and the two girls from the bar slept in his bed, the sky breaking into pink dawn in the window above them. Han's bedroom door was also open, and M cuddled a large green pillow in the narrow bed.

"I'm done," I said. "I'm done with all of it." Every nerve in my body was alive.

"Did you get laid?" Lakshman asked. "Done with what?"

"I'm done with this guru business. I can't do this. Why do you all keep using me?"

Lakshman put aside his guitar. "Calm down."

The panic rose in me. Thoughts of Julian, and Amma, and Roopa, and Vasanthy Chithy, and the woman in Delhi—they all spiraled inside my head.

"I can't do this," I said, gritting my teeth against the panic.

"Look." Lakshman pulled his laptop toward us so I could see the page he had open. It was our video, with five million views. "The band's more popular than ever. Do the prayer concert, you'll see. You're making people happy."

I sank into the couch near Jason's head. "Julian, the guy I just slept with, he has cancer. *Cancer.* And he won't get treatment because he thinks I and a bunch of crystals will save him."

"He's an outlier. There will always be outliers. You have to concentrate on the majority of people you're helping to feel better."

We sat in silence, Lakshman strumming a few notes on his guitar, and me trying to regain my breath. The jittering in my hands spread up to my chest and into my head. After Kantha Chithappa's house, Lakshman had pretended like he'd never said anything to me about his mother and how she died, and I tried to chalk it up to him being sad about all those pictures of his mother in his father's house.

"My mother died, too, you know," I said.

Lakshman stopped strumming.

"She took rat poison and walked away into the woods one night," I said. I dug my hands into the couch to steady myself.

"I know," Lakshman said. He reached over and pulled me down to him. My face pressed against his shirtless chest. I loved his smell, his deodorant, the remnants of latex paint and his sweat mixing to make something that was starting to feel like home.

"Amma wasn't sick," I said. "But I guess in a way she was."

The tears came, and Lakshman held me as I cried. I didn't know if he was crying too. I missed Amma, and Roopa, and I missed the feeling of that boy Julian's hand in mine. When I closed my eyes, I pictured him looking up at his ceiling, and what that peculiar crystalline light looked like shattered all over his skin. I sobbed into Lakshman's bare chest, but he didn't flinch from the tears and snot. He held me.

10

A week before the music festival, the band had one more gig at a dive bar called Yia Yia's, a cavernous, dark place in Hoboken that stretched the length of the block but was the width of a closet, as if it had once been an alleyway before someone had converted it into a venue. Brick ran along both walls, the whole room covered with framed mirrors etched with the flags of every state. The light inside was eerie and red.

As I helped the band set up on a tattered stage squeezed in front of a bay window, I noticed two men standing at the bar and looking out of place. They were both Indian, one tall and lanky and the other short and squat. They both wore striped polo shirts tucked into khaki slacks. They looked young, and I would've assumed they were fans of the band if not for the meticulously drawn red and white Namams on their foreheads.

They were looking around, not drinking anything, and I tried to keep busy threading the mic around Lakshman's ancient mic stand, which had a loose knob held on with electrical tape. When the men spotted me, they rushed over, bowing and holding their hands in prayer.

"Kalki Sami," the taller one said. His hair was oiled and parted, reminding me of the Deputy. "Kalki Sami, we found you."

They both bowed to me, and I stood waiting. I didn't know what they wanted—whether they were fans from before, or fans now. They came up close to me. Lakshman, M, Han, and Jason, who were also setting up, watched us carefully.

"I'm Rengaramachandran," the tall one said.

"I'm John," the short man said. He had a face like a pug, with extra folds everywhere for no apparent reason, as if his skin was bigger than the rest of his body. "We came to your pooja."

"At the temple in Queens."

They both had strong Indian accents.

"John used to be a Christian," Rengaramachandran said.

"But then I heard of you," John said, with an expression of reverence.

"And now he's one of us."

I waited for them to continue. I still didn't know what they wanted. But they waited, too, as if they wanted me to respond.

"Can we help you?" Lakshman said, coming up to flank me.

"Kalki Sami," Rengaramachandran said, ignoring Lakshman.

"We want you to know how much you mean to us," John said.

"You are the savior of the world."

"You are a god to us."

I didn't know where this was going, but we had attracted the attention of some of the bar patrons, who swiveled their stools around to watch us like we were a better show than the college football game playing on TVs all over the bar.

"Please, Kalki Sami," Rengaramachandran said, oblivious to all the eyes. "You must come back."

"There are thousands of followers waiting for you at the ashram," John said.

"They're waiting for you."

"You must come back."

It was like each one knew what the other was going to say, like they were talking to me with one mouth. It was as if they'd practiced.

Rengaramachandran grabbed my hand, and I was so shocked that I didn't pull it away. He pressed my hand to each of his eyes in turn. I imagined the ashram swarming with thousands of people.

"Please, Kalki Sami. Your devotees need you."

"Yes, Kalki Sami. We are waiting for you. Thousands of us, back at the ashram."

Thousands of people couldn't stay at the ashram. It could house no more than forty at a time, and even if people camped in tents, there would be space for no more than a few hundred. I snatched my hand back from Rengaramachandran.

"You must come back, Kalki Sami. Your followers are missing you."

"Your father is missing you."

At the mention of Ayya, my body braced itself. But before I could say anything, Lakshman wedged his body in between me and the two men, puffing out his chest.

"His father sent you?" Lakshman said. "You're not welcome here."

Now the two men took full notice of Lakshman, and also of Jason, who was standing to his full height on my other side. Rengaramachandran opened his mouth to respond, but Lakshman walked forward so both men were buffeted back.

"Leave," Lakshman said. "Now."

The men caught each other's eyes. For a minute, I thought they were going to stay, try to fight, but they turned around and left the bar, whispering to each other in Tamil.

Long after the show, after many drinks, late at night as we shut down the bar, the two men waited for me outside. As I carried a guitar case out to Jason's van, they pulled up in a sage-green sedan. John and Rengaramachandran opened their doors and jumped out.

They ran at me, and in my shock, I dropped the guitar case. The band was still inside, grabbing stuff to take out to the van. No one was around. It was after two in the morning.

Rengaramachandran pulled my arm, dragging me to the back door of the car that John held open. I yelled out. John joined him, and together they were too much for me. They dragged me by the arms, back across the street toward the car.

They got me to the door and pushed me into the car. I screamed, holding tight to the edges of the door opening. The world looked bright and full of fire.

M, coming out of the bar with an amp clutched in her arms, shouted, and Jason came running to me. He pulled Rengaramachandran off me and pushed him to the ground.

John threw his weight on me to get me into the car. My fingers slipped off the edge of the door. I fell into the backseat, and the man fell on top of me, knocking the wind out of my chest.

Someone pulled him off—Lakshman, who pushed John up against the car and punched him hard in the mouth. Rengaramachandran was curled up on the ground as Han kicked him. Jason and M tried to restrain her, though she kept flailing her legs as Jason struggled to pick her up. She kicked Rengaramachandran once more in the head.

"Hey! Hey!" yelled a rough voice.

I climbed out of the car. The bar's ex-cop manager—we'd met him earlier in the night—pulled Lakshman off John, whose nose was broken and bleeding.

"That's enough!" the man said, shaking Lakshman. "Enough."

Jason had finally heaved Han away from the other man, who was starting to stand. He had an ugly red bruise forming on his forehead.

M ran to me. I was still dazed, my head bursting. Sweat covered my chest.

"I'll call the cops," the bar manager said.

But John and Rengaramachandran had already jumped into the car. They drove away, peeling down the street with a squeal of tires.

"Jesus," Lakshman said, his chest heaving as if he'd run miles. His lip was cut and bloody, and he clutched the side of his waist.

My knees buckled. I fell into M's arms. She lowered me to the ground, and Jason put his arms around both of us, humming us a calming melody.

Ayya had always been capable of much more than I believed, but I hadn't thought he'd resort to kidnapping. This was unsustainable— me staying one step ahead of Ayya, and him escalating his attempts to make me come home.

11

We drove upstate for the music festival in Jason's van. The concerts took place on a twenty-acre plot in upstate New York, two months after my arrival at Lakshman's apartment. A hedge fund billionaire was throwing the festival for his Hudson Valley friends. Lakshman was excited because rich people would hear about the band.

"Fans are great and all," he said in the van, "but *rich* fans help pay the bills."

We were going to stay in a huge tent Jason owned and sleep on air mattresses. I helped the band set up camp, and we walked around the fair area, where artists and craftsmen hawked their wares in an open-air market. There were tents full of tie-dyed shirts, silver jewelry, and a lot of skirts and tunics that looked vaguely Indian. The women dressed in bikinis and small shorts that showed their buttcheeks. Some of them wore pottus and what looked like large Indigenous headdresses, and others had locked their blond hair. I had to keep myself from gawking. I'd never seen so many white people in one place before, not even in the city, because at least the city had diversity. Here, the handful of darker-skinned humans were diluted among the sea of white faces.

"Ugh," M kept saying. "I hate these festivals. So. Many. Whites."

"I thought music festivals were banning headdresses," Han said.

But nothing could ruin Lakshman's mood. He was bouncy, flowing, engaging with everything and everyone. He bought us all funnel cakes, which tasted like giant dry jalebis with powdered sugar on top. Jason told us jokes through a full mouth as we walked.

One woman had a large collection of what looked like brown snakes on a table. "This is sea salt pumpernickel," she told us as we walked by. On a cutting board, she carved the head of a snake off. Apparently, it was bread. She offered it to us. "I also have caramel brioche, sage baguettes, and goat's blood rye." She offered us each a piece as she said it.

I eyed the goat's blood rye.

"He's vegetarian," Lakshman said. "Mostly."

"Oh, don't worry," she said. "It's goat cheese and beets for color."

It tasted dry and salty, and I swallowed it with difficulty.

At the next tent, a white woman in a long skirt and headscarf offered palm readings. Another in a tent next to her measured people for custom-made cloaks. A man was getting measured, standing with his arms like a crucified Jesus and wearing a violently purple velvet cloak while the woman stooped low to pin the hem.

"Hey," the man getting measured said. "I know you. You're that guru guy. From the Internet." Ignoring the woman trying to pin up his cloak, he walked toward us.

I got ready to shake his hand, but he stopped short, his bloated white face turning red.

"Word is that you're a fake," he said.

"Whose word?" Lakshman asked, stepping out in front of our group, blocking me with his body.

M held him back slightly with a hand.

"It was all over Twitter this morning," the man said. "The gig's up, man. Someone leaked that news story about you. You're not Indian."

The bread I'd eaten sat like a stone.

Lakshman looked like he wanted to keep talking, but Jason steered him away.

"Shit," Lakshman kept saying. "Shit. I didn't think to check."

In all our excitement about the event, none of the band had checked the Internet. We went back to our tent, and all three of them pulled out phones.

"Oh fuck," Lakshman said, staring deep into his. "Who the fuck found that story?" At my confused look, he said, "The one of your birth in that West Virginia newspaper. How did someone dig it up?"

But there it was, a picture of the full story circulating on Twitter, the same one Lakshman had printed out for me when he found me at the temple in Queens. The band's Twitter handle had been tagged four hundred times. I sat while the three of them read out tweets to me.

I always knew this dude was faking it.

Looks like blue skin's the only thing that's real about this guru.

This man needs to accept our Lord and Savior Jesus Christ.

More like Blue-Skinned Frauds. Wonder if they lip sync, too.

Blue dude, blue dick?

"This is fucking absurd," Lakshman said. "Assholes."

But on Facebook and YouTube, our diehard fans rallied behind us, throwing themselves into the foray of comments sections.

Everyone has skeletons. Don't judge.

He's still hot, though.

I still believe in you, Kalki.

"Wait, how do people still believe you're a god?" M asked. "This is incredible."

"People are idiots," Han said.

"Some people want to believe that badly," Jason said.

My hands slipped with sweat. Lakshman still wanted me to go forward with the prayer after the concert.

"These are *our fans*," he said, waving his hand like he was encompassing all the hundred thousand people around us. "We never asked them to believe you're a god. But some of them clearly do. They love us. They want to believe in you."

I couldn't stop thinking about Kantha Chithappa sitting in a house full of pictures of his dead wife, stooped over his whiskey. I'd been lying for so long. Before I knew the truth, I lied without knowing it. But after I'd found out, I'd still lied—and that was all on me.

Our concert was better attended than we could've hoped for. About an hour out from the performance, people started filling the large field.

"This is amazing!" Lakshman said, peeking out of the stage curtains. "There's half a football field of people."

The band tuned the instruments while I helped them set up. The last performance had left a layer of glitter on the stage floor that we couldn't sweep up. I'd never sung in front of this many people before, and though I had practiced until my voice had gone hoarse, I was still dizzy from nerves. I kept wiping my wet hands on the tight, ripped jeans Lakshman had made me wear. None of the other band members had used blue paint, but we'd deepened my skin color with indigo dye, like I used to do. We had nowhere to take a bath, so Lakshman and Han had donned latex gloves and rubbed me down with dye in the tent. On top of the indigo, Lakshman had piled his usual costume jewelry onto my chest, and Jason had lined my eyes with black liner. I'd tried not to get a glimpse of myself in the small mirror we had in the tent, but M held it up before I could turn away, and I had glanced at my reflection. I looked like a parody of myself, punked-out and hollow.

"Careful," Lakshman said, rushing over to help me with the mic stand. "This thing is ancient." He showed me the exposed, mean-looking metal knob halfway down, where the electrical tape was starting to unravel.

"We're making money," I said. "You can buy new stands."

He clapped me on the back. "Yes we can." He parted the curtains and peeped out at the field. "Look! Some of them painted themselves blue."

I peered out, too, and sure enough, small groups of people clustered with their skin painted electric-blue.

"I don't know if I'm flattered or offended," Lakshman said, watching them.

"They're—they're—" I couldn't make up my mind what I thought they were.

"They're fans." He looked me straight in the eye. "You ready?" This he asked in Tamil, which calmed my jitters. "Let's do this."

When we finally walked out onto the stage, the crowd erupted in applause. It was hard to believe so many people had turned out to watch us. If not for Ayya's training on how to manage stage fright, I might have fainted or run off altogether. A tiny frog was stuck inside my throat.

Most of the concert was a blur. I remember the first few notes that Han and Jason played, M's drumbeats getting deeper, and then it's all fuzzy in my memory. I sang without really thinking about it, thinking forward to the prayer and wondering what I'd say. The time dragged on, but our set was over before I was ready. The audience applauded, and in front, I spotted three blue-painted men jumping up and down and screaming.

"Thank you all for coming out to see us!" Lakshman said. His microphoned voice boomed out across the field. "Kalki is going to lead you all through a prayer meditation to get our chakras aligned after so much fun." A hushed silence. Apparently, people didn't know what to make of this. The meditation was supposed to be a sampling of what I could do, so that I could charge money for healings and prayers later when people requested private ones.

"We are the Blue-Skinned Gods!" Lakshman shouted with his fist up in the air.

The crowd roared. I took the mic he shoved at me. All four of them stepped back, and the gaze of the silent audience followed me.

I closed my eyes and tried to imagine Rama and Krishna onstage with me. If I could convince myself, put myself in a mental state that mirrored the one I had at the ashram—before I found out the truth—I could give these people the guru they wanted.

"Let's all close our eyes," I said into the mic. I pictured myself back at the ashram, leading the visitors through morning meditation. This wasn't any different. "Think of the sun in the sky, your body below." I half-lidded my eyes, tried to enter the trance state that Ayya had taught me.

A tingle traveled through my veins, starting at the tips of my expanding fingertips, traveling to my head and toes. It was the same feeling I'd had as a child when I thought Rama was present. I imagined his soft hand on my shoulder, urging me onward.

"Feel your body soaking up the sun," I said, "which has chosen to shine on you. Feel the warmth on your skin." Through my squinted eyes, I saw most of the crowd following along. Some had decided to sit, and others bowed their heads. Still others looked around, confused, and I spotted a few of them weaving through the crowd to leave. "You are one with the universe, suspended on a miracle planet."

Miracle had been the word that Ayya liked to use. But this didn't feel like a miracle to me, standing sweaty in the heat on a stage in upstate New York. Some of the crowd fidgeted, more of them looking up to see if it was over.

"Some of you may have seen Twitter this morning," I heard myself say.

This was it. My time to come clean. I was ready. I knew that, as sure as I knew I wasn't a god.

The crowd held its breath, and my voice rang clear and true into the field.

"The story claims that I'm a fraud—that I wasn't born in India. That I was born here, in the United States, and taken to India as a child."

No one had their eyes closed anymore. I didn't look at Lakshman or M or Han or Jason. I expected them to take the mic from me at any moment, but they didn't. The crowd swelled with excitement.

"It's true," I said. "All of it. I'm not a god."

The crowd was so silent, we could hear the clashing tunes from two other concerts happening acres away. I turned away from the masses. Han was standing right behind me, her face slack with surprise. Lakshman looked mutinous. The bread I'd eaten earlier was going to come back up at any minute. I tasted the bitter bile at the back of my throat.

I pushed past Lakshman, who tried to stop me from leaving the stage. I ran down the steps and almost out to the field before I realized that I'd have to cross the mass of people to get back to the tent, and if I did, I had no way to get back to the city.

I sat on the steps behind the curtain that led to the crowd.

"Kalki Sami, in his wisdom, has given us a test," Lakshman said into the mic, his voice resonating across the field behind me. "Who still believes? Clap for me."

A small smattering of applause, but it was building, building, and then—slowly, impossibly—breaking into cheers.

"Do you still believe?" Lakshman yelled.

The crowd screamed and clapped. I couldn't feel anything now, not my hands or face.

Lakshman left the audience shouting and ran backstage. He thundered down the steps, seized my arms, and spun me around.

"What the hell?" he asked, shaking me. "What the absolute hell?"

He shook me harder, and I let him. The energy had drained from me.

"Lakshman," M said. She tried to pull him away. "He's your brother. He's your brother."

Lakshman stopped shaking me. He was out of breath. Sweat coated his face and dripped down the tips of his hair. He put his forehead on my shoulder, catching his breath.

Slowly, he started laughing into my skin. "You're such an asshole," he said, and kept laughing.

"Guys," Jason said, coming down the steps with Han to where the three of us were crowded. He had his phone out and was smiling. "Guys, Kalki's a genius. An asshole genius. Look."

We gathered around his phone. On Twitter, people were raving about the nobility of my confession, how it was a test and how they still believed I was a god.

"How is this possible?" Lakshman asked.

I didn't have the words to answer. Anger seeped up from under the numbness. The little fire in my chest was back. This was absurd. How could they believe, after all that?

Our controversial performance got us an invite to play at the house of the billionaire sponsoring the music fest. I didn't want to go—I wanted instead to lie in the tent under a mound of blankets and wish I was back in the city. If I could fall asleep, I wouldn't wake for days.

But Lakshman convinced me to go.

"The afterparty," he said, as if he couldn't believe it. "We get to play the afterparty. Wow."

M's argument was that our following was bigger than ever before, and if I did this thing, they could get some rich people interested in the band. After that, it was up to me how much I wanted to be involved. I'd been spending Lakshman's money for weeks, living hand-to-mouth. I needed to give the band something sustainable.

My guilt at riding on Lakshman's goodwill outweighed my desire to crawl into a hole and never come out. I went to the afterparty.

We arrived at an isolated mansion at ten at night in Jason's van, which clanked and whirred as it drove. The other cars in the parking lot shined wet and expensive. The stuccoed house—giant in its imposing facade as it loomed down upon us all—was lit up bright. We drove around to the back, where we unloaded equipment and handed the keys to a valet.

The house inside was spacious and lush—velvet curtains, thick wood furniture, tufted leather seats, granite countertops, glittering chandeliers. When I tried to take off my shoes at the door, Lakshman ushered me along. It felt strange to be inside a house with shoes on. I looked around to see if I'd dragged in any dirt.

The party was in full swing in the front part of the house, but the back, where we stood, was deserted, thanks to velvet ropes that held the crowd away.

"There they are," a man said, walking up to us. He was blond and white, wearing a pinstriped suit that strained against his belly. He addressed me. "And there *you* are! The famous Kalki."

I coughed. "I'm not that famous."

He chuckled and clapped me on the back. Up close, he smelled like expensive cologne that made me want to sneeze.

"I'm Tony," he said, shouting over the din of conversations and piano music coming from the other part of the house. Tony shook hands with all of us except M, whom he hugged close for too long.

While we dragged the equipment to a sitting area that he indicated, Tony poured the six of us tequila shots and brought them over on a tray with lime wedges and salt.

"It's Gran Patrón," he said. "Five hundred dollars a bottle."

"Shouldn't we sip this?" Han asked.

"Bottoms up," Tony said.

We took the shots, one, two, three in a row. I knew the band was used to performing tipsy, but this would likely put me over the edge. I hoped I wouldn't have to perform. We had never decided if that's what Tony wanted. "Game-time decision," Lakshman had said.

"Why don't I introduce you while they set up?" Tony said to me. I coughed from the tequila. Lakshman savored his last shot.

"Sure, famous guru," Lakshman said. "We got this. You go on."

"See?" Tony said, ignoring the sarcasm. "Let's go on."

Still trying to calm the burning in my esophagus, and still not sure if Lakshman was angry or happy, I followed Tony to the velvet ropes in the wainscoted ivory corridor. He unhooked the ropes, and we walked through.

The tequila started to hit me. The room wobbled while he led me with a hand in between my shoulder blades.

My first impression was of glitter. Everyone wore something that shone or sparkled. Sleek-haired, red-lipped women tottered in stilettos and tight, bright dresses, long tassels dangling from their ears as they talked. Suited men lounged on leather sofas, their legs crossed and wiggling to display expensive sneakers on their feet. I'd never seen so many manicured, well-cared-for people in my life. I felt silly in Lakshman's ripped jeans and Blue-Skinned Gods band T-shirt, which felt like a costume as much as my panchakacham veshti and jewelry had been back at the ashram.

Tony introduced me to a handful of men who were passing around a joint. One of them leaned over to put it in my mouth. Dark-skinned and afroed in a powder-blue suit, he smelled like cinnamon and cloves. I breathed in the smoke.

"Are you going to sing tonight?" he asked me. His teeth were white and bright.

"If you ask nicely," I said. It was something I'd heard M say to Lakshman. I puffed on the joint and passed it along.

In the corner of my eye, I caught a bluish blur, and when I looked that way, I thought I saw Krishna. The men continued their conversation, and Tony led me away with his hand on my back. I looked around for Krishna, but he had vanished.

We sat with some women who clustered on low, swooping couches. I was grateful to be sitting. The world turned watery, and closing my eyes seemed both terrifying and perfect. I nodded along to some questions.

I must have drifted off because Lakshman was suddenly next to me, shaking me awake and laughing for the others, his grip strong and pinching.

"Time to sing for our supper," he said into my ear. "Can you stand up?"

Without waiting for my answer, he pulled me up with him. The equipment was ready. It materialized around me. People gathered, clutching their dainty drinks, shifting their weight from one foot to another.

I looked around at the crowd, and in the corner stood Krishna—his hair shorn into a modern Western cut, dressed in jeans and black boots. His T-shirt had a picture of what looked like Amma's painting in Roopa's old room at the ashram. Next to him—I squinted to see—stood Rama, dressed in a checkered suit and lime-green tie. They smiled, made their way toward me, and climbed onto the stage.

The band started the set, but I'd forgotten my words, too distracted by Rama and Krishna flanking me on both sides. I must have looked strange to everyone in the crowd as I turned my head, wide-eyed, back and forth, looking at the ghosts who weren't there.

I stumbled over the first few words of the song, missing my cue. Krishna chuckled to himself.

I looked at Lakshman for help, and he stepped up to his own mic and sang the lyrics I should've sung. I was an idiot, standing up here with them. *A fake guru who can't even sing, can't even remember the lyrics to a single song.* Everything I tried to hold onto fell through, my mind a sieve.

"Don't worry about it," Krishna said. "They still love you."

Tony stood in the front of the crowd, watching me. Lakshman's singing brought back some words and I mumbled them into my mic. The song was endless, torturous, all wrong.

We'd planned a whole set, but as soon as the first song was over, Tony ran up to the mic I was at, and, clapping above his head, said, "Why don't we hear from Kalki?"

The applause died away. The air turned expectant, but I didn't know what I was supposed to do. I wheeled my head to Rama and Krishna.

"Give them what they want," Rama said.

"You want a sermon?" I asked into the humming silence. "Or a song?"

Tony smiled with his glistening teeth. The light reflecting off of his gelled hair was so shiny that I couldn't look at him. "Why don't you tell us why you corroborated that Twitter story? Is it true? Are you not a god?"

I saw some smiles in the faces watching me, but they weren't kind. One woman looked so thin, she seemed to be disappearing. She reminded me of Julian, the boy with the crystals.

"She's dying," Rama said.

Krishna chuckled again and said, "Everyone here is dying."

"How many of you are sick?" I asked into the mic.

People looked around at each other. Some of them raised their glasses and drank deeply.

"All of you are dying," I said. "And you're looking to me to heal you. I look out at you, and I remember a young girl and the way her father carried her in his arms. That was many years ago. He laid her at my feet, and there was so much pain in his eyes."

The room was quiet, the crowd breathing together.

"I see that pain in your eyes," I said, gazing out at them. "You need medical help. Doctors and psychologists. You don't need me."

"So . . . are you not a god?" Tony asked. He was so close to me, I smelled his minty alcoholic breath.

At this question, Rama and Krishna laughed.

"You!" Krishna said. "A god!" And he laughed harder.

Their laughter spun and wrapped around me, circling tighter until I couldn't breathe.

"I'm a fraud," I said into the mic.

I needed to sit. I tried to push past Tony to the couches beyond the crowd, but he held me in place at the mic stand. We struggled, me pulling away and him trying to keep me up there.

I felt my balance go, and I tripped. On my way down, I reached out for the mic stand to keep me upright.

Pain seared through my right thigh. Black edged my vision of the crowd, threatening to invade my eyes. People chattered all around me. Someone dropped a glass on the stage. Rama and Krishna swam into my field of vision, hovering above me and looking amused. The adjustment knob of the mic stand had lost its makeshift electrical tape cover, hooked onto my outer thigh, which was exposed by the rips in the jeans, and pulled the skin, right over my old scar from trying to heal myself as a child.

Two pairs of hands helped me up. For a second, I thought it was Rama and Krishna, but it was Lakshman and M. Through my blurry vision, I saw Jason and Han holding everyone else away. My thigh wound dripped wet onto my leg.

"That's gnarly," Tony said. "Guess you bleed after all."

"Gods don't bleed," Krishna said.

The crowd talked louder, the murmuring building. My blood, thick and black, spilled onto the floor and soaked my jeans.

"See?" I said to the room. "I'm a fraud. I bleed." The walls started to whirl around. I held onto Lakshman for support.

"Your blood isn't red," someone said from the crowd. "Humans bleed red."

"And you can heal," someone else said. "See? You're already healing."

I looked at my thigh, but it looked the same. A deep, straight cut that dripped black blood onto whatever expensive carpet lay below. Vishnu in his proper form had hundreds of arms—what was one cut compared to all that flesh?

"You're a con man," Krishna said. "You've tricked these people for too long."

"But they won't believe me," I said.

"Make them." Rama pointed toward the shards of glass on the stage. "Show them you're not a god. Show them you don't heal."

I understood what I had to do. Rama and Krishna laughed again, and my mouth laughed with them.

My hands reached down toward the glass. Before Lakshman or M could stop me, I grabbed a shard, stuck it into my cut, and pulled. The skin of my thigh tore more, right down and down to my knee, and blood spurted and pooled into my shoes, so black against all the blue.

"See?" I said to the room.

Darkness ate itself in from the edges of my vision. So many loud voices, and there were hands on me, pulling this way and that. I looked around for Rama and Krishna, but they were gone, leaving the echo of their laughter in my ears.

12

Someone shook me awake. Lakshman. His face blurred in and out of focus. He was yelling something too fast in English.

"No, no, no," he said. "Don't call an ambulance. What the fuck did you lace that weed with?"

Something pinched at my leg. My eyelids drooped. Someone was stitching up my thigh with a needle and string, like I was a piece of torn fabric.

"Kalki." Lakshman's voice. "Kalki. Kalki. Kalki." He held open my heavy eyelids. "Stay awake."

I woke up on a bed in a lavish room I didn't recognize. My leg, wrapped in gauze, lay propped up on two pillows. The ache in my thigh throbbed from the skin to the bone, but even that was minimal compared to the sharp, clanging pain in my head. Someone else was in the room. I rubbed my eyes into focus.

Lakshman sat on the bed near me, his elbows on his knees.

Through the darkness of the closed curtains, a slice of sunlight cut a path through the room.

"What the fuck?" he said, seeing me awake. "You need to figure your shit out, Kalki."

I sat up, holding my head steady.

"Where—?"

"One of Tony's guest rooms." I couldn't sense how angry Lakshman was through all the fuzz in my head, but he must have been. "I can't believe you."

Slowly, the events of the night came back to me. Rama and Krishna—I'd seen them, and they'd goaded me into this. But they weren't real, I reminded myself. And if they weren't real, it meant I had decided, all on my own, to shove a piece of glass into my own leg and cut myself. I'd made an embarrassing spectacle in front of important people, and in front of Lakshman.

Shame flooded in. I wished I was back at the ashram. I wished I could turn back everything that had happened. I wanted Roopa. I wanted Amma. I wanted to be folded back in again, to walk in the rice paddies around the ashram, to feed and ride my horse. I wanted to disappear.

"I'll go," I said.

"Go where?"

It didn't matter where. I was no one—not a god, not a singer, not a guru. I was making Lakshman's life so much harder. I could go back to the ashram, tell Ayya I was sorry.

Lakshman spread out his palms and took my hand in them. "You're not going anywhere, Kalki."

I shook my head. A sharp pain jangled in my skull every time I moved.

"You stay with me," Lakshman said.

I tried to sit up further. My body ached. I couldn't really see the way forward anymore, what I was supposed to do.

Lakshman's voice was gentler. "Let's go home." He reached for a bottle of pills on the nightstand, shook one out, and handed the capsule to me. "Vicodin," he said. "I couldn't give it to you while you were asleep. It'll help the pain."

Bricks filled my limbs. I struggled to raise my arms to hold the cup of water he handed me. As I drank and tried to force the pill down my dry throat, he kept talking.

"When we get home, I'll take you to the walk-in clinic. I can't pay for the hospital. But you're okay, right?"

I tried to nod, and even that was hard.

"You're okay," he said. "You'll be okay. You will be."

"I'm sorry," I said.

"You'll be fine."

"No, Lakshman." I needed him to understand, to remember the way my thigh looked dripping blood onto Tony's floor, the faces of the guests—incredulous, amused, shrewd. Guilt melted into a watery feeling. "I'm sorry. For all of it. Your band—I ruined it."

Lakshman surprised a laugh out of himself. "Ruined it? No, Kalki. You made us. You *made* us." He pulled out his phone and showed me the band's account on Twitter. Thousands of tags, some with pictures of me, my leg bleeding, the word FRAUD in capitals below.

But Lakshman continued to look happy. "Don't you get it? It doesn't matter if people think you're real or not. Now they know our name."

"But they don't like you."

"I don't know about that. The band's better than famous." He held out his arms like he was going to hug me. "We're infamous! You made us."

M, Han, and Jason picked us up at Tony's house. Tony was nowhere to be found. I knew I should apologize, at least for messing up his carpet. Lakshman, apparently happy to not have to speak to anyone, ushered me out of the house while a maid silently mopped the living room floor. The Vicodin made me groggy but numbed the pain so I could at least link some thoughts together.

"I want to see Ayya," I told Lakshman as I sat in the back of Jason's van. "I need to see him."

"You want to go back?"

"No, but I need to see him."

I couldn't avoid him forever. Like he'd found me at our shows, like he'd sent those two men, Ayya would keep after me. He would follow me wherever I went, chase me across the world. I needed to confront him on my own terms. It was the one thing I still had to do before I would be free to do nothing.

Lakshman nodded. "I'll come with you. And after, I'll take you home."

"Yes!" Jason said. He turned around from the front seat and wrapped a hairy brown arm around his headrest. "You have to have the confrontation, Kalki. Kill the father, and all that."

"What?"

"You know, kill the father. Freud?"

I shook my head, wondering how serious he was about murder.

"Freud thought all sons want to kill their fathers and marry their mothers," M said, not looking away from the road as she drove.

"Well, not that last part," Lakshman said. "But the first part. It's everywhere. You can't become a man until you kill your father."

The pain in my thigh beat a soft rhythm into my bones.

"I should kill Ayya?" I had tried once. I had folded my hands around Ayya's neck after Amma's funeral, ready to choke him. I had been so filled with rage. It was what he'd deserved, for everything he'd done to Amma. It was what he deserved now, for everything he'd done to me. "I should kill Ayya," I said.

Lakshman, Han, and Jason shared a glance. Jason unwrapped his arm from the headrest and turned back around to face the road. Lakshman scooted closer to me.

"I didn't mean you should literally kill him," he said. "It's a metaphor."

"But he's a monster," I said. "A monster. He killed your mother. He killed mine. It's what he deserves."

Lakshman sat back in his seat and sighed, looking resolutely out the window. In the silence, I formed a plan.

The next day, Lakshman helped me send Ayya an email, telling him to rent a room at a hotel in Queens. Part of me was afraid Ayya would have moved on, gone back to the ashram at least. But I trusted that the devotees were still willing to host him, even after two months, and if I knew him at all, I had a feeling that he would have stayed, waiting for me to come back like he always thought I would. I was his meal ticket, after all.

In the email, I told him I'd visit him, and I would bring lunch. I told him I was thinking of going back to the ashram. I told him I wanted to talk. He answered immediately and said he'd be there.

The next day, Lakshman and I bought Kung Pao tofu from a Chinese place near the hotel and picked all the peanuts out of it. At the hotel, I got a key from the front desk, like I'd told Ayya to arrange, and opened the door to his room without knocking. Ayya sat at a small table, dressed in his veshti and shirt, a red and white Namam on his forehead. His body startled when we opened the door, but he tried to act nonchalant.

As we stood in front of him, he looked me up and down. I leaned on Lakshman, and there was no way to hide my limp or my gauzed-up leg.

Ayya's eyes flickered to Lakshman, and I saw his note of recognition, but he quickly blinked back to me. "I've seen the video," he said. He walked to me and stooped to inspect my leg. "Why would you do this? Your escapades on the Internet." Ayya touched the gauze on my thigh. "Those terrible videos." He straightened up, and though he looked and sounded calm, I knew he was unsteady inside. His anger simmered under the surface and would soon boil over. "I'm ruined, you know. Everyone is calling me a fraud. All the visitors have left the ashram."

He waited for me to say something. I'd practiced a speech, but I'd forgotten it. Instead, I limped over to the table and unpacked the takeout boxes.

"You're degrading yourself," he spat. "You need to come back."

"You're a liar." I turned around to face him. "You're spinning flowers in my ears, like you've always done." I threw down the last box of takeout. The smell of food filled the room. I felt rooted to the ground by my feet, rooted to the Earth and deep down below.

The calm facade of Ayya's face cracked, and for a second I saw the real Ayya—terrible, ugly, and full of hate.

He raised his arm like he was going to hit me, but Lakshman stepped forward, and Ayya dropped his hand. Lakshman dwarfed Ayya when they stood together.

"You don't talk to me like that," Ayya said.

Lakshman pushed him back, away from me.

"Don't you know who I am?" Lakshman said. "Don't you recognize me?"

I could see the wheels turning inside Ayya's head. He'd recognized Lakshman instinctively, but still hadn't figured out who he was. Lakshman looked very different than the nine-year-old Ayya had seen last, and he'd always been in costume makeup onstage under dim lights whenever Ayya had come to the band's shows.

"It's me, Lakshman. You let my mother die."

"Lakshman?" Ayya didn't seem to understand at first, but then his eyes grew, and his mouth slackened. "Lakshman." His voice sweetened, getting that slight lilt he had when he interacted with rich foreigners. "Lakshman, it's so good to see you."

Ayya made a move to hug him, but Lakshman smacked away his hands. "Don't touch me."

"Let's sit," I said through my teeth. I took a breath and let it out. "Let's all sit down and eat before we say something we can't take back."

Lakshman crossed his arms and took a seat. He stuck a fork in his food, lifting a huge portion to his mouth.

Ayya slowly lowered himself onto a chair. I sat facing him. I took deep breaths to calm myself.

"Please, let's eat," I said.

Ayya's face bloomed in blotchy patches of red. He scooped up a bite of Kung Pao tofu and ate. Victory trumpeted in my heart.

"How long are you staying in the US?" I asked him.

He looked up, chewing angrily. As I'd planned, he coughed. And he kept coughing, doubling over in his seat.

Lakshman put down his fork.

"What?" Ayya wheezed, his fingers scraping at his throat. "What's in that food?"

"Peanut oil," I said. When I'd imagined this scene, I'd thought I'd smirk, like a supervillain who'd just won. But I didn't feel like smiling at all.

Ayya slid from his chair onto the floor, his body shuddering.

Lakshman went to his side, panic clear on his face. "Kalki, do something. This was wrong. We need to do something. We can't let him die."

I stood over them both. "He deserves to suffer."

Lakshman gawked up at me. He flapped his mouth like a fish, but no sound came out.

When I'd first mentioned my plan to feed Ayya peanuts, Lakshman had agreed to help. He had as much rage toward Ayya as I did. But he'd made me promise that I wouldn't let it go too far. Lakshman had forgotten the extent of Ayya's peanut allergy, having never seen it triggered, and I'd let him believe it was mild.

"Why did Amma kill herself?" I asked Ayya. "Answer me."

"She—she was depressed," Ayya said. He coughed and wheezed, his face red with the effort of talking.

"Why did you burn all of her paintings?" I asked. My anger buoyed me up, let me keep my head above the water when I was sinking. "Why did you send Roopa away?"

I breathed away my tears and the burning inside my nostrils. I wanted Ayya to know that I wasn't his anymore. I didn't need him. I knew the truth.

"All those lies," I said. "Why did you do it? Why did you lie to everyone? Why did you lie to me?"

Ayya pounded the ground with his hand. His face had swollen, and he looked like a cartoon character. "I wanted to—to give you a good life."

His voice was barely a whisper now. Rage filled me with fire. But I was giving him a chance to explain himself. His face started to turn blue. I swayed on my feet. Lakshman stood up and put his arm around me to keep me steady.

"We need to stop this," Lakshman said.

Ayya scrunched his eyes shut and wrapped his arms around himself—a bloated, purple version of my father I didn't recognize.

"He has a bag next to the bed," I said. "There's an EpiPen in there. Get it."

Lakshman ran to the bag, frantically searching inside. He dumped the contents out, found the pen, and brought it to me.

I took it. I slowly kneeled next to Ayya. I turned his face toward me, dark and swollen. I plunged the EpiPen into his leg. We waited while the color drained from Ayya's face and his skin deflated to its normal size. He panted, crawling on the ground.

"I'm sorry," he said between gasps. "I'm sorry, Kalki. My son. My son. Come back. Come back home with me."

I laughed in his face. Standing in front of Ayya, I no longer cared what he thought or what he wanted. He was a sad little man trying to nurse a dream that was already dead. I was free of my father. Finally.

Finally.

Lakshman walked to the door and waited for me.

"I'm leaving," I said to Ayya. I thought hard about what I could say that would make him the most furious.

He was still on the ground, clutching his neck. Lakshman put his arm around me. We walked out, but before we did, I said, "I forgive you, Ayya."

ACKNOWLEDGMENTS

A big, big thank you to all the early (and late!) readers of *Blue-Skinned Gods*, including: Mikayla Ávila Vilá, Annie Bierman, Brandi Bradley, Etkin Camoglu, Jennifer Dean, Sakinah Hofler, Elise Hooper, Kate Kimball, Jonathan Mundell, Dyan Neary, Laura Roque, Eric Schlich, Lindsay Sproul, Milinda Stephenson, Danilo Thomas, and Sean Towey.

A special thank you to my dissertation committee at Florida State University—Elizabeth Stuckey-French, Skip Horack, Pam Keel—and especially my wonderful and helpful chair, Mark Winegardner, for your guidance and support in finishing this novel.

Thank you to my professors at Florida State University, especially Robert Olen Butler and Barry Faulk, and my professors at the University of Nebraska–Lincoln, especially Amelia Montes, Timothy Schaffert, and Joy Castro, for your encouragement and love.

Thank you to Tony Amato, for giving me the prompt that led to this book.

Thank you to my colleagues at the University of Toronto for your support and friendship, especially Daniel Tysdal, Andrea Charise, Andrew Westoll, and Jeff Boase. Thank you to my RA, Noah Farberman, for your expedient and diligent work on this launch, and to the University of Toronto Scarborough for the funding to hire Noah in the first place.

Thank you to my current and former students for your inspiration and support. I can't wait to watch you change the world. And a special thank you to Zora Squish Pruitt, for your thoughtful emails and correspondence.

Thank you to my writing group, SLACK, for helping me think about this novel in ways I couldn't have imagined: Amy Denham, Laurel Lathrop, Colleen Mayo, and Karen Tucker. I love you all so much.

Thank you to Sam Majumder, without whom I'd be utterly lost. Thank you to Scott Schneider, Heather Bailey, Rita Mookerjee, Ev Evnen, Drew Ramos, Rini Kasinathan, Chris Michaels, Anthony Lucio, Jared Lipof, Sarah Fawn Montgomery, Avni Vyas, Rob and Jackie Stephens, Todd Seabrook, Annie Bacon, and Jeremy Mulder for your unwavering friendship. Thank you to my poker night weirdos for bringing weekly joy to my life during this pandemic: Marianne Chan, Clancy McGilligan, and David James Brock.

Thank you to my sensitivity readers, Mimi Mondal and Nadika Nadja, for your tremendous help as I ventured outside of my own identities and lived experience in this book. Thank you also to my accuracy reader, Kiran Rajagopalan, for helping me ensure the accuracy of the details of Kalki's life.

Thank you to my parents; my brother, Varun; my in-laws, Linda, Jeff, and Courtenay Bouvier; and to my cousins, especially Ishy, Athish, and Rishana; and to my grandmothers, aunties, and uncles for all your love and for keeping me grounded.

Thank you to my agents, Erin Harris and Jeff Kleinman, for foreseeing the best version of this story and helping me get it there, and for never giving up on me. Thank you to my editor, Mark Doten, and the whole team at Soho Press and Legend Press, for believing in me and in Kalki.

Thank you to my partner in life and in writing, Geoff Bouvier, for the tremendous work you put into helping me realize my vision, and for your meticulous and beautiful line editing. Thank you, also, for loving me day after day, even when I make it difficult.

LAND ACKNOWLEDGMENTS

I wrote this book while living as an immigrant in a settler-colonial state built on the stolen ancestral lands of the Apalachee, Yustaga, Miccosukee, and Tocobaga peoples. And, it pains me to say, I was also working as a teaching assistant at an institution that boasts a Seminole warrior as its mascot, despite repeated agitation to change. I would also like to acknowledge that the United States and Florida in particular, where I wrote this book, have built their wealth and power on the labor of enslaved Black people kidnapped from their homelands.

Soho Press is located on the stolen ancestral lands of the Lenape, in a city built by enslaved Black and indentured immigrant labor.

At this book's publication, I reside on the traditional lands of many nations including the Mississaugas of the Credit, the Anishnabeg, the Chippewa, the Haudenosaunee, and the Wendat peoples, which is now home to many diverse First Nations, Inuit, and Métis peoples, in the Tkaronto territory that is governed by the Dish with One Spoon treaty.

Please read and support Indigenous authors, such as Kateri Akiwenzie-Damm, Kenzie Allen, Cherie Dimaline, Louise Erdrich, Brandon Hobson, Randy Lundy, Tommy Orange, and Tommy Pico, among others. I also urge all of us to learn more about the histories of the lands in which we live and work, including the traditional Indigenous stewards of these lands. We need to ensure that land acknowledgments such as this one are not empty gestures, but are supported by meaningful actions toward justice and peace for Indigenous peoples, and toward forging healthy relationships between the land and those who call it home.

Thank you to Kateri Akiwenzie-Damm and Randy Lundy for their invaluable advice and guidance in writing this land acknowledgment.

For book club discussion questions on
SJ Sindu's *Blue-Skinned Gods*, please visit
sohopress.com/blue-skinned-gods-discussion-questions/